WILLIAM WILDE
⋘ AND THE ⋙
LORD OF MOURNING

THE CHRONICLES OF
WILLIAM WILDE

DAVIS ASHURA

OTHER BOOKS BY DAVIS ASHURA:

The Castes and the OutCastes:

A Warrior's Path

A Warrior's Knowledge

A Warrior's Penance

Omnibus Edition (only available on Kindle)

Stories for Arisa (short-story collection)

The Chronicles of William Wilde:

William Wilde and the Necrosed

William Wilde and the Stolen Life

William Wilde and the Unusual Suspects

William Wilde and the Sons of Deceit

William Wilde and the Lord of Mourning

To the folks with whom I work. Without their help, I doubt I'd ever have the time, patience, or sanity to write a single paragraph, much less an entire series of books.

ACKNOWLEDGMENTS

Acknowledgments

I've mentioned this before, but while I write the books, it isn't as if I manage all this without any help. And this book required a lot more help than usual. I started the story in a dark place, a few months after my father's passing. He'd been suffering with a long illness that lasted over five years. It was a wretched thing, and it took the heart of him. That grimness might have bled into this work (and probably everything else I've published), especially at the beginning. Thankfully, I have a wonderful wife who made sure I had time to write this book and supported me through all my grief. My extended family, even those I haven't seen in years, came together and made a difficult situation so much easier to handle. I'll always be grateful for what they did for my mom when she needed them the most. In fact, I doubt I could have even started the book if they hadn't been there.

In addition, some author friends of mine, specifically Bryce O'Connor of the fabulous The Wings of War series and Dyrk Ashton, creator of the epic Paternus series, did more than they'll ever know at helping me learn to smile again. Diann Reed continues to be an editor extraordinaire, and Tom Burkhalter, the Master of World War II Aviation Fiction, helped turn this book into something I believe does justice to William's story.

THE PILGRIMAGE SO FAR

The Pilgrimage So Far

William Wilde and the Necrosed (Book One)

I n the winter of his junior year of high school, William Wilde is orphaned by what's thought to be a simple car accident on an ice-slick road in Ohio. The truth, however, is far different. His family—his parents and his brother—were murdered by Kohl Obsidian, a necrosed, an undead, shambling monster akin to a zombie who seeks out and destroys anyone who possess magic. William is one such individual, although he doesn't know it. In addition, his magic is unawakened, and as a result, Kohl lets the boy live. The necrosed reasons that he can consume William once his magic comes to life. However, Kohl uses his own dark magic to change William, making him sturdier and stronger but also more prone to anger.

William recalls none of this. His memory of the accident is

absent. All he knows is that his parents and his brother are dead. Being effectively orphaned, and rather than move in with distant aunts of uncles, William chooses to remain in his hometown of Cincinnati, Ohio. He moves in with his best friend, Jason Jacobs, and Jason's grandfather, Mr. Zeus, and life continues.

However, William's world changes on the first day of his senior year of high school at St. Francis. He meets a new girl, Serena Paradiso. She's beautiful, mysterious, and most exciting of all she seems to enjoy William's company. She is accepted by all of William's friends, including Daniel Karllson and Lien Sun, a Chinese foreign exchange student who lives with Daniel's family. But Serena has secrets. She is on her pilgrimage from her home, the island of Sinskrill, and William is her final test to see her rise to the rank of mahavan, a Sinskrill master.

William, Jason, and the others, including Mr. Zeus, are unaware of Serena's actual motivations and take her into their homes and hearts. This causes Serena a great deal of doubt and remorse. She enjoys the company of William and his friends, their banter, and their obvious friendship and love for one another. She wishes she didn't have to deceive them. Her home of Sinskrill is a hard place, and this is the first time she's ever experienced such interactions. However, her path is set. She has to complete her pilgrimage. If not, her younger sister, Selene, might pay the price for her failure.

As the late summer turns to fall, the school year advances and William is confronted by his long-time nemesis, Jake Ridley, a bully and a popular boy at school. They never have gotten along.

Later on, Mr. Zeus explains the truth to William. He explains that he and Jason are *asrasins*. So are Daniel, Lien, and Daniel's parents. Mr. Zeus and Jason also explain the ongoing war between magi and mahavans, between Arylyn and Sinskrill. It is much to take in, and more will be revealed during the Christmas holidays at a *saha'asra*—a place of magic—a wild meadow in the woods of West Virginia. However, shortly after their arrival at the *saha'asra*, Kohl Obsidian, who had been tracking William, attacks. Mr. Zeus, Daniel, and Lien escape to Arylyn by means of an anchor line.

William, Jason, and Serena are unable to follow and flee from

Kohl, barely escaping the necrosed's claws. William is confronted with further hard truths. His magic has awakened, and he can no longer stay for long in the Far Beyond, the world beyond the borders of Arylyn and Sinskrill. In addition, during the attack in West Virginia, Kohl Obsidian touched William. The contact means William can sense the presence of the necrosed.

William, Jason, and Serena drive to Cincinnati, seeking to regroup and flee farther from Kohl. Serena, maintaining the web of lies that she's a simple high school senior rather than a denizen of Sinskrill, is forced to go with them since Kohl has touched her as well. As they prepare to leave Cincinnati, Kohl attacks once again. This time his presence is witnessed by Jake Ridley and his friends, late at night in a darkened park. William, Jason, and Serena battle Kohl and manage to escape once again. They drive into the night, putting miles between themselves and the necrosed.

However, Kohl can also travel by anchor lines, the mystical links that connect various *saha'asras*. He's able to transport himself instantly from one part of the world to another. As a result, they have to avoid the anchor lines, including any that might transport them to Arylyn and safety.

William comes up with the bright idea of joining a circus, *Wizard Bill's Wandering Wonders*, to hide from Kohl Obsidian. The necrosed doesn't like large animals, and *Wizard Bill's* has plenty of them, including elephants and bears. During their time in the circus, William Serena grow closer, but all the while, she is lying to him. Remorse rises within her at her actions.

Their time in the circus introduces them to Elaina Sinith, a young woman who states that she's a witch from a village called Sand. She claims that William's brother, Landon, is still alive and seems to sense the truth about Serena. William and the others are discomfited by her presence.

They eventually leave the circus in Arizona. This had always been their intention, to journey to a *saha'asra* that contains an anchor line connected to Arylyn. During the long drive to the *saha'asra*, they encounter a kitten named Aia. She can speak to them telepathically, a talent Jason has never known anyone to possess. Neither has Serena.

They bring the kitten along since she states that 'the Shining Man' placed her in their path in order to help them with their task. She also claims they'll have help defeating Kohl.

They eventually reach the *saha'asra*, and Kohl is waiting for them. He's tracked their movements through the connection he has with William and Serena. A battle ensues, and during the heart of it, a man steps through the anchor line.

It is Landon Wilde, William's brother. During the long-ago attack on William's family, Kohl shredded Landon's memories, his sense of self, replacing some of them with who the necrosed had once been, a holder named Pilot Vent. The necrosed was certain Landon would die shortly thereafter. Instead, Landon somehow lived through the torment. His sense of self fuses with that of Pilot and a new being arises: Landon Vent, the first holder in generations, and the only being who can kill a necrosed. The battle resumes, and William and Landon, working together finally manage to kill Kohl with strange lightning that pours off William's hands.

After the battle's conclusion, Mr. Zeus arrives through the anchor line. William has a choice of whether to go to Arylyn now or wait a little longer. He chooses the latter. He wants to finish high school first.

William Wilde and the Stolen Life (Book Two)

WILLIAM and his friends return to St. Francis after the terrifying events of the Christmas holidays. They come back more sober and with a greater sense of age in comparison to their fellow students. Right before the beginning of the school day, they meet Jake Ridley and several of his friends—Sonya Bowyer and Steve Aldo—in the parking lot.

All seems normal. Jake and his friends appear to have no recollection of Kohl Obsidian. Jason tells William why. Mr. Zeus visited everyone who'd seen Kohl Obsidian and placed a weave, a magical spell, on them that obscured their remembrances of that night. However, Jake *does* remember, and he knows that everyone else doesn't. He stares after William and his friends and wonders who or what they really are.

The school year progresses, and Jake remains cordial, although he shocks William with his knowledge of *The Lord of the Rings*. Later, some of the seniors are tasked with cleaning a church in Over-the-Rhine, Cincinnati's ghetto, as part of a field trip. Within the parish hall, they catch sight of Jessira, a tall, blonde freshman they met at the beginning of the school year. With her is an Asian Indian-appearing young man named Rukh Shektan.

Weeks later, William comes across information about what might have happened to him in the *saha'asra* in West Virginia. He learns that Kohl's blood must have mingled with his own during that battle, making him stronger and faster than before.

Worse, Jake confronts him, explaining that he knows the truth about the night when Kohl attacked everyone in the park. Jake demands answers, and William reluctantly agrees to bring his former nemesis to meet Mr. Zeus.

During all of this, Serena continues to struggle with her deception, but she sees no way out of her dilemma. She also learns that Jake is also a potential *raha'asra*. It is an amazing find, one that will grant both her and Isha great success in Serena's bishan pilgrimage.

Jake has dinner with Mr. Zeus, William, and Jason and is told the truth about *asrasins* and Arylyn. He takes the information well but needs time to figure out what to do with it. Afterward, Jake's car won't start, and William offers to take him home. On the way, Serena, Isha, and mahavans from Sinskrill attack and capture them. They whisk them away to Sinskrill by anchor line.

Sinskrill exists in the Norwegian Sea, a stony island held tight in the iron-fisted rule of the Servitor, Serena's true father. Serena is greeted warmly on her return to the mahavan island while William and Jake glare daggers at her. They also learn that Adam Paradiso is actually Serena's paternal uncle, the Servitor's true brother.

On Sinskrill, William and Jake are worked as farmers, something akin to drones, the peasants who make up most of Sinskrill's population. They will only be accorded greater rights and status if they master their *asra*.

Their instructor in this is Fiona Applefield, Sinskrill's only *raha'asra* and a hard-hearted women of limited patience. She torments rather than teaches, and her brutal techniques almost result in William's and Jake's death at the claws and teeth of the unformed.

Weeks pass, and Serena continues to regrets what has happened to them. She seeks a means by which to help them. The easiest way is protecting them, something she can only do if she attains higher rank within the mahavan community. She cultivates allies in Brandon Thrum and Evelyn Mason, two young, ambitious mahavans. She also speaks to Travail, a troll—also a woven—who is trapped on Sinskrill. She convinces him to take on the task of instructing William and Jake.

Meanwhile, on Arylyn, Mr. Zeus and Jason search for a way to save William and Jake. No magi has ever discovered the location of the mahavan home island, just as no mahavan has ever discovered Arylyn, but Mr. Zeus has a plan, though. In addition, there are two new members of the Arylyn community: Rukh and Jessira.

On Sinskrill, Travail begins instructing William and Jake. Serena visits them now and then, all the while harboring a dream to escape Sinskrill. The island was never the home of her heart, and she now sees a way out. She can sail away on her dhow, *Blue Sky Dreams*, and carry with her Selene, Jake, and William. However, they can't simply sail into the sea with no place of safety awaiting them. They need to get to Arylyn. Serena reasons that William can likely contact Mr. Zeus through a dream, a means of communications amongst *asrasins* who are either family or very close. *Blue Sky Dreams* can get them free of Sinskrill, and Mr. Zeus can bring them the rest of the way to Arylyn.

William's feelings for Serena begin to change when he meets Selene, Serena's little sister. Selene is a young girl of ten and innocent, and William now understands Serena's motivations. He also picks up on Serena's hints of escaping from Sinskrill. Later on, Jake meets Selene, too, and is also made aware of Serena's plans. Other secrets are revealed to William and Jake. They learn that Fiona's grim, unforgiving persona had all been a ruse. Fiona hates Sinskrill. She'd been kidnapped to the island decades earlier and also trained by Travail. She has witnessed much trauma during her time on Sinskrill.

William and Jake come to care for Fiona. However, while she wishes she could come with them and flee Sinskrill, she cannot. She wears a *nomasra* necklace that only the Servitor can remove. It will sever her head if she ever leaves Sinskrill. Travail can't leave either. He has a deep terror of the ocean and would likely tear *Blue Sky Dreams* apart if he were in it on the sea.

On Arylyn, Mr. Zeus gains a sense of Sinskrill's location and leads a rescue attempt. He takes Jason, Daniel, Julius, Rukh, and Jessira to the Faroe Islands. From there, they'll travel by boat to Sinskrill. In addition, Mr. Zeus and William are able to share dreams, and they co-ordinate their actions.

Before they escape Sinskrill, Serena is led by Selene into the Servitor's study to grasp hold of Shet's Spear. When she does so, her Spirit is transported to the mythical world of Seminal. There, she is confronted by Lord Shet, the god of all mahavans. He is tied to a mountain with chains thick as oak and black as his heart. From him billows a river of *lorasra* that somehow crosses the vastness between worlds. He is the true reason for Sinskrill's depth of *lorasra*. In addition, Shet promises to break the chains that bind him, enslave Seminal, and then come for Earth. He pronounces five years as the time for when he will arrive on Earth, his first home.

The terrifying knowledge is enough to spark terror in Serena's heart. She and the others have to go. They flee, but their plan is found out. Nevertheless, William and the others manage to escape Sinskrill, fighting their way out to sea, chased by the Servitor in his flagship.

Thankfully, Mr. Zeus, Jason, and the others have arrived by yacht and manage to save William, Jake, Serena, and Selene. They return to Arylyn. Weeks later William tells Serena of his plans for the future. His feelings toward her remain cool, but he also recognizes that Serena needs a purpose. William asks her to join him in his: he intends on returning to Sinskrill and rescuing Travail and Fiona.

William Wilde and the Unusual Suspects (Book Three)

WHILE WILLIAM IS DETERMINED to return to Sinskrill and save Travail and Fiona, he and Jake continue to struggle with the traumatic horror of their lives on the mahavan island. One thing that helps is that the two of them maintain the ritual of running that Travail had instilled in them during their time under his tutelage. Joining them are Jason and Daniel, both of who are stunned by the changes in William's strength and stamina.

In addition, they are also expected to attend classes and learn about Arylyn's history and culture. Serena joins in these lessons. During one class, they learn about Lord Shet's great enemies: Shokan, the Lord of the Sword, and his wife, Sira, the Lady of Fire. Legend states that they killed Shet and were instrumental in the founding of Arylyn. Serena doesn't believe the story because she's met Shet. She knows the mahavan god lives and that he's coming back in five years. Her statement is met with disbelief and derision by Jason, but William and Jake think otherwise. They believe Serena.

However, belief doesn't equal trust. William and Jake have learned to accept Serena's actions, but they remain distant with her. Cruel even, but Serena handles their barbs with mahavan-coolness. She doesn't let their insults cause her hurt, telling herself that her heart is a stone. It's a lie, and she knows it.

Seeking to find a place of belonging—although she would never put it that way—Serena seeks out Lien and learns to play enrune, Arylyn's national sport. While Lien isn't exactly friendly, she does offer Serena a small olive branch.

Over time, William and Serena reach an understanding. They even go surfing together, Serena under the tutelage of Jean-Paul Gascon, a flamboyant Frenchman, and William under Jason's instruction.

William and Jake's training resumes, and they take instruction from Arylyn's two *raha'asras*, both of whom are elderly: Sioned O'Sullivan and Afa Simon. The training goes well for Jake since he quickly learns to use his abilities and forms braids with ease. William struggles, though. He cannot master the simplest of weaves.

During all this, Selene, the young girl William and Jake have come to think as a little sister, finds her place on Arylyn. One afternoon, William has lunch with Selene and Serena, and the meal results in another small moment of peace between them.

William devises an experiment to put flesh on his hypotheses that Shet is real. It will require visiting a *saha'asra* linked to Sinskrill, and Mr. Zeus agrees to let him go and check on his ideas. However, he's also instructed to take a competent group with him in case anything unexpected occurs.

Accompanying William are Rukh and Jessira along with Daniel, Jason, and Mr. Zeus. They make the journey to a *saha'asra* in Australia that is linked to Sinskrill. Part of William's theory is proven correct, but there is no time to celebrate. A group of mahavans exit the anchor line and attack. Rukh and Jessira single handedly defeat them. The Servitor arrives next, and they all flee before him.

They return to Arylyn, and life progresses. William is eventually sent to learn from Ward Silver. He makes immediate progress and is overjoyed. Serena takes up farming with Sile Troy. Something about the soil, growth, and life calls to her soul. She loves it. Meanwhile, Jake merely wants to master a weave that will allow him to go home and see his family. They each manage to achieve these small victories. In addition, William spends more time with Serena when she teaches him to sail his newly built dhow, *Blue Sky Dreamer*. They develop a friendship that deepens.

William's desire to free Travail and Fiona never faded and he puts together a plan to do so.

It is a complicated two-pronged attack and involves a number of magi. Despite some setbacks, they achieve their goals. Travail and Fiona are freed.

The battle almost costs Jake his life, though. He takes a sword thrust through the chest, courtesy of Adam Paradiso, who is now the Secondus and likely the next Servitor upon his brother's death.

Jake barely survives his injury, only managing to do so thanks to the actions of Jessira and Rukh. Again, the two possess skills no one else does. They create a weave, a Healing, that saves Jake's life.

The Healing also allows Jake to see part of their lives. Later, after he recovers, he asks Rukh and Jessira about what he saw. He saw visions of them where they stood on the hills of a different world, Arisa, a world of Castes and OutCastes. Crowds bow in adulation to them.

However, all is not well because the Servitor is determined to have his revenge upon Arylyn. Twice the magi have stolen what he considers his property, and they must pay. And they will because the Servitor has discovered Arylyn's location. Shet has told him.

William Wilde and the Sons of Deceit (Book Four)

AFTER THE BATTLE TO rescue Travail and Fiona, Jake, who was badly injured at the hands of Adam Paradiso, struggles to heal. He hates his life on Arylyn, but a visit to his family and his brother goes a long way toward ending his antipathy. In addition, Jessira heals Jake's brother, John, of a degenerative neurological condition.

Shet, meanwhile, is not idle. He calls for his servants on Earth, letting them know of his awakening. One of the first to hear and heed the call is Sapient Dormant, the powerful Overward of the necrosed. He vows to do Shet's will and bring strife to the magi. He comes to know of William, believing him a holder, and infects him with savage anger. He also discovers that someone had killed Grave Invidious, the first necrosed and defender of Shet's sword, *Undefiled Locus*. The blade is missing, and Sapient mistakenly assumes the killer and thief was William.

The Servitor is similarly busy forwarding his plans. He will answer the magi's bold raid of his home. He readies an army to invade Arylyn, going against the advice of his Secondus, Adam.

War is coming.

William knows this. So do Rukh and Jessira, and Arylyn's first army, the Irregulars, is formed. Many volunteer, including William and his friends, but life isn't all about training and fighting.

During moments of quiet, Serena stretches her wings and becomes a better friend to Lien and several other women on the island, including the sisters Daniella and Karla Logan. Serena is happy and at peace in a manner she's never before known.

William feels otherwise. In training with the Irregulars and others, he finds himself struggling to overcome his anger. His fury evolves, becoming more volcanic, leaving him ready to rage at a moment's notice. Rukh notices this changed behavior, and offers advice. So does Serena. She convinces William to seek help, and he asks Travail for advice. He also seeks the opinions of his elder *raha'asras*, Afa, Sioned, and Fiona.

William is eventually healed of his anger, although it still simmers in the background. Nevertheless, he's finally able to tell Serena of how he truly feels about her and is overjoyed that she feels the same way.

Meanwhile, the Servitor sends a scouting force into Arylyn. Leading this scouting mission is Brandon Thrum. His unit spends time on Arylyn, unnoticed and undetected. However, despite express orders to leave no trace of their presence, Evelyn Mason, one of the mahavan scouts, wants to send the magi a message. She murders a farmer, Jeff Coats, leaving easy evidence that warriors of Sinskrill have been to Arylyn.

After Jeff Coats' murder, the Irregulars hasten their preparations. However, fate seems to smile on them when William discovers a slim pamphlet, *Treatises on Ranged Weapons*. It describes the construction of what can only be described as a cannon, one powered by Elements. It's a critical discovery since guns and modern artillery don't work on Arylyn.

However, unbeknownst to them the discovery is inspired by Sapient Dormant under the orders of Shet. The god wants the mahavan and magi to attrit one another. To this end, Shet sends the same information to the Servitor. The god also continues his plans to conquer the world of Seminal. He has a fierce warrior, Cinder Shade, and his elf companion, a female named Anya Aruyen, hunt down and bring to him the Orbs of Peace. These ancient globes block the abilities of all humans on Seminal, preventing them from accessing their *lorethasra*. The Orbs also work on Shet and his titans, the Holy Seven.

However, Cinder and Anya have their own plans. Cinder was once known as Rukh Shektan and Anya was Jessira.

Meanwhile, the Servitor launches his fleet. He'll command the ships while Adam will command the ground units, a mix of maha-vans and unformed. They reach an unoccupied beach on Arylyn's northern border. He plans on getting to Lilith as swiftly as possible and bring ruin to the village while the Servitor attacks by sea.

Unfortunately for them, William's senses have been unwittingly enhanced by Sapient Dormant. The anger that Afa's weave corralled warns William of danger. He recognizes that something deadly has entered Arylyn and informs Rukh and Jessira. Scouts are sent, and they confirm the enemy's presence.

The Irregulars travel north under the command of Rukh, while Jessira remains at Lilith, defending the village from a possible sea assault. In addition, more allies arrive on Arylyn. The Kesarins Aia (who first appeared in *William Wilde and the Necrosed*) and her brother, Shon, who are bound to Rukh and Jessira, respectively, arrive on Arylyn. They'd been helping William's brother, Landon Vent, but came when they sensed their Humans' need. They aren't yet what they'd once been on their home world of Arisa—still far smaller and slower—but they're beginning to recover their once great power.

The forces collide, and the Irregulars are victorious, but Daniel is killed during the battle. There is only one mahavan survivor: Evelyn Mason. She mocks Rukh, but Aia, who can pick through her thoughts, discovers that Adam has split his forces. The unit just destroyed was meant to slow down the Irregulars while another set of mahavans makes a mad dash toward Lilith. They have most of the Sinskrill cannons.

Ward's unit is informed, and they rush back toward Lilith. They arrive too late. The mahavans have already reached the fields outside Clifftop and begun raining down destruction onto Lilith. The village is in flames. Ward's unit attacks, and many Irregulars are killed, but in the end, they prevail. The mahavans are wiped out.

In the meantime, Jessira discovers how to penetrate the mahavan's shields. The gray globes protecting each ship are destroyed, and the Irregulars at Clifftop swiftly take the battle to their tormenters. The Servitor seeks to counter by sending warriors to the beach. Jessira fights them off, but at the last, right before she was about to destroy all the mahavans, the Servitor attacks from afar, knocking her unconscious.

It falls to Serena to defend Jessira. She does so and even captures Brandon Thrum. In the end, the Sinskrill fleet burns. Only the flagship, *Demolition*, is still afloat. The Servitor witnesses the destruction of his forces and vows to inflict as much harm as he can on Lilith. He launches a final payload. It arches over the village and explodes in a shower of seeming snow. Those touched by the white flakes lose years of their lives or are stripped of their magic. Selene and her friend, Elliot, are two such individuals.

Afterward, the magi take stock of their situation. It's a somber reckoning. The island is devastated. While they repulsed the mahavan invasion, they lost hundreds in the attack. For Serena it's especially bittersweet since Selene is no longer able to live on Arylyn. Because she's been stripped, the island has become poisonous to her. In the end, she and Elliot are sent to live with Jake's family.

1

PULLING TOGETHER

D ecember 1990

WILLIAM WINCED when the wooden practice blade cracked him in the shoulder. The weapon mimicked the length, shape, and heft of the longswords most magi used, and while Rukh might have pulled the blow, it still stung. William stepped back, rolling his shoulder and trying to work out some of the soreness. He also needed to catch his breath. While he wasn't winded, for some reason fatigue weighed him down.

Rukh didn't have that problem. He never did. He held his sword in a firm grip, looking as relaxed as a tiger in a sunny field. His brown skin—Indian in color, just like his features—remained dry and unblemished despite the warm morning.

The dew-laden grass scintillated as clouds drifted slowly in a bright, blue sky. A mild trade wind gusted intermittently, the breeze containing the mineral-water smell of River Namaste and the buzzing noise of lumber being cut. The latter came from Lilith, where men and women sought to repair the damage done to the village during Sinskrill's recent invasion.

William shifted his gaze back from Lilith to the enrune fields on which he and Rukh trained. He watched his fellow magi labor. They still had so much work to do, and the crews had already been at it for four weeks. His jaw tightened. The mahavans had destroyed his home, demolishing bridges, wrecking homes, and leaving piles of bricks in the place of buildings. The ruins reminded William of a lovely smile ruined by bludgeoned-out teeth.

It was true that some beauty remained. For instance, lustrous rainbows continued to soar from the water to the sky, and the cataracts formed from River Namaste still plunged down the five Cliffs upon which Lilith was built, rumbling and washing the terraces in a wispy spray. But with all the nearby devastation, the natural vistas no longer served to inspire as they once had. Their loveliness held a sense of mockery, an affront to the broken village.

Broken. William reflected on the word.

It sounded like a perfect description for what his people had endured, which was far worse than destroyed structures. After all, buildings could be repaired and bridges could be rebuilt, but lives lost were forever gone, and that stung the hardest. The final tally had been horrific. So many dead and injured. All told, a full fifteen percent of the island's inhabitants had been killed or injured in Sinskrill's assault.

Anger gave way to sorrow, and William sighed.

Rukh moved to stand alongside him. "Do you need a break?"

William shook his head. "I'd rather train."

He caught Rukh eyeing him askance. "You sure that's what you really need?" the other man asked.

"What do you mean?"

Rukh faced him fully. "We've been sparring for an hour now. You haven't done very well."

William frowned. It was true. He *hadn't* done well. He hadn't landed a single strike against Rukh, which wasn't much of a surprise. Not once in all their hours of training had he ever managed to touch the other man. Still, he could usually do better than this morning's pathetic showing. So far all he'd done was defend a few quick strikes and then Rukh would land a blow William should have normally been able to evade or block.

It might have been frustrating but William's mind was elsewhere. His wooden sword drooped.

"You're thinking about Selene," Rukh correctly guessed.

William nodded. "Yeah. Her. Everyone. It's all I ever think about. Ward, too."

"Ward made it," Rukh reminded him. "He was one of the lucky ones. We thought he was dead, but . . ."

"I know. He was only mostly dead." William's mouth twitched into a faint smile, even though he knew Rukh wouldn't get the joke.

Jake and Jason would have. Same with Daniel, but Daniel *was* gone.

A familiar ache built in William's chest, the despair of losing someone he loved. He should be used to it by now. His parents murdered by Kohl Obsidian . . .

He swallowed heavily and tried to shove the pain to the back of his mind. He didn't want to remember what had happened. Selene's life ruined. Daniel's death. All the fires, the dying, the killing. William suppressed a shudder. He could see the dead whenever he closed his eyes. Their blackened bodies, their broken limbs. Daniel's shattered corpse at the base of a rocky hill. The blood. Sometimes he could see it all even with his eyes wide open.

The visions from the battle, the remembrances overcame him then, and he swayed on his feet, unmoored like a ship set adrift, blinking back tears, trying to think about something else.

Rukh's hand landed softly on his shoulder, squeezing it in support, and the gesture of sympathy almost unmade William. He stiffened, struggling to hold in the emotions.

"How do you do it?" William asked in a soft voice once he had his feelings under control. "Why doesn't any of this affect you?" He gestured toward Lilith.

Rukh took time to answer. "It does affect me," he said. "Every life I've ever taken, every loved one I've ever lost, those who died by my command . . . I remember them all. But I keep going because it's necessary. I do what I must so no one else has to live with the burden of killing. The sin of it. And during it all I grieve. I always have."

"Really?" William stared at him in confusion. "It doesn't look like you grieve at all."

Rukh smiled faintly. "That's because I've had practice at it. I grieve in my own way."

A spark of hope lit within William. The lethargy inspired by what he'd seen and done, the depression, always weighing him down, and he was tired of it. He wanted to feel good again. "What do you do?"

"I submit to the grief, the pain of it, and I make myself think about what I did." Rukh said. "Then I pray for forgiveness, and I ask to have the burden lifted from me." He shrugged. "Sometimes that's enough. Sometimes, it's not."

William considered the answer in disappointment. Time and hard living had robbed him of his faith in prayer's power, but it hadn't always been the case. Once he'd been a firm believer. No longer. After everything he'd experienced, the shine of his devotion had long since tarnished. He now considered it as broken and wrecked as Lilith itself. "I'm not good at praying," William said, recognizing the bitter cast to his voice and not caring.

"Not everyone is," Rukh said, "but if prayer doesn't work, consider some other means. Meditation works, too."

"Meditation?" William shook his head in disapproval. It sounded like some New Age nonsense.

"Meditation," Rukh repeated. "Or talk it out with someone. The point is finding your own way to healing. Your soul needs to heal."

"And if someone blames me for what happened?"

Rukh's gaze sharpened. "Who blames you?"

William took a swift step back from Rukh's anger, inhaling sharply. Seconds later, he realized that Rukh's fierce protectiveness was on his behalf. His heart warmed at the knowledge. Grim and terrifying were good descriptors for Rukh, but so were kind and devoted. "No one blames me," William said.

Rukh nodded, a single bob of his head. "Good. They have no right to blame you for anything that happened."

William eyed Rukh in worry. A strange note in the other man's voice caught his attention. He realized that something bothered Rukh and immediately guessed what it might be. "Karla still blames you." She had been one of the earliest and loudest of those critics who believed Rukh and Jessira were responsible for the death and destruction Lilith had suffered.

Rukh scowled briefly. "I've been blamed for worse."

It was William's turn now for fierce protectiveness. "But she shouldn't blame you. No one should. It's not fair."

Rukh shrugged in dismissal. "Sometimes it's easiest to blame the person who's most available," he said. "But, yes, it's not fair."

"It also isn't right," William said, his own troubles forgotten as he considered what Rukh and Jessira must have faced since the battle with the mahavans.

Rukh managed a strained yet humorless smile. "It's fine. I can take the anger. After all, it's the price of leadership. All I truly care about is protecting the people of Arylyn."

"They're not really your people, though, are they? You're from some other world. Arisa."

"My people are who I choose them to be. They're the ones who accept me. Right now, that's the magi of Arylyn."

It was an odd concept, and William tilted his head in thought.

"Remembering those who died," Rukh said, continuing the prior thread of their conversation, "accepting our role in what we caused is something we all have to come to terms with. If prayer and meditation aren't right for you, find someone to whom you can speak."

William considered Rukh's words and realized their wisdom. He *did* need to talk to someone about his troubles, and he had the perfect person in mind. In this case, a troll. Travail would listen.

Rukh went to a nearby small barrel that contained a variety of weapons. He drew out a pair of blunted longswords, steel this time, and tossed one to William, keeping the other.

"Can you set it alight, like you did when you fought the Servitor?" Rukh asked.

William recalled that long ago battle against Kohl Obsidian and the more recent one against the mahavans. The *Wildness*. That was what it was called when his sword glowed like a lightsaber and lightning forked along his arms. It was a rare talent, one supposedly only possessed by the long-dead holders.

Then why can I manage it? William didn't know, probably never would, but he'd thought long and hard about what he'd done those few other times and practiced until he could call the *Wildness* at will. He nodded his answer to Rukh's question.

"Show me," Rukh said.

William sourced his *lorethasra*, allowing it to fill him. Only then did he reach for *lorasra* and create the complex weave of Fire, Air, and Spirit. *The Wildness.*

His sword glowed, white as the sun, and lightning intermittently crackled along its surface.

"Your eyes go white when you conduct that weave," Rukh said.

William hadn't realized, and he didn't know if it meant anything. Likely not, and even if so, he didn't much care.

Rukh readied his sword. "Go!"

William battled hard, but in the end Rukh still disabled him. Seven strokes this time. It was still a defeat, but it was better than before. William thought of it as a victory.

THE LATE MORNING sun blazed down from amongst stray clouds in a rich, blue sky. It brought unwelcome heat to the scarred fields, wrecked crops, and scorched earth of Janaki Valley, Arylyn's heartland and the source of most of the island's food. During Sinskrill's recent attack . . .

Serena briefly halted her labor, her hoe held poised above a ruined stalk of corn. Had it really only been four weeks? It felt vastly longer, ages since these very fields had been ravaged, some of them salted and set alight. She shook her head in disbelief at time's slow passage before resuming her tilling. She worked alongside a number of other farmers as they struggled to make right what the mahavans had ruined or burned.

The latter was the reason for the stench of smoke still clinging to the area. It swirled invisibly, pushed about by a vagrant breeze, and

Serena maintained a small weave of Air to filter out the smell. She could disregard many things—the day's heat, the sweat dripping down her shirt, the blisters forming on her hands from hours of tilling—but she couldn't disregard the smell of burnt crops. It agitated her sense of right and wrong in a way that death and killing never had.

Odd that.

A half hour later, Serena paused again, needing a break. She leaned on her hoe, wiped her brow, and gazed at the farmers in their distant fields. She observed children helping parents, spouses assisting one another, and friends and neighbors pulling together to fix what should have never been made wrong. And they weren't alone in their labor.

Those at Lilith were also drawing long hours, everyone trying to restore the village to some semblance of sanity and order. Even now Serena knew that workers were clearing streets filled with rubble, repairing others that had been gouged into potholed uselessness, or collapsing buildings too damaged to be left safely upright.

Too bad the dead and injured couldn't be sorted out as easily.

Serena blinked away tears as she recalled Selene. Her sister . . . Her teeth clenched in anger. *No.* She wouldn't let herself give in to weakness. She inhaled deeply, using her mahavan training to push the sadness aside. She didn't want to think about it.

Seconds later, her thoughts cleared, and she could focus again on the tilling. The work needed doing. Her hoe bit into the moist earth. She tossed aside the root ball and burnt husk of a stalk of corn.

From the corner of her eye she caught Jessira working as well, moving in a smooth, non-stop rhythm like a metronome. The other woman dug into the ground, flung aside some dirt, dug into the ground, flung aside some dirt. Over and over again. Never slowing down, never tiring, never needing to rest. Her forehead remained smooth, unmarred by troubled thoughts or perspiration. Jessira, tall, beautiful, and possessing golden hair and a ruddy undertone to her skin, could have been taking a leisurely stroll for all the strain the work caused her.

Maybe farming was her way of praying. Jessira had once

mentioned that in Stronghold, her original home, farming had been considered the most noble and sacred of occupations. She'd also mentioned how much she'd always wanted to be a farmer.

Jessira spoke then, never breaking off her work. "You're pulling away from William."

Serena didn't reply. She didn't want to talk about William. She wanted to work, which she did, digging her hoe into the ground and cutting out a burned stalk of corn.

"You'll eventually have to face the truth," Jessira said. "You can lie to the others but not to yourself. Or me. I know you too well."

"Would it help if I told you it's none of your business?"

Jessira remained intent on her work, head bent low, but Serena caught the flash of a smile. "Of course. I can leave you alone to your troubles." She straightened then, resting a hand and her chin on the butt end of her hoe while facing Serena. "But you might do better to take my advice."

Again, Serena didn't immediately answer. Instead, out of the corner of her eye, she noticed Sile Troy, the farmer to whom she was apprenticed, prowl by. He carried a shovel on his shoulder, and his jaw clenched and unclenched in obvious anger. Sile and his wife had come through Sinskrill's attack relatively unscathed, but their fields had been destroyed, burned *and* salted. He reckoned it would take months to heal the damage, maybe longer.

"What advice do you have?" Serena asked.

Jessira's response was unexpected. "Put away your sword."

Serena stopped hoeing, blinking in surprise. "Why? I know we drove the mahavans away, but there's hundreds more of them on Sinskrill. And Shet's still coming for us."

"I meant in a figurative sense," Jessira replied. "When you first came to Arylyn, you kept to yourself, remained private, hardly speaking to anyone. You had your reasons, but I wonder what they are now."

Serena didn't know what Jessira meant. She spoke to people all the time. Her confusion must have been evident because Jessira explained further. "You're retreating into a shell of a different sort.

You're pulling away from William. It's not a healthy response given the horrors we've all experienced."

Serena resumed her work and made her features drone-flat. Nevertheless, she couldn't control the blush affecting her face as anger surged like lava through her arteries. Who was Jessira to question her motivations or tell her what to do? It was none of her business how Serena lived her life.

The anger continued to course, but Serena also realized she didn't have a ready response to Jessira's accusation, especially because it was true. She *was* pulling away from William, but it was a truth she didn't want to face, or maybe one she wasn't ready to face.

For some reason, in that moment she remembered the advice Adam Paradiso had once given her: attack when at a verbal disadvantage. When she considered her former Isha, a stray thought also flicked through her mind. Adam would now carry the surname 'Carpenter' since he was the Servitor's Secondus. However, according to Brandon and Evelyn, the formal investiture had never taken place.

Regardless, his advice remained sound. Serena sought to deflect Jessira's attention. "It's not as easy for some of us as it is for you. Nothing bothers you. The battle with the mahavans might as well have not happened for all the anguish it caused you and Rukh."

Serena immediately wished she could take back the words. They were deeply unfair and untrue. Jessira was a woman of passion, love, and empathy, and while she might not readily display her pain, she couldn't have been unimpacted by what Sinskrill had done to Arylyn.

"I've lost and suffered much in my life," Jessira said, her voice quiet. "The people I had to kill, the ones who died because I couldn't protect them; those are actions I'll have to live with for the rest of my life. You have your own millstones to bear, but you won't be able to survive them unless you acknowledge their existence." Jessira's lips pursed. "You struggle hard to be strong, but such strength is brittle. You'll break. You almost did once before, and it was William who helped bring you back. Do you remember?"

Serena glowered. Her attempt at deflection had failed, and she didn't want to recall her early months on Arylyn when William of all people had been her only real friend.

"I think you need him," Jessira continued, "and he needs you. Remember, he can break, too."

Serena had only distantly recognized the pain William was likely feeling, and guilt slowly replaced anger. He'd loved Selene, too—like a little sister. And he'd also loved Daniel. He'd lost every bit as much as she had, maybe more, and the reminder washed away the last of her heat. Jessira was right. He needed her.

"What do you think I should do?" Serena asked.

"Put away the sword. Don't worry about it, or Sinskrill, or Shet. Heal. Search for the courage to offer your love and support to those who need it."

Give yourself for others. That's what Jessira was saying. "How?"

Jessira went back to clearing the field. "In the past, prayer always brought you solace. Perhaps prayer is what you most need now."

Serena stared into the distance, considering the advice. After a moment, she spoke again. "Perhaps it is."

She resumed her tilling, but her thoughts remained on Jessira's words. Prayer *would* work. Jessira was correct about that. So would talking. She briefly considered telling her struggles to William but immediately dismissed the notion. He had enough burdens to carry without adding hers to the load.

Maybe Fiona would listen?

～

JAKE LEFT the confines of Mr. Zeus's home and stepped onto the front porch, out into a free, peaceful night. The stars twinkled in night's curtain with no moon to dim their shimmer. A gentle wind blew, and the ceaseless waves of Lilith Bay rushed and receded against the sand. The clean scent of flowering jasmine filled the air. Jake inhaled deeply.

The floorboards creaked as he made his way to the stairs. Somehow Mr. Zeus' home had survived Sinskrill's bombardment intact and undamaged, which seemed a minor miracle given the destruction suffered by the rest of the village.

"Heading out?" a voice said from a darkened corner of the porch.

The red light of a match bloomed, briefly bringing Mr. Zeus' face into relief. The scent of pipe smoke overwhelmed that of the jasmines. Until now, Jake hadn't noticed the smell or Mr. Zeus. The old man, similar to Gandalf or Merlin in appearance, puffed quietly on his pipe. The habit lent him an even greater similarity to a wise wizard of legend.

"Daniella and I are having dinner," Jake answered.

The bowl of Mr. Zeus' pipe brightened momentarily, and a second later, a fragrant whiff of smoke wafted out of his mouth. "Do you have a moment to talk?"

Jake examined the night's darkness past the porch. He knew he had time, but he really didn't want to talk to Mr. Zeus. He didn't want to talk to anyone.

"It won't take long," Mr. Zeus promised.

Jake held in a sigh of annoyance and paced closer to where Mr. Zeus sat. Once there, he leaned against the porch rail, arms folded. "What did you want to talk about?"

Mr. Zeus didn't answer at first. Instead, his seamed face held a thoughtful expression. "I wanted to tell you how proud I am of you," he said after a few seconds of silence.

Jake blinked in surprise. He hadn't expected Mr. Zeus to say that. He'd expected something else, a tongue lashing maybe or a reprimand to stop being such an ass. The words would have been deserved, too. Jake *had* been an ass. He knew it. Everyone did. He eyed Mr. Zeus in silent speculation. "Why are you proud of me?"

"We've all endured much pain," Mr. Zeus said. Again, the bowl of his pipe brightened, and a waft of smoke trickled out of the corner of his mouth. "We've all lost loved ones, but you've never let it slow you down. You've worked as hard as anyone to bring our village back to life. You've cared for those who needed it." He pointed at Jake with his pipe. "That's why I'm proud of you."

Jake still wasn't sure how to respond. "Thank you," he offered in a hesitant tone.

"I just hope you've taken time to care for yourself." Mr. Zeus leaned forward. "You've suffered more than most anyone I've ever known."

"Tell that to those whose children are dead," Jake said, his tone somber.

Mr. Zeus' nodded agreement, and his pipe went back between his teeth. "I did say *most* anyone, but I still worry for you."

"I'm fine," Jake said, pushing off the railing. He sensed what Mr. Zeus was trying to imply, and he wanted nothing to do with it.

Mr. Zeus harrumphed. "Are you? I remember the nightmares you used to have when you first came here from Sinskrill. I had to take them away from you. You're crying out in the night again. It isn't a sin to ask for help or to desire joy."

Jake trembled with a burst of rage. He knew Mr. Zeus was only trying to help, but he didn't want help. He wanted to work hard enough that he didn't have time to think or remember.

Mr. Zeus' face took on a disappointed cast. "Do as you wish," he said, waving Jake toward the porch steps. "I'm here if you change your mind."

The anger left Jake as quickly as it entered. Mr. Zeus had taken him in, taught him, saved him really, and he deserved respect. "If I change my mind, I'll let you know."

Mr. Zeus dipped his head. "Of course. Enjoy your evening."

Jake nodded and departed Mr. Zeus' home. He took Cliff Spirit's Main Stairs and headed for Daniella's house. He had to detour around rubble and broken steps since large sections of Lilith's terraces had been ripped apart. Bridges and stairs linking different Cliffs and levels had been blasted into uselessness along with many homes and too many lives.

Jake tried to shake off his morbid thoughts. He wanted to enjoy the evening, but he continued to brood as he ascended the Cliffs. In a few weeks, he planned on visiting his family. Selene would be there. Maybe it would do him good to see her, his parents, and his brother. He unconsciously nodded his head. *Yes. Home. It'll do me some good to go back.*

He eventually reached Daniella's home, which was in the American Craftsman style. It, too, had only suffered minimal damage—some singed plants, missing roof tiles, and a broken fence out back but nothing more.

Daniella sat waiting on the porch. She grinned in greeting when she saw him, and once again, Jake found himself thinking that she had the prettiest smile he'd ever seen. It lit her face, brightening it into something magical.

Her humor faded when Jake approached, and her brows lifted. "What? No flowers?"

Jake drew up short, wondering if she had really expected that.

Daniella laughed, her blue eyes sparkling. "I'm teasing." She stood, giving a quick tug on her strapless green dress until it slipped down, draping her athletic form.

"Are you ready?" Daniella asked.

Jake managed the all-American grin he knew she liked. "I was born ready."

Daniella chuckled. "I'm sure you were." She tucked a hand into the crook of his arm. "Where are we going? Jimmy Webster's restaurant is still out of commission."

"How about Ms. Maxine's?" Jake suggested. "Her place didn't take any damage."

"Dessert for dinner?"

"Do you mind?"

Daniella shook her head.

They left her home and ascended the Main Stairs of Cliff Earth, where her house stood, and minutes later, reached Clifftop. No one else was about, and they walked in unaccustomed quiet. The village was normally alive at this time of day with folks out for an evening stroll, but not now. Now, Lilith lay still and darkened since most of the lampposts had been wrecked.

"I've missed you," Daniella said, breaking the hush between them.

Jake eyed her in surprise. "We see each other a lot."

"Not like this. You're always working. We both are. I don't think either of us have had any time for peace and tranquility."

"Peace." Jake muttered the word bitterly.

Daniella frowned at him, and he mentally winced, worried he'd offended her.

"Peace is a good thing," Daniella said. "Maybe the best thing."

"Hope is better."

"What better hope is there than peace?"

Jake scowled. "What hope do any of us have? The Servitor destroyed our home." He gestured to the broken buildings. "Hundreds are dead. And Shet's still coming."

"If we had no hope, why are you taking me for ice cream?" Daniella challenged.

He didn't have an answer. He was taking her because he liked her. He liked being around her. She kept him calm.

Daniella took his hand and drew him to a halt. "You can still have hope, and you can still have peace. We all can."

Jake considered her advice, about what Mr. Zeus had said. Hope and joy? Maybe he could still experience both. He hoped so. *God, I'm tired of hurting.*

Daniella must have seen something in his face because she smiled. "You're welcome," she said, giving him a slight shove with her elbow.

The motion didn't move Jake, and he drew her closer into a hug. "Thank you."

2

THOSE WHO DESIRE HEALING

D*ecember 1990*

TRAVAIL AND WILLIAM sat on the edge of a cliff that overlooked the ocean. The luminescent hills of Janaki Valley rose at their backs. Surf rolled perpetually, recalling the unspooling minutes of time as waves endlessly smashed against the black boulders and dark stone of the escarpment. Spray splashed into the air, pounding, arching into a rainbow rising from the mist. A wind, lush with the aroma of brine and minerals, blew gustily. The sun, early in the sky, warmed their spines and the stone on which they sat.

Travail and William came here often. It was where they discussed matters, both deep and mundane, difficult and simple. Their feet dangled over the cliff's edge.

Travail gestured to the world all around them. "This is a lovely place, yes?"

William glanced about, apparently unimpressed. "It's nice," he allowed.

Travail glanced down at William, unsurprised by his lack of

enthusiasm. The boy clearly had a matter that troubled him. It was as obvious as the horns branching from Travail's head or the potential for *lorethasra* swirling in William's mind. A secret known only to trolls was that they could see the *lorethasra* of all *asrasins* and woven. It was a large part of what allowed them to function as Justices. Travail sometimes pondered whether the *asrasin* who created trolls had truly intended the gift given to them, or had it all been mere luck?

He set aside his curious thoughts. "What ails your heart?" he asked.

William cracked a smile. "I thought Jake and I taught you how to talk right."

Travail didn't know what William meant. "Talk right? What species of ill grammar is this? Please don't tell me your speech has devolved into such silly chatter."

William still smiled. "There you go again. All stiff and formal."

Travail finally understood the jape and barked laughter. "Well done. I'll seek to 'talk right' from now on." He allowed a peaceful silence to build between them before speaking again. "What is it you wanted to discuss?"

A stony-eyed demeanor took the place of William's prior wan humor. He flung a stone into the raging surf. "Rukh thinks I should pray or meditate or something like that."

Travail waited a beat for William to say more or explain himself more fully. However, the boy apparently had nothing further to add. "Perhaps you should start at the beginning."

William wore bewilderment on his face. "Starting at the beginning of time might take a while."

"You're prevaricating," Travail chided. "Be forthright. What did you wish to discuss?"

William glanced up at him. "Rukh says that I need help dealing with my grief. After the battle and everything, I sometimes have dreams I'd rather not have. I see things I don't want to."

Travail stared at the young man he'd trained and of whom he was justifiably proud. No troll suffered the kind of ailments that William implied—the guilt and grief of trauma—but he'd read it was a common malady amongst humans, both *asrasins* and normals. It had an unclear relationship to suffering, and worry for his friend gripped his heart. "How can I help you?" He made his voice gentle since it tended to calm the boy, and he could tell William required soothing.

"I don't know how to pray any more, and I need advice on what to do if I can't. Can you help?"

Travail dipped his head in thought. He knew how to pray, but a troll's type of prayer was meant for trolls only. It wasn't something they shared with others. However, the notion of faith was something he could share. First, he needed more information. "Why can't you pray?"

"Because I lost my faith somewhere along the line. After everything I've seen and lived through, it's gone."

Travail's curiosity piqued. "Do you want it gone?"

William reflected on the question. A thousand emotions and deliberations flitted across his face. He answered. "I'd rather believe."

"Then choose to believe. Choose to have faith."

"It's not that simple."

"It can be," Travail said. "Faith is a leap into a vast unknown that is richer and deeper than words, brighter than light, more pure than a newborn's soul." In that moment, a span of time measured in flashes, an image flickered in his mind, a memory maybe, of immolation beneath the awful power of a bruise-colored cloud. A singing light calling him home, and a choice he'd taken.

The memory faded from Travail's mind, and he shook off his disquieting thoughts.

"What do you mean?" William asked.

"I mean exactly what I said. Faith is a choice, a decision to hope, to trust in that which is beyond us."

"Trust broken isn't easily repaired."

"No. I suppose not," Travail mused. "But consider what you truly no longer trust. A just world? It never was. You lost nothing by coming to that realization. A loving God? If He exists, which I think He does, we can never know His vast ways."

"The priests at St. Francis said the same thing," William said. "They used to talk about how suffering has no real answer. It exists, and we don't know why."

"I believe they are correct," Travail said. "The everyday hurt experienced by people and woven throughout the world has no answer. Why does God allow it?" He knew his tone had become professorial, but he also couldn't help himself. Teaching was his great passion. "It is easy for me to say 'have faith for there is an answer', but I suspect my words are cold comfort to those who have wretched lives of little joy."

"Which is why I can't pray," William said, sounding dejected rather than triumphant.

"Which is why you *must* pray," Travail countered. "The suffering has to have meaning, even if we can't perceive it. Therefore, I choose to have faith that the loving God to whom I pray has a reason to allow pain and suffering. Without my faith, I have nothing but nihilism."

"Not everyone believes what you do," William said. "They'd say you're basically someone who's afraid to face the harsh truth: that there is no God, that the universe doesn't care, and we make our own morality. It comes from within all of us. It's individual."

It was an old argument, one Travail had purposefully *chosen* to disregard. "Perhaps, but it cannot be known one way or the other." He filled his features with the power of his belief. "The question becomes: what reality would you prefer to hope is true?"

William's expression grew thoughtful, a shade less troubled.

WILLIAM AND JASON had been assigned to work on Clifftop, and their task was to help tear down the last buildings too badly damaged in the mahavan raid to easily repair. Other crews also labored nearby, calling out orders and questions while they hauled debris to Linchpin Knoll. There, the broken remnants of what had once been homes and places of purpose were to be reduced to soil and ash by other magi. Eventually they'd have Clifftop cleaned up, and afterward, they'd head down to sort out the mess that was the terraces.

The day was hot and muggy, and William wiped his forehead. He observed the Triplets in vague hope. Gray clouds crowned the trio of green hills to the northwest, promising to bring rain and relief from the scorching weather. The precipitation would also wash away the fog of crushed rock and dust stifling the air.

William shook his head, hoping for rain before returning to the job at hand. He held tendrils of Earth and Water in his hands and studied the crumbled wall he intended to tear down. It was all that remained of a once-elegant townhome on Clifftop.

"That's not going to work," Jason said, his tone gruff.

William glanced at his friend, who stood with arms folded in obvious disapproval. The latter was a regular feature on his face these days. Long gone was the laid-back, blond-haired friend William recalled from their days in Cincinnati. Jason had grown ever more bitter since Sinskrill's attack. It had actually started months prior to that, but the battle had definitely exacerbated the changes. William wished the old Jason would come back.

"You need a thicker weave," Jason said. "That wall's too thick for those spindly little threads you plan on using."

William studied the wall, eyed his braids, and realized that Jason was right. He needed stronger weaves. He sourced his *lorethasra* more deeply. The scent of mint drifted briefly as he thickened his threads. From an artery of *lorasra* he drew the corresponding Elements of Earth and Water, attaching them to the braids he already held.

"That's better," Jason said. "It takes more energy my way, but it's also faster. You should have done it that way all along. We'd have been done by now."

William shrugged, irritated by Jason's condescension and complaints. An instant later, he shook off his annoyance. He had work to finish, and he didn't need Jason's moodiness distracting him. William placed his weave against the wall, tunneling root-like coils into the mortar and pockets of air between the bricks. Once the braid was set, he sent a pulse of Air and Fire along its tendrils.

Seconds later, with a sharp report, the wall exploded in the middle and came crashing down. A cloud of dust rolled outward, and William quickly wove a braid of Air to protect his face.

Jason wasn't as quick, and he hunched over, caught in a fit of coughing.

"You all right?" William asked.

"I'm fine," Jason said around a final cough.

William waited for the dust to settle, realizing he'd pulled down the entire wall. Not a single section of the structure remained upright. Jason was right: a thicker weave was faster. "Sure would be nice if we could close Seminal's anchor line as easily as we can tear down walls."

Jason wore a puzzled frown. "What do you mean?"

"The anchor line from Seminal to Sinskrill," William explained. "Keeping Lord Shithead out of our world."

Jason scowled. "No one can do that."

"I don't know. I found a book, remember? *Treatises on Travel—A Translation.*"

Jason snorted in derision. "With our luck, you'll end up ripping the anchor line wide open, and Shet will stroll straight to Linchpin Knoll."

Something growled in the back of William's mind, the anger Sapient Dormant had cursed him with last year, a red-eyed beast. Afa Simon had created a weave to weaken and cage the creature, but nothing could entirely banish it. Nothing short of killing Sapient, maybe.

William took a calming breath, but the anger still bubbled. He took another breath. He really didn't want an argument right now. "Then what do you think we should do? Give up?"

While William didn't want to argue, Jason apparently did. "No," Jason snapped. "What I mean to say is that our luck sucks. We do one thing, and something boomerangs and kicks us in the teeth. If we'd never gone to Sinskrill, the mahavans would never have had a reason to come here."

William's anger stirred further, and his tone became harsh. "If we'd never gone to Sinskrill, Travail and Fiona would have still been trapped there." His nostrils flared. "Or are you saying you wish you'd never come for me and Jake?"

Jason's jaw clenched. "No, I'm not saying that. Of course not. But think about everything that's gone wrong in our lives. It begins and starts with *asra*."

William wanted to smack him. "You sound like Jake used to."

Jason shrugged. "Maybe Jake was right."

"You don't believe that. You love Arylyn."

Jason's face fell into the familiar lines of bitterness. "Love has nothing to do with it. This place is beautiful, but it costs too much to live here."

William didn't know what to say. Jason's sentiments made no sense, and he eyed his friend in worry. The silence pressed. "What's really bothering you?" he eventually asked.

Jason shook his head. "Nothing. Forget it. What's next?" He gestured to the approaching clouds. They'd covered half the distance from the Triplets to Clifftop. "We might be able to get some more work done before the rain arrives."

"You know—"

"I don't want to talk about it," Jason said.

William frowned in disappointment. If anyone needed to talk about whatever was bothering him, it was Jason.

Jason chuckled then, pointing at the prison in which Brandon and Evelyn were housed. "We should pull *their* building down with them inside it."

William found himself taken aback, not by the sentiment, since he often thought the same thing. No. It was Jason's laughter. He hadn't seen his friend show amusement in so long he'd forgotten he actually could. William forced a laugh, hoping to maintain Jason's good mood. "Better not let Rukh here you say that?"

"Why? He'd probably agree with me."

William thought about it and realized Jason was right. Brandon and Evelyn only lived because . . . William wasn't sure why. Maybe Rukh thought they might still have some useful information? William doubted it. Anything further those two had to say would be lies wrapped in deceit. It was the mahavan way.

William got back to work—they had a bakery to disassemble this time—but he stopped when Jason sighed. He viewed his friend, who was staring at Mount Madhava towering in the distance. A sense of longing filled his face. "Is this all there is to life?" Jason asked. "Killing? Planning for battle?"

William held his tongue, sensing that Jason's question didn't require an answer.

Jason faced him. "Is this who you wanted to be back at St. Francis? Is this what you hoped would happen?"

William shook his head. "No, but it's what it is," he answered. "And you're wrong about *asra*. Shet was going to come whether you ever used *asra*, whether any of us ever went to Sinskrill. In fact, *asra* might be the only thing that keeps us alive."

Jason chuckled, the bitterness back. "What a messed up world we live in. *We're* messed up."

"Rukh says the same thing," William said. "He also says that we all have to find our own way of recovering from what's happened."

Jason eyed him in curiosity. "He says we can recover?"

William hoped Jason would hear him out. "He says that for some of us it requires prayer." He continued on carefully, feeling like he was walking through a minefield where Jason was concerned. One wrong word could set him off. "Others need to talk it out or meditate. I do a bit of everything. It's helped."

He held his breath, hoping that Jason would show some interest in what he had to say.

Jason's expression thankfully remained curious. "How?"

AIA CROUCHED LOW, downwind of the goats she hunted. She needed to get closer or the prey might escape her claws. Right now, the tasty meal was too far away for a certain kill, especially since they were uphill of her current position. Aia eased forward, eyes focused in intent study, searching for the weakest animal. She narrowed her concentration, localizing on a ram. Older and slower. *Yes.* He was the one.

She darted forward, ten feet closer, maintaining her attention, ears perked, eyes intent, careful with the placement of her paws. Another small dash. A slim nugget of sunlight lit the sky. Night would fall soon. This would be her last hunt for the day. Then she'd have to retire to Lilith.

The old ram lifted his head, nose sniffing. Aia didn't move. She held herself as still as a statue until the goat's gaze settled down. Another few steps forward.

Almost there. Almost time.

But first, she had to plan her attack. Rukh had taught her that.

Aia studied the area she'd have to cross. The goats commanded a rocky rise, holding a position fifty feet higher in elevation than her own. Boulders obstructed her path. She mentally traced a way through them. In prior times, she wouldn't have worried about such planning. Her unmatched quickness and agility would have allowed her to easily close the distance.

No longer.

Since coming to Arylyn, while she'd rapidly regained much of her height, mass, and power—once again, she stood taller than Rukh with a length of body to match—she lacked her prior speed. She'd recover it as well—she felt certain of that—but until she was fully herself, she had to count on guile rather than blistering swiftness.

Speed. It was what set her kind, the Kesarins, apart from all other creatures. That and the ability to speak to one another, thought-to-thought.

The wind changed. It swirled, possibly carrying Aia's scent to the goats. She stiffened, watching and calculating, her eyes trained on the goats. Thankfully, the dull creatures never noticed her presence, but she didn't relax until the wind resumed its prior direction.

Any luck? a voice called in her mind. Her brother, Shon. Arylyn had been good for him, too. He had also reclaimed his prior size, which meant he was bigger than she. But Aia was still Shon's older sister. Among Kesarins, it counted for much. Shon had to listen to what she had to say, and he often had to do as she instructed.

It's not easy hunting these hills as big and slow as we are, Shon complained. He'd chosen to seek prey several ridges away.

Aia flicked an ear in irritation. *Shush. I'm about to prove you wrong, I have a prize in mind.*

She felt Shon's presence fade away, and once more, she concentrated fully on the ram. She shuffled forward another couple of steps.

A final few more. Eyes locked. Tail twitching behind her. Muscles primed. *Ready.*

Aia charged. The goats scattered. She kept her attention pinned to the ram. He darted from her, racing to the right. Aia shifted course. He twisted again. She adjusted, closing. She readied to clip his legs.

The ram threw himself down the slope. Aia followed on his hooves. He bounded down the hill. Aia had the angle. The ram twisted away, cutting across the hill. Aia struggled to shift her momentum. Seconds burned. She managed it, but the ram had opened the distance. Aia snarled and dug deep. From somewhere within, a sense of fury rose. The goat wouldn't get away.

She picked up speed. Faster. She darted around boulders. Leapt others. More speed. Ever faster. The distance rapidly closed. The goat tried his downhill trick.

It didn't work. Aia turned smoothly, as smoothly as she ever had on the Hunters Flats. She realized she was running faster than she'd ever managed since coming to Earth. Joy filled her heart.

Again, the ram sprinted uphill. Now downhill.

Aia stayed on him. An instant later, a flick of her paws tripped the goat. The ram bleated in terror. He stumbled and fell, tumbling end over end.

Aia was on him immediately. She pinned him to the stony ground with her claws, and with her teeth, she clenched him fiercely about the throat, quickly ending his life. Once it was done, she lifted her head and roared triumph. *I am a Kesarin. I am a hunter. All should fear me!* Hot blood dripped from her teeth and claws.

You caught a goat, Shon said in her mind, sounding amazed. He must have heard the thoughts in her mind.

I ran it down, Aia answered. *The creature had no chance.*

I think you must have caught an old, slow one, Shon said in a petulant tone. *Mine were all young and full of swiftness and agility. They changed directions too quickly. I couldn't stay with them when they moved like a bat through the air.*

I managed it, Aia said, not trying in the least to keep the smugness out of her voice.

Was it your speed? Shon asked in a hopeful tone. *Did you recover it?*

Aia replayed the hunt in her mind. *No.* She wasn't as fast as she had once been, but she was getting there. She said as much to Shon.

How? her brother asked, his tone plaintive.

Because I'm older and wiser.

Aia sensed Shon's growl of irritation and he fell silent. A heartbeat later, *Can I have some goat?*

Of course, Aia replied, all magnanimity. It wouldn't do to rub her accomplishment into her little brother's nose *too* hard. Nevertheless, she couldn't wait to tell Rukh about her success and Jessira about Shon's failure.

She reconsidered the last. Maybe she wouldn't tell Jessira. It might irritate Rukh's mate, and Jessira had the most wonderful fingers. Aia would never admit it to anyone, especially Shon, but Jessira had the best fingers of any human for rubbing a Kesarin's forehead.

3

SECRETS AND MYSTERIES

D*ecember 1990*

BRANDON THRUM FLOPPED about on his thin mattress, annoyed by
the damp heat of his cell. A single, barred window allowed a stray
breeze to drift inside now and then, but otherwise the air in the
room remained as humid as a swamp. At least the cacophony of
noise from shouting magi busily breaking down crushed buildings
or removing rubble was done for the day. For a short time, blessed
quiet had reigned until the evening song of rasping crickets picked
up at sunset. Brandon shifted again, and he stared outside to where
clouds drifted high above, far away and freer than he reckoned
he'd ever again be. Perhaps it was better that way. Perhaps it was
justice.

After what he'd done to Lilith, the magi would have been well
within their rights to kill him on sight and without a trial. Instead,
they'd hastily constructed this prison into the back of what had been
a butcher's shop, housing him and Evelyn Mason, the only other
mahavan survivor of Sinskrill's attack. The faint stink of old meat

pervaded the heavy air, pressed into the stone walls of the cell, but Brandon had long since gone noseblind to the stench.

By habit, he reached for his *lorethasra* and was instantly halted by the lock placed around it, a barrier resembling a wall of fiery iron. Nevertheless, he pressed harder, and the obstacle slowly heated up. He pushed even harder until the lock figuratively burned his senses, causing him to quickly withdraw.

He scowled at the failure and the pain.

It had been the same result for weeks now, endless efforts of fruitlessly struggling against the lock, trying to break through but never succeeding. He didn't know why he bothered. The barrier was impenetrable.

But he needed his *lorethasra*. He had to have it. As a result, he continued to reach for it, not caring how unlikely it would be for him to actually reach it.

"Are you awake?" Evelyn asked.

Brandon didn't reply at once. Instead, he rolled over to face his fellow mahavan and studied her. She lay in the prison's other cell. Iron bars separated them, thick and fastened firmly to both floor and ceiling. The darkness hid her features, but not her fiery, auburn hair, which no longer moved about as if on an unseen breeze. She used to do that when she could access her *lorethasra*, a foolish affectation by a foolish woman. Thankfully, imprisonment had dulled some of her more stupid notions. Unfortunately, it had done little to dull her tongue. She talked too much.

"Are you awake?" Evelyn asked again.

Brandon still didn't answer.

"Well?" Evelyn persisted.

"I'm awake," Brandon said.

"I think I've chipped a piece off my lock."

Brandon perked up. "Are you sure? William put them on us. Whatever else, he's a skilled *asrasin*."

"William." The name came out as a curse from Evelyn's lips and with good cause.

William was the author of many of Sinskrill's recent setbacks. He had escaped from his captivity on the mahavan island, taking with him Jake, Serena, and Selene. Then he'd caused further chaos by stealing away Fiona and Travail. More recently he'd helped defeat the mahavan forces who had attacked Arylyn, was instrumental in their destruction, including Evelyn's capture. Other than Serena, there was no one his fellow mahavan hated more.

Brandon reconsidered. Maybe she despised Rukh and Jessira more. Brandon thought about the two magi. The World Killers. The husband and wife who had decimated countless unformed and mahavans; the magi who had battled the Servitor and overcome him. *Undefeatable.* So it was said by many mahavans about the two of them. The whispers about Rukh and Jessira had been present on Sinskrill well before the Servitor had launched his ill-fated attack on Arylyn. Brandon wondered what the mahavans said about the World Killers now.

"Are you sure?" Brandon repeated his question.

"There's a weakness to one side. If I push on it, sometimes it gives."

Brandon's interest increased. He hadn't been happy with what he'd been forced to do to the magi, but he was even less happy with his imprisonment. "How long will it take to break it?"

"I'm not sure," Evelyn hesitated. "A few weeks. Maybe a few months."

Brandon silently cursed as hope fled. "It'll take too long."

"Why?" Evelyn asked, her tone petulant. "A few weeks of picking away at it, and I'll be free. Then I'll free you. We know where their anchor lines are. We can use them to escape from here."

"First, we don't know the keys to any of their anchor lines."

"We can learn them. Any one of them will do."

"Second, we'll have to hope William never inspects the lock."

"It can still work if you distract him whenever he comes here," Evelyn insisted.

She hadn't listened to a thing he said, and Brandon imagined the all-too-frequently seen mulish grimace on her stupid face, the one she used to express whenever her desires became frustrated, a dull-witted expression of idiocy. "I can do my best to distract William, but

I wouldn't count on him forgetting to check on it. He isn't stupid." *Unlike you.* "He'll test the lock."

"At least I'm trying to come up with a plan," Evelyn huffed.

"I'm sure you are," Brandon said, "but right now I see no way out of our predicament."

"The Servitor will—"

Brandon surged upright, fury filling him too swiftly for his mahavan training to control. "The Servitor is the reason we're imprisoned," he snarled. "He got all our people killed."

Evelyn gasped. "You can't talk about the Servitor like that."

"I'll talk about him however I want," Brandon said. "He's been a disaster for our people. You heard the magi. Other than a few unformed, we're the only ones who survived. Over two hundred mahavans dead. And the Servitor is the reason."

"They're lying," Evelyn said. "All of us couldn't have died."

Brandon laughed at her naiveté. "You were there when Rukh crushed your forces. I was there when Jessira destroyed our ships and the mahavans who fought her on the beach. Our people were killed. All but the two of us."

Quiet fell over the prison, and Brandon's thoughts drifted toward his parents, of all things. They'd been drones, and despite Sinskrill's harshness, they'd loved him. He hadn't recognized it until coming to Arylyn, and he missed them.

Once more, Evelyn spoke. "I'm going to make the magi pay for what they've done."

"We've already done plenty to them," Brandon said, his tone dry. "I heard their losses were even greater than ours." Guilt crawled through his stomach at the thought. He liked this island, the people who lived here, their culture. He'd never been happy with the Servitor's plans for Lilith, but he'd carried out his orders like an obedient mahavan should. Now he wondered if he would have been better off asking the magi for asylum. He could have done so when he'd first scouted the island. It might have even worked. After all, Serena had been granted sanctuary. Why not—

Brandon cut off his thoughts with a sigh. It was too late for that now. He'd ruined any chances for a life here. There could be no forgiveness after what he'd done.

~

"YOU KNOW, I never liked the ocean very much," Fiona said in her patrician English accent. Her gray hair hung loose from its usual clip and whipped about her seamed face.

Serena smiled at her grandmother. "You grew up in England, an island. You lived most of your life on Sinskrill, another island. And now you live on Arylyn, a third island."

"True, and by my way of thinking, it's an even greater reason to hate the ocean." The wind continued to whip Fiona's hair, and she quickly tied it off with a length of ribbon she had secreted in a pocket of her dress.

Serena eyed her in surprise. She sounded serious. "I would have never guessed that."

Fiona shrugged in disregard and gestured to the rocky, river gorge in front of them. "Deep waters and mountains were what I dreamed of as a child." She faced Serena. "Now. Why are we here?"

The two of them stood at the base of Cliff Spirit, on the crest of the Guanyin, a silver-hued bridge spanning River Namaste where the waters re-collected after thundering down the escarpment's base. Before them stretched a narrow ravine lined with steep cliffs and titanic statues. Time, water, and wind had worn away their stern visages, but a few could still be made out. The figures were of once famous individuals from Arylyn's past, men and women of myth and legend, most of whom were no longer remembered.

The statues had always caused Serena unease, the judgment she imagined on their faces and in their stony eyes. She'd never spent much time looking at them. In fact, she usually hurried across the Guanyin, making sure to never stare too closely at the figures. They bothered her that much.

But yesterday, she'd deviated from her rabbit-like scuttle across the bridge and paused to inspect the statues more carefully. Perhaps her actions had been inspired by Jessira's words from a few days ago.

Maybe she wanted to face her fears and accept her losses. Or maybe curiosity had decided the matter. Whatever the reason, Serena had stood here and studied the statues, in this area of thundering noise and spraying mist where the unruly waters tore through the gorge and out to sea.

She wished she hadn't, but she couldn't unsee what she'd noticed.

The wind keened then, a high-pitched sound of pain or longing, and Serena shivered.

"What is it?" Fiona asked.

Serena pointed to a place deep in the ravine, where shadows ruled even now, at midday. "Do you see those statues, the man and woman with hands clasped above the river? They're the only ones holding that pose."

"Yes," Fiona said. "What of them?"

"Form binoculars and focus on their faces. See past the shadows and moss. You'll understand what I mean."

Serena sensed Fiona source her *lorethasra* when the heady smell of roses filled the air, the aroma of her grandmother's magic. Threads of Air and Water were quickly woven onto a foundation of Spirit. A moment later, Fiona gasped. "Their faces. Rukh and Jessira." She exhaled heavily. "How can this be?"

Serena chewed the inside of her cheek. "I have my suspicions."

Fiona faced her, letting go of her weave. "Tell me."

"I think Rukh is the Lord of the Sword and Jessira is the Lady of Fire."

Fiona's face grew puzzled. "Why?"

"Shokan, the Lord of the Sword. Rukh is from *Ashoka*. Sira, the Lady of Fire. *Jessira*," Serena explained. "I think if they can come to us from another world, why can't they also have lived a life before this one?"

Fiona's brow creased in thought. She gave a slow nod. "It's possible," she said. "Does anyone else know of this?"

Serena shrugged. "I don't know, but you're the only one I've told."

"Not even William?"

Serena shook her head. "Not him, and certainly not Rukh and Jessira."

"Why 'certainly' not Rukh and Jessira?'"

"Because who knows if they came here directly from their world or were reborn from their past lives? There's much about them that we still don't know."

"You don't trust them?" Fiona asked.

"It's not that," Serena said, growing frustrated at her inability to properly convey her thoughts. "They've done everything we could ask, done as much as anyone can, carried burdens no one else could. But do we really want them to have this additional weight to carry? That they once were Shokan and Sira?"

"Or that they will one day *be* Shokan and Sira," Fiona added.

An odd notion, and Serena mentally shrugged it off. "I don't think we should give them the chance to find out," she said. "I think we should blur the faces off the statues so no one else can learn about it."

"Not yet," Fiona said. "Let me talk to Odysseus first. I'll speak to him tonight. I don't want to defile something the magi might consider sacred. We'll only do it if there's no other option."

It always took Serena a moment to figure out who Fiona meant when she said 'Odysseus.' It was Mr. Zeus. He and Fiona were a couple, finding love late in life.

"What if—"

Fiona held up a hand. "Many things can happen, but if no one else has noticed the resemblance by now, it's unlikely anyone will in one evening." Her grandmother's face became certain. "Odysseus will know what can be done."

Serena reluctantly acquiesced. Rukh and Jessira deserved peace and acceptance, neither of which would happen if the faces on the statues became general information.

"Was there anything else?" Fiona asked.

Serena's thoughts went inward, and she frowned. She did have something else to discuss, something Jessira's words had inspired. Serena simply wasn't sure she was ready to face it yet, and she hesitated.

Fiona's gaze sharpened. "What is it?"

Serena exhaled heavily. *Face her fears.* "Jessira believes I'm pulling away from William. She thinks I'm . . ." She stumbled to a halt when

Fiona began nodding before the final syllable left her lips. "Is it that obvious?"

Fiona smiled, warm and generous. "Only to those who know and love you. You aren't able to hide your emotions like you once could."

Serena unconsciously hunched her shoulders. "Does William know?" Guilt made her voice weak and small, and she hated herself for it.

"Perhaps," Fiona said. "More likely he's too lost in his own pain to notice yours. Or maybe he does but doesn't know how he can help."

Serena exhaled heavily, the guilt thickening inside her like cold molasses.

"What's wrong?" Fiona asked. "Something else bothers you."

"I'm tired," Serena said. "I'm tired of all the fighting, the killing, the losses. Daniel, Selene, Elliot. I wish it was over, that all of us could live our lives as we see fit. Joyful."

Sympathy filled Fiona's features. "Life is never so easy. You know this. Sinskrill's lessons were brutal, but they also contained a kernel of truth."

Serena *did* know, but Arylyn had changed her. It hadn't made her weaker as she'd once feared it would. Instead, it had made her life far richer, but that same richness could also lead to sorrow and regret, emotions that many mahavans didn't often feel.

Fiona took her hands. "What did Jessira suggest you do?"

"She said I should pray. She also said I should consider talking to someone willing to hear me out."

Fiona reached forward, tucking a stray strand of Serena's hair behind her ear. "I used to talk to my grandmother all the time. She was the only one who would listen to a child's laments."

"I'm not a child," Serena said.

"No. But you are my granddaughter. Tell me what you need me to hear."

Serena closed her eyes and prayed for courage. While a lifetime's habit of crushing her emotions, shoving them into a box where they could never hurt her wasn't so easily undone, it could be done. Serena opened her eyes, breathed deep, and spoke of her grief.

JASON SAT HIDDEN AWAY in his quiet area of solitude, resting on a stone bench concealed behind a gauzy curtain of falling water. It was a cave pressed into Cliff Air, and from it he could view Lilith, the village's image distorted by the window-thin waterfall formed by a cataract tumbling down a bulbous protrusion of rock that pushed into the blue sky. Less charitable folk might have called this place a damp closet, but Jason didn't mind. He loved it here, the privacy. His sanctuary, and the mineral scent that filled the cave reminded him of something living and earthy.

But Lilith wasn't alive. The village glowed like a jewel in the late day sun, but the image was a lie. Lilith was broken and burned, and Jason wondered if it village would ever be set to right.

He sat straighter when he heard someone descending the slick staircase, which was the only means of reaching the cave. He had an idea who it would be, and he gazed expectantly toward the entrance. Moments later, he congratulated himself on his guess when Mink turned the corner.

"Mind any company?" she asked. Her short, brown hair and native-dark skin glittered with droplets of water. There was no way to reach the cave without getting splashed.

"Come on in."

Despite her slight frame, Mink still had to duck her way under the low-sloped entrance. She settled herself on the bench next to Jason, pressing into his personal space like she always did. "What are you doing here?" she asked. "Brooding?"

"You know me. I like to be alone," Jason said in amusement.

"So you can brood?" Her warm brown eyes twinkled with bright laughter.

While Jason had been curt with everyone else—he knew it and was unable to stop himself—he couldn't behave that way toward Mink. In her presence, he couldn't remain irritated.

He laughed. "I could ask you the same thing."

Mink viewed him with disbelief. "In all the time you've known me, have you ever known me to brood?"

"Maybe you're better at hiding your brooding than I am."

"You know that's not true." She nudged him in the shoulder. "Tell. What are you doing here?"

Jason sighed. When Mink got it in her mind to learn something, she could be a real pest, badgering a body until he gave in and told her what she wanted to know. It was a contest Jason had never won, and he figured it meant he never really wanted to. Mink was his first and oldest friend on Arylyn. He'd missed her deeply when he'd spent the better part of three years in the Far Beyond with Mr. Zeus.

"Well?" Mink persisted.

"I was thinking about something William said last week. He said I should meditate or pray or something. He thinks I need help with my grief."

"William's wiser than you. You should listen to him."

Jason grunted in reply. It wasn't what he wanted to hear.

"Are the two of you still arguing?" Mink asked. "You've made that a habit with a lot of people lately."

Only a good friend—his best friend—could have said that to him without repercussion. Anyone else, he would have bitten their head off. Not even Mr. Zeus could have gotten away with speaking to him like that. Worse, Mink was right. "I know," Jason said, regretting all the arguments he kept getting into with his friends.

"Then do something about it. You're being an asshole. No. Wait." Mink pursed her lips. "You're being a jackhole."

"Rukh and his fragging sayings," Jason muttered.

"Jessira, too. She uses the same curse words."

Jason shrugged. "You really think I'm being a jackhole?" he asked although he already knew the answer.

Mink's brows lifted as if to say *"Are you serious?"*

Jason hunched down. "Life hasn't been too good for me lately." He knew the excuse was weak before he finished saying it, and he mentally winced when he saw the fury and maybe disgust on Mink's features. She surged to her feet, and he knew she was going to let him have it.

"You think you're the only one who's had it hard? We've all lost a lot. You're not the only one suffering. Lots of people died. Lots of families are grieving. It's time you stopped being so goddamn . . ." She trailed off.

"So goddamn what?" Jason asked, anger at her words rising. He stood as well. Mink could say most anything to him, but sometimes she pushed too far. "What am I being?"

"Pathetic," Mink finished, definite disgust in her voice. "You're being pathetic, acting like you're the only one who's ever lost anything."

"That's easy for you to say. Your family is fine."

"So is yours," Mink fired back. "Who died that you loved? Daniel? We all loved him. Lien and his parents loved him most of all, but they aren't acting as tragic as you're pretending to be."

Jason breathed heavily and glared at her. She glared right back.

"You don't understand," he eventually said.

She still glowered. "Maybe not, but there are those who do. And there are those who can help you. Maybe you should try asking them."

Jason knew she was right, but he didn't want to listen to her. He didn't want to listen to anyone. He wanted to remain angry at the world, to let his hate and spite fester. In the midst of his bitterness, a memory floated to the surface of his mind, one where he had laughed without regard, carefree and happy. Where had that version of him gone? *Could that person ever come back?*

The silence between them stretched as Jason thought about what she'd said, about who he wanted to be.

He recalled something else then. "The only things in life worth keeping are love and innocence," he said, quoting a saying Rukh had once told him.

Mink frowned. "What?"

"Love and innocence," Jason repeated. "I wish I could be innocent again. Life would be a lot easier if I could be."

"Maybe. But without experience, who are we? Are we really people?"

Jason didn't know, and he didn't care. Innocence sounded great after everything he'd experienced.

"Besides, love didn't die when your parents kicked you out," Mink continued. "It didn't die when the mahavans attacked us and killed so many. It's still there, but you have to want it."

Jason resumed his seat on the bench. "You think it's that easy?"

Mink smirked. "If it was easy, none of us would be in pain."

Jason stared at her in surprise. "Even you?"

She nodded. "Even me. I hurt like everyone else." She walked to the curtain of water and pressed her hand into it, letting her fingers trail in its wetness. "You really should take William's advice. Talk to someone. Meditate. Pray. Do whatever it takes to heal."

Jason watched her let the water flow around the obstruction of her hand. "Maybe you're right."

For some reason, a small pinhole of light beamed into his heart when he said the words.

4

TENSION AND RUSES

J*anuary 1991*

"SOMEONE CHECK THE ROLLS," Mr. Zeus shouted.

"I'll take care of it," William replied.

"Careful of the stove," Jason said. "I just let off the Fire to one of the burners."

"Got it," William said. He carefully reached into the oven and pulled out the rolls. All of them were golden-brown, and he salivated at their delicious aroma.

He caught Mr. Zeus peeking over his shoulder and rubbing his hands in glee. "Excellent."

The old man had invited some people over for dinner tonight, and he wanted everything to be perfect. It would be their first hosting since the Sinskrill attack, which had been five weeks ago now but sometimes it still felt like yesterday. The Karllsons and Lien were coming, and so were Ward and Julius. Serena, Daniella, and Fiona said they'd be here tonight, too.

Mr. Zeus moved on from the rolls and checked the salad on the butcher-block island. He stirred a dish of roasted red potatoes, tested the bacon-wrapped asparagus crusted with parmesan, and sampled the corn salsa. After tasting the last, he withdrew the spoon from his mouth with a flourish and made a noise of appreciation. "Almost there. The salad only needs the candied pecans."

"I've got them," Jason said.

Jake sauntered in. "Anything I can do to help?" As usual when it came to cooking, he was late, which was probably a good thing. Jake was known to burn peanut butter-jelly sandwiches.

"Set the table," Mr. Zeus said.

"The salad's ready," Jason announced.

"Great." Mr. Zeus clapped his hands once. "Let's get the food outside and clean the dirty dishes before everyone arrives."

With the four of them working in unison, they soon had everything prepared and ready to go.

Mr. Zeus quickly took one last inspection of the kitchen, likely looking for anything out of place. "Someone make sure we didn't miss anything else. I want the house spotless."

"I'll do it," William said. He started in the front of the home, in Mr. Zeus' study and the large living room. From there, he went to the single open area situated in the back that contained the kitchen and the dining room. His head swiveled as he searched for overlooked clutter or an undusted table. A short while later, he was done. "We're good," he told Mr. Zeus.

Minutes after he finished his inspection, someone knocked on the front door. William went to let in the first arrivals. Serena and Fiona. William greeted them and tried not to stare. Serena wore a blue dress that showed off her long, tan legs.

Fiona cleared her throat, clearly noticing his preoccupation with Serena. William flinched. While Fiona could have passed for someone's favorite grandmother, his first memories of her had been back on Sinskrill when she'd been an unholy terror to him and Jake.

"I made cookies," Fiona said, lifting a covered platter she held.

William stared hungrily at the tray. Other than Ms. Sioned, no one made better cookies than Fiona. He took the cookies off her hands and led them through the house to where Mr. Zeus and the others waited in the backyard.

A strip of grass and a flagstone patio contained an unlit firepit and several chairs. Water dribbled down the cliff face at the rear of the property before collecting into a small pond lined with mango and orange trees. A half-moon beamed through ivory-lit clouds while votive candles floated on the water, and several lights hung from the jasmine-wreathed pergola.

Everyone else soon showed up, and they congregated in the back, snacking and sharing conversation.

William spoke to Ward, who sat by the firepit. "How's the leg coming along?"

Ward grinned up at him. "It hurts, but it's getting better. In another couple of months, I'll probably be able to ditch the crutches." He pointed to the items in question.

"You got out of the last battle with the devil's own luck," Jake said, standing nearby. "When I saw you on the enrune fields, I thought for sure you were dead."

Ward chuckled. "You'll get no arguments there. I broke my leg in three places, punctured a lung, and ruptured my spleen. Any one of those should have killed me."

"They would have if Rukh hadn't been there," Jake said.

William winced, hoping Jake's words didn't carry. Mr. Karllson still blamed Rukh for Daniel's death, and the large man was standing close at hand.

No such luck.

Mr. Karllson, originally from Sweden and with the build of one of his Viking forebears, growled. "I do not wish to ever again hear that man's name."

William noticed Jake slink off, and he considered following him.

Mrs. Karllson, elegant, tall, and with white teeth contrasting against her dark, Ethiopian skin, touched her husband's arm. "Now isn't the time. Our son died fighting to keep us free."

"Our son died because an arrogant man ordered an attack only a fool would have countenanced."

While William vehemently disagreed with Mr. Karllson's assessment, he held his tongue. Speaking up now would only cause an argument, and it was one he couldn't win.

"Daniel didn't die for nothing," Lien said. She stood nearby and had obviously heard the discussion.

"No, he didn't die for nothing," Mr. Karllson agreed. "But he should have never died."

"His death wasn't Rukh's fault," Mrs. Karllson said. Her voice and posture indicated this was an old argument. "It was the mahavans. They are the ones we should hold accountable. If Rukh and Jessira hadn't convinced our people to fight, trained them, we might have all been killed."

Mr. Karllson shook his head, his jaw slowly clenching and unclenching. "We didn't need them. William had as much to do with protecting Arylyn as those two did. Maybe more."

William didn't want to be drawn into the exchange, but it looked like he had no choice. "We did need them. Some of us could fight, but not enough of us, not the right way. Rukh and Jessira trained up an army."

Mr. Karllson snorted. "Then he failed as a teacher as well as a general."

"That's not fair," Ward murmured.

"This argument is going nowhere," Lien said. "I'll always honor Daniel for his courage. I also won't blame Rukh and Jessira for not being infallible. Some things are impossible to predict and prevent."

William regarded her in surprise. If anyone should have blamed Rukh and Jessira for Daniel's death, it was Lien.

Mr. Karllson muttered something inaudible under his breath and marched away to a different part of the courtyard, an empty part. Lien and Mrs. Karllson watched him leave and spoke softly to one another.

Julius and Jason approached.

"What was that about?" Julius asked.

"Mr. Karllson blames Rukh for Daniel's death. Still," William answered.

Julius grunted. "Well, it kind of is his fault. Rukh's arrogant. We all know that. It leads him to make mistakes. He acts like he can do anything, beat anyone, but what about the rest of us? We're not him, and we got our asses kicked. If that's not his fault, then whose fault is it?"

William glared at Julius, shocked by his sentiments. Julius was a lieutenant in the Irregulars. He'd earned Rukh's trust. How could he betray him like this? "That's bullshit, and you know it. We lost a lot of people, but we both know how much worse it would have been if Rukh wasn't here."

"Plus, the mahavans had cannon," Jason said. "How was anyone supposed to expect that?"

"A wise general would," Julius said, his jaw thrust out obstinately.

Lien, who remained nearby, responded. "No one could have known. Only prophets, maybe. Or do you think that's another one of Rukh and Jessira's failings?"

"I'm allowed to have my own opinion," Julius said.

William shook his head in disagreement. "Not if you insult our commanding officer and undermine his authority."

Ward chimed in, speaking to Julius. "William's right. If you really think Rukh is incompetent, you need to bring it up to the Village Council or resign from the Irregulars."

Julius' eyes widened in surprise. He clearly hadn't thought through the implications of his beliefs.

Ward pinned Julius with his hard gaze. "You better figure out what you want and who's really to blame for what happened to Arylyn. Mistakes were made—Lord knows I made my share of them —but being unable to predict the impossible isn't one of them. And we don't need mouthy crybabies whining because things didn't go our way. We got hurt bad, but we also crushed the mahavans."

Julius opened his mouth to respond. "I only believe. I mean, I wish—"

Ward cut him off. "That's your problem right there. We aren't dealing with wishes and beliefs. We're dealing with reality, and the reality is that war sucks. War is hard and people die. *I* almost died. I had to send men and women to their deaths."

William found himself nodding in agreement to Ward's words. Rukh had said pretty much the same thing during the months of their drilling before the mahavan invasion. Command required the terrible willingness to send good people to their deaths. He wondered how Rukh and Jessira lived with it.

～

"YOU READY?" William asked Julius.

A couple of nights ago, at the dinner held at Mr. Zeus' house, they'd agreed to meet at Arylyn's library and repair a broken leyline that had ruptured several buildings over. Usually Ms. Sioned would have handled a task like this, but with her failing health, those kinds of jobs fell now to the other *raha'asras*: William, Jake, or Fiona.

Not that William minded. The work was easy enough, a lot like knitting. But first, they had to clean out the *theranoms*—the terracotta urns holding *therasra*, polluted *lorasra*. This was where Julius came in. He was a powerful Water adept, and while *raha'asras* could do a lot, none of them could wash away *therasra* as well as Julius.

"I brought some coffee," Julius said, passing William a mug.

For some reason, the gesture felt like a peace offering, and William took the steaming mug with a nod and a word of thanks.

"Where's the building with the busted leyline?" Julius asked.

William searched about, squinting when the morning sun shone in his eyes. He and Julius stood atop Cliff Air, upon a promontory paved with a walkway of pale, yellow flagstones bordering a square lawn. Beyond the green grass rose Arylyn's library. The building had always struck William as resembling a church rather than a place of books. A finger of River Namaste plunged downward on one side of the buckle of stone, raising a drifting mist.

The building . . . where was it?

Ah! There it is. William finally located the building, pointing it out to Julius. He gestured to a nondescript brick building on a corner lot, three stories tall and with most of its windows smashed in, giving it a lost, lonely appearance. It used to be an artisan's shop, but the artist in question had been killed in the Sinskrill attack.

"Listen, I want to apologize for what I said the other night," Julius said before they started toward the building.

"What do you mean?" William asked, distracted by the work they needed to do.

"The other night at your house."

William studied the building where they'd find the ruptured leyline. "What about the other night?" he asked, still distracted. He wondered how much work it would take. Could he could repair the leyline, or would he have to entirely rebuild it?

Julius made a sound of frustration. "I need to apologize for more than just the other night. I need to apologize about how I've behaved every day since the attack. I've been an ass."

William had no idea what Julius was talking about, and he faced his friend, giving him his full attention now. They'd all been asses—especially Jason—but it was understandable. "Don't worry about it. It's been rough on all of us. Mr. Zeus says it's common for people who've suffered trauma."

Julius shook his head. "It's not that. It's what I've been saying about Rukh and Jessira."

William made an *'Oh'* of comprehension. "About how you've been blaming them for what happened?"

Julius reddened, clearly abashed. "Yeah, that. I . . ." His sentence trailed off.

"I get it," William said. He put a hand on Julius' shoulder and gave him a supportive squeeze. Rukh always did that to him, and for some reason it helped. "Sometimes we want to blame someone for the bad things in our lives. It's a normal emotion."

"That's the thing," Julius said. "I didn't think I was being emotional. Mr. Karllson is being emotional. I thought I was being rational."

Julius' statement threw William, and his head rocked in surprise. "How do you figure?"

"I thought about everything we did during the battle, all the decisions we made. Over and over again, and I figured our biggest mistake was when Rukh ordered Ward's forces south. He should have done it sooner. If he had, Ward could have stopped the mahavans who made it to the enrune fields and shelled Clifftop. They were the ones who caused the most damage."

William had also thought of that. Ward's position at the north end of Janaki Valley had made sense at the time. Everyone expected the mahavans to take Sita's Song through Janaki Valley, but instead they'd taken a far harder path, a twisting trail amongst the rugged hills to the northeast of Lilith. Their route brought them into Janaki Valley only a few miles from Lilith, but it also meant the mahavans must have sourced their *lorethasra* the entire time they marched. They couldn't have managed the trip any other way. It was suicide, since they'd arrived at Lilith's northern border with hardly any reserves and two options: shell the village or get to the harbor and escape. They didn't have enough energy for both.

That information had come from Evelyn. She had been there when Adam had presented the choice, and the mahavans hadn't hesitated. They'd chosen death.

"Did you read the report from Evelyn's interrogation?" William asked.

"I did," Julius said, sounding reluctant. "I wanted her to be lying. I wanted to believe that Rukh should have known to reposition Ward sooner than he did."

"And risk the mahavans burning the northern end of the Valley? And with no certainty of the makeup of their forces? What if they hadn't split their forces, and all of them attacked Ward while the rest of us were running around Arylyn's interior? Farther south, Ward couldn't have barricaded Sita's Song. He would have been overwhelmed, and the mahavans would still have had free rein to reach Lilith."

Julius stared off in the distance, toward Lilith Bay and the Pacific Ocean. "There weren't any good choices, were there?" he said softly.

William shook his head. "None. We were stuck between a rock and a hard place."

Julius sighed. "Do you think Rukh will forgive me?"

A sinking feeling filled William's stomach. "You didn't say this to anyone else, did you?" *Julius is an idiot if he did.*

Julius shook his head.

"Then Rukh never has to find out."

Julius managed a weak grin. "This is Rukh we're talking about."

William understood. Rukh would find out. He had a weird way of learning things he had no right to know. "Then I guess you better tell him first before he hears it from someone else."

"Great," Julius muttered. "Can't wait for that conversation."

RUKH ENTERED the prison where they kept Brandon Thrum and Evelyn Mason. He was vigilant before he ever opened the front door. He didn't trust these two, especially the woman. He kept his attention focused on the mahavans when he walked into the area with the cells. Dust motes floated in the air, highlighted by a ray of sunshine beaming through the room's single window, and the building stank of stale sweat. There was only an occasional breeze to breathe life into the stifling space. Otherwise the prison baked beneath the afternoon sun. It couldn't be comfortable.

Too bad.

Rukh opened the door to Brandon's cell and observed the mahavan, who pretended to doze on his bunk.

"Get up," Rukh said to the supposedly sleeping figure.

Brandon didn't stir.

Jessira, who had also entered the prison, stood at Rukh's side, arms crossed in obvious irritation.

Evelyn lay on her bunk, and Rukh caught her watching them through slitted eyes. She winked when he glanced her way, proffering a smug smile of satisfaction.

Rukh ignored her and went into the cell where Brandon had yet to move. He used the tip of his boot to nudge the mahavan hard in the hip. "Get up," Rukh repeated.

Brandon yawned lazily, stretching and arching his back. He sat up leisurely, taunting them as if he had all the time in the world.

Rukh growled with impatience. He sourced his *Jivatma*—his *lorethasra* as the *asrasins* named it—and used it to power his muscles. He grabbed the mahavan by the shirt collar, jerked him upright, and flung him out of the cell. Brandon soared five feet through the air and landed awkwardly on his feet, falling over an instant later. Rukh noticed that Evelyn's self-satisfaction was no longer present. Instead, she wore the flat-eyed, blank stare that mahavans used to hide their emotions.

Rukh addressed Brandon, who was rising shakily to his feet. "Next time I tell you to get up, you'll get up like your ass is on fire. Nod if you understand."

Brandon's face had also gone flat and unreadable, but he nodded.

"You don't need to be so hard on him," Jessira murmured. Her voice carried, and Rukh saw a smirk replace Evelyn's blank features.

"You're weak, even if you're powerful," Evelyn said.

Rukh smirked right back at her. "Aia sends her regards."

Evelyn's face emptied of emotions again, but Rukh could see the fear in her eyes. Upon their first meeting, Aia had delved deep into the mahavan woman's thoughts, discovering the plans that Adam Carpenter had put in place during Sinskrill's attack. Without that information, hundreds more might have died.

"Let's go," Jessira said, gently guiding Brandon out of the prison.

Rukh followed on their heels, and they entered a bare room that contained a simple desk and three wooden chairs. Stacked gray stones formed the walls, except for the front. There, a bank of windows that had once opened onto Clifftop had been bricked closed. As a result, the only light in the room came from a single lamp on the desk.

Rukh shut the door leading into the room containing the two cells and Evelyn.

Brandon slumped into one of the chairs and winced. "That really hurt," he complained. "Did you have to throw me so hard?"

Rukh chuckled, and his grim demeanor fell away. "Consider it part of your penance for the deaths you inflicted here."

"I still think this is stupid," Brandon muttered. "How is smacking me around supposed to help anyone?"

Jessira paced forward until she stood in front of Brandon. Her prior charitable manner was no longer in evidence. "It helps those whose lives you destroyed. They would see it as justice."

"That's not justice," Brandon said. "That's revenge."

Rukh's brows lifted in surprise. He hadn't expected the mahavan's response, especially since the man was mostly right. Applying pain for no reason wasn't justice. It wasn't even revenge. It was torture, and Rukh wouldn't allow that. However, *pretending* to hurt Brandon was something else entirely. It was a ploy meant to maintain Evelyn's trust; not toward any magus—she'd never be that foolish—but toward Brandon.

Jessira's response to Brandon's statement was a narrow-eyed, unforgiving glare. "If we wanted revenge, we would have killed you." Her hand moved to a dagger sheathed at her hip. "Slowly."

Brandon shifted in his seat, and he moved his gaze away from Jessira and toward Rukh. "What do you want?"

Rukh answered. "What do you think we want? You've already told us everything you know about Sinskrill, right?" He made his features go hard, which wasn't hard. He hated what Brandon represented: murder and savagery. "Or do Aia and Shon need to verify your truthfulness."

Brandon's mahavan skill at hiding his emotions failed him, and he paled. He spoke in a rush. "I told you everything. I promise."

Rukh smiled, pretending warmth he didn't feel. "There. Now that wasn't so hard, was it?"

"Has Evelyn mentioned anything of importance recently?" Jessira asked. "Any plans? Information about Sinskrill, things of which you were unaware?"

Brandon shook his head. "No. She's an idiot. She thinks of nothing other than her hate." A beat later, he started. "Hold on. She did mention something the other night."

Rukh waited for Brandon to continue. It was usually best to simply let the man talk without interruption. Brandon clearly considered himself bright and personable and apparently enjoyed the sound of his voice.

"She said she thinks that she's chipping away at William's lock," Brandon said.

Rukh stiffened. Neither mahavan could be allowed their freedom. "Be clear. Tell me *exactly* what she said."

"Evelyn believes there's a weakness on one side of her lock,"

Brandon said. "She thinks that given enough time, she can wear it away."

Rukh's jaw clenched. A weakness could allow Evelyn to escape. Who knew what carnage she would commit then? He shared a glance with Jessira, who appeared equally unhappy.

"We'll make sure William strengthens the lock," Rukh said to Brandon. "Is there anything else?"

The mahavan shook his head. "There is one other thing," he said, sounding diffident.

Once more, Rukh waited for him to speak.

"Is there any chance I can join Arylyn? Become a magus? The others here accepted Serena."

Rukh started shaking his head before Brandon even finished his question. "Think about what you're asking. You helped murder hundreds. There's no coming back from that."

Brandon's face went mahavan unreadable. "Then when this is all over, let me go. Send me to some faraway *saha'asra*. I don't care where. Leave the lock in place."

"You'd die outside of Arylyn or Sinskrill," Jessira reminded him.

"Better to be dead than enslaved," Brandon said. Anger and regret laced his voice.

Unexpected sympathy welled within Rukh. He'd gotten to know Brandon over the past few weeks. He still hated what the mahavan had done, but much of it had been because Brandon had never known anything different. He'd never considered anything different.

But in a different world, he would have. Perhaps he would have been a better person. He recalled Arisa in that moment, the thousands of years of war against Suwraith and Her Chimeras. He remembered the honor and grace of Li-Dirge and Li-Choke. He smiled when he remembered Chak-Soon, a Tigon, the first of his kind to learn empathy and love. And if Chak-Soon could overcome his training in hatred, why not a mahavan?

5

RUNNING TO HEAL

J *anuary 1991*

WILLIAM BREATHED SMOOTH AND STEADY, his strides taking him across the dew-glistening grass. Jake and Jason ran alongside him through the empty enrune fields. No one was playing, not yet anyway; maybe in a few more weeks. At least William hoped so. Or maybe not, since most everyone who used to play had enlisted with the Irregulars. They all knew what was still needed: invade Sinskrill and stop Shet. Rukh wanted them ready to go by September. Any later, and the weather on the mahavan island would make a beach landing too difficult. Then they'd have to possibly wait as long as the spring, which would be too late.

The dawn sun pinked the sky, and the only sounds were those made by the three of them running across the fields. No birds or insects made any noise, and even the trade wind blew softly, quietly. William imagined he, Jake, and Jason were the only ones awake at this hour. Only they could appreciate this morning's peace.

Peace. A heavily weighted word. A state of being so hard to obtain, and so deeply desired. William wasn't alone in wanting peace in his life. Jake and Jason felt the same way.

William breathed deep of the cool air, unconsciously pulling ahead of the others, imagining himself letting go of his anger and sorrow. It helped, and every day the pain lessened.

Moments later he reached Lakshman's Bow, the closest bridge to Lilith that crossed River Namaste. The wide span had a set of black and white flagstones crafted to create the yin and the yang. On the far side, a road, Sita's Song, traced a line through Janaki Valley.

William halted at the crest of the bridge. River Namaste grew turbulent here, swirling with eddies and frothing whitecaps, as it raced for Lilith's waterfalls a mile away. He followed Sita's Song with his eyes. It twisted a winding path, occasionally coming close to River Namaste, which flowed through the center of Janaki Valley. He lost the road as it meandered northward, but he knew it where it ended: at the base of Mount Madhava, the island's only mountain. His gaze went there. Snow lingered on the peak's rugged shoulders all year long.

Another thought occurred to him. Meldencreche, the dwarven village. It lay within Mount Madhava, home to the Dwarven Memory. He remembered the village's sublime peace.

Again that word. William wondered if he should visit Meldencreche and talk to the Dwarven Memory. The dwarves had been created to provide solace to those in need. Maybe they could help him. Better yet, maybe they could help Jason. He certainly could use some solace.

Jake and Jason arrived.

"Slow pokes," William said.

"Slow poke yourself," Jason groused. "Not all of us were infected by a necrosed."

William chuckled in amusement, glad that Jason's tone hadn't contained its usual measure of bitterness.

"Why are we out running this early anyway?" Jake asked.

"You know why," William answered.

Jake brandished a fist in mock threat. "If you say Shet, I'll throw you in the water."

William leaned over the railing and scanned the river. It was a long fall. "Lucky for me, that's not why I wanted to take an early morning run."

"Then why?" Jason asked.

"Because it's fun."

"You think running is fun? Jason barked laughter. "You idiot."

"It is when it's with the two of you. We used to do this all the time, remember?"

"Yeah, but even then, it wasn't any fun," Jake said. "You were the only one who thought it was. The rest of us hated it."

Jason's humor fled. "Plus, it was also with Daniel."

"Yeah, but maybe we can start a new tradition," William suggested. "In Daniel's honor. He'd like that."

Jason snorted. "A tradition where you run us into the ground until we puke?"

"We've barely covered two miles," William protested.

"And I'm already ready to lose my lunch, you dumbass," Jason said.

"No," Jake corrected. "He's a dumbShet. That's what he always talks about." His voice went up an octave. "Shet is coming. We're doomed. What do we do?" He clutched his cheeks as if terrified.

"I don't talk like that," William said.

Jason took up where Jake had left off. "Oh, Serena. How can I ever trust you again?"

William reddened. "Come on. That's just low."

Now it was Jake's turn. "You hurt me so terribly, Serena."

William's embarrassment and annoyance deepened. "Lay off. That's enough."

"I love you, Serena," Jason said. He made kissing motions and sounds.

William gave up trying to shut the other two down. There was no winning this one. He watched as Jake and Jason broke out in laughter. Part of him was embarrassed by their jokes. *Is that really how they think I act around Serena?* But a larger part was glad to see them relaxed and happy, like they'd once been. If it meant he was the butt of their jokes, so be it.

They continued to wheeze more humor at his expense for a few minutes longer until Jason's laughter trailed off. "Daniel would have loved being a part of this."

A wistful smile replaced Jake's laughter. "Could you imagine how epic it would have been to give him grief for how he acted toward Lien? Wish he was still here with us."

"We all do," Jason said, "but time moves on, and we've got to also."

William did a double-take, stunned by Jason's sensible statement.

Jason noticed, becoming sheepish under William's shocked scrutiny. "It's ok. I know how I've been. I'm not saying I'm fine, but I'm better. I want to be better."

Relief for his friend lifted William's heart, and he wondered if someone had finally spoken some sense to him. "What changed your mind?" he asked.

"Mink talked to me," Jason answered.

William shared a grin with Jake, glad that the mockery shoe was about to be laced up on another foot.

"What?" Jason asked.

"Nothing," William replied. "It's just that you must really trust her judgment."

"I do."

"And that's all there is?" Jake asked, his innocent question ruined by his knowing leer.

Jason sighed. "Of course that's not all there is. She's my oldest friend on Arylyn. She's special."

Jake piped up. "She sure is, and I bet you wish she could be more than a friend."

William spoke up. "But she can't because, you know, you're such a dork."

Jason sighed. "Can we move on to some other topic?" he asked, his tone plaintive. "Something not related to my love life?"

"Or lack thereof," William said.

"Interesting," Jake said. "You're saying you have a love life when you talk about Mink?"

"Drop it," Jason said.

William laughed, unexpectedly happy like he hadn't been in weeks or months. "I miss this. Hanging out with y'all."

Jake burst out in laughter. "You hick."

William drew himself up, affronted. "What'd I say?"

"*Y'all*," Jake said, drawing out the word in a thick-as-molasses drawl.

"Shut up and run," William said, smiling to take the sting out of his words. He really had missed this.

WILLIAM EXAMINED *Blue Sky Dreamer's* tell-tales. They swirled about, shifting as the wind moved. "Sheet in," he called to Serena.

The two of them had the afternoon off and had decided to go sailing, setting off from Lilith Bay. The escarpment upon which the village nestled loomed behind them, petrels rode the blustering breezes, crying out now and then, and the wind blew hard, spraying salty water. *Blue Sky Dreamer* rode the rushing current, darting across the bay, lifting and skipping across waves like a thrown stone. Rainbows rode her wake.

William brought the helm to port, watching the leading edge of the sail as Serena had taught him. It might as well have been another life when she had. Back then all he had to do was learn to sail. Serena gripped a cleat when the bow came about and the motion of the deck altered. William brought *Blue Sky Dreamer* farther to port. The dhow's movement steadied, and she ran with the wind.

"Sheet out," William said to Serena.

The dhow picked up speed, heading across the water and thudding westward now, toward the setting sun.

"You act like you've done this a few times," Serena said, easing her way to his side by the tiller. She grinned at him in that way she had in which she seemed amused by something only she knew.

"I had a great teacher." William eyed her up and down. She wore green shorts and a loose-fitting T-shirt, both of which contrasted nicely with her dark hair and her Mediterranean-dark skin. "She was really pretty, too."

"Was?"

"Is."

Serena laughed. "Smart correction. And I'm sure that's all you thought of her."

William pretended to consider her words. "Now that you mention, she *was* pretty, but she was also a pain in the ass. Always bossing me around. I couldn't stand her."

"And what do you think she thought of you?" Serena edged closer, a single brow lifted in challenge.

William shrugged. "I never could tell. She had this way of hiding her emotions like a Vulcan. Plus, she'd do this stupid thing of raising one eyebrow, like Mr. Spock or something. I think she might have even had green blood."

Serena's mouth dropped, confusion and outrage evident. "What?"

William chuckled. "Vulcans have green blood. You know, *Star Trek*."

Serena sighed in disappointment. "For what it's worth, I hear she thinks you're a nerd and will always be one."

William grinned shamelessly. "Guilty as charged. But I have to wonder: as big of a nerd as I am, what does it say about the woman that she likes such a nerd so much."

"Nothing good, I'm sure."

William chuckled at her answer. "This is nice."

"What? Sniping at each other?" Serena tucked a lock of hair behind an ear, and William's breath caught. Something about that simple movement had always entranced him. It still did.

A single eyebrow arched again, and he realized she was waiting for him to answer her question. He quickly gathered his wits. "No. Joking with each other. We haven't done it in a long time."

Her amusement faded a bit. "We haven't had much to joke about in a long time."

William nodded agreement, and they sailed on, saying little. Serena hummed a familiar song, "Gloria," by U2.

She spoke again several minutes later. "I saw statues that look like

Rukh and Jessira in that gorge," she said. "The one near the Guanyin. There's a pair of statues there. They reach across the river and hold hands. They have Rukh and Jessira's faces. I told Fiona about it," Serena said. "I thought we should rub out the faces. That way no one can figure out who they look like, but—"

"Too late for that."

"—and she said she'd check with Mr. Zeus, but he says . . ." Serena stumbled to a halt. "Wait. You already know about them?"

William nodded.

"Who else knows?"

"Rukh and Jessira. They were with me when we saw them."

"When was this?"

William shrugged. "A couple weeks ago. They asked me not to say anything to anybody."

Serena's eyes slitted, and William found himself on the receiving end of her disconcerting focus. "You realize what this means?" she asked.

William sighed. He only wanted to go sailing, not talk about Rukh and Jessira, Sinskrill, Shet, or anything else. "I know. So do they."

"What are they going to do about it?"

"Who cares?" His voice came out more curt than he intended, and he mollified his tone. "Let's just sail. I want to take a day off from worrying about anything."

Serena eyed him in momentary consideration, her features inscrutable, but she eventually nodded agreement.

"I'm sorry," William said a few minutes later.

"You don't have to apologize."

"Yes, I do. I haven't been a very kind person in a long time, and I want that to change."

"None of us have been kind," Serena said. He noticed her gazing over the water, and her voice lowered, barely audible over the wind and rushing waves. "We've worked hard to rebuild Lilith. We had to, but it means we haven't taken the time to care for one another the way we should have. I'm just as guilty of that as you."

William didn't understand what she meant, and the confusion must have shown on his face.

"I pulled away from you. I suffocated my emotions because I figured that way I wouldn't hurt any more. It was stupid." She smiled wanly. "The trouble is, suffocated emotions never really die. They grow up into monsters."

William shrugged, not sure how to respond to her words. "If it makes you feel better, I worked non-stop for pretty much the same reason."

"I notice you're taking time off now. What changed?"

"A couple of things. First, Rukh pointed out my behavior, and then I talked to Travail."

"Talking to Travail is always a good idea," Serena said. "What did he have to say?"

"He told me to have faith and to pray. I'm trying to do both, but it isn't easy."

"Faith and prayer never are," Serena said.

William eyed her askance. "What about you? You said you *had* been hiding your feelings. What changed your mind?"

"Jessira and Fiona," Serena said. "They helped me see the truth."

"Which is?"

"Something private."

William took the hint and dropped the matter. Earlier, their sailing had been fun and full of banter, but now it felt somber, and a notion of how to recapture their happier mood came to him.

"The tell-tale is shifting counter-clockwise."

Serena glanced toward the top of the sail. "No, it's not. It's clockwise."

William readied to put the tiller over, wanting to juke the dhow into the path of a wave. The spray would hurl into *Blue Sky Dreamer* and soak Serena. It was a joke he'd pulled a few times on her in the past.

Serena caught on, though. She clutched his arm before he could change course. "You're not fooling me again with that trick," she said with a laugh. "I'll leave your boat with my T-shirt dry, thank you very much."

William lidded his eyes, and imagined Serena in a wet T-shirt.

Serena noticed his faraway stare and somehow guessed his thoughts. She rolled her eyes. "You're incorrigible."

"Which is why you like me."

Serena surprised him by kissing him on the cheek. "That's only part of the reason," she said, "but you better swing us about. We're about to reach the edge of Arylyn's *saha'asra*. I didn't bring a *nomasra*."

RUKH LEANED into Aia's side and watched the last light of the sun before it dipped below the horizon, leaving streaks of purple, red, orange, and gold spreading across the sky, maybe feathered from the brush of a heavenly painter. The brilliant colors glowed above Janaki Valley's verdant hills. A wind gusted, lofting the aroma of the mineral-scented spray that dashed against the water at the base of the cliff far below. A final blazing sunbeam lanced across the sky, and Rukh basked in its warmth.

I like it here, Aia said.

Me, too. Rukh lifted an arm and draped it across Aia's broad shoulders. She nudged him with her large head, and he braced himself to keep from falling over. His Kesarin had regained all of her stature and her strength.

Are you content? Aia asked after a moment of quiet.

I am, Rukh said. *It's a beautiful evening. Jessira said she'll bring dinner, and for once I don't have anything to do.*

In that case, my ears itch. Aia nosed him, pushing her head into his hand.

Rukh laughed even as he petted her calico-colored fur, soft as down, and ran his fingers from her forehead to the ridges of her spine. Aia purred, bending low to make it easier for him to reach the spot in question. He scratched between her ears, and her purring grew louder. He focused on the area around her right eye, where black fur looked like a pirate's patch. Her eyes closed, and her neck stretched. The line of her mouth flattened. She rumbled, sounding like an engine from the Far Beyond.

My ears itch, too, a voice complained.

Shon.

Aia's eyes snapped open. *"Then Jessira should scratch them,"* she said to her brother.

Rukh glanced down the hill to where his wife and her tawny-furred Kesarin ascended toward him and Aia. Jessira had left her bicycle next to his, and she carried a large, covered basket, moving with the grace of a trained dancer. She'd tied her blonde hair in a ponytail, and it swayed with every elegant step she took. Her hips swayed, too, and he suddenly found himself wanting to see her in a dress.

Her green eyes twinkled when she reached him. "I'll wear one when we get home," she said. As usual, she knew his thoughts without his needing to voice them.

Rukh took the basket from her. He smelled fish. "Salmon?"

Jessira nodded. "Along with cheese, wine, and fresh fruit."

"What about us?" Aia asked.

Rukh pointed. *"Those sheep look tasty."*

Aia and Shon perked up, and their heads swiveled as one as they focused on the ovines.

Shon took a hesitant step toward the sheep. *"The farmers won't mind?"*

"Of course they'll mind," Rukh said, feeling mildly guilty for tricking the Kesarins.

"They why did you tell us to eat the sheep?" Shon sounded honestly perplexed.

"He didn't," Jessira replied. *"He only said they look tasty."*

"You tricked us," Aia accused, sounding affronted and hurt.

Rukh wasn't fooled. The Kesarins enjoyed playing pranks on one another all the time. *"There are some wild goats a few hills away. You mentioned smelling them earlier,"* he said to Aia. *"Why don't you go hunt them?"*

Shon's eyes focused on the basket. *"Fish are tasty, too."*

"Goats," Jessira ordered.

With a final grumble, the Kesarins meandered away.

After they departed, Rukh helped Jessira sort out the food. He poured her a glass of wine and set out the plates while she sliced the block of cheese.

"We start training in a few weeks," Jessira said.

Rukh paused in what he was doing. "Yes." *Another group of people to teach to kill.* He wondered again if there would ever come a time when he and Jessira could set aside their blades and battles and live simply as husband-and-wife. Nothing more. Nothing less.

"Our blades and battles aren't so easily set aside," Jessira said softly.

Rukh sighed. "No, they aren't."

She withdrew a mandolin she'd packed into the basket. "Play for me."

"Sing with me?"

Jessira smiled, and Rukh strummed the strings of the mandolin. His fingers plucked the chords of a song from home, from Arisa on their wedding day. She knew it and her voice lifted. She sang of a time of peace, when Trials were a thing of the past, and the world was fresh, and life was lived joyfully.

"It's a sweet song," Jessira said after Rukh played the last few notes. "But it's part of the past. It's painful."

"Our past is painful," Rukh said. They'd left their world, their family, their children, everything and everyone they knew and loved, for what he more and more considered a fool's errand. The statues in the gorge . . . Another future awaited him and Jessira. Their battles on this world wouldn't end even if they defeated Shet in this time. They'd have to fight him again in another era, however that came to be. The thought baffled him. Furthermore, they made him wish they'd never left their children.

Jessira took his hands in hers. "You're wishing we'd never come here."

Rukh nodded. "This didn't have to be our battle."

She ran her fingers through his hair. "You were never a person to stand aside when evil threatened. Neither am I."

"Our curse." Rukh didn't bother hiding his bitterness.

"And our great strength." Jessira cupped his face, making him meet her gaze. "We have each other. We'll survive this and the times to come. Have faith. We'll see our family again. In time."

Rukh smiled acceptance, her words bringing him comfort like they always did. Sometimes when doubts crept across his mind, Jessira was the rock that kept him upright. And sometimes it was the other way around. They were like that: a true union, and he was grateful.

6

WORLDS APART

F*ebruary 1991*

WILLIAM AND SERENA jostled their way closer to the gazebo centered within the Village Green. Newly-laid bricks paved the walkways, which formed borders for the freshly placed sod. Recently planted gardenias and other young shrubs and trees—all of them stimulated to quick growth by Lilith's gardeners—filled the flower beds that surrounded the gazebo and edged the Green's perimeter.

All was restored to how it had once been, back when Arylyn knew nothing but peace. Except for the cannons still mounted on the Green. They remained wary sentinels, watching over Lilith Bay, and a harsh reminder of what the people of Lilith had endured.

William felt Serena pull on his hand. "This way," she said, tugging him along through the horde of people who shared the Green with them.

William followed her, taking in Serena's blue dress, her bright smile. She'd pinned her hair up, and it fell softly around both sides of her lovely face, displaying a pair of silver earrings. She looked happy and at peace.

So did everyone else on the Green. They all seemed to be having a good time; talking, drinking, or laughing while they waited for the celebrations to officially commence. Workers had spent the past few days preparing the Green, decorating it with strings of lights, tinsel, and floating candles. The smell of popcorn, candy, and searing meat suffused the air as a number of food wagons did a fair business, handing out food and drinks.

After the Sinskrill invasion, the magi hadn't been able to celebrate the Christmas or New Year's holidays—the Western one anyway. They'd been occupied by other matters. By now, though, enough of Lilith had been restored for the Village Council to declare a day of rest and renewal, a festival. The date in question happened to fall on Groundhog Day.

William thought the decision amusing. Really? A groundhog to figure out if there would be six more weeks of winter? On Arylyn? A place that didn't have a winter, except on the highest slopes of Mount Madhava?

William's eyes automatically went to the mountain's snow-covered heights. Under the glow of a waning crescent moon, he could barely make out the peak, and he shifted his gaze higher, noticing the stars sparkling in the firmament. *So majestic. So mysterious. Who else lives up there? How many worlds?*

Serena returned his attention to the here and now, squeezing his hand and urging him onward. They pushed carefully past other people, moving closer to the gazebo. She apparently wanted a front row seat for when Mayor Care re-lit the street lamps.

William leaned against her tugging hand, pulling her to a halt. "We don't have to get there all at once. Slow down. Take it easy." He grinned. "An old janitor told me that once."

Serena tilted her head to the side in consideration, disbelief on her face. "Really? An old janitor?"

He maintained a grin. "Yup."

"You said something like that to me before. It was when we cleaned that church in Over-the-Rhine."

William's eyes widened in surprise. He hadn't expected her to remember.

Serena chuckled. "And the advice doesn't fit you. You've never been one to relax."

William's humor fled into disappointment when he realized she was right. He didn't know how to relax. Ever since coming to Arylyn he'd pushed himself hard, always facing a new challenge after the last one was overcome.

Serena squeezed his hand in support. "You'll figure it out." She gestured to Rukh and Jessira, who stood under the eaves of a darkened building. "Remember what they looked like back in Cincinnati? We thought they were freshmen."

William pushed aside his disappointment and recalled the first time he'd seen Rukh and Jessira. Even then, with his baby-fresh features, Rukh had carried a sense of hidden power and coiled violence, and Jessira had been his match. "I don't think anyone could have ever mistaken them for freshmen."

His eyes narrowed when he noticed where Rukh and Jessira stood: on the edge of the crowd, in a shadowed vestibule, unseen, like they didn't want to be noticed. William knew why. Too many still felt like Mr. Karllson, blaming Rukh and Jessira for the losses the magi had suffered. His jaw clenched in anger.

"I know," Serena said, apparently recognizing the direction of his thoughts. "It's not right, but give it time. People are starting to come about."

"They're not coming about fast enough," William said.

"Come on." Serena tugged on his hand again, getting them going forward. "Tonight isn't about them. Tonight is about having fun."

William nodded agreement, but his annoyance with Rukh and Jessira's situation still surged through him in waves even after he lost sight of them. He practiced Travail's teachings then, inhaling and exhaling deeply while thinking about something soothing, something that made him happy. He ended up thinking about Serena, remembering his dance with her last year. It had been the Chinese New Year. He'd loved holding her in his arms.

She glanced back at him then, and something in his features must have given him away because a sloe-eyed smile of pleasure lit her features.

How does she always know? William affected a nonchalant posture.

Serena continued viewing him through lidded eyes for a moment longer before facing forward again and drawing him deeper in the crowd, always toward the gazebo.

While they walked, William noticed a silver anklet chime with every step Serena took. He'd given it to her during their time at St. Francis. He smiled when he saw it and pointed it out. "You still have it."

Serena shook her foot, jingling the anklet. "Of course. My first and best friend gave it to me."

"I'm glad I'm your best friend." He leaned close. "You're my best friend, too." The words said, he realized they were true. He liked Jake and Jason, but he liked spending time with Serena even more.

Serena merely nodded, and they continued on, finally reaching the gazebo. Most of the Village Council were gathered upon it. William tried not to scowl when he saw Zane Blood, the Councilor for Cliff Spirit, and his ally, Break Foliage of Cliff Fire. Both were native-born magi, and both were cowards who would hopefully be voted out of office in the next election. Those two were perfect examples of what Rukh meant when he said that politicians the worlds over were useless.

Then again, there was Bar Duba, the Councilor for Cliff Air, a tall, stout man, and native-born like Zane and Break. Unlike them, he actually had a brain in his head. So did Seema Choudary, a small, quiet Indian woman, and Lucas Shaw, a tall man of patrician breeding from Charleston, South Carolina.

Several minutes after William and Serena arrived at their spot near the gazebo, Mayor Care, a former English governess, stepped forward and held her hands up for quiet. The crowd slowly settled down. "I don't have much to say. We've had a terribly difficult year, and I doubt you've come here to listen to me speak anyway. We've lost many good people, too many of our loved ones, and life has been hard. But despite these losses, Lilith is coming back to life!" Her voice, which had faded into pained reminiscence, gathered strength. "The proof is this rebuilt Village Green and your own presence. We survived, and better times *will* come!"

The crowd cheered, and William shouted agreement as loudly as anyone else. As usual, Serena was more sedate in her response.

Mayor Care continued, "And although terrible dangers still threaten and the enemy remains unbowed, we should give over our worries this night. On this night, let us celebrate and dance!"

The mayor stepped back, and a band—two guitars, an upright bass, and a fiddle—began playing. People paired up.

William recalled what almost happened last year—Chinese New Year. He'd nearly lost his chance to dance with Serena. Fear had held him back. This year would be different. He wouldn't give way to cowardice. He held out his hand. "Care to dance?" He eyed Serena in challenge.

Serena didn't reply with words. Instead, she graced him with a smile, the one of secret amusement, and took his hand. He drew her closer, and she flowed with the movement, pressing close, closer than the dance needed. She kissed him, a peck on the lips, before pulling away. "I'd love to."

SAPIENT DORMANT KNELT before the Servitor's Chair in Lord Shet's Hall. He pressed both fists against the onyx stones that formed an aisle leading from the gray double-door entrance, through a forest of overwrought gold columns, and to this point in the room: the dais holding the Servitor's Chair and Shet's Throne.

High above, stained-glass pictures and mosaics from Sinskrill's holy book, *Shet's Counsel*, decorated the vaulted ceiling. The images displayed the Lord holding various visages: violent, patient, hardened, calm, or resolute. Sapient preferred the ones in which Shet smote his enemies.

The Servitor sat upon his Chair, two steps up the dais, his features inscrutable. Sapient flared his nose, flicked his low-lying ears, and darted his black tongue past pale lips, all of it a pretense of nervousness. Let the mahavans think he feared their Servitor. He mentally scoffed at the notion even while he studied the room.

The Servitor watched him, and across his lap lay a white spear carved with glowing, red runes: Shet's Spear. Sapient kept himself from staring at the weapon . . . or the throne. He could sense the Lord's *lorasra* flooding from the one, and as for the other—it wouldn't do for the Servitor to learn about its importance.

He twisted his gaze past the Servitor and the Lord's empty throne, beyond them both to a titanic statue of Lord Shet looming at the far end of the hall. In the figure's three right hands, the god grasped a khopesh, a mace, and the Book of the Dead while the left ones held a bow, a spear, and the Knife of Woe. The jaws of a crocodile crowned the statue's head.

The Servitor leaned forward, an intensity coming over his bland features. "Why are you here?"

Sapient spoke, the timbre of his voice rich and pure, unlike his decaying body. "As I once vowed obeisance to your ancestor, so I vow and bow to you."

The Servitor eyed him for a pregnant moment before dipping his head in acquiescence and rising to his feet. "Then stand and be welcome amongst Shet's army on Sinskrill."

Sapient stood, unlimbering himself to his spindly eight-foot height. As a result, he met the Servitor's gaze nearly at eye level. The mahavan's jaw clenched briefly in obvious annoyance, and Sapient constrained a sneer of pleasure. The Overward of the necrosed ran a four-fingered hand over his bald pate. "It is good to be made welcome. Should I call for my brethren?"

"No," the Servitor said, the word sharp and final. "There is no need for any other necrosed when we have you, the Overward." He gestured to a mahavan who stepped forward. "My Secondus, Adam Carpenter, will show you to your quarters." The two men shared enough features to be brothers.

Sapient bowed, a brief bending at the waist, enough to show respect but not deeply enough to demonstrate obeisance. "As you command, but I'll journey elsewhere. I prefer the solitude of the forest, and I'm sure your fellow mahavans would, too. With the over-abundance of tasty *asrasins* walking around, I fear I may allow my hungers to overcome my discretion." He eyed the Secondus in challenge and let the man see his appetite.

Adam didn't flinch, and Sapient viewed the man in fresh respect. The Secondus either had exquisite self-control, or he actually thought he could stand against a necrosed.

The Servitor cleared his throat. "If you wish a journey, then perhaps one of a different sort might be more to your liking." He offered the Spear's haft. "Hold this and be transported to Seminal. Allow the Lord to know of your loyalty to him . . . and to me."

The fool actually thinks I fear to stand in the Lord's presence. Sapient grinned. Seeing the Lord again . . . nothing could make him happier. He grasped the Spear, knowing what was needed. He sourced his pustulant *lorethasra*, and his Spirit separated from his body. A rainbow road opened in front of him. It quickly transitioned into a black tunnel. Sapient's senses collapsed into nothingness. Distance became meaningless. *He* became meaningless. He threatened to come apart. Dissolution beckoned. Death's dawning. Sapient urged it on.

Almost . . .

The travel ended with a disappointing jolt, and Sapient found himself floating above a different world, a strange one, one populated by a variety of nightmarish woven. Wild necrosed hunted the land, packs of unformed crawled like parasites across the hills, and vampires drained *lorethasra* from their helpless victims. Sapient's gaze moved to a range of hills. They reminded him of gnarled teeth, and beneath them, armies of ghouls ruled dead cities.

Sapient laughed at the wonder of it all.

A voice spoke on the wind, surprised and overjoyed. "My long-lost, beloved child, come to me."

Shet. Sapient focused on his master's call, knowing it would guide him to the lord. He swiftly made his way to a fortress carved onto the shoulders and ledges of a mountain that was taller and grander than all the others.

As it should be.

The citadel merged menace and beauty, protected by tall towers and thick walls. A slender road ribboned along the outskirts of a dark valley. Staring into those shadowed hollows, disquiet stirred within Sapient, a rare emotion for him. Something dangerous possessed the valley.

He threw off his thoughts when a courtyard, one open to the skies, came into view. The Lord waited for him there, upon a dais, standing in front of a throne made from the open jaws of a dragon. He clasped a rune-wreathed black spear in a firm grip and wore a glad smile on his face.

Sapient responded with a beam of pleasure, his features twisting into an unaccustomed display of happiness as true joy filled his heart.

He paid no mind to the other woven arching outward in waves of importance from his Lord. They mattered not. None of them did; not the slumbering, tawny dragon curled close by or the handful of black-eyed demons huddled about Shet's dais. Only the Lord signified worth.

Sapient marched past them all, crashing to his knees before Shet, his homage complete and total. The Lord had created him, and the Lord would complete him by overcoming Shokan's curse. He had promised he would, and any doubts as to Shet's ability to make good on his vow departed when Sapient beheld the Lord's charisma and power. *This* was a being worth serving.

"Welcome, my old friend," Shet said, his voice warm and commanding. "What news do you bring? Tell me of your life."

Sapient knew better than to tell the Lord of his millennia of slumber or the occasional woven he'd consumed over the unspooling years. His life since Shet's departure from Earth had been pathetic. Instead, he spoke of more recent events.

Shet's visage grew grim as Sapient spoke of what he'd witnessed. "Grave Invidious is slain and *Undefiled Locus* is stolen?"

"Yes, my Lord. I have my suspicions as to who might have performed such profane acts."

"Indeed?"

"A young holder by the name of William Wilde."

Shet tsked. "The holders have always been pests. Cockroaches they are, scuttling about and hiding, barely avoiding their richly deserved demise."

"They are vermin," Sapient said by way of agreement. He thought he and his brethren had hunted the holders to extinction. He'd certainly believed it to be the case when he'd killed Pilot Vent, thereby birthing Kohl Obsidian.

But then had come William Wilde.

Sapient mentally scoffed at the ridiculous name. But the young holder's skills weren't ridiculous. He'd already killed Kohl and Grave.

Shet smiled predatorily. "Thankfully, I've found the exact warrior to rid me of those insects." His voice rose in timbre. "Seminal will be purified of their curse. It will be done."

Sapient's curiosity got the better of him. Overcoming a holder was no easy task, even for a necrosed, the mightiest of Shet's woven. "Which of your followers is puissant enough to accomplish your will, my Lord?"

Shet gestured languidly, toward a couple lingering near the courtyard's perimeter. "He and his elf-mate stand over there. They bark and yowl, but in the end, they will do as I bid."

Sapient looked to where the Lord pointed and stilled. *It couldn't be.*

"Something disturbs you?"

Sapient forced his eyes away from the man and the woman, making himself meet the Lord's gaze. Shet wore a patient visage but a shrewd calculation filled his eyes. "Surprise only, my Lord. The man is merely human, and the woman is an elf. On Earth, elves were never a match for a holder."

Shet nodded, and the sense of testing faded from his eyes. "On Seminal, matters are somewhat different." He laughed. "I will speak to you more of this when I again stride my birth world."

Sapient laughed with the Lord. "I look forward to the day with great anticipation. All my brethren do, when we're made whole again."

Shet's smile faltered for an instant before he quickly restored it. "Of course. Your restoration will be my first act."

Sapient maintained a grin, but he hadn't missed the Lord's slip. "I should return to Earth."

Shet waved him off. "Certainly. We shall grasp forearms soon, just like we did when I ruled Earth and counted you as one of my greatest servants."

"I am still your servant," Sapient said. He bowed low and then rose into the air. As he ascended, his eyes went back to the man and the elf-woman. Shock filled him anew.

Shokan and Sira. They lived when Shet had assured him they'd been killed.

And Shet didn't see it. If he had, he would have immediately killed them. His hate for them was volcanic. If Shet couldn't see what was so plainly in front of his face, what else was he missing? What else might he be lying about? Sapient hadn't missed the Lord's stuttering tone when he'd mentioned the notion of being restored.

Doubt stirred like a rustling serpent in Sapient's heart.

SHET MUSED about Sapient after the necrosed left. There might have been something unusual in his servant's features, something that spoke of anger. Worse, he couldn't tell if he saw the truth of the matter or if his suspicious nature was raising doubts where none should exist. Sapient had been the second of his kind ever created and had always been loyal. He still should be. Certainly, the joy on his face when he'd seen Shet hadn't been feigned.

The Lord threw off his doubts and called for Sture Mael, the greatest of his Holy Seven, the general who had vanquished mighty Aia, Shokan's cursed steed. Sture, Shet's trusted brother from when they had started this journey together, with Sture as the teacher, the isha and Shet as the student, a bishan. Of course, the student had long since eclipsed the teacher, thereby becoming the master, and it spoke of Sture's quality that despite the alteration in their positions, he never wavered in his allegiance, never varied from following the Lord's commands.

Sture, standing nearly as powerful and massive as Shet, shouldered aside a cluster of gathered woven, parting them as a shark does minnow. The titan attired as usual in a kilt, halted before the Lord. A set of broadswords formed an 'X' across his back, and short-cropped hair the color of a bloodless corpse contrasted with his dark skin. A scar carved a canyon across his face, running from the corner of his mouth down to his collarbone. It had been a near-mortal blow—should have been—delivered by Shokan when Aia had died.

Shet spoke to his general. "We still have one more Orb to retrieve and destroy. Only then can our full plans be set in motion. Earth's poisonous aether . . . you know what it does."

"A final Orb, and we save Earth and Seminal both," Sture said, a questioning note in his voice. He couldn't see the aether as Shet could, could not see its flow.

"Of course," Shet agreed. "It should have never been left to this late hour, but what is done is done." He tsked. "When the anchor line between the two worlds was sundered, neither I nor Shokan accounted for Earth's aether, that world's quintessence. It has contin-uously leaked into Seminal for the past seven millennia. The poison must be expunged."

"Yes,' Sture agreed, "and afterward, we will rule our lessers as dharma dictates." He paused then. His gaze went to Cinder and Anya, and he silently observed them. The human and the elf-woman stood against the courtyard's wall, unobtrusive and alone. Unsurprisingly, the woven didn't bother them. Both individuals gave off an aura of constrained deadliness that the monsters recognized and respected. "We truly need them?" Sture asked after a few seconds of apparent thought.

"We do."

"I worry about them. They are too powerful, too proud. There is something about them, a stench of priggish morality." Sture's mouth curled. "Do they not remind you of Shokan and Sira, utterly certain in their self-righteousness?"

Shet descended the dais, not speaking until he stood at Sture's shoulder. He leaned close, not wanting his next words to carry. "We require their aid," he whispered. "You know why."

Sture's frown deepened. "The Calico dragon protects the final Orb."

Shet smiled. "Which is why we will send Cinder and the elf princess to steal it. They are pawns to be sacrificed, if need be."

"And if they live?"

"Then I will have other uses for them. You know the holders seek to gather allies against us."

Sture crossed his thick arms, still unhappy, and Shet sighed in impatience.

"Can you not send your own dragon to fetch it?" Sture asked, gesturing to the tawny beast who had one eye cracked open. "And was he not red last season?"

Shet waved aside the question. "Dragons change colors as the mood suits them," he reminded Sture. "And I won't risk Charn. He's the first dragon I have ever mastered." His eyes went to the great dragon, who blinked once before resuming his slumber. He'd never had a pet, but Charn reminded him of a cat, and he found himself growing ever more fond of the creature.

Sture shrugged and resumed his study of Cinder and Anya. A second later, a pleased smile flitted across his face. "Sira."

"What of her?" Shet asked, disliking hearing the name of his enemy.

"Shokan's screams at her dying was lovely. Do you recall them?"

Shet chuckled. "I do." Well did he remember that day, but further recollections caused his humor to fade. He also recalled what came next when Shokan deflected the power of *Undefiled Locus* against him and the Seven, banishing them to Seminal. Tumbling across unspooling centuries. Awakening, finding himself unmoored in time, losing thousands of years, and finally re-engaging with the world. The final humiliation occurred a bare score of years later when the great dragon Antalagore and the cursed Mythaspuris bound him and his surviving titans to stone and mountain, wracking them in chains of *lorasra*. They'd been locked away for eons.

It wouldn't happen again. Shokan and Sira were dead, and their allies, the great cats, Aia and Shon, destroyed.

Sture gestured at Cinder with his blunt jaw. "You don't fear the boy might become a rival power once the final Orb is destroyed?" he asked. "He has the potential. I last sensed such latent greatness when you were my bishan."

Shet had already considered the possibility. Thankfully, there was a way around the matter. Cinder loved the elf-woman, loved her to the very depths of his soul. And though she denied it, she loved him just as deeply. It was as obvious as the scar on Sture's face, and like a scar it marred perfection. Properly trained, Cinder could have indeed challenged the Seven, but he would never attain such a future.

"He has the possibility of power," Shet agreed, "but not his elf lover. I will make it his undoing."

Sture's grim visage broke into a smile. "The wise warrior crushes the heart of his enemy."

"And Anya is Cinder's heart. Threaten her, and he will be brought to heel."

Sture continued to smile, but the pleasure soon left him.

"What is it?" Shet asked, irritated that his greatest servant still questioned his plans.

"What if he does as you and I did? He might still become a power we can't provoke or too swiftly dismiss."

Shet shook his head in disagreement. "You know how we came to be as we are. Do you really think that boy has the strength of will to accept such pain?"

"Shokan could."

Shet's mouth curled down. He was truly annoyed now at the naming of his other great enemy. "Thankfully, Shokan never had the opportunity."

"Thankfully, indeed."

Shet no longer wished to discuss the matter. He ascended the dais and resumed his seat on his throne. "Enough. All of this is immaterial. My will shall be carried out."

Sture hammered a fist to his chest. "By your will and words, it will be accomplished."

Shet's mouth thinned, still angry at Sture's continual questioning. Nevertheless, he accepted the ancient words of a vassal to his lord.

7

PLANS AND CHOICES

F*ebruary 1991*

ADAM WATCHED Sapient Dormant exit Shet's Throne Hall. The Over-ward all-but strutted his way out the door. The creature had completed his journey to Seminal, and afterward there was something odd in his features. Fear or shock perhaps. Adam couldn't tell, but then who could truly read the emotions of a necrosed? More importantly, why did it matter? The undead monsters were a plague on existence. They should never have been created.

Still . . . Adam pondered what had transpired between Sapient and Shet. What had they discussed?

An instant later, he shook off his musings. He'd never learn what had happened, which meant it was inconsequential. He had more important matters to attend.

Adam faced his brother, the Servitor, who, despite the setbacks he'd suffered in the past few years, retained an unmistakable presence. A circlet graced Axel's forehead and a rich, fur-lined cloak confirmed his majesty. They did nothing to soften his coarse features or his obvious frustrations.

"Ensure our privacy," Axel ordered, his breath frosting. Winter's chill permeated the room.

Adam sourced his *lorethasra* and wove a pattern of Air to create a block, a braid meant to prevent anyone from listening in on their conversation.

"What do you make of Sapient?" Axel asked.

"He lies," Adam said without hesitation. "He pretended to show obeisance to you, but I'm sure you caught the mockery on his face."

Axel nodded impatiently. "Yes, but what do you suppose occurred during his journey to Seminal. Did you not notice how troubled he seemed when he returned?"

Adam hesitated. He wasn't sure what he saw. "I don't know. He appeared upset."

"I agree," Axel said, "but what to make of it?" He sighed an instant later, slouching in the Seat as he kneaded his temples.

Adam had no response and watched his brother in silence. "Perhaps it's best to leave it for another time," he suggested. "Several tribes of unformed have arrived. I sent them north."

"I heard. Jeek Vosh will have to manage them. He'll either displace their primes or will himself be displaced."

Adam understood the Servitor's reasons for bringing the woven monsters to Sinskrill, but he still harbored significant doubts as to the validity of the plan. His own strategy—allying with Arylyn—struck him as a wiser course of action. Surely the magi would see the futility of attacking Sinskrill. Not when a far greater threat loomed. It would be both ruinous and irrational for the magi to attack Sinskrill. He'd dreamed as much to Serena since she knew the truth about Shet.

"Several vampires have also answered my call," Axel said, interrupting Adam's thoughts. "They'll flow to the island tomorrow afternoon."

Adam's mouth curled. Vampires. *Parasitic vermin.* He'd met a few in his life. They held themselves in an arrogant fashion, as if refined gold flowed through their veins. In truth, they were nothing more than rats.

"You disapprove?" Axel said.

"You know my feelings toward vampires."

Axel grinned. "I share them, but in this case, we need them and possibly their blood-slaves."

Adam still disagreed. Of all the woven, vampires were easily the worst: lazy, pretentious, and not particularly powerful. "What use are the blood-slaves if they're normal humans and not even woven of some kind?"

"They also have a few unformed, a plethora of ghouls, and even a few elves."

Adam's gaze shot to him. "Elves? Surely not. I thought their kind extinct."

"The vampires have kept a small *sithe* alive, in a *saha'asra* deep in the bowels of the earth. Somewhere in Romania." Axel shrugged. "They may bring the blood-slaves or they may not. I don't care, so long as the vampires answer my call."

Adam still didn't believe the vampires and their blood-slaves would be of use. He didn't think any of the woven monsters would, but he couldn't disagree with his brother. Axel was the Servitor, and the Servitor's will was law. To challenge it was to court death. "Is there anything else?" Adam asked.

Axel rose from the Servitor's Chair. "There *is* one other thing," he said. "I've discovered the relics of a demon, the final war machine an ancient Servitor brought to Sinskrill. Salachar Rakshasa was her name. She was likely the last of her kind on Earth, but it'll be months before I can fully repair her shell. Even then, her body will be an empty vessel since her aether is yet trapped in the realm of the Rakshasas. It will take time to master the braid that will recall her from that plane of existence, but do not worry, I will manage it."

Adam broke into a sweat. "You mean to awaken a demon?"

Axel nodded. "Demons were Shet's greatest warriors, standing only below the Seven in power. Compared to them, the necrosed were mere drones."

Madness.

Some of his horror must have showed because Axel slammed the heel of the Spear against the ground. "The decision is made. You will support it." His eyes blazed.

Adam nodded, but turmoil continued to consume his thoughts. This Salachar Rakshasa could be as powerful as Axel believed, but what was to stop the demon from killing them all and await Shet's return amongst a forest of dead mahavans? "Are you certain this is wise?" Adam dared to ask. "Why not help William destroy the anchor line to Seminal? Was that not your original intention?"

"It was, but I lack the knowledge of how to break an anchor line, and I've never discovered it. Such knowledge is lost," Axel said. "Or have you learned what I haven't?"

Adam shook his head.

"Then it is Salachar who will serve and save us. I can control her. I can bend her to my will." Axel leaned toward Adam. "You don't know all the secrets a Servitor possess. Nor my power. With the demon, I can also control Sapient and prevent the Overward from bringing any more necrosed to Sinskrill."

The plan still sounded dangerously mad. "If you can control the demon, why can't you control Sapient?" Adam asked. "Bend him to your will, and the demon becomes unnecessary."

Axel shook his head. "I can do as you say, but I still need the demon's power to defend Sinskrill. We have to be in command of the situation when Shet arrives. He'll kill us all otherwise." Axel peered at him probingly. "Are we clear on the matter?"

Adam pushed away his emotions, allowing no hint of his horror to show on his face. "Yes, my liege, we are clear." He bowed low. "I have matters to attend. Do I have permission to depart?"

"You may go," the Servitor said.

Adam bowed low again and left. He strode out of the Throne Hall, through the corridors of the Servitor's Palace, and the entire time he considered the situation at hand. Axel was insane. The fool would kill them all. Adam couldn't simply step aside and watch the Servitor bring Sinskrill and the world to ruin.

He neared his quarters and came to a decision. Serena had to know what was coming. He'd dream to her tonight. A part of him wondered how long he would maintain his courage. Probably not much longer than it took to send Serena the dream. He knew himself a coward.

SERENA KNEW SHE WAS ASLEEP, but even while slumbering, she managed to groan in frustration. Another dream from Adam? How many would he send? She'd long ceased responding to them.

But this one was different, filled with stranger images. A white staff with fiery, red runes. *Shet's Spear*. It summoned creatures of forever shifting forms. A hundred of them. Serena recognized them. Unformed. Another image. This one of a pale creature, tall and spindly. His arms extended past his knees. Bald, and eyes like gangrenous stones. Malice filled his features. *Sapient Dormant*. The Overward disembarked a rainbow bridge—an anchor line—and marched onto a land of clouds, hills, and giants. *Sinskrill*.

Another final vision had been sent. This one was of a being lying upon a slate slab with eyes closed. Standing, she'd be taller than Sapient. Powerful with chitinous skin, matte-black like a gun. A head like a bullet. The Spear touched the creature, and its eyes opened. Red fire blazed.

Serena's sleeping mind recognized the being. *A demon*.

She awoke with a gasp, sitting upright. Her heart pounded. It took her a moment to collect herself, and she stood on shaking legs, stumbling to the window of her bedroom. She gazed at the beach just beyond the front porch of her cottage. The golden sand glowed ivory under the light of the full moon. A vagrant breeze billowed the window's lacy curtains, moving it languidly about Serena's still form. Waves washed against the shore.

The gentle sounds and scene brought Serena no calm. She understood the import of the dream Adam had sent her. Her father had brought a horde of unformed to Sinskrill. Worse, he'd brought Sapient Dormant as well. The last image, though, was what terrified her the most. She continued to struggle to believe she'd actually seen it. Was it really what Adam sent? Was she interpreting his vision correctly? A demon?

It couldn't be. Until now, Serena had always thought the creatures a fable, a terrible nightmare from a dead world, but if Adam was to be believed, a demon still lived.

And her father planned on awakening the monster.

A thirst filled her, and Serena went to the kitchen, poured herself a glass of water, and tried to be as quiet as possible.

Fiona must have heard her anyway because she opened the door to the cottage's other bedroom. "I thought I heard someone moving around the kitchen," she said. Her eyes immediately sharpened, apparently noticing Serena's troubled mien. "What happened?"

"I had a dream," Serena said. "Adam sent it."

Fiona stepped forward, her demeanor calm. "Tell me."

Serena explained what she'd seen.

Fiona found a seat on the couch, her face having gone drone-unreadable. "You believe him?"

Serena sat beside her, fully considering the question. "I do," she said, even while struggling to understand her reasons for believing Adam. "It had the flavor of truth."

Fiona stared out the window, toward the lagoon and the peaceful setting of a full moon shining on calm waters and ivory sand. "Only you can say if Adam dreamt you the truth or a lie. Only you knew him well enough to tell."

"I think he sent me the truth," Serena said, her mind filling with further certainty as she more closely evaluated the dream.

Fiona's frustration overcame her mahavan training, and she glowered. "But why? Why would he tell us what we face? And a demon, of all things."

"I think he's frightened of the demon. It terrifies him. He thinks it's wrong to bring the creature to life. He feels the same about Sapient Dormant."

"The Overward and a demon." Fiona snorted. "Which one do you suppose is the greater threat?"

Serena shrugged. "I don't know, but the stories about demons . . ." Little information remained about the creatures. All she knew were fables of their legendary power. No one knew if the creatures were woven or something else, something that predated the ancient *asrasins*, but all stories agreed that the creatures had been viciously evil and possessed the strength to move mountains.

"You understand what this means?"

"It means we're in trouble."

"Yes, we are." Fiona shook her head in apparent disbelief. "I never believed the Servitor could be arrogant or foolish enough to rouse a demon."

Serena didn't harbor such doubts. "My father is many things, and arrogant is most certainly one of them."

"And foolish?"

For all that her father had done, and now this, raising a demon? Foolish didn't begin to describe his actions. "Idiotic and cowardly is more like it," she said.

"Yes," Fiona agreed. "What will you do with the information?"

Serena had already made that decision. She knew who to tell. "I'll speak to Rukh and Jessira first. Mr. Zeus, too. After that, I'll inform the Village Council." She needed all their advice.

"A good start," Fiona said.

Serena shook her head in disagreement. "A good start would be an end to this war."

JESSIRA SAT on one of the hard benches that faced the rectangular table behind which sat Lilith's councilors. Today's meeting was scheduled to take place in the Municipal Center of Arylyn, a place as nondescript and bland as the rest of the village was evocative and lovely. This windowless room with its boring color palette of tan-on-tan could have easily served as the jail in which Brandon and Evelyn remained imprisoned.

Jessira figured the uninspired decor was a gentle reminder that the Village Council was intended to be as ineffectual as possible. In this regard, it brought forth memories of the Magisterium, Ashoka's city government. It, too, had been meant to do as little as possible, and she figured the people of Rukh's home would have appreciated a popular phrase on Arylyn: *One bureaucrat is a necessity, two are a nuisance, and three are a reason to fetch tar-and-feathers.*

The pontifications of Break Foliage, the rat-faced Councilor for Cliff Air, interrupted her ponderings. His partner in vainglory, Zane Blood, the Councilor for Cliff Spirit, nodded his bald head at every statement Break made. His glasses occasionally slipped down his nose when his head bobbed too vigorously.

At least Bar Duba, the thick-set Councilor for Cliff Air, could be counted on to see reason. Same with Lucas Shaw, Mayor Care, and the quiet Seema Choudary. The small, Indian Councilor for Cliff Earth shared some features with Rukh and could have even passed for one of his aunties.

Jessira smiled to herself at the thought. In many ways, she and Rukh were older than Seema.

Her husband, who was seated beside her, quirked a questioning eyebrow, catching on to her humor. Almost from the first, the two of them had been able to know the other's thoughts without the need for words, an unexpected gift from the First Father.

Rukh leaned close and whispered in her ear. "She would be the tiniest of aunties."

Members of Rukh's Caste, Caste Kumma, were universally tall, and Jessira stifled her laughter, covering her lips with a fist.

Once she had her humor under control, Rukh spoke again. "You really should pay closer attention to the Council," he whispered. "Who knows what pearls of wisdom they'll put forth."

Jessira shushed him, paying more attention when Break finally finished his soliloquy. Maybe now the Village Council would make a decision.

A moment later, she rolled her eyes at her naiveté. No such luck. Now it was Lucas Shaw who needed time to blather on and on about something, rambling in his elegant yet slow cadence.

Jessira mentally groaned. *This was taking too much time.*

She stretched her legs, slouched deeper into her seat, and folded her arms. As she'd feared, the councilors insisted on reviewing every speck of Serena's testimony in tedious detail, over and over again.

The girl had already recounted her dream three times now, and she had yet to be dismissed from her position as a witness at the podium. Her face had gone blank a long time ago—hours it felt like—and was empty of emotion. Nevertheless, Jessira saw the irritation reflected in Serena's stiff carriage, which was perfectly under-standable.

Jessira twisted in her seat to get more comfortable, but the move-ment caused a twinge of discomfort, a lingering effect from the blows to the head she'd suffered during the Sinskrill attack.

Rukh eyed her again, this time in concern. "How bad is the pain?" he whispered.

"Tolerable," Jessira said. She recalled how frightened Rukh had been when she'd been delivered into his hands after the battle.

It served him right after all the times he'd scared her. She remem-bered when he'd almost died, single-handedly destroying a Chimera breaching tower. Or when he'd saved the Trims during the Advent Trial from the Sorrow Bringer's unexpected presence.

"I wasn't that bad," Rukh muttered, obviously aware of her thoughts.

Jessira didn't have time to reply. Lucas Shaw had paused his rambling speech, apparently asking a question of one of the other councilors.

"I really think we should reconsider the ridiculous notion of a demon," Break began.

Jessira's patience threatened to snap. They'd already discussed the demon—thrice! She wanted to stand and order the idiot councilors to make a decision.

Rukh must have felt the same way. Generally more composed than she, he stirred in his seat, arms folded as he stared at the Village Council in obvious annoyance, especially at Break, who apparently caught onto Rukh's irritation and stumbled to a halt.

The toady councilor swallowed. "But perhaps we've discussed the matter enough."

"Thank all that's holy," Serena said. "Can we please move on and vote on what you'd like me to do?"

Zane Blood leaned forward in his chair and peered over the rim of his glasses. He wagged a finger at Serena. "Now, listen here, young lady. We will not be—"

Jessira couldn't take any more, and she erupted to her feet. "Enough!" She glared at the Council. "We've wasted enough time. Vote and move on."

"We still have much to discuss, many questions," Zane said.

"Then discuss them yourselves," Serena said. "I've already told you what Adam dreamt to me. Answer the matter and let me know what you decide." She made to leave the Council chamber.

Jessira flashed Serena a wink when she passed by. Rukh rose to his feet as well, muttering about the stupidity of politicians.

"Wait!" Bar Duba called. "I move that we vote on the matter."

Serena halted her departure.

"Second," Mayor Care spoke up.

"What are we voting on?" Lucas asked, sounding confused.

"Whether Serena dreams to Adam and asks for more information," Bar said. He addressed Serena. "Is that what you wish to know?"

Serena wore a long-suffering visage. "Yes. It was what I asked when I first told you of the dream. It's all I ever wanted to know." She muttered under breath. "I didn't think it would take two hours to find out."

"All in favor?" Mayor Care asked.

A unanimous set of 'Ayes' met her question.

8

DECEPTIONS AMONGST ALLIES

F *ebruary 1991*

SAPIENT DORMANT SAT ALONE on a black rock, feet dangling over the edge of a cliff as he watched the deep waters of Lake White Sun, and beyond it the Norwegian Sea. He rested in a small clearing, blood leaking down his claws. A blustery wind blew, but he paid it no attention. A drizzle fell, icy like pinpricks, and he ignored that as well. Other thoughts occupied his mind.

In his four-fingered right hand, he held the corpse of an unformed. He'd already consumed the creature's *lorethasra*. Tepid as it was, it would have to do. The rest of the creature's tribe would shortly arrive. Sapient would kill them, and from their carcasses he could likely harvest limbs aplenty to supplement his decaying flesh, possibly replace the dying vision of his cataract-infested eyes and maybe even a corrupted lung. Sapient scrutinized his fingers. Deformed and broken, and he only had seven left. A fully-fingered set of hands would also be handy.

The Overward smirked at his pun. Shokan had hated puns,

detested them actually. So did Sira, but they both had laughed anyway because they'd loved the holder who Sapient had once been.

His humor faded. The holder he'd once been had been a fool. He had voluntarily gone to Clarity Pain, Shet's first and greatest fortress. He'd gone there against Shokan's advice, unable to sit still while the god tortured his fellow holders. He went there thinking he could free his brethren. Instead, he'd quickly succumbed to capture, been tortured, brought near death, and then revived. An endless cycle. Over a period of months, the pain and trauma had transformed a noble warrior into a killing machine, one made to love his tormenter. With Sapient's first breath as a necrosed, love for Shet had filled his soul, no different than air filling his lungs.

Sapient had then marched from Clarity Pain, full of fervent vigor, a slave to Shet's will, and addicted to the god's *lorethasra*. He, Shet, and Grave Invidious had battled the mighty Antalagore the Black along with Sira and her powerful steed, Shon. Sapient lost consciousness during the conflict, and when he awoke, he learned that the great dragon had been sent fleeing to Seminal while Sira and Shon had been killed.

Shokan had paid him back for the murders by casting a curse upon all the necrosed, committing them to a life of unending decay and slow death. Shet had promised to lift the malediction, but Shet lied. Sapient knew the truth now. Sira lived. Sapient had seen her and Shokan—another who Shet claimed to have slain—alive and hale on Seminal. That fact and Shet's absence for the past seven thousand years had allowed the last of the Overward's love for the god to finally die.

For the first time in millennia, Sapient was truly free to do as he desired.

The necrosed pondered what that might mean for his future, but his thoughts cut off when he sensed a tribe of unformed arrive. They were kin to the one whose blood still stained his claws. Sapient stood, taking the time to stretch his gangly limbs. He clenched his fists, rolled his shoulders, and loosened his jaw. Jagged teeth could work as well as claws. He smiled in anticipation when the tribe entered the clearing. Only six of them. Their Prime, wearing the aspect of a

Siberian tiger, snarled when he saw the dead unformed at Sapient's feet.

The Overward smiled wider, gesturing the Prime forward. *Come on.*

The Prime took the bait. He charged, leaping for Sapient's neck. The necrosed stepped aside. His fist flew out, catching the Prime in the shoulder. The unformed crashed to the ground. Before Sapient could go after him, the rest of the tribe attacked.

An eagle raked at his face. Sapient snatched the unformed by the neck and ripped off the creature's head. He quickly inhaled the unformed's *lorethasra*. A rhino charged. Sapient leapt above its goring horn and landed on the animal's back. A hooking punch to the side of the beast's chest shattered ribs. Sapient's claws also dug deep, furrowing out flesh. The rhino collapsed.

Sapient took in this one's *lorethasra*, too, and when he slipped off the beast, he flexed limbs that were suddenly stronger.

Something slammed into him. *A buffalo.* Sapient flew through the air, crashed heavily, and tumbled across the ground. Before he could regain his balance, hooves pounded into his head. Sapient's vision went gray for a moment.

He growled, pushing past the injuries. He sensed the hooves ready to crunch him again. *A horse.* He caught a leg and threw the beast aside. It transformed in mid-flight to an eagle, who flapped above his reach.

Two buffaloes charged.

Sapient hunched low, driving strength into his limbs as Shokan had long ago taught him. He hurled forward, twisting to dodge one buffalo. He spun and smashed into the other one. For an instant, he strained against the creature. He lifted, and the buffalo lost its footing. Before it could transform, Sapient was on it. He ripped out the beast's throat with his teeth.

Again, he stole the creature's *lorethasra*.

Pain tore through him. Claws and teeth dug into his back and neck. Sapient threw off whatever had attacked him. *The Prime, still a tiger.*

Sapient used some of his stolen *lorethasra* to heal his wounds. He snarled silently as the remaining three unformed arrayed against him.

The Prime transformed into a tall, thickly built, naked man. "Why do you attack us? The Servitor commands us to maintain peace."

Sapient sensed fear in the creature's eyes. He'd already killed three of the six unformed, and he knew these final few wouldn't last against him. "I attack because it is my wont," Sapient replied. "And the Servitor is not my master. I serve no one but my own needs."

The words spoken, Sapient recognized the truth in them. Shet had created the necrosed, but he'd also betrayed them, leaving them trapped in this lingering, half-life. Sapient would no longer serve the so-called god, and he certainly wouldn't pay obeisance to the pathetic Servitor.

"You may kill us, but the Servitor will learn of your perfidy," the Prime said. He gestured, and one of the unformed transformed into an eagle. The woven winged away southeast, in the direction of the Servitor's Palace.

Sapient briefly watched the creature retreat, unconcerned. Let the wretched Servitor learn what he had done. He didn't fear the man.

His gaze rested on the last of the unformed, the Prime and another, and he taunted them by licking the blood off his claws and grinning. Once again, the fools took the bait. The Prime bounded forward, a tiger again. Same with the other unformed. Sapient launched himself at the tigers. He crashed into the Prime, hurling him to the ground, and quickly hamstringing him. The Prime was out of the fight.

He faced the final uninjured unformed, a female. The creature backed up, glanced at her Prime, dipping her head in seeming sorrow before taking to the air as an eagle. She rose swiftly out of reach, heading north.

Sapient scowled as she flew away. He needed her flesh. He took his frustration out on the Prime, tearing out the woven's throat. *Lorethasra* flowed into him, and his anger eased as he sighed in appreciation.

Afterward, Sapient arranged all the dead and pondered how best to use their flesh. He could use his newly-stolen *lorethasra* to force a few of the unformed corpses to transform into their human shapes. Then he could replace his fingers. The tiger's claws would fit well on his feet. And the eagle's eyes would make a good replacement for his current pair.

As he set to work, Sapient wondered how the Servitor would react to today's events. While the Overward didn't fear the *asrasin*, he respected the man's power. The Servitor would prove a dangerous foe. Apologies and perhaps abasement would be needed to earn the man's forgiveness.

Sapient smiled as a plan took shape in his mind.

The Servitor would be angry, but the man would soon face far greater worries. Not just Shet, but the magi. The mahavans feared them. Sapient could taste the terror they felt for their brother *asrasins*. What deliciousness then to give the key to Sinskrill's anchor line to the boy, the holder who had killed Kohl Obsidian and Grave Invidious. William Wilde was his name. Sapient could pass the information to him, and if was lucky, two enemies would kill one another.

He chuckled as he harvested the corpses.

AXEL PACED through the by-now familiar open air courtyard of this fortress of menace and power, this place called Naraka. Mountains soared all around, but none overtopped the peak upon which Shet had forged his black citadel. A gusting wind blew, but Axel didn't feel it. His body hadn't made the journey to Seminal, only his Spirit. Despite the inability for any being here to harm him, Axel stayed vigilant, cautious as he eased his way past the cacophony of creatures: the various necrosed, ghouls, and handful of monsters that could only be demons. No reason to upset those who dwelt here. When he reached the dais at the end of the courtyard, he bowed low to Shet, who sat upon his black throne.

At the god's command, he'd come to explain the situation on Sinskrill and Earth. It was a meeting Axel had tried to delay as long as possible since he didn't want to tell Shet of his failure on Arylyn. He would have avoided coming here altogether, except he'd already delayed too long as it was. He could no longer ignore Shet's summons, which had come through the Spear, the focus and source of a Servitor's power. Upon their ascension, all Servitors were remade, gifted with great power, and like all gifts they could be taken back.

Axel noted Shet's black spear. Rune-carved and glowing blue fire, it could have passed as the opposite twin to the Servitor's own weapon.

"It is good to see you," Shet began, his voice bland but the sharp tang of disappointment unmistakably present. "Perhaps you can explain why you've delayed your attendance for these many moons."

The plethora of woven monsters gathered in the courtyard rustled upon hearing Shet's statement, many of them hissing threats. Axel mentally sneered at their taunts. Had they dared speak to him in such a fashion on Sinskrill he would have eradicated them without a second thought. He had the power to do so. "I was unavoidably delayed, my Lord. I have sent my Secondus in my place to keep you apprised of our status."

"Your status as the one who has failed me?" Shet asked, his voice still bland.

Axel held his features still, yielding no sense of the turmoil raging through his mind, the outrage. The unfairness of his life pierced him like an arrow then. Prior to Shet's re-emergence, Axel had ruled Sinskrill, his voice and will heeded without the need to consider another's point of view or opinion. Now, he had to couch his words, appease a greater power, and he hated it.

"Failure is a powerful word, my Lord," Axel said, his tone as mild as he could make it. "I think we were successful in our endeavors on Arylyn."

Shet smirked. "If that was a success, I tremble to learn what you think a failure."

Failure is the millennia-long imprisonment you suffered, fool, the Servitor thought.

A tawny dragon lay at the base of the dais, curled like some giant cat. The beast sat up then, emitting puffs of smoke from his nostrils. The Servitor found himself fixated by the dragon's hypnotic gaze. He broke the creature's stare with difficulty and resumed his attendance of Shet's assessment.

The god leaned into the back of his throne and wore a flat, unfriendly expression. "One should never stare a dragon in the eye. Neither should you seek to deceive your god. You were dealt a defeat on Arylyn, no matter how many you killed. The magi are far more numerous than your mahavans. They'll come for you and kill every one of your kind."

Axel dared disagree with Shet. He had to. He couldn't allow the god to believe him weak. "No," he contradicted. "Whatever history's judgment, the attack on Arylyn was a success. They no longer outnumber us, not warrior to warrior."

"Truly? That isn't the case based on my reckoning." Shet tilted his head as if in thought. "Or do you expand your lies in order to further hide your incompetence?"

"I speak the truth," Axel vowed. "I've called a number of woven to Sinskrill: all the necrosed, unformed, and vampires remaining on Earth. I've even begun the process of rousing the last demon, Salachar Rakshasa. All told, to my six hundred mahavans, I'll add over two hundred woven."

"You think to control so many, including a demon?" Shet sounded skeptical, "especially one as mighty as Salachar?"

"With my powers, the ones possessed by all Servitors, I will manage them," Axel replied, his voice ringing with certainty.

Shet appeared impressed. "Then perhaps my gifts have not been put to waste." An instant later, his gaze sharpened and he leaned forward. "Or perhaps I've been too generous with them."

Axel had no easy reply to such an accusation. He settled for simply dipping his head and awaiting Shet's next words.

The god leaned back in his chair again. "Step away from the throne and await my judgment."

Axel bowed low once again and retreated the appropriate twenty feet. The entire time he remained facing the god. He straightened and found a relatively quiet place, one empty of the woven monsters who clustered in the courtyard.

A cowled man sidled up to his left, graceful as a jaguar. A sense of deadliness emanated from him, reminding Axel of someone. Who was it? He tried to peer at the man's features, but the cowl denied his attempts.

"You are brave to disagree with him," the man said.

Axel nodded, not trusting this fellow. He'd never before seen this stranger, and he had no use for his admiration.

"The lord's power is impossible to overcome," the man continued. "You would be wise to talk more softly in his presence."

The advice was as obvious as an observation that dark clouds brought rain. "Thank you for your wise counsel," Axel said, keeping his voice flat.

"The lord is inured to pain," the cowled man said. "It is how he obtained his great power: through suffering. Any who wish to throw off his yoke must embrace pain as well."

"Who are you?" Axel asked, facing the man fully. He didn't like this man who gave advice that sounded a shade below treason. "I am not the faithless servant whipping the workers when the master isn't in attendance."

The man shook his head. "You misunderstand. I am not Shet's servant. For now, he and I share similar ambitions. Nothing more."

The man faced him, and Axel frowned. He knew this person. He felt more sure of it now.

"Cinder," an elf called to the man. "Shet will require our presence soon." Unlike most elves, who tended to be slight, she was tall and powerfully built, standing nearly the same height as the man, and her green eyes were lit with intelligence. She also moved with a deadly grace, her blonde ponytail swaying with every smooth step.

The man bowed to Axel. "Pain is power," he whispered before moving to stand next to the elf.

"Axel Carpenter," Shet called. "Attend us and learn your fate."

Axel stepped forward, and he couldn't help it: his heart seemed to race, an echo of his fear. He bowed when he once again stood before the lord.

"You will be spared," Shet said. "You will return to Sinskrill, continue your preparations, and await my coming."

Axel bowed. "As you will, my lord."

Shet waved him off with a sneer of disdain. "Depart."

Axel rose from the courtyard, headed back to Sinskrill. The man who'd spoken to him earlier—Cinder—his face came into focus. He could have passed as a close brother to the male World Killer. And the elf woman could have been sister to the female World Killer.

Axel stared down at them. *Who are they?*

CINDER WATCHED Sinskrill's ruler ascend into the sky, and he remembered his past battles with the man. In some he'd fled from the Servitor, barely escaping with his life. In others, he and Jessira had trounced the man. The memories remained distant, though, shaded as if seen through the mirage of a heat haze. Cinder clenched his jaw in frustration, wishing he could recall his true self more clearly.

Anya waited nearby, the two of them standing in Shet's courtyard. A horde of monsters surrounded them, including several demons, who prowled about, probably hoping to find someone to eat. An arrogant vampire idled close by, handsome and proud as only his kind could be. He winked at Cinder and offered a lazy smile of bared fangs.

It was enough of a challenge.

"When will they learn?" Anya muttered in annoyance. "Make it fast."

Cinder confronted the vampire, sword unsheathed and leveled. The vampire's eyes widened in fear and surprise. He stood no chance. Cinder took the vampire through his gaping mouth. The creature died with a gurgle.

A demon pressed forward, a patch branded into his chitin indicating his status as a Warden. "What happened?" the black-shelled monstrosity growled.

Cinder answered. "The vampire smiled at me. He bared his fangs."

The demon grunted. "Foolish. He must have been new." He pondered, sighing an instant later. "I suppose you haven't broken Shet's peace." He sounded disappointed, and he held up a cautioning finger, one that ended in a claw longer than a bear's. "But this is a warning. You are not to kill any who challenge you. Bring it to my attention first."

"No," Cinder said. "That would only invite the others to consider me weak. I'll protect myself and *then* bring it to your attention."

The demon bristled, but settled down when Anya approached. He'd likely seen her put down two necrosed by herself. He rightly respected her. "Don't break Shet's peace," the demon warned before retreating in the face of Anya's clear annoyance.

"Did the Servitor have anything of note to tell you?" Anya asked.

Cinder had no chance to reply. Shet had called for him. "I'll tell you later," he whispered hastily before leaving to attend the god. His stride remained steady, and he bowed when he reached the dais. "What is your bidding?"

"You spoke to the Servitor," Shet said. "What did you discuss?"

"I told him of your path to power."

Shet's eyes contracted, and the scent of gardenias filled the air. He held a coruscating weave of Fire, one hot enough to boil a sea. Cinder mentally sighed. Not this again. He grew tired of Shet threatening to undo him. With their every conversation, the threat was made and never carried out.

Cinder let none of his irritation show, though. He couldn't allow the god to know his true feelings toward him. Not yet anyway.

"What exactly did you tell him?" Shet demanded.

"I told him that the path to power is the acceptance of pain."

"Why?" Shet asked. He still hadn't released the weave of Fire.

Despite the clear threat, fear didn't touch Cinder. It rarely did. Only the gravest danger brought forth that emotion. In fact, for years following his first death he'd never truly known that sensation. He'd literally been unable to conceive of it. It had been as impossible for him to feel as it was for an eyeless man to see. A few years ago, however, fear had re-entered his life. It was when he more fully remembered his past, his true self as Rukh Shektan.

Still, while he lacked the muscle-melting fear others might feel, it didn't mean Cinder was incautious. He knew when to step warily.

Cinder spoke a lie he knew would assuage the god's concerns. "I wanted to see his hope rise and die."

Shet took in the words, and after a moment of thought, he barked a single laugh. His weave, though, remained coiled in his hands. "You never struck me as one who torments others."

"The Servitor's arrogance offended me," Cinder said, which was the truth.

Shet smirked. "You surely didn't feel such a sentiment on my behalf."

Cinder shook his head. "On my own behalf. I offered him sound advice: to not contradict your judgment. He ignored my words. Thus was born my irritation."

Shet grunted, and the weave dissolved. "Was there anything you wished to discuss? I didn't expect you and Anya for at least another month."

"We've spoken of the final Orb. It will be no easy task. You know who guards it. We believe your dragon could help us obtain it." Cinder glanced at the tawny dragon curled at the foot of the dais. The creature stirred, hissing at a passing demon. Cinder pitied the creature, bereft of intellect and memory, mute and unable to communicate. *Soon we'll free you,* he sent to the great dragon.

"Why do you require Charn?"

"The Orb is held by the Calico." Again, the tawny dragon stirred. Cinder held the creature's gaze, and it was the dragon who looked away first.

Shet's face twisted, and Cinder noticed fear flash across the god's face. It took place in the space of a blink, and likely no one else saw it, but it had been present. Cinder knew. Shet feared the dragons, even his tawny pet, Charn. The god tried to hide his dread, but his scowl gave away his feelings. "The *asrasins* erred when they created the woven. They made some of them too powerful. You cannot steal from her."

"She sleeps, and rumor states she often slumbers for years at a stretch."

"Where?"

"A deep cavern, high in a mountain far from here. A solitary peak in a small island rising from the ocean."

Shet said nothing for a long time. Instead his gaze went distant, as if he beheld a curious type of insect. He finally cleared his throat. "What do you need?"

Anya stepped forward, bold as she had ever been. *Jessira*. A longing filled Cinder. He wanted to dance with his wife. "We seek to steal from a dragon. For that we need a thief."

"And to complete our theft, we need a rapid means of escape," Cinder added, sensing Anya's thoughts as he always could. He pointed to the tawny dragon. "He'll do nicely."

AFTER SHET AGREED to let them borrow his pet dragon, Anya bowed to the so-called god, hating the humbling gesture. She despised paying obeisance to this wretched being, but she hid her distaste, and once she and Cinder had retreated the proper twenty feet from the god, they straightened and left the courtyard. Only after they'd left behind the assorted woven monstrosities did she allow herself to express the disgust she felt every time they came to Shet's citadel.

"Easy. We aren't free yet," Cinder whispered.

Anya, who had once thought of herself as Jessira, viewed him in surprise. In that moment the inflection in his voice, the tone, the words themselves . . . they reminded her of Rukh. Unsurprising, since Cinder had many of Rukh's memories, mannerisms, and skills. But he wasn't Rukh. Rukh was gone.

"You're wrong. I *am* he," Cinder said.

Anya viewed him in bland dismissal. He'd first made the claim a year ago, but she hadn't believed him then or since. Now, however . . . had he truly guessed her thoughts? Her heart briefly raced with burgeoning hope. Only Rukh had been able to do that. Could Cinder—

No. Anya crushed her hopes.

She had spent decades praying her husband would return to her and decades after hating his absence. She had learned to live without him, accept her station, and no longer desire his presence in her life. At least that's what she told herself.

As for Cinder's guess, he'd likely known the direction of her thinking due to all the years they'd spent together. It was over a decade now since she'd discovered him in the Third Directorate, his incomparable grace and skill, helped train him. Yes. It was familiarity that must have bred the knowledge to tell Cinder the angle of her thoughts. Nothing more.

And yet . . .

Cinder was so similar to the man she had once loved, but he wasn't her husband. And even if he was, she didn't know if she would have accepted him back in her life. Years of loneliness had embittered her heart. More importantly, those same years had taught her the folly of hope: Rukh was gone. She'd long since accepted the truth and possibly come to hate her husband for it.

Cinder flicked her a wry smile. "Memories don't entirely make the person. Neither do attributes. They are merely a part, but the personality is the core."

Anya glared at him. She didn't need his explanation to tell her who he was or wasn't. Nor would she allow him to believe this falsehood about himself. "You think yourself him? You are nothing like Ru—"

"Ears listen," Cinder hissed, cutting her off. He gestured with his eyes to a group of goblins coming their way.

Anya faced forward, marching past the bat-eared woven. The creatures stood no taller than her shoulders, wearing leather armor the color of ash to protect their spindly limbs. Fingers ended in talons, and a line of inch-tall chitinous serrations extended from their lateral wrists to their elbows. *Warriors.* The breeders and workers didn't have such defensive features.

"We will speak more when we leave this place," Anya said.

They marched through Naraka's white-washed halls, many of which were capped by vaulted ceilings, past lovely murals painted by the scourskin: peaceful bucolic scenes from all parts of Seminal. Anya glared at the artwork. Their beauty mocked the citadel's dark purpose. She took in images of verdant hills and fog-shrouded valleys, an unruffled mountain lake frozen in winter's embrace with snow on the trees, and a village built on an escarpment with an endless tropical ocean at the base. The last reminded her of Lilith, a place where she and Rukh had known peace and some measure of happiness.

Remembrances decades in the past. Maybe centuries. Too many wonderful people she'd known, loved, and lost. Family, friends, her own children. Where were they now? Would she ever see them again? Did she dare see them? Anya trembled. She'd lived too long, and the price of her memories weighed her down. Rukh could have carried some of the burden, but he had abandoned her.

"He is here for you now, and he can carry them again," Cinder said.

Once more, Anya viewed Cinder in surprise and speculation. That time it had been more obvious. He'd also completed her thought when they'd spoken to Shet. Again rose the hope, and again, she shoved it down.

She couldn't ask him any questions yet. Not here in Shet's fortress. She had to bide her time, bite her tongue as they continued through the citadel. They swept through lovely rooms with stained-glass windows that beamed colored pictures onto marble floors, scenes again of evergreen forests or solitary lakes under the moon. They also came across more woven—poisonous ajakavas with their scorpion tails raised as they shuffled along, echyneis who normally resided in the water and waddled gracelessly on land, tusked erawans, who resembled stunted elephants, and ketus with their snakelike lower body and human torsos with four arms. The last two reminded Anya of a strange breed of Chimera from her home world of Arisa.

The only woven not present were dwarves, elves, and trolls, none of whom had ever believed Shet's lies. There were humans aplenty, though. The god promised to restore them to their lost heritage of might. For thousands of year, humans had been denied access to their *lorethasra*, leaving them with short, brutish lives and prey to every other sentient being on the planet. Ironic, since humans had created the other woven and should have been the most powerful of all the races.

While they pressed onward, questions about Cinder rose and fell in Anya's mind, hope crested and receded. She needed to know why he sounded so much like Rukh. She knew part of her husband resided within Cinder, but only a part. The rest was missing. Or might she be wrong? She doubted it. Cinder was a mere shell of man, a living weapon. More likely her current doubts and questions arose from a deep-seated desire because she wanted something so badly that she made herself believe it was true even when it wasn't.

They entered a broad courtyard. A line of barracks lined one side of the space and a row of stables the other. A cacophony of grunts, curses, thudding flesh, and clashing swords filled the area as kobolds, ogres, and orcs trained under the watchful gaze of Garad Lull, one of the Holy Seven. The titan, nearly as tall as Sture and Shet, had dark hair and dark features married to a languid grace and breezy demeanor. Handsome and arrogant. Anya remembered his cunning on Earth, how he'd tricked the first set of holders into a failed inva-sion of Clarity Pain. Thus had been born the necrosed.

Anya and Cinder didn't pause to speak to anyone, including the titan. They hated this citadel and all its denizens. Instead, they went straight to their horses in the stable, saddled them, and minutes later were on the road leading away from Shet's fortress.

Miles passed, and the questions in Anya's mind continued to roil her thoughts. She had to know. She formed a bubble of Air to hide their conversation and dismounted. "Why do you keep saying you're Rukh?"

Cinder quirked a grin, so like Rukh's. "Because I am."

Anya glowered. "No, you aren't."

"I have his memories, but not all of them. Not the important ones. You know the ones of which I speak."

Anya had an idea: the private moments between her and Rukh: their weddings, the nights in Ashoka when they'd tasted the city's wonderful fare, simple moments of love. "They are not for your perusal. I won't share them with you as I have his other memories."

"Nor would I wish you to. I'll either remember them or I won't," Cinder said. "But tell me this: did you know who I was when we first met?"

Anya nodded. "I knew who you most closely resembled, but you are not him. Besides, by the time I first saw you fight, I was no longer looking for my husband. I was looking for a weapon. I found you."

Cinder wore a pensive air. "I was a shell of a person when you found me. I grew up. I had hopes and dreams, but there always was an emptiness inside, a longing for something that kept me incomplete. When you awoke my memories of Rukh—"

"I *gave* you his memories," Anya corrected. "Part of them."

"No," Cinder contradicted. "The memories were already there. You gave me your remembrances of Rukh, but they only served to awaken what I already possessed."

"If the memories were already there, then . . ." Anya stiffened. *Then Rukh was within him all along. With her all along.* "Why didn't you tell me?"

"I didn't realize until a few weeks ago how it truly came to pass."

"You've been trying to understand what it means," Anya added, finishing his thought. She gasped. *I finished his thought.* Anya's thundering hope tore all notions from her mind. *Rukh.* Her eyes welled, and she allowed him to draw her close. He even smelled like Rukh. She'd never noticed that before.

Anya scrutinized Cinder as she never had before, and her brow furrowed, her eyes focused. "How did you learn this?"

"Aia. She no longer sleeps."

Anya's face twisted in confusion. "Who is Aia?"

"She was once my Kesarin. She is sister to Shon."

Anya's puzzlement deepened. She knew those names, but from when? It was important . . .

As if a dam exploded, a torrent of memories flooded her mind. *Shon.* Her Kesarin. How could she have forgotten him?

"When we scouted Aia's cave a few weeks ago, she spoke to me. She helped restore what memories she could." He shrugged. "The rest will soon come back. At least, I think they will. So will yours."

Her memories? His words made no sense. "I'm not the one who can't recall the truth," Anya said.

"You couldn't recall Shon and Aia."

Anya had no answer to his statement.

Cinder stepped closer. "Memories aren't the entirety of a person, but they're a start. And I was always far closer to being the person you remember as Rukh than you ever allowed yourself to accept."

Anya took a full step away from Cinder, discomfited by his proximity. "You and he are similar, but you are not the same. There are differences."

"Are we ever the same person we once were? Are you the same person I first knew in the Third Directorate? I'm not the Rukh you knew on Earth or Arisa, but nevertheless, I am he."

Anya shook her head by way of disagreement. "None of this matters."

"It does matter." Cinder eased forward, standing too close again. "I know who I am, and I know what's most important to me: I love you. I have always loved you, even from when we first met and you were injured. I carried you across the Hunters Flats. *Priya.*"

Anya inhaled sharply. That word. How long since she'd heard it? A lifetime, and she'd forgotten it, its beauty, its meaning: *beloved.*

"I said it to you when you took me to Stronghold," Cinder said, his voice soft. "It was our last night alone."

"You meant it as a joke."

"But I meant it in truth."

Anya's heart trembled, but an instant later it firmed with a surge of anger. *He abandoned me!* She pushed Cinder away, full of fury. Her rage was unreasonable but she didn't care. She couldn't simply forget her decades of loneliness, over a century, the betrayal of it. Such bitterness didn't wash away in a single conversation.

"*Priya—*"

"No." Anya chopped the word aside. "I am no longer your beloved. You lost my heart long ago."

She mounted up and left him. He could catch up on his own.

9

REBUILDING LOVE

F*ebruary 1991*

"THANKS FOR HELPING me rebuild the house," Julius said to Lien.

Lien shrugged, a motion of boredom and eloquent disregard. "No worries. It's not like I was using it."

Julius thanked her again anyway. Regardless of her dismissive demeanor, he still thought it was kind of her to help him restore the townhouse she'd once shared with Daniel. He'd recently asked for the property, since she was still staying with the Karllsons and his own home had been flattened. Ever since Sinskrill's invasion, he'd been living with friends, and it was time for him to find his own place.

Lien's townhouse was perfect for him. It perched on the edge of Cliff Fire and had made it through the mahavan shelling mostly intact. The yard had been chewed up, and the front porch needed replacing, but otherwise the structure was good to go. Nothing a little bit of elbow grease couldn't fix.

Right now, he and Lien were working on the front porch, framing it under the heat of a blazing hot afternoon sun. Sweat beaded on Julius' forehead, dripping down the center of his nose and the center of his back. Thankfully, a stiff trade wind gusted now and then, bringing relief from the heat. The breeze also swirled the rich aroma from the roses blooming in a resuscitated flower bed. Bees buzzed about the blossoms.

Julius had always loved the smell of roses. Beyond the obvious romanticism of the scent, he found the aroma soothing.

The playful breeze blew again, this time carrying a hint of coolness, of impending weather. Julius scanned the Triplets, where a bevy of dark clouds perched. They'd have rain soon.

He grinned when he considered what was going on up on Clifftop. "Looks like the poor saps out working today are going to get doused."

Again came a dismissive shrug from Lien.

She didn't seem to be in a talkative mood, but Julius didn't like working in silence. He liked conversation and laughter. More importantly, he worried for Lien. Her quiet attitude was unlike her normal demeanor, or at least unlike how she used to be. "How are the Karllsons?"

"About what you'd expect. They cry a lot. Daniel was their only child."

"Even if they had ten children, losing someone like Daniel would hurt."

"Daniel was special," Lien said. She smiled fleetingly, and Julius took heart, pleased to have drawn her out of her shell, however briefly.

"Yes, he was," he agreed. Remembrances of all who had died drifted into the forefront of his thoughts, and with it came the familiar anger. It raged in him, and in all this time he couldn't find a way to rid himself of it. He hammered a nail into a post, needing only two strikes to bury it.

Lien paused in her work. "Why are you angry?"

Julius grimaced sourly. "Because of everything that happened."

"But it happened. Staying angry won't help." She tilted her head in thought. "Or is anger how you grieve?"

Julius sighed, the passion washing out of him as swiftly as it rose. His shoulders slumped. "I don't know. I guess?"

"I still grieve, too," Lien said, "but I can't change the past, and I don't want to stay buried in sadness."

Julius resumed hammering. He'd spoken to others like Lien, those who had recovered more quickly from the grief they all suffered. They weren't joyful, but they weren't mired in misery, either. They could laugh and joke, talk about Arylyn's losses without growing furious. Julius didn't understand them. He couldn't find a way to let it go.

"I like the roses," Lien said, interrupting his thoughts as she gestured to the flowerbed. "Daniel and I could never figure out what to plant there." Sadness flitted across her face.

Julius didn't know what to say or if he should say anything at all.

"Anyway, Daniel would have approved," Lien added.

They got back to work, hammers pounding nails and saws cutting wood to length. An hour later they finished framing the porch. Julius stepped back and regarded their work.

He dipped his head in approval. "Looks good." A couple more afternoons and the porch would be done. Then it would be time to move on to the interior and maybe the lawn.

"I've got other things to get done, but if I'm free I can help you finish up," Lien offered.

"You don't have to do that," Julius said. She'd already done more than he had any right to expect.

"Work keeps me busy," Lien said. "Creating helps me heal."

Julius fell silent, once more unsure how to respond.

Lien abruptly faced him. "Promise me you'll fill this home with laughter and children."

Family was the last thing on Julius' mind. Too much needed doing first before he could plan his future, although having children would be wonderful. "I can try for the laughter part," he said, "but the children part isn't in my control. I'd have to marry the right woman, someone I could have children with who would also be *asrasins*." He chuckled. "Besides, the townhome is fine for a single person or a couple, but not a family."

"Then you'll have to find a family home when you're ready."

"Only after I find the right woman."

"We all need that."

"The right woman?"

Lien laughed. "Definitely that." Sadness stole her humor. "The right man would do. I had him, and I miss him."

LANDON VENT SAT IN A WIDE, leather chair in the front room of his single-story log home, sipping coffee. A fire burned cheerily in the hearth, bringing welcome heat and driving off the morning chill. A table and chairs acted to separate the front of the house from the kitchen in the back, and a long wall lined with shiplap partitioned the home's only bedroom and bathroom.

He took a sip of coffee and wondered again how Aia and Shon were doing. He thought about William also.

My brother.

Since he'd last seen William, some of Landon's memories had recovered. Not many, but enough. He could now recall happy reminiscences of holidays, summers, and everyday events involving William. But somehow they continued to feel separate from him, like they were the remembrances, recollections, and emotions of someone else.

Maybe it was because he also recalled the memories of Pilot Vent, the other half of who he was now. He had Kohl Obsidian to thank for his strange state of affairs, for his double memories. Landon shook his head at the notion. A necrosed had created him, mistakenly taken two broken beings and forged them into one. In some ways, though, Landon still felt fractured.

He sighed. It was done. He was who he was.

Restlessness, so much a part of his essence now, caused him to stir. He rose to his feet and padded to the front door, making sure to remain quiet. His wife, Elaina, still slept.

His breath frosted when he stepped outside into a cold, wintry morning. The weather was typical for Sand, a village huddled and hidden in the mountains of Idaho. Snow buried the eaves of his home, water dripping into icicles that reached like stalactites toward the ground. His cabin nestled amongst a small copse of pine and aspen, detached to a certain extent from the rest of Sand, and it was how Landon preferred matters. He enjoyed his privacy.

He took another sip of coffee, staring at the village where he'd finally found a place to rest his restless flight.

Snow covered the landscape all around him, including Sand's roughly fifty cabins, the wide avenues of soft grass separating each of the log homes and the brick-lined streets. Curling smoke lifted off most of the chimneys. Folk were up. In warmer times, there would be the villagers mingling in the streets, sharing friendship and fellowship.

My people. *The Wrin.* They were a race of woven, similar to elves, dwarves, necrosed, or holders, but also different in a key manner. Long ago they'd been created from normal humans, those without *asra*, possibly by Sira, the Lady of Fire. At least their legends spoke of her. Regardless, an *asrasin* had created the Wrin.

Asrasins.

Landon's lip curled. *Asrasins* and their wars. *Would they never end?* Even without the dreams troubling his sleep, Landon could sense the coming conflict. He felt it in his bones, tasted it on the cold, dry air, heard it like a faint whisper on the wind. It was similar to the sensations which had warned him of the unformed, the ones who'd attacked Sand and her surrounding villages last year.

War was coming, and Landon was afraid.

The holder in him studied Sand, the placid scene around him, searching for danger. There was none, but he needed to make sure.

He exhaled heavily, praying for patience when he saw Granny Castor, Elaina's grandmother, hobbling toward him with her ever-present mouth-pinched scowl of irritation. She needed a cane to help her get around and glasses to see, and maybe her lack of sight was the reason she wore such an ugly assortment of oversized coats and bright scarves. Dressed as she was, she reminded Landon of a rainbow-colored marshmallow. However, underneath all that plethora of clothing and disregarding her fragile physical build, Landon knew he'd find a wiry woman who was tougher than stone.

Perhaps she was the danger his instincts warned him about. Granny Castor was a force of nature, and woe onto her foes. Landon was glad she'd finally come to accept him.

"We need to talk, boy," Granny Castor said when she reached the porch.

Landon wordlessly opened the door and ushered her inside.

"Elaina still asleep?" Granny Castor asked once she was inside.

"She had a late night," Landon said.

"I bet she did," Granny Castor cackled. "I'm guessing both of you had late last nights, eh? I won't ask why."

Landon blushed.

Granny Castor cackled again. "Newlyweds. I bet you two could give bunnies a lesson."

Landon blushed further and did his best to collect himself. "Would you like some coffee?" he asked, hoping to distract the old woman.

"You know I can't stand that stuff," Granny Castor said. She rapped her cane on the ground. "Besides, I didn't come here for a social call. Trouble is brewing."

"You feel it, too, then," Landon said, unsurprised at Granny Castor's insight into what he sensed. She had an uncanny ability to read the future.

"I feel something." She peered at him through her thick glasses, shrewd and intent. "What do *you* feel, boy?"

"War," Landon replied without hesitation. Hiding the truth from Granny Castor, even shading it, was never a good idea.

"War?" she said, her lips sneering in distaste. "Like last year with the unformed?"

Landon shook his head. "Worse. Something more dangerous. Evil awakens."

Granny Castor's face stiffened. "Necrosed? They can't enter Sand. We don't have no anchor lines here, and Sira, blessed be her name, placed us beyond the world's reach."

"We do have an anchor line," Landon said, softly, hating to bring more worries to the old woman. "One. It's linked directly to Arylyn, but I can take it anywhere."

Granny Castor gasped.

"The necrosed know of it, but something in their nature won't allow them to use it." Landon tapped his head. "Pilot remembers that."

"How long have you known?"

"Since last summer when I sent Aia and Shon to Arylyn."

Granny's mouth puckered like she'd sucked on a lemon. "I never did understand why you'd do such a fool thing as that. We could use those two if the unformed ever come back."

"They wanted to go back to their humans," Landon said. He didn't bother adding how much he missed the Kesarins, missed rubbing their foreheads and hearing them purr.

Granny Castor stroked her chin. "Are those folk they went to good people?"

"They'd have to be for Aia and Shon to love them as much as they do." Landon also didn't further explain the inexplicable kinship he himself sensed toward Rukh and Jessira.

Granny Castor grunted. "What about the war you think is coming?"

Landon hated having to tell her the rest. "It's a war among *asrasins*. We should be unaffected here but not forever."

Granny Castor's gaze sharpened. "How do you know this, boy?"

"I can sometimes hear William's dreams."

"Truly?" She sounded both surprised and nervous. "He's a magus. You're a holder. How's that possible?"

Landon shrugged helplessly. "I don't know, but a few months ago, William suffered terribly. He still does. It leaks into his dreams. I saw images of a battle. I also got the sense it's not done."

"It is for us," Granny Castor declared. "We have nothing to do with *asrasins*. They'll enslave us like their ancient masters did. All their blood flows the same."

"The magi are different," Landon protested. "William is."

"Maybe. But we're Wrin. They're *asrasins*. They can snap us in half."

Some of what Granny Castor believed about *asrasins* was true, but Landon didn't believe it applied to the magi, at least not all of them. He also had a final piece of information to tell the old woman, but he hesitated. "Shet is the cause of the war. It's the name that is foremost in William's dreams."

"Shet is a myth," Granny Castor scoffed.

"William thinks otherwise. He's certain of it. *I'm* certain of it. The holder in me is certain."

Granny Castor focused her attention on him, as intense as a wolf staring down a rabbit. She probably hoped to see a lie on his face. Landon stared back, allowing her to read the truth of his words. The blood drained from the old woman's face. "Brightness save us," she whispered, still studying Landon. "What will you do?"

"I'll fight," Landon said. "I have to. It's part of who I am. Holders. Shokan wrote it into our dharma: sacrifice all so others need not."

Granny Castor nodded understanding. "Will you tell Elaina?"

"Tell me what?" Elaina stood in the bedroom doorway.

SERENA SAT ON A RATTAN CHAIR, her feet propped on the railing of the front porch to her beach cottage. She watched the waves gently lap against the lagoon's golden sand, washing and receding, back and forth perpetually. She found the ocean's steady motions soothing after a hard day of training. The late afternoon sun lit the waters, causing them to sparkle, but Serena remained shaded under the porch. A breeze stirred the air now and again, bringing the loamy scent of moss and decaying vegetation from the surrounding jungle. The smells mixed with other aromas, those of the many flowers blooming in her gardens.

William exited the cottage and handed her a glass of guava juice. Serena sat up with a groan and accepted the beverage with a tired "Thanks." Today's training had been their first in months, and Rukh hadn't been easy on them. Neither had Jessira. They'd pushed the new recruits and veterans of the Irregulars hard, forcing them through a series of exercises meant to build stamina and strength.

Running, jumping, and pushups, followed by more running, jumping, and pushups. Then had come a hellish exercise consisting of carrying logs up and down a cursed hill.

Serena's whole body ached. She needed a shower and an early night of sleep. Her eyes drifted closed. Maybe the sleep first.

"Serena." William woke her.

Her eyes snapped open. "I'm awake."

"Why don't you take a shower and call it an early night?" he suggested.

"If I sleep now, I'll wake up in the middle of the night, and I won't be able to go back to sleep."

"Then how about a shower?"

"Do I stink that bad?" She took a whiff of her sweat-stained T-shirt and quickly pulled back. *Ugh.*

William had already showered and donned a fresh T-shirt and shorts. He filled them out nicely, handsome ever since he'd decided to keep his hair cut short. He no longer resembled a long-haired hippie. As for his shadow of a beard, she didn't yet know if she liked it. Short as it was, it still tickled when he kissed her.

Serena levered herself upright. "I'll be back in a bit."

"I'll get dinner started," William said.

"Don't worry about it. I've got some leftovers from yesterday in the icebox."

"Then I'll have that ready."

Minutes later she finished in the bathroom, coming out clean and wearing fresh clothing. It felt like she'd shed a hundred pounds of weariness as new energy filled her.

William waited in the single room that served as the cottage's kitchen, dining room, and living room. He stood at the counter, heartily smacking away at a pomegranate with the back of a spoon. Seeds flew into the dish positioned underneath the fruit.

"You had cold chicken but it needs something to go with it," he said.

Serena rested her elbows on the counter and watched him work. She liked the way his muscles moved under his T-shirt, the fierce, tight-lipped concentration on his face, and the way his mouth pursed when he worked. She wondered what he was thinking about. Probably something martial. It was where his thoughts always ran to these days, a far cry from the naive high school senior she'd first met. At the time, she'd been a mahavan in training, a bishan, and their early history together hadn't been kind—at least for him—so many hard times to endure, and now . . . Now she wished they could stop the world and simply love one another.

Her mind froze when she realized what she was thinking.

Love. Was that what she felt for William? She wasn't sure. Maybe. She wanted it to be. It was what Fiona and Mr. Zeus shared. Thinking about the old couple made Serena smile. They were obviously and deeply in love and about to marry in the next few weeks.

"What are you smiling about?" William asked.

Serena tucked a strand of hair behind an ear. He always liked when she did that. She also changed her smile to the wry one he thought indicated her amusement at the world. "I was thinking about Fiona and Mr. Zeus. They're getting married."

William grinned. "I'm happy for them. We could all use a bit of joy with everything else going on."

Serena nodded agreement but didn't say anything else. She didn't much want to talk about everything that had happened. She'd already brooded about it enough.

William soon had the pomegranate seeds mixed with the cold chicken and a bed of spinach, and they sat outside to eat while the sun set over the lagoon. They didn't speak much over dinner. Serena was too tired, and William, while he probably wasn't feeling the same degree of fatigue given his necrosed-infused blood, apparently had his mind on other matters.

After they finished, Serena helped collect the dishes, setting them in the sink.

"I can clean up," William offered. "You look beat."

He nudged her toward the couch, where she settled down. Her eyes began to droop. Without meaning to, she dozed, snapping awake when William flopped down next to her.

"Sorry," he said. "I didn't mean to wake you."

"It's fine," Serena said. "I need to stay awake anyway." She curled up close to him and, despite her best intentions, she closed her eyes again, resting her head on his shoulder. Her thoughts grew hazy with impending sleep, but she noticed that William's breathing had deepened, becoming more controlled and steady. "What are you doing?" she mumbled.

"Meditating."

Sleep beckoned, but Serena sat up, not sure she'd heard right. "Did you say meditating?"

He nodded.

"Why?"

His response surprised her, briefly dragging her back to full wakefulness. "Because I need to. It's how I pray or heal or whatever."

"You do that a lot," Serena noted.

"Only around you. It's when I feel the safest. Maybe it's because I love you."

Serena smiled, kissing him softly. Once again, she rested her head against his shoulder and closed her eyes. "I love you, too."

10

PLANS TO TRAVEL

M*arch 1991*

JASON SAT at the kitchen table in Mr. Zeus' home, sipping his coffee, content since the waffles and bacon he'd made for breakfast had him pleasantly full. He patted his belly in satisfaction. He took another sip, watching Jake clean the dishes while William dried them. No guilt stirred his heart at observing their work while he did nothing. After all, he'd made breakfast. Let them do the cleanup.

Mr. Zeus was present as well. He leaned against the counter, a cup of coffee in hand, talking about his upcoming wedding to Fiona. "She wants to wear white, which I don't mind, but she wants me in a tuxedo," he said, sighing forlornly. "I haven't worn formal clothing since the Roosevelt administration."

"Which one?" William asked.

Mr. Zeus frowned. "What do you mean?"

"He means which Roosevelt administration," Jake said. "Teddy or FDR?"

Mr. Zeus harrumphed. "The only one of import: Teddy." Another sip of his coffee. "I met him once, you know? Did I ever tell you?"

Jason smiled while Mr. Zeus recited an unlikely story about the Rough Riders and the Battle of San Juan Hill. It was good to see Mr. Zeus happy. In all the time Jason had known him, his grandfather had lived a life alone. He deserved better.

The wind chimes in the rear courtyard rang, and Jason glanced outside. The sun was hidden behind a rolling line of clouds stretching from horizon to horizon. It promised to be the start of a wet, gloomy day, a rare occasion for Arylyn, but it also seemed apropos. Gloomy thoughts occupied Jason's mind. Or at least he felt like it might become gloomy if he didn't do what he had long since considered an important part of his healing.

"Can I come with you to the Far Beyond?" he asked Jake.

A flicker of uncertainty crossed Jake's face.

Embarrassment caused Jason to redden. He shouldn't have asked. There'd only be questions. "It's all right—"

"No. It's fine. You can come," Jake said. "It's just that you've never wanted to before. Why now?"

Jason shrugged, unable to give voice to his true desires.

Mr. Zeus' mirth faded. "What's this about?"

William, to whom Jason had confided in the most, knew what he couldn't say and bailed him out. "It's something Jason needs to do. He'll tell us if he wants to."

Mr. Zeus' features cleared in apparent understanding. "I see."

Jake remained confused. "Am I allowed to know or is this supposed to be super-mysterious?"

"Let it go," William said softly to him.

Jason spoke to William, appreciating his effort at discretion but not needing it. "It's fine. I'm not going to break," he said before addressing Jake. "When my *lorethasra* came alive, my parents told me to never come home. They're pretty religious folk, and they said I was a witch. You know what the Bible says about witches? That's what they told me."

Jake's mouth dropped. "Are you serious?"

Jason nodded.

"Man, that sucks. Sorry I brought it up."

Jason shrugged. "You wanted to know. Anyway, I don't want to see my parents, but I have brothers and sisters. A few older than me. I haven't spoken to any of them since I left home. I thought I could call them."

"How long's that been?" Jake asked. "Ten years?"

"A little more than that."

Again, Jake whistled. "I couldn't imagine my family never wanting to see me, or not getting to see them for that long."

Jason moved about in his chair, uncomfortable with the ongoing attention about his plans. "Anyway, I thought I'd call them, and see how they're doing."

William tossed a dry towel at him. "Enough about you." He smiled, taking the sting out of his words. "Help us with the dishes. I swear you used every single one of them to make breakfast this morning."

Jason grinned, grateful for the change the conversation. "You can make your own breakfast next time."

William laughed. "No problem. I think I'm burning more calories drying the dishes than I could have gotten from eating your food anyway."

Jake spoke to Mr. Zeus. "Why aren't you and Fiona having a bigger wedding?"

"We're old," Mr. Zeus answered. "Neither of us has the energy or inclination to invite anyone other than close family and friends."

William sighed. "Selene would have loved to be a part of it."

His words threw cold water on the conversation, and the room quieted. Jason remembered seeing Selene and Elliot and all the others who had been caught in the final volley launched by the Servitor. He recalled the dead and injured. The engagement he'd commanded with Tam Emond.

"Sorry about that," William said. "I didn't mean to be such a mood killer."

"You weren't," Jake said. "I was thinking about her anyway. It's a big part of why we're going to the Far Beyond. I miss her."

"Same here," Jason said.

Jake eyed him in surprise. "I didn't know you were close to Selene."

"I wasn't," Jason said. "At least not like you and William, but I still liked her and Elliot. I want them to know they're loved by a lot more people than they realize."

"Amen to that," Mr. Zeus said.

The rest of the dishes were quickly cleaned, and afterward Jake went to hang out with Daniella, Mr. Zeus retired to his study to read something, and William and Jason sat on a pair of chairs on the front porch.

"I'm glad to see you back to your old self," William said. "You're more relaxed now, more like the guy I used to know."

Jason came to the startling understanding that William was right. He *was* more relaxed. Happier, too. He liked that. In the privacy of his thoughts, he once again thanked Mink for the kick in the ass she'd given him.

～

RUKH GLANCED up from the book he'd been reading when Jessira entered their flat. She had gone to the farmer's market for some groceries and set down burlap sacks containing fresh vegetables, fruit, and some kind of fish wrapped in wax paper on the kitchen counter.

Their flat contained a single space for the kitchen and dining room, a living room delineated by a small partition wall, and a small bedroom. In some ways it reminded him of their apartment in Ashoka, except this one contained no personal items. In fact, it might as well have been unoccupied since it wasn't and never would be home.

It had to be this way. Arylyn wasn't his and Jessira's final destination. They had more work awaiting them.

"Need some help?" Rukh asked, rising to his feet and walking to where Jessira was busily emptying the bags.

"I've got it," Jessira said. She lifted her nose and sniffed in his direction. "Did you forget to shower after training today?"

Rukh shrugged, knowing he smelled of sweat and dirt. "I didn't forget. I just got distracted by this book." He gestured to the coffee table, pointing to the slim volume he'd been reading.

Jessira shook her head and smiled fondly. "You and your books." She stood on her tiptoes to put away some dishes, and as always he admired the line of her legs. His eyes traced their length from her ankles to her waist.

"You'll want to think about something else," Jessira said, not bothering to turn around.

Rukh chuckled. She always knew when he was admiring her beauty.

She faced him with a knowing grin, guessing his thoughts without him needing to say them. "Admiration? I thought it was lust."

"Can't it be both?"

Jessira laughed. "In your case, it always is." She paced to the couch where he'd been seated a moment earlier. She saw the slender book lying on the coffee table. *Treatises on Travel.* She made a surprised sound, apparently appreciating the incongruousness of what she was reading. "The title is written in Arisan."

"I recently found out that William has been trying to read the translation of this book for the past year," Rukh explained. "He finally tracked down a copy of the original, and he's been asking around for anyone who can read the language."

"You believe one of us wrote it."

"No one else could have. I only wish our past selves or future selves, whatever they are, would have been clearer in what they wanted us to know," Rukh said in frustration.

Jessira snorted in amusement. "That would make things too easy, and our lives and easiness don't exactly go together." She tapped the book's cover. "Have you learned anything?

Rukh shook his head. "Nothing of any use. I've already read it from front to back twice. The only interesting thing it states is that an *asrasin* can stand athwart an anchor line and force a traveler coming in the other direction to halt."

"Is this going to be another *Book of the First Movement*?" she asked in a teasing tone, referencing a text Rukh had once spent months studying.

"I hope not, but I've got to think it's important since *we* must have written it."

"Mind if I take a look?"

Rukh gestured for her to go ahead. "I'll get dinner started."

While Jessira read, he chopped onions and potatoes, crunched kale and seasoned the fish—trout in this case. Next came oil in a cast-iron skillet, and while he waited for it to get to temperature, he peeled and sliced a mango.

Jessira had her feet propped on the coffee table, concentration evident on her face.

"Want some mango?" he asked. He tried to keep his mind blank for the joke he planned on playing. He popped a slice into his mouth and tried not to grin.

Jessira loved fruit of any kind. She set the book aside, rising to approach his offering. She was about to reach for the bowl holding the mango, but at the last instant she pulled away. "Oh no, you don't."

Rukh reached for her anyway, but she sidestepped his grasping hands and resumed her seat on the couch. It was an old trick. Rukh would get smelly and sweaty, and when Jessira wasn't paying attention, he would try to pull her close and get his stink all over her.

"I never understood how you did that," Jessira commented without glancing up from the book. "Go from frustration to light-hearted in the blink of an eye."

Rukh waggled his eyebrows. "Consider it part of my charm," he said, resuming the dinner preparations. Minutes later, it was ready.

"What did you think of the book?" Rukh asked before they started eating.

"I think it's obtuse." Jessira grinned. "Which means you were the one who wrote it."

"Obtuse? Or maybe it's too deep for your illiterate, OutCaste mind?"

"This OutCaste just read the book, which means I can't be illiterate."

Rukh laughed. It was another old joke.

They began their meal, and Jessira spoke a couple minutes later. "I found the part in the book you mentioned. Where the author talks about standing athwart an anchor line. It mentions aether will hinder aether, except . . ." She viewed Rukh. "The way it's written, it uses *Jivatma* and aether interchangeably."

"I noticed that, too. Any idea what that means?"

"*Jivatma* is our soul. At least as we think of things. Aether must be the same thing, but the closest they have to something like that here is Spirit. The only problem is that Spirit is only an Element of our *lorethasra*, which also isn't entirely the same as *Jivatma*. They aren't identical."

Rukh pondered her insight. "You're right, but it still doesn't answer the question of how *Jivatma* is removed from a body or anything else."

"Unless it's as plain as the writing states. Remember, Serena said her *Spirit* traveled to Seminal. Same with Adam in the dreams he sent. But our *Jivatmas* traveled from Arisa to Earth. We couldn't take our bodies. To exist here, we had to find the bodies of people who were recently deceased. I wonder if that's what's meant by aether?"

Rukh's mind lit with understanding. "Maybe all the anchor lines between worlds are like that. We can block Shet from coming here if we're present when the anchor line between Earth and Seminal opens." His budding optimism faltered. "I don't remember how we separated our *Jivatmas* from our bodies. Do you?"

Jessira shook her head. "No. But at least we know that our past selves knew of a way to stop Shet from entering this world."

The task persisted as seeming impossible, but Rukh grinned. "Which means all we have to do is invade Sinskrill, learn where the Seminal anchor line is focused, and stop Shet. And get it done by September."

Jessira grinned as well. "All in an afternoon's work."

~

SERENA SAT ON THE GROUND, leaning against her backpack full of gear while waiting atop Linchpin Knoll for Jake to trigger the anchor line. He never could do it as smoothly as he could most everything else, which was strange. Jake was a fine *raha'asra*, skilled and talented, but for some reason, triggering an anchor line always caused him trouble. It made no sense. Opening an anchor line was one of the easiest braids to form.

Lilith lay quiet below them, the homes and shops darkened for the night. Crickets chirped. A warm trade wind blew steadily, building to a gust now and then, and a half moon rode a cloudless sky. However, Serena smelled the mineral-rich scent of impending rain. She could also see it in the thick clouds bracketing the Triplets.

William and Jason stood alongside her, the two of them sharing a low-voiced conversation. It sounded like a discussion about an undiscovered country. She had no idea what they were talking about, and it took her a moment to realize it was about *Star Wars*. Or was it *Star Trek*?

Who cares?

Serena ignored their nerd conversation, her attention going again to Selene. She wondered how her sister was doing. She'd see her again today for the first time in months, and she couldn't wait. The only oddity was that Jason would accompany them. He hadn't been particularly close to Selene or Elliot, or to Jake's parents or brother for that matter. But he'd asked to come, and Serena hadn't pressed him on his reasons why. She understood the need for privacy.

"Are you nervous?" William asked, interrupting her thoughts.

Serena shook her head. "No. Should I be?"

"What about the Ridleys?"

Her stomach roiled with disquiet. She *was* worried about the Ridleys. During her last visit to see Selene, they said they'd forgiven her for what she'd done to Jake . . . at least to a certain extent. She said as much to William. "They say they've forgiven me," she said, hoping they really had, "but I doubt they'll ever like me much."

"I think they like you more than you realize."

Serena shrugged, trying for a nonchalance she didn't feel. "As long as I can visit Selene, it doesn't matter."

"They're good people. So are you. They've seen the change. Give them a chance."

His praise made her uncomfortable, and she wanted to change the conversation. She pointed out the first thing that came to mind: his longsword. It poked out of his bag. "Expecting trouble?"

William grinned and gestured to her belongings. Clearly visible was the hilt of her *jian*. "Why don't you tell me?"

Serena bubbled laughter. "Rukh and Jessira?"

William nodded. "When they found out we were going to the Far Beyond, they insisted we go armed. They said the same thing to Jake and Jason." A second later, a broad grin broke across his face. "It's about time."

Serena understood what he meant.

Jake had finally managed to open the anchor line.

Praise God.

A vertical slit split the air. It rotated until a two-dimensional doorway revealed itself. It contained a kaleidoscope of colors that formed indistinct shapes. Jake's cut-grass *lorethasra* flared when he sent a braid of Fire into the anchor line. The stink of sulfur drifted on the air. A deep-toned bell sound rang out, and the colors and shapes within the doorway solidified into a rainbow bridge extending into infinity.

"I hope she's happy to see us," Serena said. "She was so angry the last time we saw her."

"Selene's a teenager," William said, as if that explained everything.

Serena smiled wryly. "We're not far off from being teenagers ourselves."

William exhaled heavily. "Yeah, but . . ." He trailed off. "I guess I feel a lot older than a teenager."

Serena nodded agreement. She felt the same way: old beyond her time. "Do you think she'll ever be happy in the Far Beyond?" she asked. She privately doubted it, but maybe William saw the situation differently.

He disappointed her with a grim tightening of his mouth. "I don't know. I think she can be happy, but it won't be easy. She lost paradise."

"It won't be easy for Elliot, either," Jason said, apparently over-hearing their conversation. "It's time to go. Jake's waiting."

Serena tethered to the anchor line and traveled.

11

BATTLES AND TRIBULATIONS

M *arch 1991*

WILLIAM STEPPED into the familiar West Virginia meadow, stumbling from the disorientation of journeying along an anchor line. Once his disequilibrium faded, he took the time to survey the first *saha'asra* he'd ever encountered. *A long time ago in what felt like a galaxy far, far away.*

He and the others had left Arylyn in the middle of the night, but it was only creeping into early morning here.

Cabins huddled along one edge of the field, but for some reason, they appeared strangely unoccupied today. They also usually had lights on. This morning, though, all the windows were darkened and no smoke rose from any of the chimneys. A dreary rain pattered on fallen leaves and branches that were still winter-bare. William's breath misted in the cold wetness.

A warning bell clanged in William's mind. Something didn't feel right.

"Where is everyone?" Jake asked, rotating as he viewed all the cabins. He appeared troubled, too.

The sense of danger increased, and William peered around, trying to figure out what had him spooked.

"Let's get to the car," Serena suggested, her gaze darting about. She looked every bit as unnerved as William felt. "We can figure it out on the road." She put a hand on the hilt of her *jian*, ready to unsheathe it.

"Yeah. Let's," Jason urged, nervousness affecting him also.

William led them toward his hot-rod red T-bird, which he always left in the *saha'asra's* parking lot.

"Why do you luscious dishes scamper away so swiftly?" a voice rasped. "We have much to discuss."

William spun around, his hand going to the hilt of his sword. A creature minced around the massive oak centered within the meadow, ducking under a branch. She—probably a she—straightened to her full height. She was at least seven feet tall and built like a tank. Her hands hung to her knees and ended in black talons. She grinned around a mouthful of broken teeth. The smell of a corpse wafted off her hideous form, and her unkempt hair, white as alabaster, wriggled like a horde of maggots.

A necrosed.

William sourced his *lorethasra* and drew his sword. He disregarded the drops of rain trickling down his back, controlled the fear pounding through his heart. A life and death battle loomed. He braided weaves of Fire, Air, Water, and Earth, ready to kill this creature. He glanced at the others, who all had their blades bared and weaves at the ready.

"Peace," the female necrosed said, holding her hands up. "I bring information from the Overward. He believes it might be of use to you." She grinned. "I disagree with him. I see it doing nothing but hastening your demise."

William eyed the necrosed, wondering if they could take her, or at least slow her down long enough to get to the T-bird and escape.

"What information?" Serena asked. She held her *jian* in a steady grip.

"Straight to the point," the necrosed crooned, unaffected by their threatening postures. "Where's the fun in that? Don't you want to play first? I know so many wonderful games. The armless *asrasin*, the headless magus . . ."

"We're not interested," William said. The red-eyed beast in the back of his mind, the anger with which Sapient had cursed him, rumbled to life. William let it come. He needed it, welcomed its strengthening rage. "Sapient told you to give us information. Give it and leave."

The necrosed smiled in response. "You would speak to me so rudely? When I can tell you the secret to Sinskrill's anchor line?" The necrosed inched toward them, pausing after a few feet. "I'll whisper it in your ears." She hunched forward several more yards. "And then I'll rip them off and eat them." She cackled.

William was no longer listening. The red-eyed beast snarled. He sent a weave of Earth rumbling at the necrosed. She shuffled out of the way, graceful despite her bulk.

"A dance? How sweet. That's a game I love. I'll show you my favorite. But work first and then play. Observe." A flashing series of Fire played across her hands. "Do you remember it? It's Sinskrill's key. You need to see it once more? Fine." She sounded fond—the fondness of a cat tormenting a mouse—but again flashed the Fire.

In spite of his fear about the necrosed, William made himself pay attention. He didn't know why she was really here, but if there really was a chance to learn the key to Sinskrill's anchor line, he'd take it.

All amusement now fled from the necrosed, William found himself the focus of her attention. "Now, we shall play. The Overward said I can't kill you, but I'm sure he didn't say anything about your friends." She rushed forward, her feet steady despite the slippery grass.

William ignited his sword. The Wildness roared up the blade until it glowed like the sun, too bright to look at directly. Speed and power coursed through his veins. He felt like he could uproot a tree, and his red rage seemed to quail.

The necrosed halted her charge. She licked her blood-red lips with a wormlike tongue. "The Wildness." An instant later, anger replaced her short-lived concern. Twin short-swords, black like her claws, formed in her hands, extruded from her body. "No matter. I'll kill you anyway."

William had enough of her talk and taunts. He attacked with a diagonal slice, rolled beneath a counter strike. Jason protected his back. William leapt forward, blade thrust like a glowing arrow.

The necrosed leapt over his blade, landing behind him.

Serena and Jake defended him. One of them went high. The other went low. The necrosed defended smoothly, shunting aside their blades.

William joined his friends in attacking the necrosed. He lunged, but the monster spun away, back-flipping to gain further distance.

A weave of Fire roared from Jason's hands, engulfing the necrosed. She thrust her arms to the side, swords pointing up. Her face lifted to the sky, her attitude one of delight. She cackled again, and her hair stood out, whipping around her features like a pallid flag. "Thank you for the Fire, little *asrasin*. It felt *good*."

"Try this," Jake snarled. A boulder cracked the monster in the back of her head, causing her to stumble.

Serena took advantage. She was closest to the creature, and she slashed at the necrosed's exposed neck, but her sword bounced off the monster's skin. The creature quickly recovered from both blows.

Serena tried to disengage, desperately withdrawing. She slipped on the slick grass. A backhand from the necrosed sent her flying. Serena landed heavily, plowing into the ground and rolling. She groaned, tried to rise, but couldn't make it up.

The monster didn't give any of them room to breathe. She leapt forward, sending a flurry of strikes at Jason. He gave ground. William took the pressure off him with an attack of his own. The necrosed defended, and he growled in frustration. Whatever the Wildness could do, it wasn't enough. He couldn't get past the monster's guard.

Jake entered the fray with a thrust. The necrosed slipped the blow, stepped forward, and cracked her knee into Jake's head. He went limp, unconscious. The monster prepared a killing thrust.

William used a blast of Air to give him greater force and speed. He tackled the monster to the ground and immediately wanted to vomit. Up close, her corpse-like stench was overwhelming. The monster's face filled with fury. William snarled in response. He knew what she intended, and he quickly braided Earth. He trapped the fist she'd meant to use to cave in his skull and scurried away from her.

He heard a groan from where Serena had fallen. She attempted to sit up again, and this time she managed to gain her feet before sitting right back down.

The necrosed stood, rolled her shoulders, and smirked at William. "Is that all you have? I expected more from the one who killed Kohl Obsidian and Grave Invidious."

Grave Invidious? Who the hell is that?

William had no more time for questions. Here came the necrosed, straight at him. Red rage threatened to overwhelm his thoughts. He controlled his anger by sourcing more deeply. The Wildness brightened, focusing his fury, imbuing him with greater strength. Again the necrosed slowed her charge. Jason used the distraction to slash at her thigh. His attack did no damage, and in reply, she kicked him in the torso. He landed five feet away, clutching his chest.

William faced the necrosed alone. Fear might have unmanned him at one time, but he and fear had become bosom friends over the past few years. Plus, he had his red-eyed rage and the Wildness. He readied himself for what was to come.

The necrosed attacked. William called on all his skill, all the training with Rukh and Jessira. He defended, parrying blows, slipping those he couldn't block, and dodging gracelessly when he couldn't evade. The blows came harder and faster.

William bit down and reached deeper still. More Wildness. More strength. More power. Speed. Balance. Controlled rage fueled his defense. The wet ground didn't hinder his movements. The glowing Wildness also dulled the impact of the monster's powerful attacks.

On they battled, ranging across the meadow.

Finally, William saw it, the moment he'd been hoping for: the necrosed flashed frustration. An opening revealed itself, and he took it. A sidekick cracked the necrosed in the side of her knee. She stumbled away from him, shaking out her leg. William gestured her on.

She took his challenge, howling. *Good. An angry warrior will fight foolishly*, he could almost hear Rukh saying.

Again William did nothing more than parry, keeping up with the necrosed. He waited again for his opportunity. *There!* William slid aside when the necrosed overextended. She lunged past him, and he sent a downward slice. It took the creature's arm off in the middle of her biceps. She screamed. Black blood pumped like sludge from the wound. Wherever it landed, the grass died and the ground bubbled and hissed.

Jake somehow was back in the battle. So were Serena and Jason. All of them staggered about, unsteady on their feet, but resoluteness filled their eyes. William attacked the necrosed, the other three following.

This time it was the necrosed who was hard pressed. She retreated. William sensed her reach for the anchor line. He acted on instinct, creating a weave. It was one triggered by knowledge his anger seemed to know.

He locked the necrosed out, and she gasped, eyeing him with shock. "How did you—"

William didn't bother answering. He went low, a slash at her knees. The necrosed parried. She couldn't block Jake's thrust. It thudded into her chest but didn't penetrate. Still, the necrosed reacted. Her guard opened. William used it. A horizontal strike ripped across the abdomen. More blood oozed. The monster's remaining arm sagged. William filled himself with the Wildness, and he spun, sword arcing. The blow cleaved the necrosed's head from her neck.

Her body slowly collapsed to the ground.

Silence filled the meadow, and William tried to absorb what they'd just done. *A necrosed. We killed a necrosed!* He roared in triumph.

～

"WHAT DO we do with the body?" Jake asked.

William eyed the necrosed's corpse. Blue eyes. He hadn't noticed that before. They'd also never learned the monster's name, but her dead body remained as gruesome in death as she had appeared in life. The maggot-like hair lay unmoving, and her hideous features, scarred with pustules, held an enduring sneer. At least the black blood no longer oozed from her wounds. He nudged the necrosed's body. It felt like pushing against hardened rubber. *Rigor mortis? Already?*

"Burn it," Serena said. She wobbled on her feet.

"I think you better sit down," William said, easing her to the ground.

Jason hunched over, clearly in pain. "I think I cracked some ribs."

"Should we go back to Arylyn?" Serena asked.

William considered it. He didn't want to. "I think we should use the satellite phone and tell them what happened," he said. "But Selene is expecting us. I don't want to disappoint her."

"I can heal you some," Jake said to Jason. He managed a grin. "After all the healing Jessira put me through, I figured a few things out."

"You sure?" Jason asked, his voice uncertain.

"I'm sure." Jake placed a hand on Jason's chest and sourced his *lorethasra*. The scent of cut -grass flittered through the air, washing away some of the grotesque aroma wafting off the necrosed.

William closely observed Jake's braid. It was a delicate weave consisting of all the Elements, each thread like a line of silk. William knew he couldn't recreate something so detailed and fine. He lacked the skill.

Serena, still resting on the ground, must have been watching, too. She whistled appreciation. "You've gotten a lot better," she said to Jake.

"Ready?" Jake asked Jason, who nodded.

A narrow band of lightning bled from Jake's hands and into Jason, who stiffened. His mouth gaped. Less than a second later, the lightning faded.

"Son of . . . Ow! That hurt," Jason complained.

"How are the ribs?" Jake asked, his demeanor curious and intent.

Jason took a careful inhalation. A moment later, he took a deeper pull and grinned. "Better. No pain at all."

Jake grinned. "It worked."

Jason shook his head. "Yeah, but you've got a ways to go before you can heal like Jessira. I wish she was here."

William chuckled "You only want Jessira around because she's Jessira."

Serena harrumphed.

William cleared his throat. "I mean it would have been great to have her help fighting the necrosed."

"I'm sure that's what you were thinking," Serena replied.

Jason grinned and made a whipping sound.

"Shut it," William said.

"I wish someone could help me with my headache," Jake said. He glanced at Serena. "Can you stand?"

She nodded, rising to her feet. Again, she swayed.

"Do you need me to heal you?"

Serena shook her head. "I'll be fine."

William sourced his *lorethasra*. A pine scent filled the meadow. He created a braid of Fire. The weave crackled around his forearms. "Step away from the corpse."

"Hold up," Jason said. He retrieved the necrosed's severed arm, holding it with his fingertips. He gagged, looking like he was about ready to vomit. Next, he kicked the head closer to the rest of the body. "Go."

William unleashed a white-hot blaze of Fire at the necrosed. The corpse went up with a whoosh, and seconds later nothing but remained but ash. *Wow.* He found himself impressed by his own work. *That was a powerful weave.*

Jake stroked his chin. "Huh? Why didn't Fire work on her before?"

Jason slapped him on the shoulder. "Because she was alive then, stupid."

"How are those cracked ribs?" Jake asked.

"Sorry," Jason muttered.

"Let's get out of here," William. He still didn't understand why the surrounding cabins seemed empty. There should have been lights on.

Someone should have heard their battle with the necrosed. The quiet left him unsettled.

They quickly got on the road, with Serena making the call to Arylyn.

"What did they say?" William asked after she hung up.

"Rukh and Jessira are going to wait in the *saha'asra*. They figure if another necrosed shows up, they'll kill that one, too. One less enemy for us to fight on Sinskrill."

Jake laughed. "I almost hope another necrosed *does* show up. Serve them right to eat a pile of death pie."

William rolled his eyes. "Death pie?"

"It's a thing," Jake said with a grin.

"You think this is how life will always be?" Jason asked, anger lacing his voice. "Fighting all the time?"

"Easy," Jake said. "We survived. I call that a win."

"I wish we didn't have to survive anything," Jason said. "I wish we could live our lives without monsters, mahavans, and gods bothering us."

"We will," William said. "But you better not backslide and become all mopey. Mink will kick your ass if you do."

Jason managed a chuckle. "Anything but that."

AFTER THEY GOT on the road, Jake tried not to think about the recent battle. They'd killed the necrosed and survived. That was enough. Instead, he tried to think about the coming excitement and joy of seeing his family.

Several hours later, they rolled out of the West Virginia mountains and into Ohio's low-lying hills, and by the time they neared Cincinnati's outskirts, Jake had largely succeeded in his efforts to forget about the necrosed.

The others seemed to have pushed aside the terror and pain of their recent battle, too. At least Jake figured they had, based on the eagerness in their voices as they talked to one another, especially when they started seeing signs for the city.

A half hour later, a weight of worry and weariness lifted off Jake's soul when familiar sights became apparent. A thousand memories from a childhood running wild through these streets came over him. Setting firecrackers off in mailboxes, scaring girls by giving them bags full of worms . . . he'd been a little hellion. They soon entered his subdivision of tree-lined streets and small mansions on large lots.

Home.

Or at least the home of his heart. But so was Arylyn. He loved both places, but it hadn't always been the case. He was glad it was now.

Jake grinned more broadly when they reached his parent's house, a tan, two-story modern structure with a peaked roof. He exited William's T-bird almost before the car came to a full stop, grabbing his duffel bag and trotting up the front steps, where he knocked once and unlocked the door.

"Mom! Dad! We're here," he called out.

The others followed on his heels, all of them pausing to wait in the large, two-story foyer. A glass chandelier scintillated above, and to the left a curved staircase ended at a catwalk, leading deeper into the second floor of the house. From the rear, which held the kitchen, dining room, and family room, Jake heard glad noises.

Seconds later, his parents arrived along with John, Selene, and Elliot.

His dad, a big, balding man who Jake ruefully realized he'd resemble one day, reached him first. "Come here, bud," he said, pulling him into a bear hug.

Jake's mom tugged his father aside. "Enough of that. You're going to break him, Steven," she warned. Jake had long grown used to being taller than his mom, but somehow she still seemed bigger than him. She gripped him tightly in her arms, and he kissed the top of her head where her once-blonde hair had gone gray.

John, a smaller version of their dad, came next. He walked without a hitch in his gait. It meant more than anything to see his brother walking like this, and Jake grinned. "John." He pulled his brother into a hug every bit as tight as the one his dad had given him.

Jessira had Healed John last year, saving him from a disease, which had slowly been destroying his nervous system.

He gave his brother a final clap on the back before turning to Selene. William was in the middle of saying something to her. She reddened but chuckled.

"Hey, Tiny," Jake said to her.

"Hi, Jake." The past few months had seen Selene fill out some of her lanky frame. She was a little shorter than Serena but every bit as beautiful. He figured she had every boy in St. Francis drooling over her. She tried to hold a serious mien, but he could see the grin lurking at the edges of her lips.

"That's all you have for me? 'Hi'? Come here." He embraced her as well.

Elliot Dare, a youth the same age as Selene who had also suffered the loss of his *lorethasra* during the Servitor's final attack, stepped forward with a shy smile. He had a lanky build and paler skin than most native-born, a likely heritage of his Slavic grandmother.

Jake shook hands with him. "How are you doing, Elliot?"

Elliot shrugged. "I hate the weather, don't like the cafeteria food, but school is fun."

"You know, I used to think I was smart until Elliot came along," John said.

Jake eyed Elliot with fresh appreciation.

"Nerds," Selene said with a rueful shake of her head.

"Nerds rule, Tiny. Best get used to that," William said to her.

"Yeah, and aren't you the one who's always bothering Elliot for help with math?" John asked her.

"Like you don't?" Selene countered.

Mom cleared her throat. "Why don't we let everyone get settled? We've got food waiting in the kitchen." She pushed John, Elliot, and Selene toward the back of the house.

Jake smiled fondly as he watched them leave, mumbling in teenage argumentation.

"You four look like you've been in a fight," Dad said after the kids were out of earshot.

Jake shared an uncertain gaze with the others.

Mom wore an unhappy frown. "What happened?"

William explained, wisely making it seem like it wasn't a big deal. Jake knew his parents would have freaked out if they knew the truth.

"You're okay?" Dad asked, staring intensely. "No injuries." Jake found him pinned by his parents' gazes of concern.

"I'm fine," Jake said. "We all are."

Mom continued to peer at him, studying him and the others. Jake shifted on his feet, uncomfortable under her scrutiny.

"Isn't there a way to avoid these kinds of things?" Dad asked.

"I wish there was," Jake said, "but it's part of the world we live in." The bitterness he once felt was largely absent. He figured it meant he'd grown used to what it meant to be an *asrasin* and a soldier.

"It'll be like this until we defeat Shet," William said. "After that, things will probably be a lot more peaceful."

"Shet, necrosed, unformed." Mom muttered the names like they were curses.

"How's Selene doing?" Jake asked, not wanting to talk about the recent battle any more.

Again came the exchange of an uncertain glance between his parents. "She's doing as well as can be expected," Mom said. "She and Elliot spend a lot of time alone in their rooms. We worry about them."

He caught the sharpness in Serena's gaze. "Why are you worried about them? Beyond the obvious."

Mom took over the explanation, and for a wonder she took Serena's hands in hers.

Jake wanted to crow in triumph, proud that this parents had forgiven Serena. They were good people.

"They're struggling," Mom said. "They're trying to fit in, but it hasn't been easy. The three of you being here should help."

"But it's not all doom and gloom," Dad added. "Like Elliot said, he likes school. He's doing well. They both are. We just have to give them time."

12

TEENAGE TROUBLES

M *arch 1991*

THE DAY after their arrival in Cincinnati, Serena decided she and Selene should take a walk. William and Elliot accompanied them, and they drove to French Park, a lovely place near Amberley Village, one of Cincinnati's wealthier suburbs. Winton Woods was closer but it held a *saha'asra* and an anchor line, one that Kohl Obsidian had once used to track them down. After yesterday, no one felt like lingering near a place where another necrosed could easily find them. Serena went so far as to bring her sword, hiding it in a long, cardboard tube meant to hold posters and slinging it over her back.

William walked ahead, similarly armed, while talking to Elliot.

Yesterday's rain had tapered off some time in the middle of the night. Sunshine beamed down, reflecting off the still-wet grass. The day promised to bring spring warmth, but the morning remained chill. Serena's breath frosted, but she disregarded the cold air. The strength to ignore inclement weather, lessons learned from her training on Sinskrill, hadn't yet faded.

Serena tried not to stare at Selene, who paced beside her. Her sister was fourteen now and growing into a lovely young woman, one who was currently either unhappy or bored. Serena couldn't interpret Selene's demeanor and an unspoken tension marred their stroll. Serena remembered what Jake's parents had said about Selene and Elliot yesterday, and she wondered what she could do to ease her sister's burdens. "How are you fitting in?" she asked, hoping the question would break the stiffness.

"I'm getting by," Selene grunted, not bothering to elaborate any further.

"Jake's parents say you're having trouble finding your footing."

Serena rocked in surprise when Selene glared at her. She'd never seen her sister so angry.

"Finding my footing? Of course I can't find my footing. Everything I love is gone. I've been banished, and it's my own father's fault."

"It's not all gone," Serena said in what she hoped was a soothing tone. "I'm still here. William and Jake, too. Elliot."

"You think I love Elliot?" Selene scoffed. "He's a friend, not my brother."

Her sister refused to be mollified, and Serena didn't know what to say to her to make her feel better. Instead, she took a deep breath, praying for patience.

"Are you going to hum 'Gloria' now?" Selene asked in a sarcastic tone. "It's what you always do when you think you need help." She snorted derision. "God doesn't exist."

Serena's patience snapped. "Enough. You have food, a home, and safety. It is more than you had in Sinskrill. Accept what is and make it what you need."

"I don't have my family or my *lorethasra*."

"And for that I'm sorry," Serena said, wondering how the conversation had gotten so out of control. "But understand this: your life could be much worse. On Sinskrill you would have long since been chewed up. By now, you would have become a drone, given to some favored foreman to do with as he chose."

"I could have become a mahavan," Selene countered.

Now it was Serena who snorted in derision. "And become a

murderer? Like those who attacked Arylyn? That's who you would wish to be?"

"No, but maybe I'd rather be given to a foreman than live here," Selene muttered.

"You'd rather live the life our grandmother was forced to endure?" Serena scoffed, and the mahavan in her reared its head. "Don't be stupid as well as weak."

"That's easy for you to say!" Selene shouted. "You have everything you've ever wanted."

Serena noticed William and Elliot viewing them in concern. She shook her head, not wanting their intervention. "My apologies. I mistook you for someone rational," she said to Selene, angry and embarrassed at her sister's outburst. "You are a child with a child's tantrums. Talk to me when you're no longer sulking."

"I won't talk at all. How about that?" Selene asked. "No family. No home. No magic. I might as well be dead!"

Serena mentally hummed "Gloria," trying to drive away her frustration with her sister or at least control it better. After a few minutes of quiet, she could think again. "The Ridleys can be your family."

"They aren't family."

"But they can be. They don't want to replace me or Fiona, or William and Jake. They only want to love you." She spoke softly, imbuing her words with as much caring as she could. It must have worked because Selene didn't snap at her, which Serena took as a good sign. "And if you haven't noticed, they have a nice house, a home they're willing to share with you."

Selene smiled faintly. "Did you ever watch TV on a big screen when you spied on William?"

"I hardly watched TV at all," Serena replied. "Isha wouldn't allow one."

A few more minutes of quiet followed.

"I'm sorry," Selene said. "I don't like it here, but I'm trying. Really."

"I know," Serena said, drawing her sister into a brief embrace. "And you have no reason to apologize. What you've experienced is something no one should have to endure." A beat later. "And I'm sorry for calling you stupid and weak."

"And calling me a child?"

"You're barely fourteen," Serena said. "You *are* a child."

Selene nudged her with a hip. "I won't always be one."

The rest of their walk passed by with less tension. Nevertheless, Serena continued to worry for Selene.

AFTER RECEIVING the report from Serena about what had occurred in West Virginia, Jessira and Rukh had decided to investigate the meadow, especially the mystery of the uninhabited cabins. The two of them worried that the necrosed who William and the others had killed might have done something horrific to the people living near the *saha'asra*. They intended to find out what had happened.

Of course, the Village Council had tried to object. They worried over the two of them. Everyone remembered that the necrosed tended to congregate at a *saha'asra* where one of them had been injured. Zane Blood—the hypocrite—had gone so far as to claim that Arylyn might not survive in their absence.

Their concern was appreciated but unnecessary. Jessira intended nothing less than the utmost discretion and care. They could have taken more warriors—she'd argued for it—but Rukh had disagreed. He feared that bringing others would merely place them in danger and they'd be unable to do much more than get in the way.

His decision—one she eventually agreed to—didn't stem from a foolhardy nature. Not entirely, anyway. Rather it was a reflection of Rukh's giving nature, his Kumma heritage in which members of his Caste willingly courted danger in order to protect those for whom they were responsible. It was who Rukh was.

Jessira followed on her husband's heels when they exited the anchor line from Arylyn to West Virginia. She immediately took stock of their situation. The sun shone on an otherwise unoccupied *saha'asra*, the light glistening on grass still shiny with dewy frost. The cabins remained unlit, just like Serena had described. No lights in the windows and no smoke puffing from the fireplaces. A large oak tree dominated the meadow, and near it she sighted a large scorch mark. It must have been where William had burned the necrosed he'd killed. Jessira peered about. Her instincts screamed danger, and the surrounding forest seemed to hold its breath. No birdsong or small animal noises.

Something wicked waited, and Jessira sourced her *lorethasra*, her *Jivatma*, as she would have called it back home. She created a Shield and Blended. The Shield would protect her while the Blend made her invisible to most everything but an unformed. Rukh did the same and Linked with her so they could see one another.

A rustling came from the forest and out shambled a monstrosity, a stain on Creation. It overtopped Rukh by several feet, and he was a tall man. The thing—male—had a nose like an oozing sore and a cleft lip. Bat ears extended from a lumpy head topped by a ragged clump of hair. Short arms hung no lower than the monster's waist, but great claws, five inches long or more, extended from stumpy fingers. The creature's ugliness wasn't what caused Jessira's lips to curl in disgust, though. It was the sense of disease, of walking corruption emanating off the monster. This had to be another necrosed.

Rukh unsheathed his sword and held a Fireball at the ready.

The necrosed lifted his nose to the air. "I can't see you, little *asrasins*, but I know you're here." He spoke in a scratchy voice, as if unused to speaking. "I can smell your *lorethasra*. It is rich and delicious." He licked his lips, a forked tongue flicking out. "I know much. You aren't holders. You aren't the ones who killed Rue, but I'll be the one who kills you." He chuckled. "That rhymed."

Rukh let go of his Blend and the Fireball, but he maintained his Shield "Who are you?" he asked the necrosed.

The creature faced him. "Ah, there you are. Prey should never hide when there is no hope for succor." The necrosed smiled, and Jessira could see all the jagged teeth lining the monster's mouth. "As to my name, I am Charnel Blood. But you may call me your bane."

Rukh nodded. "Interesting meeting you. Do you happen to know what happened to the people living here?" he asked, his tone conversational.

"Why do you care?"

"Curiosity."

"Curiosity killed the cat, little *asrasin.*"

"But the cat died satisfied," Rukh said. "You don't mind satisfying the curiosity of a little *asrasin* like me, do you? I'm nothing but prey. I'll soon be dead anyway."

Again, the necrosed chuckled. "That rhymed, too. For that I'll answer, but only if the other *asrasin* shows herself. I know she's here." The necrosed inhaled deeply. "Yes. She's definitely a female."

Jessira briefly considered the matter. In the end, the choice was easy. She dropped her Blend.

"Pretty," the necrosed said, leering now.

Jessira didn't bother replying. The necrosed was using a pathetic ploy meant to unsettle her, throw her off balance, and make her easier to kill. It wouldn't work.

"The people," Rukh reminded Charnel.

"The people." Charnel blinked. "Oh yes, the people. They sleep. A simple weave. I'll allow them to wake once I've finished feasting on you and the pretty one."

"And if you die?" Jessira asked.

Charnel laughed. "That would be a neat trick. Why don't we find out?" He launched himself at Rukh.

Rukh waited, sword ready. Jessira had no worries for him. He could defend himself against this beast. At the last instant, Rukh shifted slightly to the side. Charnel's claws lashed against his Shield but found no purchase. Rukh's sword whipped about. Jessira sensed him harden it through one of his Kumma Talents. The blade cut a shallow line across Charnel's chest.

The necrosed fell back with a snarl of pain.

"That probably stings, doesn't it?" Rukh asked.

"You're a holder," the necrosed spat. "Sapient said you were all dead."

"Your Overward lied. We are very much alive," Rukh answered.

"A lie for which he will answer. I am gravely disappointed in his leadership." Charnel's eyes grew unfocused, became consumed by swirling rainbow hues.

The colors reminded Jessira of an anchor line as it opened. The necrosed sought to escape. She hurled a Fireball. It slammed into the creature, flinging him back ten feet. He landed awkwardly on his butt, flipped over his head, and came to rest on his chest. He rose shakily. "You are no holders." Fear filled his face.

Rukh jumped forward, covering the twenty feet between himself and the necrosed in a single bound. His sword flashed forward, aimed like an arrow, and took Charnel through the heart. He twisted the blade. "We'll mention your grave disappointment when we see the Overward."

The necrosed clutched in disbelief at the sword that had lanced through his chest. "What are you?"

"The Servitor calls us World Killers," Rukh said, "but you can name us your bane." He echoed the monster's earlier words.

The necrosed slumped off Rukh's sword, collapsing to the ground.

"That was easy," Rukh noted.

"And a little much on the drama part," Jessira said with a chuckle. "You can name us your bane?"

Rukh grinned. "It sounded more impressive in my mind."

"I'm sure it did," Jessira said.

"We need to burn this one," Rukh said. His hands filled with a weave of Fire, a braid they'd learned to create from the magi. White-hot and blazing like the sun, he set it off, and the flames incinerated the necrosed in seconds.

Jessira gestured to the cabins. "Let's see about the people here. Make sure they're waking up."

"We should probably also stay here until William and the others arrive," Rukh said. "Keep the *saha'asra* safe for them."

Jessira wasn't fooled. "You're only searching for an excuse to kill more necrosed."

Rukh grinned. "Of all the sentient beings we've ever met, they're the first ones I don't mind ending."

～

SAPIENT HAD SMILED in satisfaction when he tasted Rue's death. She had always been a thorn in his side, a painful irritant for well over three millennia. Now he was gladly rid of her. The young holder had killed the horrible fiend, just as Sapient had hoped. He'd laughed heartily when he imagined Rue's death.

Hopefully, it had been as pathetic as the life she'd once lived.

However, a day later had come Charnel's unexpected demise. Sapient had stiffened in disbelief because this time it hadn't been the boy who had slain a powerful necrosed. Sapient could tell. He could taste the faint echoes of power drifting along the lines of *lorasra* from that faraway *saha'asra* all the way here, to Sinskrill. It had been someone else who had ended Charnel, someone familiar.

He heard and ignored the angry snarls of his brethren clamoring in his mind, demanding he answer this outrage. They cared little for Rue or Charnel, but two necrosed—four when Kohl and Grave were included—dead at the hands of *asrasins* couldn't go unpunished. Sapient promised to heed their complaints but didn't bother to tell them how he would deal with the matter. He was the Overward for a reason: because he could reason whereas the others simply attacked without thinking the matter through.

He recognized that caution was required.

Sapient tasted the *lorasra*, seeking out the nature of the ones who had destroyed Charnel, but in the end, he snapped his teeth in annoyance. He couldn't ascertain the identity of Charnel's killer from his place on Sinskrill. He'd have to travel to the actual *saha'asra* and take a closer surveillance of the situation. He didn't want to. Those who wielded the power he sensed, the ones who had ended Charnel's life, inspired a rare emotion within his ravaged heart: fear. Sapient wanted nothing to do with them.

But the brethren required an answer, and it fell to the Overward to supply it.

Sapient paused before leaving. He took in the scene in front of him, Lake White Sun at night, the sun already set, the blustering breeze, the omnipresent clouds, and regular rain. Unable to delay any longer, he made himself ready and traveled to the place where Charnel had died.

He exited into a meadow held in winter's grip, but spring beckoned. Soon would come warmth, but for now frost gleamed. The sun bore a bright light. Cabins huddled like frightened children. A forest stretched all around, hushed now. Sapient inhaled deeply. Again came the familiarity of power, this time more strongly. He carefully paced the *saha'asra*, senses tuned for danger. He hissed at the fear coursing through him. It was not how a necrosed should ever approach any situation, especially one inspired by a mere *asrasin*.

Sapient came across a dead patch of grass and halted. Rue had bled here. Farther on, he neared a large, burned area, the place where her body had been burned. This had been the action of the boy, the young holder. He searched about. None of this was of interest to him.

What of Charnel's death?

He prowled about the meadow, quickly reaching another area where blackened ash replaced healthy grass. This was the site of Charnel's demise, his body consumed in a flash of heat, and Sapient trembled. Sensations flooded through him, memories stoked to life like a hesitant fire brought to burning from embers.

His eyes flew open in shock. He knew the killer. He inhaled more deeply. No. He knew the killers. He knew them both, had once been as close to them as kin.

But it was impossible. How could it be them? Shokan and Sira were on Seminal. Sapient had seen them there with his own eyes, and yet the weaves he felt in this place, the ones he could almost see . . . They were of Shokan and Sira's creation, as unique as their very *lorethasra*. If true, it was no wonder Charnel had died. His demise had likely come quickly, too. No necrosed could stand against Shokan or Sira separately, and certainly not both at the same time, which is what Charnel had apparently faced.

Sapient didn't know what to make of the situation. An unaccounted mystery had risen. Shokan and Sira couldn't exist both here and on Seminal. Not in their physical forms. Only one's aether could travel the anchor line between worlds.

Unless . . .

What if they have two shells, one on Seminal and one here? Their aethers could then travel the anchor line from Seminal to Earth and inhabit a waiting body.

Sapient immediately shook off the notion. The anchor line between Seminal and Earth remained closed. Otherwise, Shet would have long since made his presence felt.

He ground his teeth in frustration. The mystery wouldn't resolve itself here and now. Sapient flicked his gaze around the empty meadow, growing nervous. *What if Shokan and Sira returned?* The meadow appeared empty, but danger . . . it lurked. He could feel it in his gut, and a shiver traveled down his spine. Better to ponder the situation from the safety of Sinskrill.

Sapient hastily withdrew from the *saha'asra*.

13

JUDGMENT AND OPPORTUNITIES

M *arch 1991*

WILLIAM SHARED a bench with Serena at the Village Green and luxuriated in Arylyn's warmth. A few days ago, they'd been freezing cold in Cincinnati, and now they had ice cream cones in hand—courtesy of Ms. Maxine—while watching a sunset. Many villagers milled about, sharing gossip, or hauling groceries home from the recently concluded farmer's market. The mouthwatering aroma of sizzling meat from the recently rebuilt *Jimmy Webster's Restaurant* wafted on the wind. Jimmy had also installed a smoker, and he had something delicious-smelling cooking on the barbecue.

A puff of breeze swept Serena's hair, waving it about like a soft, black pennant. She placed a hand on top of her head to keep her hair from billowing about. "I really should remember to put my hair in a ponytail," she said under her breath.

"You mean like Jessira?" William teased, knowing Serena had a large dose of hero-worship for the woman.

Serena snorted. "You're one to talk with how you feel about Rukh."

William shrugged, knowing her observation was true.

"I'm worried about Selene," Serena said. "She tried to hide it, but she was sad when we left, more than she should have been."

William had also sensed Selene's melancholy, but he'd sensed other emotions coming from her: grit and determination. "She'll be fine. She's tough. She's from Sinskrill. She'll get through this."

Serena faced him. "How do you know?"

William took a deep breath, thinking of what to say. He had to tread carefully. If he acted too sure of himself, Serena would likely take it as condescension. But he also wanted her to know the depth of his certainty. "Selene's strong. She's got a lot more courage than you realize. I talked to her. Sure, she's upset and sad at everything that's happened, but she's also determined to make her way in the Far Beyond. She'll find a way."

Serena viewed him with skepticism. "She said this?"

"No. Not in so many words, but I could tell that's what's in her heart. She'll make it. She's strong like you and Fiona."

"Fiona always used to say that Selene reminds her of Cinnamon, our mother," Serena said. "You know how her life ended. She wasn't so strong." Bitterness tinged her tone.

Cinnamon had been whipped to death for some made-up crime, and Serena had been forced to watch.

"Cinnamon wasn't weak," William said. "Not the way I see things. Maybe she was naive or foolish, but she wasn't weak."

Serena eyed him with fresh interest, with that vaguely unsettling, overly intense stare she possessed.

"She had the courage to love you and Selene. On Sinskrill. Can you imagine how hard it must have been for her? Especially with what we know about the source of Sinskrill's *lorasra*."

"Shet." Several years ago, Serena had made the discovery when she'd touched Shet's Spear and traveled to Seminal. She'd witnessed the god chained to a mountain, and the poisonous *lorasra* pouring off him. It entered the strange connection between Seminal and

Sinskrill, and infected everyone on the island with callousness and cruelty.

"Cinnamon was strong, probably stronger than anyone on Sinskrill."

"Maybe," Serena said, her unsure demeanor persisting.

William tried a different tack. "If you don't believe me, then believe Selene."

"What do you mean?"

"Selene never once cried or sniffled when we visited," William said. "She was sad, but she wasn't defeated. Couldn't you tell?"

Serena's eyes narrowed in thought, her air became thoughtful. After a few seconds, she nodded as if in reluctant agreement.

"And Mr. and Mrs. Ridley have her in counseling. That's got to help." William didn't know much about counseling, but it sounded like a good idea. "They also said she's finding her footing. They didn't say she's falling apart."

Serena's attitude changed from worried to hopeful, and a hesitant smile took shape. "You're smarter than you look."

William grinned and sought to ease the last of her tension. "You're only saying that because you're hoping I'll kiss you."

Serena threw her head back and laughed. People stared, and William glanced about in embarrassment.

"It wasn't that funny," he said. Serena continued to laugh, and he found himself growing irritated. It wasn't like the two of them had never kissed before, and half the time she was the one who started it.

He was about to say something, but she silenced him with her smile, the one he loved where she seemed secretly amused with the world. "You're right. It's not funny," she said. She put a hand behind his neck, and he allowed her to draw him close. She kissed him, brief but deep and intense.

She leaned away too quickly for his liking. "Thank you. Talking to you helped." She smiled. "And you're right. I like kissing you."

William found himself lost in the intensity of her regard, in her lovely eyes, and he couldn't reply at once. It took him a moment to gather his composure, and once again, he found that *he* was now the focus of her secret smile of amusement. "I like kissing you, too," he managed.

Serena rested her head on his shoulder and sighed. "I wish we could sit together like this for the rest of our lives."

William kept himself from stiffening as he took in the import of her words. *The rest of our lives.* It didn't sound far-fetched. It sounded perfect.

Serena lifted her head and stared him in the eyes, unblinking and unflinching. He'd never seen her so willingly vulnerable or fearless. "Did I say something wrong?"

"You said everything right."

She settled against his shoulder again, seemingly pleased, but William's heart still raced. *The rest of our lives.*

WILLIAM PACED the training field and studied the Irregulars' new recruits. He'd been assigned roughly fifty of them. The Wild Ones were what he'd taken to calling them, and the name had stuck. These were the men and women he was expected to train, the folk he needed to get ready for the invasion of Sinskrill. They ranged in age from their late teens through their seventies. The older ones could have passed for forty in the Far Beyond. All of them carried a serious and focused demeanor. They understood what was expected of them.

Other companies shared the field with the Wild Ones, each group having a specific area for training. It was the same shallow swale—a place they'd named Warning Meadow—where the first Irregulars had formed and trained. Lakshman's Bow arched over the nearby River Namaste, but the enrune fields on the other side remained empty. Everyone who played Lilith's national sport had volunteered for the Irregulars.

Following Lilith's rebuilding, a total of about eight hundred magi had signed up for the Irregulars. For now, they'd been split into groups of fifty, each unit under the command of a veteran lieutenant, someone like William who'd survived Sinskrill's attack.

"Shift!" William shouted.

The squads who'd started the sparring session while facing Lakshman's Bow moved to their left, facing off against a new set of opponents. They changed positions every five minutes, since William didn't want any of them getting too familiar with their adversaries. Most used wooden swords but some had opted for the staff. They fought in small units of four-on-four, and their weapons clacked against one another. An occasional smack against flesh resulted in a shouted curse.

William watched his unit closely as he prowled the perimeter of the field. The day wasn't particularly hot, but sweat soaked the Wild Ones. Their shirts clung to their skin. They'd only been practicing at war for the past month, and many still didn't have the conditioning they would ultimately need. Some already panted, less than an hour in.

It disappointed him that this far into their training, they still weren't as conditioned as he would have expected. Had they done nothing during the week he'd been gone while visiting Selene and Elliot?

"No slacking!" William barked at those whose weapons drooped. "When we go against the mahavans, do you think they'll slack? They'll cut you into pieces if you give them a chance."

He continued observing the Wild Ones, calling out corrections in posture and technique but also wanting to find those who could become squad commanders. *Leaders.*

A short while later, he called an end to the session. Grateful groans met his pronouncement.

"Get some water and assemble here in five minutes," he said.

Again, William watched, searching out those who took control of the water barrels, the ones who made sure everyone had a chance to drink. Minutes afterward, he faced a line of still panting magi, most of whom, despite their fatigue, seemed eager and willing.

A sense of age came over William. He'd seen and done so much more than any of them. Terrible things. The blood he'd shed, the battles he'd fought. In comparison, he found the Wild Ones to be terribly young, even those who were old enough to be his grand-parents.

"You're coming along," William shouted, projecting his voice the same way Rukh did. "We've only been at this a month, but I can already see progress. Well done."

The Wild Ones straightened, some of them sharing pleased smiles with their neighbors.

"But we've got a lot further to go. Your conditioning sucks." William glared. "And it's not enough to smack each other with wooden weapons. You need to be willing to step forward into danger. Accept it, overcome it, and kill your enemy."

The smiles faded, and the Wild Ones shifted about in uncertainty.

Again came the feeling of great age. William had killed people. Ordered it. He knew what it meant. He'd been instructed in how to wage war, and he wished he didn't have to pass on his learning.

"Y'all know our ultimate goal," William said. "Invade Sinskrill and stop Shet from coming to our world. That means we'll have to kill anyone who gets in between us and our objective."

More shifting of feet.

"Sir." Derek Findlay, an older magi, held up his hand. "You were forced to fight. We all know how you ended up on Sinskrill and everything after. It's not like that for us."

"Which is why we're training so hard," William said. "If we train hard enough now, we can do mighty things."

"Is killing mighty?" Derek asked.

William didn't need to think about the answer. Killing was horrible. He hated it, no matter the necessity. "No," he answered. "It might even be the opposite of mighty. But killing may allow us to do those mighty things." He clapped his hands once. "Enough talking. There's still daylight, and there's still time for another session. Pair off. Same squads as who you ended against." The Wild Ones grumbled in complaint but shuffled to their positions. "Move it!" William shouted. They quickened their pace. William waited until they were in position. "Go!"

Once more came exhortations, shouted orders, and the slap of wood against wood.

ADAM STOOD with crossed arms and concern on his face as he watched the newly minted mahavans learn the way of the sword and the mastery of their Elements. They battled in the Crucible, and their contests made for a pathetic spectacle. None were worthy of the title 'mahavan,' but it had been bestowed upon them regardless. They rushed about like farmers wielding pitchforks, and their weaves lacked power and control. Adam mentally shook his head.

These fools are Sinskrill's hope?

He snorted in derision.

They'd all be dead inside of a single engagement with the far more powerful magi. Adam recalled how well the enemy *asrasins* wielded their weapons and their *lorethasra*. They were formidable.

From close by, Axel observed the scene as well, his demeanor equally bleak, but it was an air of judgment only Adam could discern. To anyone else, his brother might have appeared drone-flat in his mien, but Adam knew him too well. He sensed Axel's disquiet.

They watched from a viewing stand built along the northern edge of the large, lower courtyard of the Servitor's Palace. An alabaster wall rimmed the space with barracks and paddocks to the east, a raised portcullis and main gate to the south, and the Crucible to the west. It was there, where the so-called mahavans trained, that Adam focused his gaze.

For centuries, in those squares of packed dirt, mahavans, bishans, and shills had sparred and struggled. It was Sinskrill's heart, where shills became bishans; bishans became mahavans; and mahavans became noteworthy. It was where greatness rose and the unworthy failed.

But no longer.

Now with Sinskrill reduced and devastated by the poorly conceived attack on Arylyn, these wretched men and women, all of them drones given a second chance at glory, were all that was left of mahavan might.

"Create a bubble," Axel said, his voice soft. A fleeting glimpse of sorrow crossed his coarse features.

Adam did as he was bade, forming a weave of Air to prevent Walkers from listening in on whatever his brother had to say.

"Our poor, deluded mahavans will try to hold back the magi tide, but they will fail," Axel said.

Adam held back his start of surprise. He agreed with the Servitor, but to hear his brother actually say the words was shocking. Always before Axel had exuded confidence that he would somehow lead Sinskrill through this great and grave crisis to a future full of possibilities and power. To learn Axel thought their cause hopeless was stunning.

Axel smiled, a bare twitch of his mouth. "You believe this as well, do you not?"

Adam regained his equilibrium. "I do."

"What do you advise we do, my Secondus?" Axel asked, his tone formal.

"With the unformed, we might deal the magi enough damage to cause them to withdraw," Adam said, although he believed it unlikely.

"The unformed," Axel said, his tone making the words a question. "They answered my call, but I worry over who they consider their true master. They obey me now, but consider this: do they follow my commands because of respect for my office or because of Shet's summons? He sends them instructions via the very *lorasra* he transmits to Sinskrill."

Adam didn't know this. He hadn't realized this was the means by which Shet communicated with his woven. "You don't think we can rely on them?"

"We can rely on them to fight for self-preservation," Axel said, "but that isn't the same as fighting alongside us for a common cause."

Adam pondered the situation. He'd never had much faith in his brother's plan of bringing the world's woven monsters to Sinskrill in order to defend the island. It seemed he was right to be skeptical. "What of the demon?" he asked. Privately, he thought raising the demon an even graver mistake.

"Salachar Rakshasa. The last and possibly the greatest of her kind on Earth." Pleasure lit Axel's face. "She rouses. Slowly, but she should be awake in time for the battle."

Adam did his best to shove aside his discontent. "Can she be controlled?"

Axel shook his head. "No one can control a demon. No one but Shet, and even his hands rest lightly on the reins of their mastery. But they can be reasoned with, and this one has been reasoned with. I've spoken to her."

Again, Adam started. "I thought she was asleep."

"Her body only. Her mind already quests, searching and studying for a means to achieve vengeance. It was Shet's promises that caused her to battle Shokan. Shet should have aided her, but he didn't. It was in that battle that Salachar fell and faded. To waste away in the realm of the Rakshasas in perpetual, restless slumber. She has no fondness for Shet. She'll battle on our behalf, possibly even battle the god when he finally steps foot on our world."

Adam still thought waking the demon was a terrible decision, but another notion caught his attention. "I've wondered about something. If only our Spirits can cross the anchor lines between worlds, how then are we able to visit Seminal? Does it not mean that the anchor line is already open?"

Axel shook his head. "The Spear allows our Spiritual Element to reach Seminal, but it isn't what is meant by *our Spirits*. When the anchor line is truly opened, it won't be our Spiritual Element alone able to make the journey across the worlds. It will be our entirety, every portion of our *lorethasra* and more."

Something about the explanation struck Adam as odd. "But not our bodies?"

"No."

Adam's disquiet increased, and he thought aloud. "If our bodies can't cross, then Shet will need a host."

Axel smiled wryly. "What do you think the statue in the Throne Hall is meant for? It is not merely decorative. It is Shet's shell on this world. Once he passes through the anchor line, he'll wear it like a second skin." He shrugged in a dismissive fashion. "Or at least, that is what all Servitors have believed since Sinskrill's founding."

The answer to one of their greatest fears suddenly seemed so simple. "Destroy it. Break the statue to rubble."

Axel shook his head. "The statue is not stone. It was created by Shet's own will and skill, anchored to the island's roots. Nothing short of a volcano can dislodge it or his throne."

Adam's gaze sharpened. "Why is the throne anchored so deeply?"

"It is the focus of the anchor line connecting our worlds. The anchor line from Seminal begins and ends at the throne."

Adam shook his head. *Of course.* "Is there anything we can do?"

Axel nodded his head. "Dream again to my daughter. We discussed the last time you did so, after you told her about the demon."

A sly smile stole across the Servitor's face, and Adam kept his own features even and untroubled. However, his heart raced sudden worry. He hadn't meant for his brother to learn about that prior dream, but somehow the Servitor had found out about it anyway. He'd been amused by Adam's actions, approving them as if they were based on a discussion they'd already agreed upon.

But in his heart, Adam's intentions had been driven by betrayal. For whatever reason the Servitor didn't seem to care. Or perhaps his lack of concern was a ruse and the punishment would fall when Adam least expected it. He didn't know, and the lack of knowledge kept him worried.

"Tell her about the throne," Axel continued.

"To what purpose?" Adam didn't understand the Servitor's reasoning. "If you want the magi to know our plans, why fight them at all?"

Axel smiled, predatory. "You'll only tell them enough to whet their appetite. Make them believe we're weak. They'll charge straight ahead on our beaches, and we'll kill them for their lack of foresight. Shet will hopefully applaud our courage." He gestured to the maha-vans who flailed about ineffectually. "I'll take over their training myself. They'll be ready for what's to come."

Adam kept himself from gaping. As a plan, it was utterly stupid, but the Servitor was his ruler. He'd do as he'd been ordered.

"There is one other thing," Axel said. "Another tribe of unformed has been killed."

"The Overward." Adam's flat inflection expressed none of his anger with the creature. He wished Axel had never allowed Sapient access to the island. The cursed necrosed gave lip-service to Axel's rule, doing as he wished, coming and going as he pleased, and killing those he had been expressly told to leave alive. But what could they do? Sapient Dormant was the legendary Overward. No *asrasin* could defeat him.

"I overlooked one insult already, but this one I cannot," Axel said. "Have him summoned."

"Yes, my liege," Adam answered.

He privately doubted the wisdom of confronting the powerful necrosed, but he also realized there was no other option. Then again, if Axel died, the mahavans could finally make alliance with the magi and together, perhaps, they could stop Shet.

He could only hope.

14

MARRIAGE AND FEARS

 *pril 1991*

"YOU ALMOST MISSED IT," Mink whispered when Jason finally arrived at the blue pavilion set up on the warm sands of Lilith Bay.

He was late, and he knew it, and he whispered apologies to her and everyone else attending. He briefly bobbed his head to William and Jake, who sat nearby.

"I had to take care of Mr. Zeus' house," Jason explained to Mink.

"Ah. I see."

Mr. Zeus and Mayor Care stood on a raised platform in front of a single row of white chairs—all of them occupied by a small group consisting of the Karllsons, William, Jake, Daniella, Julius, and Jessira. Rukh stood in a corner, a mandolin loosely clasped in his hands. All of them had been invited to today's celebration in which Mr. Zeus and Fiona would wed. She hadn't arrived yet, but Jason had seen her standing next to Serena on the Guanyin. They had been discussing something, probably a private matter.

The sun settled toward the horizon, its evening rays beaming across a golden sky and cotton-candy clouds. The ocean susurrated, a counterpoint to the low rumble of Lilith's distant cataracts. A blustering breeze blew.

A few minutes after Jason's arrival, Fiona and Serena showed up at the pavilion. They paused at the entrance, and Rukh began strumming a tune, one Jason didn't recognize.

"It's from Ashoka," Jessira whispered to him from a few seats over. She must have noticed his uncertainty.

Fiona beamed as she and Serena sedately made their way down the short aisle leading to the dais. When the two of them reached Mr. Zeus, Serena broke off and took a seat next to William.

The vows proved to be short and sweet, words Mr. Zeus and Fiona had written for one another. Moments later it was over, and Mayor Care threw her arms open, smiling widely, pronouncing them husband and wife. Mr. Zeus and Fiona shared a kiss.

Jason grinned and clapped, making himself focus on his joy for the new couple. He tried not to notice Mr. Zeus' tremor when he offered Fiona his arm. He ignored his grandfather's stooped gait, and the new age-lines seaming his face. Mr. Zeus and Fiona paced out of the pavilion, headed for the Guanyin and the Main Stairs of Cliff Spirit. From there, they'd eventually head to the Village Green where the main party would take place. It was a long hike for the old couple, and they'd stop first at Mr. Zeus' house before making the rest of the journey to Clifftop. Everyone else would meet them there.

"It's cruel to ask them to go all the way up to Clifftop," Mink said while watching Mr. Zeus and Fiona proceed toward the gorge and the Guanyin.

Jason nodded agreement. "Yeah, but they wanted to have the party up there."

"Using a wedding as an excuse to celebrate is always a wonderful decision," Jessira said. "We used to do the same in Stronghold."

"I think everyone everywhere does that," Rukh said in a wry tone, moving to stand at her side. "We certainly did in Ashoka. Remember our second wedding? All the guests? Some were even enemies to my House."

"You had two wedding ceremonies?" Jason asked in surprise. He'd never heard this story.

"Why two?" Jake asked.

"We'll see you at Clifftop," Mr. Karllson said to the group. He gave a brief nod toward Rukh and Jessira, lips thinning. Daniel's father still couldn't bring himself to talk to the commanders, which was a shame.

As Jason figured things, the true villain behind Daniel's death wasn't Rukh or Jessira. It was the Servitor.

"We'll be there in a bit," William said, his hand entwined with one of Serena's.

Mrs. Karllson gave a smile to Rukh and Jessira, a rueful tightening of her lips. "We look forward to seeing all of you there," she said before she and Mr. Karllson headed toward the gorge.

Lien and Julius trailed after the Karllsons.

"The wedding in Ashoka was lovely," Jessira said, smiling warmly at Rukh, continuing their discussion of their weddings, "but the one in my home had greater depth of emotion."

Rukh took her hand and stared soulfully into her eyes. "You were the reason for the loveliness and the emotion in both our weddings, in all our moments together. My life would forever be incomplete without you."

It was bizarre seeing the commanders like this since Jason's only awareness of them was as his strict taskmasters. Witnessing them affectionate and loving was like watching a rabbit stand up and talk. And this amount of syrupy love was just gross.

Jake must have felt the same way. He groaned in disgust. "Oh, come on."

William was right on his heels. "Get a room."

Jessira smiled while Rukh laughed.

"He's jerking your chains, boys," Jessira said. "That is the correct phrase, is it not?"

"What?" Jason asked in shock. *Did Rukh just tell a joke? Impossible.* Jason had never known the commander to ever crack a smile. Then again, he apparently *had* told a joke based on Jessira's wry headshake.

Rukh confirmed it a moment later. "Jessira's right. It was a joke."

He addressed her, his eyes gleaming with humor. "Next time I should tell them the poem I wrote for you during our second wedding."

Jessira pealed laughter. "They would be horrified."

"Or maybe I should leer at you," Rukh said.

"Or maybe you should say something truly sweet."

"For such a strong, beautiful woman, you certainly require a lot of sweetness."

"And?" Jessira asked in an arch tone.

"And I wouldn't want you any other way."

The two of them left the pavilion, and Jason watched them wander off.

Mink piped up. "Is it just me, or does everyone else think it's wonderful that our fearsome commanders are so in love with each other?"

Jason eyed her in surprise. "What? Seriously?" He never expected Mink to have such a sentimental side.

"Seriously," she replied.

"Let's head on up," Serena said.

Everyone followed the commanders then—William, Serena, Jake, and Daniella up front and Jason and Mink trailing behind. The two of them walked in silence and reached the Guanyin. A dozen different things flitted through Jason's mind; thoughts about the future, life, peace, and love.

"You're humming," Mink said as they crested the bridge.

Jason hadn't realized he'd been doing it, and he broke off.

"It was 'Gloria,'" Mink added. "Did you pick that up from Serena?"

Jason nodded. "It used to be her way of praying. I guess it must have rubbed off on me."

"Praying is good."

"Yes, it is," Jason said. Just then, a surge of unexpected happiness lifted his spirits. "Thank you for coming with me. You didn't have to."

Mink appeared surprised. "Of course I'd come. Why wouldn't I?"

"Because you didn't have to." For some reason, Mink viewed him in disbelief, and Jason recoiled. "What did I say?"

"You're thick, you know that?"

Jason frowned in confusion. "What?" he said, hating how stupid he sounded.

"I wanted to be here because I like you. I think you like me."

Jason blinked in uncertainty. He did like Mink. He always had, but what did she mean she liked . . . *Oh.* Silence feel between them as his mud-slow mind processed the information.

The dawning understanding must have been evident on his face. "Thick," Mink said with a shake of her head.

Jason drew her to a halt and bent his head, hesitation causing him to move too slowly because Mink tugged his head down and kissed him.

SAPIENT BENT HIS head in order to duck beneath the portcullis leading to the lower courtyard of the Servitor's Palace. This was the place the mahavans labeled "the Crucible," the place where they believed their children became worthy warriors. Sapient had his doubts about whether any of the *asrasins* could make such a claim. He had seen their training and came away unimpressed.

Children playing with toy weapons.

The air held still and Sinskrill's perennial blanket of clouds appeared motionless as Sapient gazed about the Crucible. He immediately noted the lack of activity, and his wariness rose. At this time of day—early afternoon—it should have been full of *asrasins* striving against one another. Instead, Sapient saw no one else present except for the Servitor and his Secondus. They stood upon the grounds of the Crucible, eyeing him as if he were vermin. Sinskrill's ruler wore white leather pants and a matching vest that left his arms bare. He clutched Shet's Spear as if it were a lifeline and he a drowning man. The Secondus was unworthy of note.

Nevertheless, Sapient's wariness increased further.

"It is good that you have deigned to answer my summons," the Servitor said, his tone sarcastic. "I feared you believed yourself immune to my rule."

Ah. A test of wills. Sapient's wariness eased. He noticed many faces peering from the various windows surrounding the Crucible. *An audience.* The Servitor wished to discipline him for some inexplicable reason, and he wanted his people to bear witness. Sapient knew not what motivated the Servitor's actions. Perhaps it had to do with the tribe of unformed he'd killed several months ago. Or maybe the one from several days back. It didn't matter.

"I answer only to Shet's rule," Sapient said.

"And through him, to me," the Servitor countered.

"As you say," Sapient replied in a tone a shade below mockery. "And what service may I provide?"

"Your service?" the Servitor seemed to taste the question. "I do not require your service. I require your obedience."

Sapient sneered, no longer caring if it offended the Servitor. What could the Servitor do against him? Nothing. He was weak, weak like all *asrasins.* A vagrant thought flitted into his mind. *What about those who slew Rue and Charnel?* Sapient's features flattened, and he disregarded the question.

"You think I find your disobedience humorous?" the Servitor asked.

All the while the Secondus had remained quiet, and Sapient's eyes flicked the man's way when he shifted to a flanking position. He also caught the Servitor's subtle gesture, calling his fellow *asrasin* back to his side.

"I do not care what you believe," Sapient said, bored of this game. He didn't answer to the Servitor, and he didn't respect or fear the man. "Nor will I pretend any longer to obey your missives." He turned his back on Sinskrill's supposed ruler and made to leave the Crucible.

A bolt of Fire struck him in the back, causing him to stumble and fall. He caught himself on his hands and slowly straightened, turning to face the Servitor with an anticipatory grin. He would wreck this puppet king.

He smirked when he noticed the Secondus had retreated to a viewing stand. *At least one of the* asrasins *here has some sense.*

"I did not give you leave to withdraw," the Servitor said. "You *will* attend me."

"And if I say 'no?'"

The Servitor's reply was another line of Fire.

This time Sapient was ready. He absorbed the weave, and it filled him with greater energy. *Fool.* He darted forward, dodging a hissing braid of Air. He noticed too late a rustling braid of Earth, and it threw him off his feet, tripping him. He swiftly regained his balance and barely had time to bend beneath a rushing braid of Water.

The Servitor could weave quickly. He'd give the man that much. But it wouldn't be enough to save him.

Again came Fire.

Sapient paused his headlong rush toward the Servitor and took in the weave. Would the Servitor never learn? Fire fed a necrosed. Further energy fueled him, and he laughed. *Almost as good as consuming an unformed.* A thin weave of Air lanced into him. Sapient planted his feet and leaned forward, knowing what was to come. The braid couldn't penetrate his skin, which was sturdier than steel, but it could cause him to lose his footing.

His preparations weren't enough.

The Air blasted him in the stomach, hurling him off his feet. Sapient had a moment to gasp in disbelief before he smashed into the far wall of the Crucible. He grunted heavily on impact.

"You were told to leave the unformed be," the Servitor said from the far side of the Crucible, "and yet I learn that you exterminated two entire tribes."

Again came a braid of Air. It pinned Sapient to the wall, and he struggled to free himself.

The unformed. Sapient cursed to himself. *This battle was truly because of those vermin? What stupidity.*

Sapient finally rid himself of the weave holding him against the wall. Mobile again, he faced the Servitor, all trace of amusement wiped clean.

"I intended on simply defeating you," Sapient said to the Servitor. "I think I shall kill you instead and feast on your *lorethasra.*"

Now it was the Servitor who smirked. "You will learn a hard lesson today." He aimed the Spear. A thick bar of Earth rippled over the ground at Sapient.

He dodged it.

More weaves exploded at him. He continued to evade the Servitor's attack, all the while drifting closer, waiting for his moment.

Now!

Sapient rushed forward. The Servitor blocked his first punch with the Spear, but not the second. The Overward landed a fist against the man's chest, a solid strike. The Servitor flew through the air, landing more than twenty feet away, sliding another half dozen on his back.

Sapient exulted. A killing blow. His satisfaction fell away when the Servitor sat up. The punch should have staved in the Servitor's chest. Instead, blood trickled from the man's forehead and dirt scuffed his white leathers, but otherwise he was unharmed, rising easily to his feet.

Sapient gaped. *How?*

"Shet gave you strength," the Servitor said. He twirled the Spear. "I will give you humility." A whirlwind roared off his hands.

Sapient leaned into it. It was more powerful than any weave he had ever expected the Servitor to manage. Only a *thera'asra* could have created such a braid. The Servitor paced toward him. The leaf-shaped blade of the Spear began glowing. Sapient tried to duck below or around the Servitor's attack, but to no effect. Every one of his motions was somehow anticipated. He darted from one side to the other, but the Servitor kept pace with him.

Impossible.

Sapient's eyes widened. Only Shokan and Sira could match his speed.

The Overward found himself hemmed in, unable to move forward or sideways. A trickle of worry rippled along his spine. He sought retreat, but a bar of Earth cracked into his chest. It blasted him head over heels, smashing him again into a distant wall. He grunted in pain but clambered to his feet as quickly as he could manage. He found the Servitor directly in front of him. The man thrust the Spear's glowing blade forward.

Sapient gaped again. The Spear penetrated his skin, cutting deep into his abdomen. Pain exploded. Black blood pooled from the wound. Until this moment, Sapient had believed that no weapon other than one imbued with the Wildness could damage him.

The Servitor twisted the Spear, and Sapient growled, the pain cresting. He extended his arms, hoping to snare the Servitor on his claws, but the man stood too far away.

"No clever quips or superior smirks?" the Servitor asked. He yanked out the Spear, and Sapient slumped.

A whiplash of Air, thin as a hair but with the strength of a hurricane, bit into his chest. It carved a fresh wound, and once more Sapient's mouth dropped open in shock. More black blood flowed. Questions roiled through his mind. How could the Servitor be so powerful? Only Shokan could have bested him so easily. Or had the long march of millennia robbed him of more strength than he realized?

"On your knees," the Servitor commanded.

For the first time in his long life, Sapient Dormant, the Overward of the necrosed, willingly bent knee to someone other than Shet. He'd been bested, and he knew it.

The Servitor stood over him, fearless in his victory. "I spare your life only because you might yet have some small worth in the battles to come. But hear me and mark my words. You will answer when summoned. You will leave the unformed alone. You will obey. Anything less than instant obedience means death. Am I understood?"

Sapient mutely nodded. "Yes, my liege." He spoke the words, but his heart burned with anger and shame. He would find a way to defeat this petty *asrasin*. He'd defeat Shet as well. Even Shokan, wherever he was.

ADAM STRODE through the relatively empty hallways of the Servitor's Palace, his boots echoing as he marched toward his quarters. Occasionally long carpets and rugs—most of them purple or red in color —softened the white marble floors and muffled the sounds of his firm footsteps. He swept through a solarium with a ribbed ceiling, potted shrubbery, and a hearty fire burning in a hearth. It was empty of people, and Adam wept at the waste. Once, not so long ago, the Palace would have bustled with drones running hither and yon, or mahavans on errands for themselves or their betters, but there were so few now. So few to keep alive the culture and history of Sinskrill.

It shouldn't have been like this. If the Servitor had left *Demolition* and led the attack personally, it wouldn't have. Once again, Adam had recently witnessed his brother's fearsome power when the Servitor had laid low Sapient Dormant, the Overward of the necrosed, the being feared by all mahavan, magi, and woven. Axel had defeated and humiliated the legendary monster in under five minutes. Which angered Adam to no end. Why couldn't his brother have brought forth such might during his ill-planned, ill-fated assault on Arylyn?

Instead, he'd stood idly by, safe in the harbor, shelling a defenseless village while his mahavans bled and died for his cause. Adam scowled. Axel had still somehow managed to lose all the warriors manning the ships. The World-Killer, Jessira, had defeated him, while Rukh of Ashoka had destroyed the combined mahavan and unformed forces.

Adam entered a vaulted hallway with whitewashed walls and lit by regularly spaced lanterns. His scowl deepened as he neared his personal rooms. Axel had tremendous power, but somehow the World-Killers always overcame him, always defeated Sinskrill.

They—

His footsteps faltered as an idea slowly seeped into his consciousness. *Rukh of Ashoka.* He'd once asked Axel about the man's name, how similar the name of his city of origin sounded to Shokan, Shet's great enemy. At the time, his brother had shrugged off the resemblance. But what about Jessira and the Lady of Fire, Sira? Another set of similar sounding names. Was it truly but a coincidence?

Adam halted.

Or was there a deeper connection?

He continued to ponder the notion, but after a moment, he got himself going again, still thinking about the possibility but no closer to an answer.

He entered his quarters, which were properly spartan and spare.

The front room held a couch and table for guests while the bedroom contained a cot, a simple dresser, and an armoire. The simplicity was a reflection of Adam's beliefs of the true nature of what it meant to be a mahavan.

He sat on a chair, unlaced his boots, and slipped them off, all the while chasing down the recently revealed notion about the possible relationship between Rukh and Jessira and Shokan and Sira. Surely those ancients were long deceased. They'd battled Shet thousands of years ago. They couldn't still be alive

And yet, Shet, long believed to be a myth, was real, and he lived. Why not Shokan and Sira? *What had they been doing all these many years? Or perhaps they were newly arisen, awake after years of slumber.*

He didn't know, couldn't know, but the more he considered the possibility that the World-Killers might be Shokan and Sira, the more certain he believed that it to be the case.

And if he was right, what should he do about it?

Serena.

He should tell her. He could dream to her. Unconsciously, he bowed his head. Of course, he'd already contacted her a few other times now, but on those other occasions it had been either at the behest of the Servitor or involved apparently unimportant information, such as the knowledge about the demon. This time, if he reached out to his once-bishan it would be on his own behalf, and it truly would be traitorous. No. This next dream would be to save the mahavans. That couldn't be considered treasonous.

Adam's posture firmed. Indeed. It would be for all the people of Earth. For if anyone could stop Shet, it would be the Lord of Sword and the Lady of Fire.

And Serena could be the one to bring them here, through Sinskrill's anchor line. He'd tell her how.

～

SERENA AWOKE WITH A JOLT. Another dream from Adam had snapped her out of her sleep. She sat up, threw off the covers, and wandered to the windows. The white, diaphanous curtains puffed with an errant breeze coming off the lagoon. Outside, quiet reigned over the surrounding jungle. Stars twinkled in a smear of light across the vast, dark deepness. Waves washed softly against the ivory shore.

She watched the serene world outside, trying to make sense of what Adam had sent her. His dream contained information, the key to Sinskrill's anchor line. *Could it be?* Serena didn't know, and she crossed her arms in frustration. As far as she was aware, only the Servitor possessed the key to Sinskrill's anchor line. It was information no other mahavan had ever learned, although that necrosed in West Virginia, the female they'd killed, also claimed to know it. And now Adam also sent her such knowledge?

Why? What does he really want? Does he think I'll fall for his ploy, whatever it is? Then again, regret had tinged Adam's dream, including anger toward the Servitor. What was really going on in Sinskrill?

Serena tsked. Standing at the window in the middle of the night wouldn't give her any answers. She couldn't learn the truth by forcing a solution. She needed to talk this over with others.

She mentally nodded. She'd tell those who needed to know in the morning. The conversation could wait until then. Meantime, she'd go back to sleep.

She paused on her way back to bed.

What about Fiona? She could talk to her grandmother now. Serena took a single step toward Fiona's bedroom door and faltered. She'd momentarily forgotten. Fiona no longer lived here. She'd moved in with Mr. Zeus, living now with her husband.

The thought brought a bittersweet smile to Serena's lips. She had the cottage to herself. She was alone. Selene was gone, and so was Fiona. Serena blinked back tears, uncaring since no one was around to view her weakness. She missed her sister and grandmother terribly.

She sighed. The morning it was, then.

Besides, she told herself, she needed sleep. Tomorrow would be another hard day of training the recruits. Rukh and Jessira figured if they pushed them hard enough, they'd be ready to invade Sinskrill in another few months. Eight hundred magi to attack Sinskrill, who would have a complement of six hundred mahavans and several hundred woven.

The situation wasn't ideal, but . . .

Serena sighed once more. It was a problem for another day. She clambered back into bed and quickly fell asleep.

15

A MEETING OF MURDERERS

 *pril 1991*

EVELYN SMIRKED when the magus woman delivered her breakfast. She'd never bothered learning the git's name. Why should she? The girl was a drone, Evelyn's servant, directed to feed her, clean up after her, and in all other ways take care of her.

"Your food," the servant woman said to Evelyn, her tone cold.

In the other cell, Brandon had already received his food—bacon, eggs, and toast—and he was busily gorging himself.

Evelyn slowly sat up in her bunk and stretched. She knew it irritated the girl, but what could the drone do?

Nothing. She'd sulk, whine, and make threatening noises from her stupid mouth, but ultimately, she would be unable or unwilling to carry through with their warnings.

The magi were fools. They treated their enemies like royalty. Certainly Evelyn didn't enjoy being caged, but she was given shelter and regular meals, all at no cost. No requirements had been placed on her.

Evelyn gave a haughty gesture, her movements languid and bored, indicating the small table in her cell, the only furniture. "Put the food there, and then fetch me new bedding."

The tray hit the floor, the food spilling.

"You can eat the food off the floor," the girl said with a glare, "and the bedding isn't my concern."

Evelyn's jaw dropped. How dare the drone speak to her so? She surged to her feet, infuriated. She made to discipline the girl, but a note of caution entered her mind. She remained locked out of her *lorethasra*. She couldn't battle the git without *asra*. William renewed the lock every week, denying Evelyn her most potent weapon. But no mahavan was ever truly disarmed. She let the small shiv fall from where it lay pressed and hidden against her wrist and into her hand, palming it.

"What did you say?" Evelyn addressed the girl.

"You heard me," the drone said. "Eat the food off the floor. Eat it like a dog, for all I care." She turned her back, moving to the exit.

Evelyn was on her in an instant. The shiv, a stolen bread knife she'd sharpened and filed until it fit in the palm of her hand, stabbed out. It took the girl in the side of her throat. Blood spurted, and the drone gasped. Evelyn stabbed again and again. Her thoughts left her. All she knew was to kill. Destroy this vermin who dared mock her, disrespect her.

Distantly she heard Brandon shouting.

She paid him no heed. The shiv rose and fell. Rose and fell. The drone lay face down on the floor, unmoving.

Evelyn didn't stop. She continued to stab the dead girl, pouring her hatred and anger into the action.

Eventually, she tired and her blows fell more slowly. The anger ebbed.

Brandon's shouts became clearer. "What have you done?"

Evelyn noticed her hands covered in blood. Her face as well. She sat in a pool of it. The blood coated the floor of the cell.

"Evelyn!" Brandon shouted.

Evelyn rose to her feet and proudly faced her fellow mahavan. "I taught the drone a lesson. I taught all the magi a lesson," she said, no worry or concern in her voice. After all, what would the magi do? Rage and threaten? They always raged and threatened, just like the dead girl. But their weakness would prevent them from acting on their anger.

"They'll kill you for this," Brandon said, his voice and features unreadable, but Evelyn sensed satisfaction in his tone.

Certain events snapped into focus. Brandon's regular interrogations by Rukh and Jessira. Evelyn had always wondered what the World-Killers could possibly hope to learn from him after all this time. She realized now the interrogations had been nothing of the sort. Brandon had been giving them information. Information about her.

The day after I mention that I've been breaking down the lock on my lorethasra, William renews it. The day after I tell him about my first shiv, they remove it. Thankfully, I never told him about this one.

Traitor.

Evelyn glowered, and redness filled her vision again. She worked to suppress it. "You'd like that, wouldn't you?"

Brandon's flat affect left him, and he smiled in real pleasure. "I will enjoy learning of your demise."

She sneered. "You think the magi will do anything to me? They're weak. So are you, traitor." The door to her cell remained ajar, but before Evelyn could consider escaping, Rukh and Jessira exploded into the jail.

"I guess we'll find out," Brandon answered.

"What happened?" Rukh demanded. He shivered with what Evelyn realized was fury.

Evelyn faced him and Jessira, uncaring of his rage. The World Killers were powerful, but they lacked the ability to do whatever was necessary. They wouldn't kill her. They likely wouldn't even hurt her. She crossed her arms in a posture of derision and challenge.

"What happened?" Rukh asked again.

Brandon supplied the answer. "She murdered Samantha."

Samantha? A plain name for a plain peasant.

Jessira stepped into the cell, squatted and placed fingers to the drone's throat. Her jaw clenched, and she stood. "You will pay for this," she said, her voice sounding more deadly for its quietness.

Evelyn wasn't impressed, and she remained where she was, maintaining a scornful air. "I murdered no one," she answered. "I disciplined a drone, as is my right as a mahavan. She deserved—"

Jessira's punch to the gut blew all the air out of Evelyn's lungs, and she flew through the air, slamming into the opposite wall of her cell. She slumped to the floor, gasping. A blow to the cheek, and Evelyn felt a bone break. She screamed in pain.

"Don't kill her," Rukh warned. "Her judgment isn't for us to make."

Wait. Kill me? This isn't right. The magi are weak. They'd never hurt her before. Panic overwhelmed pride. Evelyn held up her hands, pleading. "No. I'm sorry. Please don't kill me."

Jessira stepped closer, staring down at her, unforgiving and colder than a winter wind. "I won't kill you."

A knee to the forehead clubbed Evelyn into unconsciousness.

WILLIAM STARED murder at Evelyn Mason. The mahavan had killed Samantha Grove and smiled about it during her trial before the Village Council. She'd laughed as Rukh and Jessira and even Brandon had testified against her.

When asked if she had anything to say in her defense, she'd grinned and told everyone present that they were her lessers, that she didn't recognize the Council's authority, that Samantha had earned her death. She'd continued to smirk as she said the last, apparently not caring that her right cheek remained swollen and misshapen from where Jessira had punched her face.

William was glad about the injury. Evelyn deserved far worse than a few punches, and now justice would be administered. He only wished that the punishment actually fit the crime. Banish her from Arylyn? *So what?* She deserved to die for what she'd done.

Since he'd been one of those tasked with imprisoning Evelyn, he insisted on being among those who would also get to see the mahavan off of Arylyn. As a result, he stood at Linchpin Knoll along-side Mayor Care, Rukh, and Jessira. The latter were kitted out with swords and bows. William wasn't sure why, but their visages were grim.

Arylyn's ever-present sunshine beamed brightly. A trade wind blew now and then, keeping the weather cool. William inhaled the mingling aromas of gardenias and a magnolia tree, both growing at the base of the hill. Clouds drifted, serene as palaces in the sky. The lovely day seemed to mock Samantha's murder, another nail in the injustice of her death. While William had never known Samantha all that well, she hadn't deserved to die like that, killed by a savage.

"Where will you send me?" Evelyn asked Mayor Care, her simpering tone at odds with the sneer on her still misshapen face.

"To the Far Beyond and far from here," was Mayor Care's answer.

Evelyn scoffed. "You think because the lock is still in place, I'll die before I can remove it?"

Mayor Care blinked, showing less emotion than a drone. "Yes, and it is said to be a most painful demise."

William had heard the same, but he still didn't understand why they were bothering to give Evelyn any chance to live in the first place.

"Maybe you're right," Evelyn agreed, grinning more widely, more mockingly, "but I'll have the lock off within a week. I can easily manage to survive that long in any *saha'asra*. Then I'll make it home."

Rukh stepped close to her, within inches of the mahavan, staring her down. "Hold on to that certainty. Let it give you hope. But know this: where we send you, two necrosed were recently slain."

William exhaled in relief. Evelyn wouldn't escape justice. She would be punished, and it would be everything the evil woman deserved.

The smile left Evelyn's face, and she took several swifts steps away from Rukh, putting distance between the two of them. Her features had gone pale as snow. "You can't send me there. The necrosed hunt any *saha'asra* where one of their kind bled."

William didn't know how she knew this, but he also didn't care. He was merely glad to see fear take away her arrogance.

Jessira nodded. "Yes, they do, and you will provide them sustenance." Now she wore a mocking grin, similar to the one that Evelyn had recently worn. "Unless you can remove the lock before one of them arrives."

"You can't do this," Evelyn insisted, terror filling her visage, breaking through her normal ability to hide fear.

"We can do this, and we will," Mayor Care said. "Or did you truly think we'd simply let you leave after murdering one of ours?"

"Kill me now," Evelyn pleaded. "Make it clean."

"Like Samantha's death?" William asked. "You murdered her, and now you ask us to provide you with a quick death?"

"Yes!" Evelyn said. "You can't give me to a necrosed. Do you know what they do to our kind?"

"I have an idea," William said. "I killed two of them."

Shock momentarily overwhelmed Evelyn's terror. "Two of them? Impossible."

William shrugged, not caring to debate the point.

Evelyn spoke to Rukh. "You're said to be noble. Give me a quick death. Please."

Rukh shook his head. "You've earned this punishment. Slavery, butchery, and murder. Samantha wasn't even the first of ours you murdered."

"I killed in battle," Evelyn shouted. "That isn't murder."

"Jeff Coats," Rukh said.

"Who?" Evelyn's face twisted in perplexity.

William wanted to kick himself. He'd forgotten about Jeff Coats, and he shouldn't have.

"He was a farmer," Rukh explained. "He had a wife and young daughter. You slit his throat, desecrated his body by cutting out his eyes. Then you threw him in River Namaste, hoping we'd find him."

"I didn't—" Evelyn began.

Rukh unsheathed a dagger, one William had discovered at the site of Jeff's murder. The knife belonged to Evelyn. "You recognize this."

Evelyn's face paled again. "I killed him in battle. You can't punish me for that."

Jessira backhanded her. Evelyn's head rocked under the blow, and blood trickled from a scalp wound. "Cease your blubbering. You're embarrassing yourself." She slapped Evelyn across the mouth this time. "Or are you really as weak as you appear?"

William viewed Jessira in shock. He never expected this from her, even after he'd heard she'd punched Evelyn and clubbed her unconscious.

"Jessira," Mayor Care murmured in disapproval.

"She doesn't need her mouth to fight," Jessira answered.

The mahavan gazed about, her eyes darting, viewing the unsympathetic, unyielding faces, and William was pleased to see that she no longer had an air of pleasure or sneering superiority. Instead, she shuddered uncontrollably, but after a few seconds she managed to regain control of her emotions. Her demeanor became unreadable.

"May I have a weapon with which to defend myself?" Evelyn asked.

"No," Rukh said. "You will evade the necrosed or you will not, but we . . ." He pointed to Jessira, ". . . will accompany you to ensure the creature gives you an easy death. We will remain with you for one day."

Evelyn made a slight moue. "What good are you against a necrosed?"

"We defeated one in the *saha'asra* where we're sending you," Rukh said. "He was an easy kill."

Evelyn stared at him, unblinking, breathing heavy. She must have finally realized the certainty of her upcoming death. A vindictive part of William was pleased.

"Why?" Evelyn asked. "Why kill me like this?"

"Because your death at our hands here would be justice," Rukh explained, "but your death in West Virginia at the hands of a necrosed, specifically Sapient Dormant, would be equal justice. It will also provide us needed information."

William viewed Rukh in surprise. He hadn't heard of this until now. "What kind of information?" he asked.

"The key to Sinskrill's anchor line. We know Sapient is there. He'll travel by anchor line to West Virginia. We can then see the key to Sinskrill."

"The Servitor will kill you all," Evelyn said in what was apparently a final flare of defiance. "And if he doesn't, Sapient will."

"He's welcome to try," Jessira said, "but we've already defeated the Servitor several times. We'll defeat him again."

Her words sounded like a promise, chill and deadly, and William shivered, glad to have never earned Jessira's anger.

Rukh opened an anchor line. "It's time."

~

SAPIENT'S EYES snapped open with sudden alertness. Something was amiss. His nose flared, searching for what had awakened him. *Was it Shet sending a command? The Servitor?* The Overward sat unmoving, waiting for a repeat of whatever it was he'd sensed.

Darkness enfolded him. For his home on Sinskrill he'd chosen a cave that normally offered a view of Lake White Sun, but he'd blockaded the entrance, not wanting any light in his hovel. The bones of animals littered the small space. The regular plop of water dripping from the ceiling echoed, but otherwise no sound penetrated the cave.

There!

A smell on the wind, drifting on the *lorasra* connecting the anchor lines, wafted to Sapient. The scent dissipated too quickly for him to identify it, but his interest intensified. It smelled of blood. Sapient's heart, which normally beat as slow and sluggish as that of a man dying on a cold winter night, tripped a little faster. His blood, thick like tar, thinned.

Sapient stretched his senses, pushing to taste whatever it was that he'd scented. He kept still, waiting for the smell to return. It would. He need only be patient.

Again it came.

Sapient inhaled deeply. He held the breath in his lungs for an instant as disbelief warred with desire. This time he knew what it was. He slowly exhaled. The blood of an *asrasin.*

Exultation brightened the necrosed's broken features. Possibilities of power raced through his mind. One of the *asrasins,* either a magus or mahavan—Sapient didn't care which—bled in a *saha'asra,* one he knew well, in the place called West Virginia. He would have to be swift, though, to take advantage of this unforeseen boon. He had to race his brethren, claim the prize before one of them did.

Sapient stretched his limbs, cracking disused joints. It was time to awaken. He'd slept long enough. In fact, he'd done nothing but slumber since the Servitor had bested him. He snarled at the memory. Once he would have crushed a dim creature like the Servitor without any effort.

How far I've fallen.

So be it. He'd lost the battle against the Servitor but not the war. This *asrasin* would provide him everything he needed to further his plans, to earn his revenge against all who had wronged him.

His stretching complete, Sapient stood, hunching because of the cave's low ceiling as he eased out into an early evening full of cold drizzle and a gusting wind. He disregarded the weather. The discomfort was immaterial. He made his way down an animal track, pushing past wet fronds and clinging branches. He needed to reach the anchor line. He needed to get to the *asrasin*. His pace increased, and soon he was running through the forested hills surrounding Lake White Sun.

Minutes later, he reached his destination: a broad field edged by a wall of fieldstones. Sinskrill's anchor lines congregated here.

Sapient slowed and hid in the shadows of the forest. He tested the air. In and out he breathed, slow and steady, taking the time to make sure no enemies lurked about. A minute of scenting told him that he stood alone. He didn't sense the presence of any mahavans or woven.

He launched himself into the field then, opening the anchor line he required as soon as he could reach it. A line of black split the darkness, expanding into a doorway filled with a cascade of moving colors. A rainbow bridge formed, and Sapient tethered to it.

An instant later he stood in a meadow, in a *saha'asra* he'd visited a scant month ago. He took in the scene, letting sensations wash across his mind. An afternoon sun bled light through a canopy of spring leaves, and silence gripped the field. Next, he tasted fear. He focused upon it, isolating it. A short time later, he had it. It came from the forest. He heard the source now. A woman, an *asrasin*. He could tell her general location. The female stumbled through the trees. She gasped in desperation, blubbering in terror.

Sapient waited several heartbeats longer. The *asrasin* couldn't escape him. He had plenty of time to track her down, but first he had to ensure that none of his brother necrosed had already traveled here. If they had, he'd have to kill them. His nostrils flared as he tasted the air. More seconds passed.

Alone.

Sapient rejoiced. It was time to hunt. He wouldn't prolong it. Sometimes he enjoyed the fear he induced, the desire for dominance, but not now. In this moment, hunger served as a more powerful motivator than pleasure.

"Run, little *asrasin*," he whispered. "You're mine. I'll feed." He raced into the forest, toward the desperate woman.

EVELYN EXITED INTO A SMALL MEADOW, staggering from the disorientation of traveling by anchor line. A broad oak spread its leaf-budding branches wide, promising to shield the field from a spring sun that had to yet fully rise. Birds sang and crickets chirped. A half dozen cabins lined the *saha'asra*. Smoke wreathed off some of the chimneys, caught in a wind that rattled the limbs and leaves of a forest full of fresh growth. Evelyn shuddered at the weather. It felt chill after Arylyn's cloying warmth.

Rukh and Jessira exited the anchor line on her heels. They both had swords at their hips, bows in their hands, and a quiver full of arrows in easy reach.

"You'll want to run or hide," Rukh advised. "From what I've read and learned about necrosed, they'll quickly sense your presence."

Jessira pointed to Evelyn's face. "Blood is the attractant."

Evelyn touched her scalp wound and her lips, the blows Jessira had recently delivered. She wondered if the clouts had been administered with cool deliberation rather than through anger. It didn't matter. If the lock weren't in place, she'd teach the so-called World Killer what it was to strike a mahavan. She'd—

"You're wasting time," Rukh reminded her.

Evelyn still couldn't believe the magi had conceived of such a punishment even as part of her applauded their plan: to punish an enemy and make the punishment useful. But more, she couldn't believe they would actually carry through with it. It was impossible. The magi were weak.

Or perhaps this was some other ploy on their part. Who knew if any of them had ever really battled a necrosed before, much less killed one in this *saha'asra?* Hope briefly crested. Yes. That had to be it. "You'll truly stand back and watch me battle the necrosed?" She made her voice scornful.

"We'll watch, and we won't interfere," Jessira said. "If you're as powerful a warrior as you believe, you'll survive the necrosed. If not, you'll die."

She said it with such bland disregard that Evelyn's fluttering hope crashed, and the first inkling that the magi weren't pulling a hoax fully possessed her mind.

Rukh nodded as if he understood her thoughts.

Evelyn swore and sprinted for the edge of the meadow. The moment she left the *saha'asra*, lethargy weighed her down. She pushed past her weakness. She'd hide in the forest and wait for the necrosed to grow impatient and leave. She could survive the Far Beyond without a *nomasra* for several days. Surely the creature wouldn't wait around that long for her?

If Rukh and Jessira . . . She flicked her eyes about. *Where did they go?* She caught the glimpse of a heat shimmer near the oak, but an instant later it was gone. *What?* She shook her head. No matter.

Evelyn plowed her way into the forest, struggling to find a path forward. She cursed as branches whipped at her face, clawed at her clothing. If she had her *lorethasra*, maybe she could have stood her ground and fought the necrosed. After all, she was a mahavan, and mahavans didn't run from anything, not even the undying woven that others feared.

Out of habit, she reached for her *lorethasra* and was shocked when she could source it. She wanted to shout with joy as options opened in her mind. She had to get back to the meadow. While she couldn't travel directly to Sinskrill, she knew the keys to a number of other anchor lines. Surely one of them would be connected to this *saha'asra*. She could escape the magi and the necrosed, make her way to Sinskrill, and bring useful information about Arylyn to the Servitor.

She raced back in the direction she had just come, but paused when she sensed the anchor line open. Evelyn was a Rider, and Water was her strongest Element, but she also had talent with Air. She wove a braid, one that brought sounds and smells to her. It wasn't as powerful as something she could have constructed in a *saha'asra*, but it would do.

Evelyn listened for whatever had entered the meadow.

All she heard were slow breaths like bellows. The noxious stench of rotting meat carried to her as well. *A necrosed.*

The creature whispered. "Run, little *asrasin*. You're mine. I'll feed." She heard it accelerate, its pounding footsteps aimed straight for her.

Fear gripped Evelyn. Her earlier courage left her. She cut a different course back to the *saha'asra*. She could still make it back to the field, open a different anchor line, and escape.

Evelyn ran recklessly, pressing as hard as she could. All the while, she listened for the necrosed. It crashed through the forest. She glanced back. Trees swayed as something large and powerful forced itself through the forest.

It was coming.

Terror lent Evelyn further speed. She dashed through the small spaces between the dense forest. Tree limbs snagged her clothes. Desperately, she pulled herself free. She took scratches from bushes. She didn't care. The pain meant nothing.

At last! She came across an animal trail and picked up speed.

The necrosed adjusted course. She could see its location from the trees and bushes shoved aside. On it came. Gaining on her.

Evelyn reached deeper, running harder, faster.

She heard a panting growl. It sounded right behind her. She could smell a fetid breath.

"You're mine," the creature whispered.

Evelyn couldn't help it. She whimpered. She followed the animal trail, hoping it would lead her back to the meadow.

Something yanked at her shirt, tugging her backward. Evelyn blindly cast boiling water. It struck an albino monstrosity in the eyes. The creature snarled, but it also let her go.

Evelyn raced away from the gruesome monster. Seconds later, she burst into the meadow. The power of the *saha'asra* brought her renewed energy and strength. She reached for an anchor line, opened it. She wanted to laugh in relief. A moment later, the anchor line slammed shut.

What?

She tried again. Something blocked her. Shock filled her mind.

The smell of rotting meat heralded the arrival of the necrosed. Evelyn spun about, trying to make sense of the creature that slowly strode toward her. It stood a spindly eight feet in height. Arms hung apelike, ending in claws that belonged on a tiger or a bear. Hairless skin, the color of bone, encased the creature. The worst aspect was its face, diseased with open pustules and a mouth like a wound. The pale eyes of an eagle viewed her with malice.

Evelyn snarled at the creature, outrage briefly overcoming fear. She was a mahavan, a Rider of Sinskrill. Glory was written into her blood, and this corrupt monstrosity dared seek her doom? *I won't go down like a lamb. I'll fight like a lion.* Maybe necrosed were as powerful as the histories made them out to be, but so were mahavans. Evelyn reached for her training, pushed aside all her fears, and fully sourced her *lorethasra*. She was ready.

The creature charged.

Evelyn flung a wall of boiling water at the necrosed. It landed flush, but the beast never slowed. Evelyn braided a tornado of Air. She wrapped the necrosed within it and sought to fling him away. He wove in response, one of Earth, anchoring himself to the ground and counteracting her braid. She strained to lift him, reaching as deep as she could. All she needed was time and space to escape.

Once again, he shrugged off her weave.

Panic finally set in, and Evelyn sent a line of Fire at the necrosed, the hottest she could manage.

He seemed to inhale it, chuckling briefly before surging forward, claws ready.

In her final seconds of life, a vague regret drifted through Evelyn's mind. She was going to die. She knew it.

The claws penetrated, and terrible pain filled her stomach and her mind. Something precious was being ripped away from her.

RUKH HAD SEEN ENOUGH. Evelyn was presently held upon the creature's claws, agony clearly written on her face. He regretted what they had done to the mahavan woman, but what choice did she leave them? She'd brought nothing but murder and mayhem to Arylyn, even when imprisoned. Death was her proper punishment, but Rukh wished it didn't have to be so painful. A wispy substance, a ghostly fog wafted from her. The necrosed's mouth stretched, and he consumed it.

"Enough," Rukh growled. He dropped his Blend and hurled a Fireball. It wouldn't hurt the necrosed, but it blasted into Evelyn, incinerating her body into ashes. Maybe she'd find grace or peace in her next life.

The albino necrosed stared at his now empty claws. "You stole her!" the creature roared. "She still had plenty of *lorethasra* to consume."

Jessira released her Blend as well. "Sorry to disappoint," she said. "Who are you?"

"Your doom," the creature growled, taking a step toward them.

Rukh rolled his eyes at the melodramatic response. He remembered the other necrosed they'd killed making a similar stupid claim. He wondered if all necrosed spoke like that. "That's too bad. We were hoping to find Sapient Dormant."

"You've found him," the necrosed said, "and if I can't have one *asrasin*, I'll have two."

"The last necrosed we fought said the same thing," Rukh told the creature headed their way.

Sapient halted, nose lifted to sniff the air and uncertainty writ large across his repulsive face. "You defeated Charnel?"

"We killed Charnel," Jessira corrected.

Sapient's nostrils flared. Further uncertainty flitted across his face followed by recognition. "Sira? Shokan? You truly live? I wasn't sure."

Shocked disbelief poured through Rukh. *How does this creature know about Shokan?*

The creature must have noticed his surprise. "I was once a brother to you. Do you not recognize me? I loved you." He gestured to himself. "You made me into what you see now."

Rukh lifted his brows in surprise. He and Jessira had come to accept that their future was everyone else's past. Until now it had been a vague sort of understanding, but here was a being who recognized them, who had apparently known them from some ancient time before. Worse, this creature had or would be a brother to them. They'd loved him, and yet somehow caused his transformation into this evil monster. It sounded impossible, but how else would Sapient know them as Shokan and Sira? He shared an unsure glance with Jessira.

She shrugged. *Be careful,* her manner seemed to suggest.

Rukh faced the necrosed, setting aside his worries. "I am sorry for whatever harm we did to you," he began.

"Save your sympathy for someone who needs it," the necrosed said.

"If you were a brother to us, you'd know—" Jessira began

"You are from Stronghold," Sapient said to her. "You had a cousin, Sign Deep, and several brothers. Your favorite was Lure Grey." He addressed Rukh. "You are from Ashoka. You had a brother, Jaresh, and a sister, Bree. You almost killed Sira when you first met her." He faced them both. "Your fondest hope is to see your children again." He shook his head. "It won't happen."

Rukh pushed aside the million thoughts racing through his mind. He and Jessira *did* share a history with Sapient Dormant. They'd loved him, had told him about their past and their dreams for the future. How could he have ended up like this?

Rukh shook off his thoughts. More necrosed might show up. They needed to finish Sapient now. "Then we have nothing more to discuss," he said. "Leave and live. Stay and die."

Sapient studied them through narrow, dark eyes, considering. "I see it now. You smell like Shokan and Sira. You even look like them, but you aren't so grand anymore. You're feeble. Time stole your power just as it stole mine."

"Test us and find out." Rukh sourced his *Jivatma* and hardened his Shield.

Jessira did the same.

Sapient charged.

Rukh strengthened his muscles and engaged as well. He blurred forward in the incomparable speed of his Caste. He knew through their link that Jessira would trail after him on his right.

Sapient matched their speed. He raced toward them like a rumbling chariot.

They reached one another and clashed. Rukh slashed with his sword. Sapient blocked with steel-like claws. A follow-up swing with his off arm had Rukh bending backward at the waist and under the blow.

Sapient captured Jessira's sword thrust in a fist. She kicked him in the wrist. He grunted and released her weapon.

Their weapons couldn't penetrate Sapient's skin, but he apparently felt their punches.

Rukh launched himself at Sapient. He aimed a flying knee at the monster's forehead, but the necrosed clubbed him aside. He slammed into the ground, his head banging hard. Rukh's Shield had softened most of the blow, but he still felt it. He shook his head, clearing the cobwebs. *Fragging unholy hells!*

Jessira sent feints at the necrosed, but Sapient never fell for them. He allowed her to circle him, spinning with her and maintaining his patience. An instant later, he darted forward, swiping at her. She took it on her Shield, which brightened, defending her, but she was still pushed back. She stumbled and Sapient kicked her, sending her flying through the air. She landed gracefully on her feet.

"Weak," Sapient said. "Sira would have handed me my head by now."

Rukh glowered. After the easy victory over Charnel Blood, he'd taken Sapient too lightly. No more. He sourced his *Jivatma* and formed a Blend. While Sapient loomed over Jessira, he attacked. He slammed his sword into Sapient's side, powering the blow and strengthening the sword. It cut. Black blood trickled out, and Sapient roared in pain.

Good.

The necrosed spun about and Rukh blocked a spinning elbow.

"You Blended," Sapient said to him. "You show wisdom . . . but I can smell you." He rushed forward, straight at Rukh, moving like an avalanche.

Rukh held his position. Thousands of hours of training offered him a hundred possible counters. He chose one at the last moment. He stepped to his right, let Sapient roll past him, and again sent a heavy blow, one that connected with necrosed's flank and cut even deeper than the last strike. More black blood flowed.

Jessira re-entered the fight. She landed a chopping blow against Sapient's shoulders. The Overward fell back, stumbling but quickly regained his footing. More blood leaked like tar from the monster's wounds.

Rukh didn't ease the pressure. He connected the flying knee he'd missed earlier, cracking the Overward in the forehead.

Sapient's head snapped back. Jessira slammed home a horizontal slash into the necrosed's thigh. His leg collapsed, but he immediately stood again, swinging his arms to gain space.

"If you were truly our brother, you wouldn't fight us," Jessira said. "You would seek a cure for your affliction."

Sapient laughed, a harsh sound like gravel rolling across a tombstone. "Affliction? What you did to me made me stronger than you can possibly imagine. And for what you did, I'll be sure to give you every last ounce of my gratitude. I'll . . ."

Rukh let go of his Blend even as he stopped listening to the necrosed, long since disbelieving the Overward. He and Jessira would never make someone they loved into a necrosed. Sapient lied.

He sourced his *Jivatma* and readied a Fireball.

"Fire doesn't work against my kind," Sapient sneered. "It feeds us."

"Charnel said the same thing," Rukh said. He heated the Fireball further and launched it from a distance of no more than ten feet.

Sapient didn't bother to dodge. He allowed the Fireball to strike him straight in the chest. He breathed deep, satisfaction filling his features. His chest swelled, and he seemed drink the Fireball through the pores of his skin.

The Fireball dimmed. Seconds passed. A rictus of effort replaced Sapient's pleasure. He must have reached the limit of his ability to consume the Fireball. It exploded in brightness, hammering into him, and smashing him off his feet. He hurled through the air like a launched boulder, crashing heavily. Smoke drifted off his burnt clothes and flesh. He lay unmoving on the ground.

Rukh carefully approached the necrosed, who coughed once before heaving himself upright.

Sapient chuckled weakly. "Perhaps not so feeble after all."

Black lightning spilled off his fingers. Rukh caught it on his Shield and flinched as stray bolts punched through. He knew Jessira would take off the pressure, and she did.

An arrow bounced off the armor that was Sapient's skin. Rukh took the distraction to leap straight up, twenty feet into the air. The black lightning didn't follow. He readied another Fireball, but Sapient had taken the brief pause to open an anchor line.

The necrosed bowed mockingly to them. "Another time." He leapt through to safety.

Rukh landed, unhappy with the outcome. Draws were fragging useless.

"I saw the key he used," Jessira said. "It was the same one William and Serena described."

Rukh nodded. At least something useful had come from today's battle.

"It's time for us to go," Jessira said.

An *asrasin* bled here and so had Sapient." More necrosed were likely to soon arrive.

16

PLAN A MISSION

M*ay 1991*

D**AWN WAS NEWLY RISEN**, and Lilith had yet to stir. The village remained peaceful and quiet, except for a few early songbirds trilling out a melody. Rukh had the windows to the flat open, and sunlight beamed into the main room of the apartment. He worked alone in the kitchen, though, stirring batter. He let it drip off the ladle, checking the thickness.

Perfect.

Rukh wasn't very good at preparing food—certainly nothing like Cook Heltin, his family's chef when they lived in Jubilee Hills in the glorious city of Ashoka—but over the years, he'd improved. Last night he'd decided to try his hand at one of his favorite breakfast meals: dosas. He'd started the preparations after Jessira had gone to bed, and this morning the batter had risen and had the perfect consistency and undertone of sourness.

Best of all, Jessira still slept. Rukh wanted to surprise her with breakfast.

Minutes later, he heard her stir in the bedroom, and a short time after she entered the main area of the flat, dressed in a robe that stopped a few inches short of her knees. Sleep still filled her eyes, and her hair was tousled.

"Morning," he said.

She mumbled a response and wandered into the kitchen.

The cooking of dosas reclaimed Rukh's attention. He poured the batter onto a hot skillet, unwinding the dollop in a circular pattern until it was paper-thin and reached the edges of the pan.

Jessira's arms went around his waist, and she rested her chin on his shoulder. "What are you making?"

"Dosas."

She inhaled, making an appreciative noise. "It smells right. It even looks like you've got the right thickness." She kissed the side of his neck. "An OutCaste could get used to being spoiled like this."

"Don't you mean a *ghrina*?" Rukh teased.

The kiss became a nip. "Purebloods should know never to use that word around an *OutCaste*." She emphasized the last word.

"I know," Rukh said, "which is why I said it."

Jessira's arms left his waist, and she moved to his side, facing him with her elbows resting on the countertop. She lifted an eyebrow in challenge. "You mean so you can vex me?"

Rukh chuckled low. "Who else can I vex if not you, *priya*?"

"You're going to burn the dosa," she noted.

Chagrined, Rukh focused on the hot skillet. The dosa was quickly crisping, and he'd have to hurry before it burned. He placed a small mound of spiced potatoes, peas, and carrots on the dosa, folded it, and let it cook for a few more minutes. Once finished, he set it on a plate, which he offered to Jessira. "Done."

"Thank you." She took a bite and made another appreciative noise. "It's delicious," she said, "but don't make too many for me. Bread puts on the weight." She ran her hands over her trim, athletic figure.

Rukh eyed her, moving his gaze up and down. "I don't think you have to worry about that."

Jessira's features warmed. "You may vex me, *priya*, but sometimes you say the sweetest things."

Rukh dipped his head and smiled. He layered out another dosa. "I've been thinking."

"Uh-oh." Jessira grinned. "I'm not sure that's a wise idea."

Rukh chuckled. "Well, this time my thinking leads me to believe I need your advice."

Jessira set aside her plate. "Oh my. This sounds serious."

"It is," Rukh said. He'd been considering this notion ever since the attacks in West Virginia. The necrosed killed by William had claimed to have the key to Sinskrill's anchor line. It was the same one Adam had sent and, more recently, the one they'd seen Sapient use.

"You want to scout Sinskrill," Jessira said, sensing the direction of his thoughts.

Rukh nodded. "The new enlistees are coming along and should be ready to go by September, but it's not enough. We need more intelligence. We have the dreams Adam sent Serena about the composition of the Sinskrill forces, but we can't trust him."

"Agreed."

"Which is why I need to go to Sinskrill myself and see what's really happening over there."

"Have you considered that Serena can gain us this information without a raiding party?"

Rukh exhaled heavily. "First, Serena's information will come from Adam, which we've already determined can't be trusted. Second, I'm not interested in raiding Sinskrill. I only want to scout it."

"You can't go," Jessira said. "Neither of us can. We're too important for the command of the Irregulars."

Rukh had expected this line of argument. "I'm also the one most capable of leading a scouting mission. It has to be me."

Jessira shook her head. "No, you're not. Your importance to training and commanding the Irregulars automatically disqualifies you from this mission. You have to trust your lieutenants to carry out your orders. You can't do all their work for them."

Rukh placed another mound of the potato mixture on the dosa and didn't bother disagreeing with her. She was right, and he'd already reasoned out her objections on his own. He'd only spoken as he had in the event that she could figure a way for him to command the scouting mission.

"You knew all this beforehand," Jessira said, her head tilted in thought. "So why are you arguing with me?"

Rukh shrugged. "I wasn't. I only wanted to hear you say the words. It makes them more definitive when they come from your lips."

Jessira's eyes narrowed in thought. "You were also hoping I would find a reason to let you go, weren't you?"

Rukh nodded, passing her another dosa. "You know how much I hate putting other people at risk."

"I do, and I feel the same way. Even after all the battles we've fought, it isn't easy."

Rukh swirled out another dosa. "No. It shouldn't be, and I'm glad it's not."

"Who do you want to send on the scouting mission?" Jessira asked.

"Remember that part about me needing your advice?" Rukh asked.

Jessira spoke without hesitation. "Send William to command the mission."

Rukh eyed her in surprise. "Not Ward? He's senior, and he's healed up from his injuries."

Jessira shook her head. "William. He's ready. He's proven himself over and over again, especially for what you're wanting done. He's smart, a good leader, and the Irregulars trust him."

"Ward has those qualities, too," Rukh said, not ready to let go of his first choice.

"Not like William, and you know it. He's young, but think about what he's been through and overcome. He has a knack for survival and for completing the task at hand. Plus, his unit, the Wild Ones, are further along than anyone else's. Send William."

Rukh considered all the events in William's life, and he recognized what Jessira meant. He passed her another dosa. "William, then." He prayed silently, hoping he hadn't just decided to send the boy to his death.

WILLIAM WAITED ALONGSIDE SERENA, Jason, Rukh, and Jessira, the five of them observing the latest recruits for the Ashokan Irregulars, the ones Jake and Lien were bringing in from an early-morning run. River Namaste gurgled in the distance. Warm sunshine beamed down, and a gentle breeze kept the morning comfortable and lovely. Despite this, sweat dripped off all the recruits. This was new to them since they were the newest members of the Irregulars, the one hundred or so who had decided to join up during a final recruitment drive last week, and the morning's three-mile run was their hardest conditioning session so far.

Jake shouted for a halt, and the mixed group of men and women stumbled to a stop, most immediately taking a knee and gasping for breath. Some heaved and threw up.

William pursed his mouth, wishing the new recruits had joined the Irregulars far earlier. They only had a few more months to train and learn. It wasn't a lot of time, and they'd likely be best suited as the reserves and support staff, like medical. Thankfully, the initial eight hundred volunteers were much further along. They'd already matriculated into more advanced training, and yesterday morning Ward, Julius, and Mink had taken them into Arylyn's interior to start them on small-unit combat drills.

"Move it, ladies!" Lien shouted in a rude fashion, speaking to the recruits. "We don't have all day. Get some water and be ready in five."

"She sure has a loud voice," Jason noted.

Serena smiled. "Would you have it any other way?"

William grinned and answered. "Not a chance." After Daniel's death, Lien had retreated, becoming a shell of her prior self, quiet and demure. Seeing her shout again, loud and brash, was a good sign as far as he was concerned.

Jake and Lien headed their way.

"It's going to take forever to get them in shape," Lien said, sounding disgusted when she arrived.

William laughed to himself at her complaint. There was the Lien he knew and loved.

"They'll manage," Rukh said to Lien. "I remember how hard you struggled early on."

Jake laughed at her. "I don't think any of us complained as much as you did. You whined nonstop."

Lien waved aside Jake's words. "Fine, but that was then. This is now. They don't have the luxury of time."

"None of us have the luxury of time," Jessira said.

"No, we don't," Rukh said. "There's much we still need to do and more we need to learn regarding the forces we'll be facing."

William wasn't sure why Rukh thought they needed more information. As far as he knew, they had everything they needed. "Adam dreamed all that to Serena. We already know what the mahavans have."

Rukh shook his head. "No, we don't. We only have what Adam told us. He's a proven liar."

"And it wouldn't be the first time an enemy sought to deceive their opposition," Jessira finished in that creepy way she and Rukh had. "In fact, it's a common ploy."

William hadn't thought of that, and he caught Serena shaking her head in disappointment at him.

"We can't trust Adam," Lien said.

Rukh spoke. "Which is why we need our own eyes on the ground there."

"Are you going to Sinskrill?" Jake asked.

"Neither Jessira nor I," Rukh said. "We'll remain on Arylyn. This isn't a mission for the senior-most commanders."

If Rukh and Jessira aren't going, then that meant—

"You plan on sending one of the junior officers and a small unit," Jason said, figuring it out at the same time William did.

Rukh nodded. "William will take a small group through the Sinskrill anchor line and infiltrate the island."

"Me?" William asked in surprise.

"We believe you would have the best chance at success in this mission," Jessira said.

William nodded acceptance, although he remained unsure why they had so much trust in him. The thought left him humbled and terrified. Going back to Sinskrill alone with a small force.

Lord, keep me safe.

"As a *raha'asra*, we think you would be uniquely qualified for this mission," Rukh said, "which should explain why Jake can't go."

"We can't risk both our young *raha'asras*," Lien said, nudging Jake. "You're our precious."

Jason did a double take. "Did you just quote *Lord of the Rings*?" He cackled. "You nerd."

"Daniel must have rubbed off on me," Lien muttered.

"What's the plan for Sinskrill?" William asked Rukh and Jessira.

"You'll enter by way of the anchor line," Rukh explained. "We'll see for certain if the key Adam and that necrosed you killed told us—and the one we saw Sapient use—truly works. From there, you'll recon the island as best you can."

"How many should I take?" William asked.

"No more than five total," Jessira said. "Everyone will have satellite phones in case anyone gets cut off. You'll recon the island and remain in close contact with a yacht we'll have parked just over the horizon."

William saw the meat of the plan. "And after we recon the island, instead of escaping by anchor line, we'll steal a boat and link up with the yacht?"

"Why not leave by anchor line?" Lien asked.

Jessira answered. "Because if they're detected going in, the Servitor will probably have it guarded."

"Who'll command the yacht?" Serena asked.

"You will," Rukh said. "You know Sinskrill better than anyone, and you're also the best sailor amongst all the Irregulars."

Go back to Sinskrill, learn what they could, and then escape undetected. They could do this. Even more, they *needed* to do this. Burgeoning excitement filled William, a sensation apparently shared by Jason, who grinned at him.

"Whoever goes, maybe they can squeeze in some payback," Jake said.

"No." Rukh said, his tone brooking no dissent. "You are to do your best to avoid any detection. If possible, I want Sinskrill to have absolutely no notion that we were ever there."

Jason nodded understanding. "I guess payback will have to wait until the actual invasion." He glowered a moment later. "Payback is going to hurt us just as much as it will them, won't it?"

William noticed Rukh's demeanor grow distant. "It usually does."

"IS EVERYTHING READY FOR TOMORROW?" Serena asked William.

He nodded. "We're as ready as we're going to be."

The two of them stood side-by-side in Mr. Zeus' kitchen, washing dishes and readying dessert—chocolate cake—for the others who sat at the table outside in the rear courtyard. A steady breeze rattled the wind chimes on the front porch and rustled the palm fronds and leaves of the trees out back.

Jake entered the house. "Do you need any help?"

"We've got it," Serena said, flashing a warning at Jake to leave. "We'll be out shortly."

He must have understood her message. He ducked his head. "I'll let everyone else know." He retreated to the back yard, rejoining Jason, Mr. Zeus, and Fiona.

Some of their friends had gathered tonight since it would be her last one on Arylyn before she left for Sinskrill tomorrow. As soon as she had her yacht in place, William would take his unit—Karla Logan, Rail Forsyth, and Tam Emond—through the Australia anchor line and from there to Sinskrill.

They couldn't use the one in West Virginia since it didn't actually link to the mahavans' island. Sapient Dormant had been able to make the connection because of his kind's ability to forge a junction between two unjoined *saha'asras*. Unfortunately, no one else had such a skill.

William interrupted her thoughts. "What's wrong?" he asked, his visage questioning. "You were frowning."

"Was I?" She recalled her thoughts and understood why she might have been frowning. "I was thinking about Sapient. I know I shouldn't, but sometimes I can't help it."

"Me, neither," he agreed, speaking softly and staring at the ground.

Serena eyed him in concern. She worried for him. He was going back to Sinskrill, a place of terrible danger. He'd be alone against the mahavans, unformed, and whatever other horrors her father had called to the island.

William exhaled a heavy breath, and his fists briefly clenched. "Let's talk about something else."

Serena nodded agreement. She didn't like to think about Sapient or Sinskrill, either. Instead, she made herself smile, the wry promise of amusement she only gave to William. "What do you want to talk about?"

At first, William only managed a tight-lipped expression, a scowl rather than a smile, and Serena noted the concern lingering in his eyes. A moment later, he managed to shake himself loose of his apprehensions and his pleasure seemed more genuine. "I'm thinking we should have invited Mink tonight."

Serena grinned. "Oh, that's mean," she said.

William feigned innocence. "I don't know what you're talking about."

Jason didn't like talking about Mink. He remained an intensely private individual—which was ironic given how much he enjoyed gossiping about others—and when it came to discussing Mink, he always found a way to quickly change the subject. Nevertheless, everyone knew that the two had formed a serious relationship, one they kept discreet and reserved with no public displays of affection. Nevertheless, it would have been amusing to see Jason's reactions to Mink during dinner tonight.

Serena still grinned. "Sure you don't." She slipped a strand of hair behind her ear, a gesture originally done for William's benefit but which had since become a habit.

He eyed her in appreciation before a considering air took hold of his face. He gestured to her hair. "Do you do that because it's become a habit or because you know I like it?"

Serena's mouth dropped in shock. *How did he know?*

William placed his arms around Serena's waist and drew her closer. "You aren't entirely the mysterious, unknowable mahavan you used to be," he said. "I've learned some of your secrets."

Serena laced her fingers around his neck. "You think you know me?" she asked in challenge.

"No chance of that," William said, his voice wry. "I said I learned *some* of your secrets."

"Really?"

"Only a few of them," William promised.

Heat slowly rose from her abdomen, tingling up her spine, into her face. Her breath became shallow. Being with William left her vulnerable. Her heart was no longer her own. Her mahavan training still screamed at her to withdraw, to pull back, to shutter away her feelings for him. She'd long since ceased listening to those unnecessary warnings.

Serena's focus narrowed to the feel of William's arms around her waist, his mouth, the twinkle in his eyes. She drew him nearer, kissing him. She fell into his embrace, loving the joy and terror of it, the promise.

William was the first to pull back, but Serena was privately pleased to see him shudder when he did so. She felt the same way, although she hid her trembling reaction better than him.

"We should get dessert out to the others," he said.

"We left them some roast. Let them eat steak."

William laughed. "That was a pretty bad mangling of Marie Antoinette."

Serena quirked an eyebrow. "The sentiment holds true." She kissed him again. Tonight could be their last hours together, and she wanted to remember it.

Again, William pulled away, this time doing so with less effort than before. "We have a lot to talk about when we get back," he said, a fervent promise in his eyes.

The moment was lost, and Serena let her hands drop. "I'll take out the cake if you brew the coffee," she offered.

William nodded, and she gathered a few plates.

The promise in William's eyes likely had something to do with the ring she'd learned third hand that he'd had commissioned. It was sized for a woman. She prayed she'd get to hear the reason for it from his own mouth.

RUKH STRUMMED HIS MANDOLIN, picking out a song from the Far Beyond, the ironically named "Ashokan Farewell," a song written by a man who'd never been to Ashoka, and yet the somber, possibly hopeful notes somehow captured the city's heart during the battles against Shet's children. The music washed over him, and he allowed the notes to lead him where they willed.

He and Jessira shared a stone bench on the edge of the Village Green. The people of Lilith tended to skirt around them—they always had to a certain extent, but now more than ever—leaving them in an unasked-for cone of privacy. As a result, though the Village Green held a crowd of folk going about their joyful activities, he and Jessira sat alone, looking out over the Pacific Ocean and Arylyn's incomparable beauty.

Rukh tried not to notice the ruined homes and scarred terraces lining the escarpment. Instead, he focused on the glory of Lilith's waterfalls and rainbows, the playful mix of water, colors, and the rush of River Namaste. Butterflies and bumblebees flitted amongst the honeysuckles and jasmines lining the gazebo centered upon the Village Green.

"We can't stay here," Jessira said.

"I know," Rukh said.

Maybe she spoke of William, whose team was mere hours away from the *saha'asra* in Australia that connected to Sinskrill, but there were other depths to Jessira's statement. The two of them would soon have to leave this place, Arylyn, and travel onward. Other tasks awaited them, their future in the past as Shokan and Sira.

Only after defeating Shet—twice, apparently—could they return home.

Rukh privately worried that they would remain trapped in Earth's history and never again see their children and family.

"I meant to say that we can't stay at the Village Green," Jessira added, although he knew she recognized the nature of his thoughts.

"Where do you want to go?" Rukh asked, ceasing his strumming. Music reminded him of love, laughter, and sharing: the good things in life. It was everything he and Jessira thought they had achieved for themselves when they'd defeated Suwraith. And for a time following the Sorrow Bringer's demise, life had been like that, simple and lovely.

Shet's children had ended all that, bringing forth a storm of war. *War ruins all.*

"I'm sorry," Jessira said. Empathy filled her lovely features, and she squeezed his hand in understanding. "I shouldn't have interrupted you. I know music allows you to forget our situation."

Rukh shook his head. "No. Music lets me remember."

Jessira's head cocked in confusion.

Rukh smiled, glad to still be able to surprise her. Their ability to sense the other one's thoughts often meant there was little he could do or say that she didn't already know. "Sometimes a song captures my heart. When I listen to it, I can remember why we fight."

Jessira's head remained cocked but realization gradually dawned on her face. "The music's spell takes you to a place of warmth and joy."

Rukh nodded. "Arisa and our family."

Jessira squeezed his hand again. "We'll get home. One day, we'll walk the green hills of Ashoka again and watch the sun rise over the Sickle Sea."

Rukh hoped it would be the case. He prayed so, every day to Devesh. *Does the Lord still hear our longings?* After everything he and Jessira had endured, he wondered how much more of life's tribulations and trauma would be required of them.

"We have to go," Jessira reminded him.

"A moment," Rukh said. He strummed the mandolin, lifting notes into the beginning of a song, one Jessira knew and loved.

She sang, a poem from Arisa, one she had told him reminded him of Ashoka's past and future. Her confident contralto reached the notes, clear and pure:

> *"Summer's last light has frayed and faded.*
> *So harvest the wheat with breaths bated,*
> *Whilst the last seritonal heat remains.*
> *Before gilded leaves are semaphore chains.*
> *Before bitter winds, a synecdoche*
> *Of winter's clutching snow and solid sea."*

AFTER SHE FINISHED, she waited on his response.

Rukh stared at her in surprise. "I never did learn when you learned to sing."

Jessira's green eyes twinkled. "Do you truly want to know, or would you rather it remain a mystery?"

Rukh thought about her question and recalled their wedding night, how it seemed as if all the glories and mysteries of the world lived in her eyes. He realized that the world's glories and mysteries still resided within Jessira, within the spark of her gladness, the kindness of her laugh, and the warmth of her embrace. "You have always been gloriously mysterious, and I wouldn't want you any other way."

Jessira stood and offered him a hand, helping him rise to his feet. "For a Pureblood, you have a lovely way with words. And I wouldn't want you any other way, either."

He held her hand as they made their way to Lilith's municipal building, which also served as the headquarters for the Irregulars. William would call soon, and the council would want to hear everything. Glories and mysteries would have to wait for war's strident call, which was a sad truth.

17

SCOUTING THE ENEMY

M*ay 1991*

W<small>ILLIAM</small> <small>HELD</small> the satellite phone to his ear as Rukh spoke to him from Arylyn, relaying last-second instructions. The rest of his team— Karla Logan, Rail Forsyth, and Tam Emond—leaned in to try and listen. The four of them waited in the parked Jackaroo, the same vehicle Mr. Zeus had obtained during the raid on Sinskrill in which they'd freed Travail and Fiona. It idled a hundred yards outside an oasis in Australia, the *saha'asra* linked to Sinskrill.

An early afternoon sun shone upon the grass, stones, and ring of encircling red hills. The perfumed aroma of golden wattle drifted on the breeze.

"We only want information," Rukh reminded him. "Nothing more."

"Yes, sir," William said. He imagined his commander's expression of forceful determination, the belief Rukh tried to imbue in all of the Irregulars, the certainty that they could do what must be done, fulfill their mission no matter how dangerous.

"Do whatever it takes to remain undetected," Rukh continued. "Do not engage the enemy if you have any other option." A slight hesitation came across the phone. "Stay safe."

"Yes, sir," William replied, sensing Rukh's concern for him and the rest of the team. The commander tried not to show it, but those who knew him well understood how much he feared for those under his command. Rukh loved the men and women of the Irregulars, and he worried for them. More, he hated sending them into danger, having them risk their lives because of his orders.

William hung up the phone, and Rail Forsyth, a young magus whose slim, tall build and long nose and jaw gave him an unfortunate resemblance to his first name, ran worried fingers through his dark hair. "What did he say?"

William relayed the information. He also wanted to go over the initial steps of the plan one more time. It never hurt to make sure everyone was on the same page. He pointed to their vehicle. "We'll take the Jackaroo straight to the anchor line. Once there, we immediately disembark. I'll trigger the anchor line, we hustle through, and hide. We have to make sure no one senses us. If at any time we're detected, we immediately call Serena's crew. They'll be waiting off shore, south of Village White Sun, but they'll change positions to whatever area is easiest for us to get off the island. Understood?"

A trio of "Yes, sir," met his query.

"Any other questions?"

No one spoke.

"Let's go then." William got the Jackaroo going, slipping through the gears. They rambled across the ragged desert floor, picking up speed. William wanted to cover the distance to the anchor line as swiftly as possible. The mahavans used to monitor all *saha'asras* linked to Sinskrill, and they still might, although Adam had dreamed otherwise to Serena.

Maybe it was true, but William didn't want to take any chances. He planned on giving the mahavans as little time as possible to scramble in case they still monitored this *saha'asra*.

Seconds later, they reached the anchor line. They screeched to a halt in a blur of clouding dirt. William linked to the surrounding *lorasra.* He instantly gagged. The *lorasra* tasted like sewage. It shouldn't have surprised him. All *saha'asras* connected to Sinskrill had Shet as the source of their *lorasras.*

His unit disembarked the Jackaroo. William hitched his pack on his shoulder. "Everyone check your gear. We move out on my signal."

Karla, a bespectacled woman with the same brilliant blue eyes as her sister, Daniella, cleared her throat. "I'm ready."

Tam, a gray-bearded magus who'd served in Korea and Vietnam as a leatherneck sergeant, spoke in a hard-eyed yet calm manner. "Let's get this done."

"Here we go," William said.

He triggered the anchor line, using a braided series of Fire. When the rainbow bridge opened, relief swept over him. The necrosed and Adam hadn't been lying.

"Hopefully, this leads to Sinskrill," Karla said.

"Ready, sir," Tam said. He tethered to the anchor line, and stepped onto it.

William went next, with Karla and Rail to follow, in that order. He exited the anchor line, shook off his disorientation, and saw Tam hunkered nearby. William immediately created a block of Air, encompassing both himself and the other magus. Only then did he have time to study their surroundings. *Empty.* Relief passed through him again, along with a plethora of other emotions: fear, loathing, anger.

He ruthlessly shoved aside his feelings. He didn't have time for them. He had a mission to complete, one he'd trained for over and over again for the past month.

They were in the right place. A ring of stones no higher than his waist formed the border of a grassy sward about a hundred yards in diameter. An evergreen forest cupped the field. It merged with jagged mountains rearing to the north and east. Clouds hid the heavens, rain fell, and fog hugged the forest floor.

Sinskrill.

"Nothing," Tam said, scanning the trees. "No birds. No animals."

Karla and Rail quickly entered the meadow, and William gestured them over. He pointed to an opening in the ring of stones, barely visible in the mist. He knew from memory that it was wide enough for a wagon. Once past the rocks, it led to Lake White Sun, and from there to the Servitor's Palace.

"Move out," William whispered despite the block of Air. "We head south along the trail. We run if we see mahavans heading our way."

The others followed on his heels, and he led them at a dead-sprint to the opening in the stones. He didn't bother raising the hood of his heavy, camouflage jacket. He needed clear vision right now more than the comfort of keeping the weather off his head. Icy rain dribbled down the collar of his jacket, and his pack bounced a bit with his gait.

Rail called for a pause once they were outside the meadow. "Need to tighten my gear." He tugged on the straps holding his pack and also checked his sword and cased bow.

As soon as he was done, they set off once more, quiet and alert. They jogged smooth and steady, spread out enough to be able to draw weapons without encumbrance but close enough to easily support one another. William scanned their surroundings the entire time, knowing the others did the same. They soon reached a rutted trail paved with blocky stones. Puddles pooled on the rocks, and weeds grew in the cracks. At least they wouldn't leave any boot prints on it.

William winced when a wolf howled. The others glanced his way.

It was Tam who spoke, though. "It's miles away. It's no concern of ours."

"We keep going," William said. Once more, he shut down his roiling emotions. The mission was the only thing that mattered.

Serena automatically maintained her balance as her ship rocked on the rippling swells of rushing waves. She kept a firm grip on the ship's wheel as she beheld the dismal colors of the Norwegian Sea, gray and roiling beneath a lashing wind. Several miles away, the water transitioned into the indigo hue of Sinskrill's massive *saha'asra*. Of course, the color was only visible to an *asrasin*. To normals, the waters would remain as gray as the dullest charcoal all the way to the shores of the island.

The blue-hulled yacht they'd rented at Tórshavn in the Faroe Islands rolled in the lashing wind and swelling waves. They'd furled the sails. Cold spray dashed over the railing, spilling onto the deck and splashing like hail against Serena's face.

She had her rain parka closed tight about her, even pulling the hood low to keep the weather off her head. Nevertheless, chill rivulets still found a way past her protections. Worse, her hands, despite the wax-sealed, leather gloves she wore, had become blocks of ice under the ceaseless wash of wind and water.

"We're drifting too close to the *saha'asra*," Jean Paul told her, having to shout in order to be heard over the sound of the roaring wind and water. "A hard blow might send us straight into it."

"We're fine." Serena told him. "The water won't take us in." She pointed. "Look. The wind has us drifting northeast. We'll skirt the *saha'asra's* edge." She wanted to keep them far enough out from the island so as to remain essentially invisible to anyone who might glance their way from Sinskrill.

Jean-Paul shrugged, apparently trusting her judgment. "You know sailing better than I do."

He moved off, keeping a grip on the railing as he swayed his way toward the yacht's bow. He slowly eased past Jason and Julius, who had come up from the galley. They held plastic travel mugs with steam leaking out of them, and Julius passed a cup to Jean-Paul while Jason worked his way aft. Serena hoped it was coffee he was bringing to her, and she maintained a solid grip on the ship's wheel while he approached.

This was her crew, the ones she'd asked to come with her to Sinskrill. All of them knew how to sail, although none of them knew the waters of the Norwegian Sea like she did. However, their knowledge of ships, waves, and wind wasn't the only reason she'd asked them to come with her. It was because of their talents as *asrasins*. Julius was a Master of Water, Jason commanded Air, Jean-Paul held Spirit, and she could handle both Earth and Fire. Together they had mastery of all the Elements, which meant they could use the cannon mounted on the ship's bow.

They'd hauled it from Arylyn all the way through West Germany —no, just Germany. The Soviet Union had dissolved during her time in Arylyn, and the two Germanys, West and East, had reunited into a single nation. From Germany, she and the others had traveled to Gdansk, Poland, and then on to the Faroes.

Jason arrived with the steaming mug, offering it to her. She took it from him with a grateful nod, especially when the heat leaking off the mug warmed her icy fingers. She took a sip of whatever Jason brought to her and breathed out appreciation. *Coffee.*

"Take a break," Jason suggested.

He reached for the ship's wheel, and she let him take control of the yacht, wrapping her hands more fully around the travel mug. It was weakness to demonstrate her discomfort, but that had been a worry during another life. For now, she was happy.

Jason must have noticed that she was cold. "You should use a small braid from your *nomasra* to keep your hands warm. A little Fire would do."

"I can't braid that fine," she said. Mahavans were taught to braid swiftly and powerfully, but not accurately or with great subtlety.

Jason looked taken aback. "Still?"

Serena shrugged, not interested in discussing the faults of her ability to weave. "Any word from the shore team?" She kept her voice steady, evincing none of the concern she felt for William and the others.

Jason shook his head. "They called when they entered Sinskrill. They said no one saw them arrive. No mahavans or unformed. Last I heard, William said they were heading to some place near Travail's old field, Rock Hill. They're going to take a breather there."

Serena considered the terrain in which William's team traveled. Rock Hill bordered Lake White Sun, with plenty of stones and boulders among which to seek shelter. It was a good place to take refuge.

"William knows the place well," she said, "and since the wind is constantly blowing there, no Walker can hear them."

Jason nodded. "They're supposed to check in again a few hours from now."

It was the plan they'd come up with on warm, dry Arylyn: scout the Lake, listen like a Walker with Air, and move on to examine Villages Paradiso and Bliss, but avoid Village White Sun. Scouting the Servitor's village would leave them at too high a risk for discovery. In addition, William's team was to check in every four hours.

The other dangers to avoid were the woven creatures. The unformed could pose as any animal, and William's team might not know of their presence until it was too late. There was also Sapient Dormant. William could no longer sense the Overward, and in turn it was believed the leader of the necrosed could no longer sense William. Nevertheless, Sapient still resided on Sinskrill as far as she knew, and he was the wildcard in William's mission, a danger best avoided.

What if we're wrong?

Serena cursed silently. She wished Rukh and Jessira had been able to kill the Overward.

"I know what you're thinking," Jason said.

Serena quirked an eyebrow, wondering if he really knew her thoughts. Only William could guess them, and even then it wasn't that often. Certainly not like what Rukh and Jessira shared.

"You're wondering if you can go down below and warm up. You're shivering."

Serena shook her head, chuckling. "Not even close."

For some reason, Jason's face fell into disconsolate lines, and he muttered, "Unreadable mahavans."

WILLIAM FINALLY RELAXED when they reached their camp at Rock Hill. This was the place near Travail's field where the troll had taught him and Jake during their time as slaves on Sinskrill. It was also the safest place on the island for the team to hole up. The Walkers couldn't hear them here amongst the hill's constantly moaning wind, and just as important, no one bothered with this empty stretch of

land. While it overlooked Lake White Sun, there was little else to
draw anyone's interest here. Nothing but an abundance of boulders,
sparse grass, and scruffy bushes.

"No fire," William said, knowing the order was unnecessary but
needing to say it anyway.

"Understood, sir," Tam said, saving him from the embarrassment
of having Rail or Karla point out the obvious nature of his order.

The others broke out their supplies. They'd hidden them after
arriving on the island, within a crevice below the lip of a tall boulder
shaped like a plinth. It was a risk to leave evidence of their presence,
but in the end they figured if they were ever found out in the open,
they could run faster without their supplies slowing them.

They settled down amongst a cluster of boulders forming a cave
of sorts. It sheltered them from every sightline, including above. Rail
drew out a hunk of bread and some jerky, while Karla prepared a mix
of almonds, peanuts, and raisins. Tam rehydrated some dried eggs,
heating them in a pan with a thread of Fire. William went to refill
their canteens from a nearby stream that emptied into Lake
White Sun.

He scratched at his stubble as he waited for the canteens to fill.
They'd been here two days now, and today they'd searched out
Village Paradiso. The place had been utterly deserted, which made
no sense. *Where did everyone go?* A pair of hawks had soared the
heights above the village, but otherwise, nothing.

Nevertheless, they'd hidden from the birds. Hawks weren't native
to Sinskrill, and as far as William knew, the only such birds would
have been unformed.

While the canteens filled, William's thoughts drifted. He
wondered how life was back on Arylyn. Warm, certainly. He also
thought about the ring he'd purchased. He'd left it back home, and
he hoped he'd have a chance to give it to Serena. He hoped she
would—

He cut off his thoughts. He needed to maintain his focus.

A short time later, the canteens were filled and William returned
to their camp. The others had the food ready, and he passed them
their water.

"Thank you, sir," Tam said.

They ate their food silently, and when they were done Rail packed the remainder away. The slender magus reached onto his tiptoes, replacing their rations within the crevice.

"The island is quiet," Karla said.

"It's also cold," Rail said. He drew his cloak closer about himself as a gust of wind blew chill.

"It's like this all year long," William said. "Cold, damp, and gloomy." In their two days on Sinskrill, they'd never once seen the sun. It remained hidden behind a perpetual layer of oppressive clouds that lay low over the island and cast an intermittent drizzle.

"How did you survive it?" Karla asked.

William had often wondered the same thing. He offered the only answer he'd ever come up with. "I got by with a little help from my friends."

Tam snorted amusement. "Didn't figure you for a fan of the Beatles?"

William smiled. "Everyone likes the Beatles."

"Look. The sun," Karla said. She gestured to the pencil-thin view they had of Lake White Sun. A late day spar of sunshine had broken through the scudding clouds, peeking through them and causing the water to glisten.

They sat in silence and watched the view.

Minutes later, the sun set and a drizzle started. Night swelled swiftly, as it always did on Sinskrill, spreading like an inky stain across the sky. Soon would come fog and mist to crowd the hollows and make nighttime travel difficult. Hopefully, they'd never have to press their luck and journey through such difficult conditions.

"Do you have any sense of why they abandoned the village?" Tam asked.

William could barely make out the older man's face in the darkness. "I'm not a Walker, but I heard some things from a couple of faraway mahavans. They lost over two hundred of their own in the attack on Arylyn. There were some people talking about how few people they have left. There's only about nine hundred total left here.

Two-thirds of them are mahavans, but according the conversation I heard, they aren't very skilled."

The last bit of information had him relieved. While the Irregulars would outnumber the mahavans, it was always good to know they'd also be much better warriors.

"What about the unformed?" Karla asked.

"I don't know," William said. "There were seventy or eighty of them when I was last here, and that doesn't include the bears on Amethyst Island." He referenced the small island on the other side of Suborn Strait. It had once been inhabited, but now only unformed bears lived there.

"We killed fifty of them during their attack," Tam said. "That'd mean only twenty or thirty left."

"Unless the Servitor really is bringing in more of them to the island," Rail said.

"He is," William confirmed.

"Do you know how many?" Tam asked.

William shook his head. "No idea."

"What about the necrosed?" Karla asked.

"I heard something about that, too," he said. "Sapient is the only one of his kind on the island." It was another relief, and William hoped they never came across the necrosed during their time here.

Rail spoke. "I might have picked up on something."

William perked up. Rail hadn't mentioned anything before. "What?"

Rail hesitated, obviously disquieted. "I heard two people talk about a demon. They said it was starting to waken."

William's mouth pursed in consideration. Serena had mentioned this from her first dream, but Adam hadn't sent any further information about the creature. All William knew was that everyone was afraid of the monsters but no one knew much about them, only the myths about their terrible power and evil. "I was hoping Adam was lying about that," he said before addressing Rail. "Did you hear anything else?"

Rail shook his head, a vague movement in the dark. "Nothing."

Karla swore. "A demon."

"The demon doesn't matter," Tam said. "It's a worry for another day. We still have a mission to complete."

William nodded thanks to the old soldier, grateful that he'd refocused their attention on what they still had to do. Right now, it was the only thing that mattered.

"Get some rest," he said to his unit. "I'll take first watch and check in with the ship and Arylyn." He briefly wondered if Serena could learn anything more about the demon from Adam. "Tomorrow we'll head south and take a quick peek at Village White Sun before heading home."

"We aren't supposed to go there," Karla warned.

"We aren't supposed to enter the village," William corrected. "We won't. We'll be far away, hidden in the forest. I want to get a more accurate count of how many people are still there, the make-up of the place, especially if they've built any defenses, like walls or road blocks on the Great Way."

"It's a good notion," Tam said.

William nodded appreciation for the old soldier's support. "After that, we'll head to Village Bliss and get the hell off this rock."

SAPIENT UNCURLED himself from where he lay in his cavern. Darkness folded him like a comforting blanket, but a line of light marred the gloom. It lanced in from the cave's entrance, a pinpoint beam shining upon the far wall. Water dripped from the ceiling, regular as a metronome, forming the first nub of a stalactite. The sound wasn't what had awakened him, though. It was something else, a scent, an aroma riding the currents, penetrating deep to where he'd made his lair. It carried the smell of someone familiar. He levered himself upright, disturbing the bones of those upon which he'd fed. The flesh of those he'd killed hadn't sated his hunger. Only an *asrasin's lorethasra* could fully quench his appetite.

Sapient inhaled deeply, trying to understand what he smelled. Another deep breath, and he had his answer.

William, the young holder. Again. He'd scented the boy several days ago, as well as yesterday. He suspected the reason why, and agitation roiled through him. Sapient didn't fear William, but he respected his power. The boy had already defeated three powerful necrosed: Kohl Obsidian, Grave Invidious, and Rue Blade, and more dangerously, wherever William went, Shokan and Sira shortly followed.

Which meant the scent Sapient detected was a trap. Shokan and Sira stalked Sapient. He knew it now. They'd already tricked him once before with that silly *asrasin* in West Virginia. Then they'd arrived to finish him off. Sapient had barely escaped with his life, and wisdom taught him to never again swallow such a lure.

The scent quickened for a beat, and Sapient glowered. He resented the intrusion of the boy's aroma. *So tempting, yet so deadly.* William had likely entered a *saha'asra*, one tightly linked to Sinskrill, a taunt to lure Sapient into attacking.

He wouldn't take the bait. Instead, Sapient lay back and tried to recover his rest. He needed it. He needed to husband his strength if he wished to overcome the Servitor. Then would come Shet. Sapient would deny the god's entrance to the world. The Overward ground his teeth in anger. Even better if he could travel to Seminal itself and kill the deceitful god.

Once more, William's scent drifted on the breeze, and Sapient nearly groaned with need and frustration.

He wouldn't chase the boy, not to some faraway *saha'asra* where Shokan and Sira waited. He'd remain here and—

The scent thickened, and Sapient's thoughts sharpened. *Wait.* He tried to hold back the growing excitement, but he couldn't prevent the thinning of his pustulant blood, the slowly accelerating beating of his decayed heart.

The aroma couldn't penetrate along the anchor lines, not like this. He sat upright once again, rising to his feet, and prowling toward the cave's entrance. Something was amiss.

Or something wonderful had fallen into his lap.

He crawled outside, moving around stones and boulders until he could stand upright. Lake White Sun spread out before him, stretching mostly to the north and west since his cave hunkered in a hill toward the water's southern border. He spun in a slow circle, trying to understand William's scent, the depth of it. Eastward, his gaze fell upon Village White Sun. It belched smoke, and the maha-vans there moved ant-like in the distance. To the south, the Norwe-gian Sea shone indigo, and past the *saha'asra's* border it became a drab gray. North, the scent thickened.

Sapient followed the invisible trail along the lake's shore, his nostrils flaring to capture the fragrance of fresh *asrasin*. He clambered up and down the rugged coast, traveling ever northward. The scent drew him onward like iron to a lodestone. The aroma grew stronger when he reached a hill populated with boulders of all shapes and sizes. They lay scattered like dice. It was strongest here, and Sapient paused.

New smells intruded. More *asrasins*. Four of them, including William. The odor of them was strong here, powerful. Sapient hurried. He reached a place on the hill, near the base, where boul-ders ringed a small opening. He shoved himself inside and discov-ered crumbs of dried meat and fruit. Nuts. His nostrils flared.

William had been here. Others as well. Questions raced through his mind. *How? Why?* It was risky for magi to enter Sinskrill. Was it magi?

Sapient only considered the questions for an instant. Their answers were meaningless. The only issue of importance was William's presence on the island. He had been here. Others had been here, too. *A feast for the taking.*

Excitement flooded Sapient's senses, overwhelming his ability to think until his heart stuttered and picked up a more rapid beat. He considered what to do. As best he could tell, William was still on the island. So were other *asrasins*, likely more magi. In addition, the scents didn't end at this lonely ring of stones. They continued east, and east Sapient followed. A truly wondrous feast might await him, and he wouldn't let it scamper away to safety.

WILLIAM LAY ON HIS BELLY, peering through the binoculars he'd formed. He and the others huddled within a copse of trees, hidden by a small rise as they observed Village Bliss. No people and no movement met his study, except for a few birds wheeling in the sky. Puffins, maybe, but not unformed, who always took the shapes of eagles, hawks, or crows. The village appeared to be as abandoned as Paradiso. Same with the surrounding fields, which were overrun by weeds.

William let go of the binoculars. "What do you think?" he asked Tam.

"I think we've seen what we came to," Tam replied, crouched next to him. "I think they must have abandoned their villages and concentrated themselves at Village White Sun."

"I still don't understand why they did that," Rail said. He huddled close by, blowing warmth into his hands. Rain dripped off the brim of his hood.

"Because it's more defensible," William said. "They've got a wall around Village White Sun, mounted cannons, and a way to funnel anyone who breaks through into a kill box."

Tam nodded. "Another few months, and they'll be dug in like an Alabama tick."

William eyed the empty village for a moment more before gesturing that it was time to leave. "Let's go," he said, scooting down the hill to where they'd left Karla to protect their backsides and their packs.

Her hand rested on the pommel of her belted sword, and she restlessly scanned the surrounding area. Despite her heavy jacket, she shivered now and then, and William could tell she was more than ready to get off Sinskrill. He explained what they'd seen.

"Will they have enough space for everyone in White Sun?" she asked.

"They should," William said recalling what he could of the village. "There were plenty of empty buildings back when I lived there. They'll be packed tight, but they'll have enough room. And that doesn't take into account the number of people they can shove into the Servitor's Palace."

"How are we going to get to the Palace if they've got cannons and a wall?" Rail asked.

"I didn't notice any cannons mounted on the Palace," Tam said. "Might be we could land at the base of the cliff and take them from that direction."

William stared at him in surprise. "You could see all the way to the Palace?"

Tam grinned. "I've got a fair bit of skill with Air when it comes to spectacles and the like. I could see, and they didn't have any cannons there. They've got a second wall and cannons at the base of the hill where the Palace stands, but everything is facing inland. If a raiding party scaled the Palace's cliff, they could open the doors for everyone else."

William nodded. It was a good idea, but now wasn't the time to plan Sinskrill's invasion. They still needed to finish their mission first. "If Village Bliss is abandoned, then the Prime's castle probably is, too. I want to search it."

"What do you think you'll find there?" Rail asked, sounding doubtful.

William wasn't sure. "Maybe some papers, information, anything to tell us how many woven are here."

"You sure we need to do this?" Karla asked, mirroring Rail's doubt.

"It's on the way to the pier anyway," William said. "If we don't find anything, we'll be in and out inside of ten."

"Then let's get it over with," Tam said.

William led the way, and minutes later they reached their destination. The Prime's castle stood on a small hill and possessed a commanding view of Village Bliss and the Norwegian Sea. It had the shape of something from the Middle Ages, made of blocks of rough-hewn stones that were interrupted by infrequent, narrow windows. William reckoned it was probably no warmer inside the building than the damp weather outside. A wall surrounded the grounds, although the iron gate normally barring the entrance rested open and already showed signs of rust.

They entered the castle, quickly opening and shutting the front door. They stood in a dark foyer, a dank, dim hallway stretching in front of them. William's heart beat faster. Excitement and tension warred in equal parts, and he listened hard for the presence of anyone else who might be inside.

Nothing.

"Hold up," William whispered, despite the block of Air he held around them. He took out his satellite phone and called Serena, briefing her on what they intended.

"Stay safe," she said.

"Roger that." William spoke to the others. "Let's move."

He led them deeper into the castle. Their footsteps echoed. Tapestries hung from the walls, but William couldn't make them out in the gloom.

"Should we make a light?" Rail asked.

William considered. "A small one," he said. "Real small. We don't want anyone seeing light coming through any of the windows."

Rail wove a blue globe, tiny and bobbing ahead of them. It provided barely enough light to illuminate a single square foot.

They explored the castle, going through a set of rooms: a tapestry lined hall, a dining room containing a long table and rough-hewn chairs; a kitchen where a loaf of bread moldered on the counter and a wooden barrel held a handful of wrinkled apples. They also came across a set of bedrooms containing dust-covered furniture and threadbare clothes.

They next ascended a set of stairs circling the edge of a turret. It led to the third floor, the highest floor in the castle, and ended at a single closed door. William pushed it open and discovered a study, a round room illuminated by the only window worth the name in the entire castle. He immediately closed the door. "Turn off the light," he told Rail, going on to explain what he'd seen.

Rail did as instructed, and the hallway in which they stood darkened. Only then did they push into the study.

On the wall opposite the door stood a pair of relatively empty bookcases, bracketing the window, which opened onto a view of the fields south of Village Bliss. To the left, a heavy desk with feet shaped like dragon claws rested in front of an ash-filled fireplace. Above the mantle hung a portrait of the Servitor. To the right hand side of the study stood more empty shelves. A bear rug covered the flagstone floor.

"Help me with the curtains," Karla said. "We need to close them so no one can see us moving around in here."

Rail moved to assist her. "Melt their edges a bit. It should glue them to the wall."

Once they finished, William created a small globe of light and examined the shelves. Tam and Rail joined him. After a few minutes of perusal, William scrutinized them in silent question. They shook their heads. The remaining books held nothing of interest.

"I think I found something," Karla said. She'd been examining the desk.

William went to her.

She held up a leather-bound accounting journal. "Whoever made this kept close notes about everything," she said. "It says here that one hundred twelve unformed answered the Servitor's call. Plus another forty-three from Amethyst."

William scratched at his stubble and did some quick math. "Which means they have around one hundred fifty-five unformed beyond the ones on the island beforehand." It was more than he'd hoped but less than he feared.

Karla continued. "It also says that after the attack on Sinskrill, there are a total of one hundred fifty-seven mahavans and drones left in Village Bliss. It also gives totals for the other villages."

"How many altogether?" William asked, peering over Karla's shoulder and reading the numbers himself.

Karla pointed to the figures in question.

Rail tallied them first. "Nine hundred thirteen."

Again, it was more than William hoped but less than he feared.

"Look here." Karla pointed, sounding more excited. "It also tells how many drones managed to become mahavans."

William's attention grew distracted. An itch formed in the back of his mind. His anger rumbled. *What now?*

"Does it have a date?" Tam asked.

The itch grew more pronounced.

"Two months ago," Karla answered.

William's throat went dry. Something was coming, something he recognized. His heart pounded fear, and he went to the curtains, peeling open a small fragment that Karla and Rail had fused to the wall.

"So the information is at best two months old." Tam grunted. "Better than I expected to learn."

William peered outside. Far in the distance, a figure loped toward the castle, a giant with arms hanging down to his knees. Claws extended from his hands.

18

ESCAPE AN AMBUSH

M *ay 1991*

WILLIAM LET GO of the curtain and stepped back. His mouth went dry, and he swallowed heavily, working in moisture. His mind raced. The others must have sensed his fear.

"What is it?" Tam asked.

William inhaled deeply, blowing out his fear like Rukh taught and steeling his resolve. "Sapient is coming. He's here."

Karla inhaled sharply. "God save us," she breathed fervently.

Rail paled. "We'll need more than a god to stop a necrosed." He trembled.

William's thoughts started to come more easily. "Necrosed can be killed. They're not unbeatable. I've killed two of them." He hoped his words would bring some spine to the fear-filled scout. "And Rukh and Jessira killed another. They almost killed Sapient, but he ran away before they could finish him off." He *really* wished they had killed him.

"But Sapient is the Overward," Rail began, panic persisting in his voice.

"Quiet," Tam told him in a firm voice. "Get yourself together. We don't have time to fall apart."

William nodded "Thanks" to the old sergeant. The nugget of a plan formed in his mind, and he spoke to Karla. "Grab the book." He addressed the team. "Drop everything that might slow you down. It doesn't matter if someone figures we were here. We have to run."

They shucked their gear—everything but their weapons: swords, bows, and quivers—dumping them in the center of the room. William led the others out of the study. They needed a way out of the castle, something other than the front door, which was Sapient's most likely destination. He'd seen a few other exits, but they opened into courtyards or open spaces. He needed something more private.

He dialed Serena as they headed down the stairs, hoping she could help them. She'd been to this castle plenty of times in her time on Sinskrill.

THE BLUE-HULLED YACHT CRESTED A SWELL, her prow lifting up and over the wave. Serena rode the rising-and-falling motion with practiced efficiency, her attention remaining upon Sinskrill. The island was nothing more than a green blur due to distance and the darkening sky. Drizzle fell and clouds swept by under the force of a steady wind. The yacht maintained a position directly outside Sinskrill's *saha'asra*, near the border where the waters transitioned from indigo to gray.

Serena had her hood up, keeping her head covered to ward off the weather. Her mind was restless, though, not focused on the drab day but on the ground team on Sinskrill, on William, Karla, Tam, and Rail. They'd checked in a few hours ago, but she wouldn't be happy until they were safe and sound aboard the yacht, and Sinskrill was leagues behind them.

The satellite phone rang.

"I've got it," Julius said, taking the ship's wheel from her. He,

Jason, and Jean-Paul stood close by, all of their attention focused upon Sinskrill, all of them wearing identical features of concern.

Serena reached into her waterproof bag and drew out the phone.

William spoke as soon as she answered, and her heart dropped when he told her their situation.

"We're still in the castle. Sapient's coming." His voice sounded steady, but a strain of stress marred its smoothness. "Is there an exit that doesn't lead out to an open space?"

Sapient. Serena's heart raced, but she pushed aside the fear. A single, deep breath and exhalation and she could focus on what needed doing. "Where are you?"

"We're near the study, heading down a stairwell in the turret."

"Go back up. Get back to the study. Behind the right hand book-shelf, there's a secret passageway. It leads to a hidden stairwell. Pull on one of the candelabras to unlock it. It'll take you to a door exiting the first floor. It opens behind a hedge, right around the corner from the kitchen. From there, take a right, and you'll have a straight shot to the docks."

"Once we reach the docks, we should be safe," William said. "Necrosed are afraid of running water."

Serena clenched her teeth. "This is the Overward. What if he isn't?" She noticed Jean-Paul eyeing her in alarm.

"I hope he is," William said softly. "We're heading back to the study. We'll see you soon."

"When you get to the docks, don't worry about finding a boat. We'll come for you."

Serena hung up the phone.

"Sapient found them," Jason guessed.

"He's right outside the Prime's castle in Village Bliss," Serena said. "William's team is trapped inside."

Oaths met her words.

"What's the plan?" Jean-Paul asked, his demeanor serious. In fact, during the entire mission he had never once evinced the flamboyant air for which he was known on Arylyn.

"Julius and I are going to take the skiff to the docks," Serena explained. "We'll pick them up there."

"Why don't we all go?" Jason asked. "Any extra magus might help if Sapient is on them before they can get to the docks."

"Because the skiff can barely carry six people as it is. We load it with seven, and someone will have to hang on to a rail on the outside."

"Not Julius," Jason said. "He can ride the water. He's a Master of Water."

Serena had forgotten about Julius' ability to surf the sea like a mahavan Rider, and Jason's advice made sense. The extra magus might be the difference between success and death. She quickly made up her mind. "Jean-Paul, you'll stay here and maintain position. The rest of us will get to Sinskrill."

"Use the extra *nomasra*s to go faster," Jean-Paul suggested. "Drain them if you have to. They won't do you any good if you're late."

"Air could also lighten the load and increase our speed," Julius said.

Serena briskly nodded. "Call it fifteen minutes to get to the docks," she mused. "Any nearby unformed will probably hear or see the skiff."

"Does it matter?" Jason asked. "If they're surveilling the docks, they'll see William's team leaving anyway."

Serena shook her head. "You misunderstand. The unformed might fight William's team. They'll slow him down long enough for Sapient to catch him." She grimaced. It was a problem they'd figure out if it ever became an issue. "Right. Let's deal with what's in front of us. We're going to be cutting it close as it is."

Minutes later, they had the skiff lowered to the sea. Serena flung the line tying them to the yacht over to Jean-Paul. He gave them a 'thumbs-up.' The skiff's engine sputtered, caught, and they soon raced across the waves toward Sinskrill.

Julius had the rudder while Jason kept a film of Air under the skiff's hull. Serena smoothed the flow around the prow. The wind whipped her hair about, but for once she'd remembered to tie it off in a ponytail.

Serena figured they were making forty knots but wished they

were going even faster. She closed her eyes for a moment, breathing a prayer for William. *Lord, keep him safe.*

"BACK UP THE STAIRS," William said.

They quickly got themselves going in the right direction. They ascended, and William explained the plan he and Serena had come up with.

Fragging hells. Why did Sapient have to find us now of all times? Why did he have to find us at all?

They reached the study they'd recently exited. Karla, Tam, and Rail immediately began yanking on the various candelabras. William, having brought up the rear, watched, not wanting to get in the way.

Rail glowered. He was pulling on a candelabra, rocking it back and forth. William inspected the right-side bookshelf, but it remained locked in place.

"I think this one might be it," Rail said, "but it's stuck."

The sound of the front door crashing open echoed through the small castle. A leering laugh followed. "Small *asrasins*. Little magi. You don't belong here."

Sapient. William silently snarled. *Fragging necrosed.*

He gestured to Tam, indicating for him to help Rail while he carefully shut the door to the study. Karla brought over a high-backed chair, and they set it under the door handle, doing what they could to impede Sapient's progress into the room.

It probably wouldn't do any good, but better something than nothing.

A click from the right bookshelf drew William's attention back into the room.

"Got it," Rail hissed, his voice triumphant.

The bookshelf's edge had pushed a finger's breadth into the study. A brief wind whispered into the room before fading away, but it left a stale odor behind.

Karla went to the bookshelf, prepared to throw it open.

"Wait," William warned. Karla held back, a questioning widening of her eyes. "The hinges might squeak and give us away."

Tam grunted. "Good thinking." He sourced his *lorethasra*, and the scent of cut wheat briefly filled the room. He braided Earth, Air, and Fire and sent the weave into the bookshelf's hidden hinges. "A bit of lubricant. Try it now," he instructed Karla.

She pulled on the bookshelf, and it opened silently, exposing a narrow spiral staircase.

"Go," William said.

The others entered the enclosed passage. Tam took point, Rail on his heels, and followed by Karla. William brought up the rear. He closed the bookshelf behind them, glad to hear the lock latch again. He took an instant to weave a blue globe to provide illumination. The others, who were arrayed down the stairs, also held small lights.

They hunched in a slender corridor narrower than his shoulders, and he had to shuffle sideways to squeeze through it. Thankfully, a few steps farther down the passageway opened up enough for William to face forward again. Dust drifted on unseen currents, kicked up by their footsteps. He blinked, rubbing his eyes.

They descended a set of stairs, and William kept his focus on his footing, not wanting to slip on the hidden staircase's narrow treads. No one spoke. They all knew not to. The only sounds came from Rail's and Karla's heavy breathing, and the whispering scuff of everyone's boots.

As one, they startled to a halt when the noise of something powerful striking wood penetrated the passage. It had come from up above.

The study door. Sapient.

Tam halted. They all did, glancing up the staircase, focusing on the noise. Rail and Karla wore fearful expressions bordering on terror, while Tam only appeared irritated. William hoped his own demeanor was similar to that of the old Marine.

Again came the booming sound. The splintering of wood. A shout of triumph followed by a roar of rage. Something heavy tumbled about. It sounded like Sapient had thrown the desk.

A voice shouted. "You will not escape me, little magi. I know you hide."

Tam got them going again, and while they hustled down the stairs William kept listening for Sapient's presence. Seconds later, heavy footsteps descended from beyond their enclosed staircase, menacing sounds like drums of doom. The noise of claws scratching the exterior wall penetrated into their corridor, sounding right next to his head, and again, they all halted.

William's heart raced harder. Sweat beaded on his forehead. Fear rose in his throat.

Sapient's menacing descent never slowed. The monster continued on down the stairs, and a low chuckle rumbled from the necrosed, but eventually his presence was no longer audible.

William breathed relief. "Go," he ordered in a whisper.

On they descended, circling around the turret. Crashes and snarls occasionally reached them from distant parts of the castle. William did his best to disregard the sound. He and the others never slowed. The stairway ended in a straight passage, twenty feet long.

At the end of it, Tam held up his hand. "Hold on."

An iron-banded door barred their progress.

The way outside.

Hope rose like a fervent prayer in William's mind. *A short run, get outside, get to the docks, and Serena will be there.* Maybe they'd make it out of this after all.

Rail bolted around Tam, reaching for the bolt holding the door locked. William tried to warn him, but too late, the slender scout tugged, and the grating cry of iron rasping against iron echoed down the hall. William winced, certain the noise sounded as loud as a blacksmith's hammer pounding an anvil.

"Sorry," Rail squeaked. His face went pale.

Tam shoved him aside. "Let me." He wove another braid like the one he'd used upstairs on the hinges to the bookcase. This time the door slid open easily and noiselessly.

A tall hedge dripping beneath a drizzly rain met their wide-open eyes.

Another crash. It still sounded distant but too close for William's comfort. He held up a hand, restraining the others from rushing outside. "Tam, Rail take point to the docks. Karla and I will hold the rear."

The others whispered "Yes, sir."

They darted outside, swiftly taking their positions.

Another roar, this one much nearer. The next room over maybe. Seconds later, a crash from the sound of a door smashing into stone from only several yards away.

SAPIENT ROARED WITH FRUSTRATION. *Empty.* The room was empty. Again, he roared, but this time his eyes fell upon the scattered backpacks lying on the floor. They could have been left behind by the mahavans when they'd abandoned this place, but he didn't think so.

Sapient smelled the dust, mold, and stale odors that lingered in buildings left unoccupied. He also tasted the scents of the many *asrasins* who had once lived here, faint like a barely remembered memory.

Except for the heady aromas of William and his fellow magi.

Their fragrance of promised *lorethasra*—so delicious—permeated the air. They had been here, not long ago, either. And the packs lying on the floor were suffused with their scents and still warm.

Which meant the magi weren't too far away. Sapient could still catch them.

He exited the empty room, descending the stairwell while straining all his senses for any indication of William's presence. He absent-mindedly trailed claws along one of the stairwell's stone walls. The scratching sound echoed through the turret.

He reached the floor holding the main living quarters and paused once more, his body quivering while he listened intently. His low-set ears flicked about. He inhaled deeply although his sense of smell wouldn't help him as much now. William's aroma filled the castle. He'd apparently explored many of the rooms, and Sapient couldn't tell which scent was the newest.

After a moment of silent scrutiny, he growled in frustration. *Noth-*

ing. He flung furniture out of the way and proceeded forward, searching through the castle, room by room, for the magi he knew were close by.

Minutes into his exploration he halted, frustrated by his own stupidity. He couldn't afford to crash through the castle like this, thoughtlessly and without a plan. William would be long gone by the time he finished his search. The boy would have certainly heard his entrance into the castle since he'd made enough noise to awaken a hibernating bear.

He thought about the scenario from the boy's perspective.

A necrosed bearing down on his weak, asrasin *flesh . . . Trapped in a castle . . .*

Sapient pondered, and realized the boy would seek an immediate route of escape. He might already be gone.

But where would he go?

Sapient considered the situation and realized where William was most likely headed. He needed to get there first. He rushed toward what he knew to be the closest exit: the kitchen.

WILLIAM DARTED a glance in the direction from which he'd heard the sound. The kitchen. It was right around the corner from them. A low-pitched growl emanated. It promised death.

"Move," William ordered. "Quietly. No *lorethasra.* He can sense it."

The others shuffled along the border between the hedge and the castle's exterior wall, all of them careful to disturb the shrubbery as little as possible. They reached the end of the hedge and exited onto a sloping field. Rain, mist, and whipping wind limited visibility, but when William peered intently, he saw a pebbled road on the far side of the field. He recognized the path. It ended at Village Bliss' sheltered cove and docks. He could see them, too.

A half mile to freedom, if there was some sort of transport to get them off the island.

Tam set off at a run. "Follow me."

The rest of the team raced after him.

"Careful," William hissed when Karla almost went down. He supported her by the elbow for a second, until she could run steadily.

Seconds into their run, a pounding sound reached them. Rail searched behind. His eyes went round with terror.

William didn't have to look back to know what the scout saw: Sapient. He felt the necrosed's feet beat through the ground, a distant rumble growing more powerful. He imagined the Overward's steaming breath on his neck, his claws ready to rip.

He pushed away his imaginings and focused on running and maintaining his balance. Adrenaline coursed through him. The sound of an engine from the cove echoed. Hope flickered. Serena was close. She'd be bringing reinforcements.

Rail shot another look back.

"Eyes forward," William snapped.

Rail didn't listen. He kept glancing rearward. It proved his undoing. He tumbled to the ground, taking out Karla who tripped over him.

Fragging idiot!

William yanked them both to their feet. Rail stumbled, crying out in pain. He couldn't bear weight on his right foot. He'd hurt his ankle, twisting it, maybe even breaking it. Karla gazed in the direction they'd come, face tight with terror. Tam sprinted back to them, taking some of Rail's weight. The red rage flickered in the back of William's mind. He crushed it. He needed to think right now, not give in to anger.

"Take his other side," William ordered Karla, indicating Rail.

"What are you going to do?" she asked.

"I'll slow Sapient. Get to the docks."

Tam and Karla hobbled off, Rail clinging to their shoulders.

William faced Sapient. The monster charged, only dozens of yards away, his mouth set in dire promise. William unsheathed his sword, sourcing his *lorethasra*, drawing deep and igniting the Wildness. Lightning crackled along his arms. The sword blazed, bright as the sun.

Sapient accelerated.

William dashed forward to engage. His jaw clenched. Purpose filled him. He'd kill the necrosed.

Several feet before contact, Sapient leapt. William's jaw dropped when the necrosed flew overhead. Anger flooded him. The red beast grumbled. *Damn it!* The Overward now had a clear shot at the rest of the team.

William raced after the necrosed, shouting warning.

Tam darted a glance back. He let go of Rail and drew his sword. So did Karla. Rail struggled to maintain his footing, but he too unsheathed his weapon. They had less than a second to ready themselves before Sapient powered into them.

All three were blasted off their feet. Tam flew several yards through the air, crashing to a sliding halt. He slowly rose, wiping blood from the corner of his mouth, a snarl on his face. Karla had spun down the hill, mostly on her back, but she managed to regain her feet as well. Rail didn't stand, and William realized with horror that he never would. The slender scout's chest had been ripped open. Blood pooled about his body.

William roared with anger.

Sapient raced at Tam, who desperately defended against the necrosed's slashes and punches. Karla tried to help, but Sapient slipped away from her blows.

William let the red-eyed beast at the back of his mind off its leash. Rage powered his motions, and he arrived with a cry of savage fury, sword aimed like a spear.

The Overward somehow sensed his presence. The albino monstrosity spun and defended, blocking with his claws. William drew deeper on his *lorethasra*, moving faster. He thrust, slashed, and hammered an overhand blow. Sapient spun around the last, his attention fully on William.

Tam landed a ringing strike against the creature's side. The sword did nothing but bounce off. Sapient didn't even grunt. Tam ducked under the return swing, a hooking blow. William knocked aside a backhand, parrying with a rumbling weave of Earth. Vines rippled out of the ground. Sapient cut them down with a slash of Air.

Shock filled William's mind, and he stepped away from the Overward. He hadn't expected the necrosed to weave against him. He gritted his teeth. *Who cares?* He'd still bring the monster down.

He sent a stinging whip of Water. It snapped into Sapient's face. The Overward glared, wiping away a line of blood trickling down his face. William sent another whip of Water, but Sapient burned it with a line of dark Fire.

The Overward's inattention allowed Karla to attack while from a distance. An arrow sprouted from the Overward's shoulder. He ripped it aside, his face expressionless. Black blood oozed from the wound, quickly drying. He disregarded William and attacked Tam again. The Overward spun, a roundhouse kick followed by a diagonal slash. Tam ducked under them both, rolling away. Sapient pursued.

William snarled. No chance he'd let this monster hurt anyone else. He slashed at the Overward's back. Again, the monster sensed his approach. Too late this time. The Wildness-powered slash cut into Sapient's shoulder, drawing more blood.

The Overward grunted.

From a distance, William saw Serena tying off the skiff. Jason and Julius disembarked.

"Go," he ordered Tam and Karla. "I'll follow."

Tam hesitated. An instant later, he gave a hard nod of acknowledgment. He fled toward the pebbled path, collecting Karla on the way.

The Overward faced him. "You'll not escape to safety. Nor can you defeat me. I've tested your power. I deem you wanting."

William didn't reply. He knew he couldn't stop the Overward, but he didn't have to. He only had to hold him off. He and the necrosed came together. William sent out questing feints and thrusts. Lightning rippled from the Wildness. Sapient blocked all his attacks smoothly, except for a hissing braid of Air that got through the Overward's defenses. It clipped the necrosed on the side of his head.

Sapient rocked, but the attack didn't slow him down. He responded with a blurring set of his own blows.

William struggled to keep his distance. He couldn't let himself get hooked on those claws. He blocked Sapient, using his sword and weaves of Air and Earth, giving ground as he worked his way down the slick slope. Another series of slashes from the Overward. William deflected or eluded them all.

A punch got through. He only partially evaded it, and the blow took him in the solar plexus. His breath blasted out as he was flung ten feet farther down the hill. He rolled another dozen.

William bit down, anger energizing him. He surged to his feet.

Sapient loomed.

William drew desperately on his *lorethasra*. He sent a fist of Earth, a shotgun blast of stones pulled out of the ground. They punched into Sapient, who smacked them aside.

It was a feint for William's true attack: a gripping weave of Air. It wrapped around the Overward, and William hurled him halfway up the slope, back toward the Prime's castle. Sapient roared fury as he soared through the air.

William wasn't listening. He sheathed his sword and took off toward the docks. Tam and Karla were a hundred yards ahead, on the road now and picking up speed once they no longer had to contend with the slippery grass. Serena and the others moved up the path from the docks, apparently intending to lend support.

"Keep running!" William shouted. "Don't wait for me." Serena shot him an expression of uncertainty but she did as he ordered. All of them sped back to the skiff.

William heard Sapient's breath like bellows, closing on him. He ran faster, hitting the road and accelerating. Tam and Karla reached Serena. They paused briefly, speaking to one another.

William risked a look back. Sapient had gained the road. He came on like a tank on jet fuel, raging faster. Yards away. William wouldn't make it, not in a dead sprint. He drew more *lorethasra* and used Air to break a branch off a nearby tree. He hurled the limb at the necrosed.

The Overward tried to smash it aside, but the limb cracked him in the thighs, slowing him a bit.

Jason and Julius had the skiff ready. Tam and Karla were onboard. Where was Serena?

William wanted to scream when he saw her. She stood in the middle of the road, bow pulled back and arrow ready. She should be on the skiff. Fear for her rose in his throat. She released the arrow.

Sapient cursed.

William glanced back. The necrosed stumbled. The arrow had

taken him in the stomach. He yanked it out, but the attack gave William precious extra yards of space. He needed more, though.

On he ran, ripping apart more branches as the opportunity allowed, lifting boulders, tossing them onto the path. Sapient had to dodge through them all. He also had to evade a few more arrows. William gained precious yards.

At last, Serena regained the skiff. The boat drifted away from the dock, into the cove.

Only seventy yards to go.

The Overward's vile stench, his fetid breath was William's only warning. The creature neared. He couldn't be more than a few feet behind. William dug deep, straining for the last ounce of speed. Something ripped at this shirt.

Sapient's snarl of frustration.

No. William put on a final burst. He reached the pier. His feet pounded. Less than a second later, the heavy thuds of Sapient's pursuit echoed on the planks.

Again, something snatched at his shirt.

William leapt for the water. His shirt tore. He hit the water and dove deep, resurfacing twenty feet from the dock.

Sapient watched from the pier, William's tattered shirt in his hand. The creature stared hatred, but a second later, the Overward flung his shirt aside, bowed mockingly, and walked away.

William wanted to shout in triumph, but then he remembered where Sapient was going. *Rail.* He was dead. William shook his head in regret, knowing he couldn't do anything more right now. He swam to the skiff, where he was hauled aboard.

19

PROPOSALS AND DISCOVERIES

J *une 1991*

IT HAD BEEN a week since the mission to Sinskrill, a week of endless debriefings for everyone involved in the scouting mission. Serena quickly lost count of the number of times she had to go over her role, which had been pretty straightforward. She couldn't imagine what it had been like for William. Rail Forsyth had died on his watch. The reason for his death was easy to explain: Sapient Dormant had discovered them, but the why or how was less easy to understand.

William had led his unit into Castle Bliss, and while they'd discovered a great deal of helpful information, some council members thought his choice was unnecessary. They argued that the knowledge acquired was something they already knew—which wasn't true—and William's decision to go to the castle was the direct reason for Rail's death. In addition, William's unit had left behind proof of their presence: their backpacks dumped in the study.

The arguments had raged, but from the beginning Rukh and

Jessira had supported William's decisions. Their opinion carried a great deal of weight amongst the Irregulars and served to quell much of the discussion. Unfortunately, the snakes on the Village Council— Break Foliage and Zane Blood—weren't as easily assuaged. Rail had been Zane's nephew, and they wouldn't let the matter drop. At another interminable council meeting they had yapped like small dogs, only giving over when the Mayor and Bar Duba managed to curtail any further arguments.

William was eventually absolved of Rail's death, but it had been hard on him. Serena knew. He'd been torn up with guilt by what had happened on Sinskrill.

Which was why she was so pleased that he'd invited her to dinner tonight. Maybe he was ready to forgive himself.

However, since privacy was at a premium at his home these days, given Mr. Zeus and Fiona's recent nuptials and Jason's and Jake's schedules, they were having the meal at her house. William had promised to do all the cooking and cleaning and to get the table and chairs set up, saying it would be a dinner on the beach next to the lagoon. He'd also told her he didn't want her help for any of it. In fact, he'd asked her to stay away while he worked. She'd even had to shower and get ready at his place.

As a result, Serena arrived at her cottage by the lagoon with few expectations, but she inhaled sharply in pleasure when she saw what William had done.

A pair of tiki torches burned cheerily on either side of a square table. The delicious aroma, asparagus, grilled eggplant, and sea bass with capers rose from two place settings of sky-blue china, pale enough to be almost translucent, and likely from Mr. Zeus' home. A pair of goblets held white wine while the bottle itself sweated in a cooler. Centered on the table rested a tall candle, white in a blue lamp the color of Arylyn's skies. It provided further, softer light.

A newly risen crescent moon wisped ivory beams amongst vagrant clouds. Stars bathed the darkened firmament. Washing waves rustled the lagoon, rippling beneath a soft breeze. William had left a few lamps on inside the cottage, and they glowed low and warm through the home's windows.

Seeing it all, unexpected butterflies flitted through Serena's stomach. The dinner itself wasn't the cause of her excitement, though, and if she was honest with herself, her trepidation. It was what she expected tonight to entail—and again, if she was being honest with herself—hoped would happen.

Serena slipped into the seat William held out for her, smoothing the fabric of the lime-green dress she wore for William's benefit. He'd mentioned once that he thought it was pretty on her, saying it highlighted her dark skin.

As for William, she approved of his attire. He'd come back from Sinskrill scruffy and beat up, but once home he had resumed the well-groomed style he'd chosen a year ago. He wore gray slacks and a long-sleeve shirt, the same caesious hue as his half boots.

"Are you all right?" William asked after he took a seat across from her. "You look, I don't know, nervous."

Serena gathered her jitteriness, imagined locking it in a bottle and shoving it out of sight. She flashed William a smile. "I'm fine."

"How about a toast?" William said, holding up his glass of wine. "To home."

"Home," Serena agreed, clinking her glass against his. She dipped her fork into the sea bass, which flaked apart. She took a bite and made an appreciative sound. He'd cooked it perfectly. She tried the asparagus and eggplant. Everything was delicious.

William watched her, amused for some reason.

"What?" Serena asked, noticing he hadn't started on his meal.

"You're so dainty when you eat."

Serena arched an eyebrow. "I believe we've discussed this before. A woman needs to maintain the polite fiction that we're more civilized than men."

William tilted his head as if in thought. "Are you sure you *aren't* actually more civilized? I mean, Jason's a slob when he eats. He's like a blender when he chews his food."

Serena laughed. "Please don't tell me you're thinking about Jason during our dinner."

William chuckled, sounding rueful. "No chance of that. I don't want to kiss Jason."

He was certainly bold tonight. Serena's heart tripped a little faster at the recognition. Maybe he *would* ask her. She hoped so, but who could ever be certain about such things? She sipped at her wine, working moisture into her mouth. "Is that what you're hoping to do?" she asked. "Kiss me?"

William remained smiling. "I believe we've discussed this before," he said in echo of her words. He leaned forward.

Serena's heart beat even faster. A deep desire to have him at her side filled her, to share her life with him. Uncertainty followed, a whisper from her mahavan training that these feelings were a measure of weakness, that *she* was weak. Her legs tensed, and the fear-fueled need to run from him swept through her like a ghost.

She did her best to ignore her feelings. "What's stopping you?" she challenged, hoping the forceful words would squash her swirling thoughts.

William quirked a wider grin. "If that's an offer, maybe I'll take you up on in it."

Serena shivered, faintly, but she was sure he noticed. Again came the worry of being thought weak. *What's wrong with me?*

Concern replaced William's prior good cheer. "Are you ok?"

Serena took a steadying breath and another sip of wine. "I'm fine," she said, forcing the words past the shudder in her throat. She loved William. She knew it, but a more powerful recognition was what she was considering: molding her life around his. What if he didn't intend the same? She'd make herself weak for no reason.

He regarded her in seeming speculation. "I was going to do this after we ate, but I don't think we should wait that long."

Maybe he sensed her roiling emotions and felt bad for her. Serena wanted to scowl at the notion. She required no one's pity.

Her worries faded when William placed a small box on the table, wooden and graven with an image of a man kneeling before a woman. Her heart raced faster. Her thoughts spun between hope and terror. She didn't know why her emotions surged so powerfully, why she wanted to cry.

William opened the box, and within it nestled what she'd hoped to see: a gold ring topped by a large diamond. Platinum millwork edged the band. He took her hands in his, and a silly thought stole over her. *At least my palms are dry.*

"Serena Paradiso, will you marry me?"

She didn't answer at once. The mahavan in her didn't trust him, even now. Instead, she reached for her Spirit and hesitantly extended a thread of it toward William. Their Spirits touched, and a new sensation washed over Serena. She inhaled sharply. *Was it real?*

William allowed her to see what he felt, to study his emotions, never withdrawing from their shared connection. He loved her, deeply and truly, in a way words could never express.

A single tear spilled down Serena's face, and she made herself think about the distance she'd come, what she'd done in her years of living, how blessed she was to have this life and to have earned a place on Arylyn as a magus, and especially finding love. She forced herself to pause before speaking, forced herself to memorize this moment, to feel the breeze on her face, the wash of waves, the smell of the food William had prepared. Mostly she wanted to forever etch the sight of William's face glowing in the candlelight, filled with hope and yearning.

Seconds passed, and when Serena knew she'd never forget the night's image, she poured all her love and trust into a single word. "Yes."

~

"YOU DARE COME to us for more warriors?" Zane Blood asked, doing little to hide a sneer. "We've already provided you with over nine hundred. How many more do you require? And how many more will you allow to die for no reason like you did Rail?"

Break Foliage leaned forward. "Or perhaps incompetence drives your requirements. A more skilled commander could make do with those warriors we've already given over to you."

Rukh bit back an oath. Break and Zane deserved to have their noses flattened, but he had to maintain his composure. Today's meeting with the Village Council was simply another kind of battle, and in battle, anger earned little for a wise warrior. In addition, military leadership answered to civilian authority, a necessary facet for a civilized people.

But it didn't mean Rukh had to enjoy speaking to conniving politicians, wasting his time in trying to convince them on how best to save their people. Rukh stood at the podium, forcing his gaze away from Zane and Break, flicking it amongst the other councilors. Their membership remained unchanged, with several of them, including Mayor Care, successfully winning re-election recently. In contrast, the thorns in Rukh's side—Break and Zane—wouldn't face re-election for another three months. He wished it was in three days. He never wanted to ever again have to deal with the fragging rats.

Lucas Shaw might have felt the same way. The patrician magus stiffened at Break's words. "You go too far," he said in his refined accent. "Point one, Rukh has never demonstrated incompetence. Point two, without his insistence, many more thousands of our people would have died in Sinskrill's attack. Point three, when invading a fortified position, it's generally best to have a three-to-one advantage. Even more if possible. To deny him what he needs is to deny him a chance at victory."

Rukh hid a smile at Lucas' supportive words. If he'd actually displayed his pleasure, Break and Zane would have rightfully taken it as a disrespectful sign aimed in their direction. Rukh mentally snorted, wondering how those two cretins could be so blind to the contempt in which the rest of the island held them.

Break or Zane—it didn't matter who—squawked something unimportant.

"Point four," Bar Duba rumbled, taking up Lucas' count and addressing Break and Zane. "The two of you will face re-election in a few months. You won't win, which is what you deserve. Everyone knows your positions almost led our people to catastrophe. I, for one, will be glad when I no longer have to put up with your idiocy."

Mayor Care rapped a gavel. "I will not have personal insults flung at our fellow councilors," she said to Bar. She gathered Zane and Break in her gaze. "Nor will *you* insult those who address the Council."

Break spoke. "But he is incompe—"

Bar cut him off. "You're a fool! Shut up when your betters speak."

Mayor Care hammered her gavel, but it was too late. The Council broke into bickering.

Rukh sighed. He didn't know how long the Council meeting would last, so he distracted himself by studying a recently painted mural on the wall behind the councilors, a scene of Lilith unspoiled: the vibrancy of the waterfalls, rainbows, and bridges; the green foliage, flowers, and sun at noon. Other than the lovely image, the chamber remained dull and uninspiring, a polar opposite to the glorious beauty of the rest of the island and village. Or at least as the village had once been. Thankfully, it was regaining its lost luster.

It took several minutes for Mayor Care to get the councilors to quiet down.

"You must think us foolish," Seema Choudary said during a moment of relative calm.

Rukh realized the small magus was speaking to him. "Only some," he said, making sure not to make eye contact with Break and Zane. If he did, it would set them to squawking again. They still glowered at him anyway, and his forbearance for them frayed. He rolled his eyes, not caring if they saw. He had better things to do. "I need another two hundred warriors to have a proper reserve force. Sinskrill will have at most six hundred mahavans, but of those I'd bet only two hundred will be effective combatants. The other four hundred have only recently started training in the use of their *lorethasra.*"

"What about the woven?" Seema asked, leaning forward. "William's report indicates there's at least one hundred and fifty unformed, and that doesn't even include the demon or anything else they've managed to scrounge up. Even if there are only two hundred effective mahavans, that gives the Servitor three hundred and fifty warriors. Will eleven hundred be enough?"

"It will have to be," Rukh said. "We don't have time to train any more, and I'm not sure how many more of our people we can divert away from the island's other needs. Plus, the woven aren't soldiers. They don't fight with discipline. They're savages, and each one is lesser than our individual magi. As for the demon . . ." He shrugged. "We have no knowledge of what it brings to the table."

Bar cleared his throat. "You mentioned that you plan on transporting cannons. How?"

"There is an old text, *Treatises on Travel*. It describes how to tether objects to an anchor line. We've mastered the required weaves. We'll have the cannons mounted on wagons drawn by horses or bullocks."

Seema settled into her chair. "As you say. You've not led us astray thus far."

"Perhaps not, but we suffered grievous losses under his command," Zane said, smooth and oily now. His chastisement at Bar and Lucas' hands must have broken through his thick skull. He no longer spoke so contemptuously to Rukh.

"And those who died should merit our concern, especially if we are expected to expose more of our people to the possibility of injury and death," Break said in a grating tone, unable to match Zane's slickness.

Rukh's patience snapped. "I was at the funerals of nearly everyone who died," he said. "I saw Bar, Seema, Lucas, and Mayor Care at every one of them. I didn't see either of you two." Zane and Break bristled, but Rukh spoke over them. He'd had enough of their short-sighted stupidity, their *politics*. Cowards and jackholes, the both of them. "I know who died, who they were, who they loved, and who they left behind. There will be more. War always takes the heart of us, but this is a war we must fight or we'll all die!" He slammed his hand on the podium. The marble top cracked.

The Council started, frozen into silence, and Rukh realized they were frightened by his angry display. He took a calming breath.

Mayor Care spoke into the silence. "You'll have your two hundred warriors."

"We haven't voted yet," Break complained.

Bar smirked. "You and Zane will vote against Rukh's proposal, and the rest of us will take the rational road and vote for it. It's a formality, and you know it."

"Motion to vote upon Rukh's proposal," Lucas said.

"Second," Seema said.

The vote went exactly as Bar said it would.

~

ONCE A WEEK ADAM took report from an unformed, getting a sense as to the state of the various tribes. He needed to know what they'd seen and heard of the happenings throughout the island. He also needed to know if they'd noticed Sapient Dormant acting in an untoward fashion. Adam didn't trust the necrosed, especially after the Servitor had so savagely humbled the monster. It had to stick in the Over-ward's craw, infuriating him, but so far, Sapient had persisted in his quiet attitude.

Today was a day for one such meeting, which was to take place at a cliff near the Servitor's Palace. It was distant enough to offer privacy from prying eyes but not so far as to require a long journey. A mid-morning sun shone through a split in the clouds, blooming light but not warmth upon Sinskrill. A chill breeze blew. Upon it floated a briny aroma, a mix of sea and fish rising to the cliff's summit.

Adam formed a block of Air as soon as he came in sight of the unformed creature. The woven held the shape of a stallion but transi-tioned into the form a naked, middle-aged man when Adam arrived at their meeting place. This unformed was new to him. Adam had never seen him before. Generally the ones he met for his reports were young. This one was mature, powerful. Adam eyed the creature in challenge, wondering why an elder had come this time.

The woven stared back at him with unblinking eyes, but after a moment he broke eye contact and dipped his head, the shallow nod of a subordinate. "I am called Prime Ash Dockles. I am at your bidding."

Adam kept his eyes from widening in surprise. *A Prime to deliver the week's report? Unusual.* He next noticed the packs resting at the woven's feet. This time he didn't bother to control his reaction. His brow creased in consideration. They weren't of Sinskrill make.

"We found this gear within Castle Bliss," Ash said.

Adam stroked his beard. He understood the importance of the items. If they weren't from Sinskrill, it meant they were from Arylyn.

The magi had entered Sinskrill . . . unless these packs were from their last excursion upon the island. It was possible, but unlikely. Bliss' Prime wouldn't have hoarded the packs in his study and told no one of his discovery. He would have spoken of them long ago.

Privately, Adam hoped it *was* the magi. If they invaded, they'd overwhelm Sinskrill. The newly raised mahavans weren't worth their name. The island would fall, but perhaps something could still be salvaged from defeat. Perhaps the World Killers had a means to stop Shet. And maybe they wouldn't slaughter the mahavans to the last man, woman, and child after carrying out their mission. From what Adam had deduced about them, such an action wasn't in their natures.

"We also found a dead human," Ash added. From one of the packs he withdrew a head, tossing it on the ground. It had been roughly decapitated and desiccated until the flesh took on the skull's shape.

Adam peered more closely, unsure what could have happened to cause the head to decompose like this. He squatted, studying more intently, trying to make sense of what he was seeing. Features came clear. The head had belonged to a man, one with dark hair and a long nose, someone Adam didn't recognize.

Adam inhaled sharply. A magus. They *had* been here. His thoughts raced, partly in trepidation and partly in excitement. "Did you kill him?" he asked the Prime.

"We did not," Ash said. "We know the penalty for killing a mahavan."

A suspicion rose in Adam's mind. "How can you tell it's not an unformed killed while in human form?"

Ash seemed to ponder the possibility. "I can't," he answered after a few seconds.

"Neither can I," Adam said, although he doubted the likelihood. He stood silent and traced the possibilities. "What was his condition when you found him?"

"His head is as you see it, as was the rest of him. Withered, as if all the water in his body was wrung out."

Adam shook his head, still unable to fathom what had happened to the man. Nothing natural could have caused this dried out state. "Where did you find him?"

"His body lay on a field east of Bliss' castle, near the docks. It was rent as if by great claws."

Adam paused. *Damn it.* He now understood what had happened to the magus. "Four claws? Was his body rent by four claws?"

Ash nodded.

Adam cursed. The decayed body, withered . . . Only one being could do this. The legends spoke of what happened to the body of a woven or *asrasin* when killed by a necrosed. They were drained of all fluid, left as mere husks.

Sapient Dormant.

The necrosed had killed the unknown magus, which meant he'd also stolen the *lorethasra* of a likely powerful *asrasin*. Who knew what Sapient could do with it? How powerful could he become?

"Return to your tribe," Adam said to Ash. "Redouble the watch on the necrosed. I want to know everything he does, and especially his appearance. Has it changed? Does he strike you as less decayed?"

"You think the Overward killed this one?" Ash asked, pointing to the head.

Adam shot him a sharp gaze. "It is none of your concern what I think," he said. "Do as I command. That is your only mission."

Ash bowed at the waist. "As you will." He straightened, blurring into the form of an eagle, and flew north.

Adam absently nudged the head with a booted foot, and glared at the packs. Axel would be furious about the intrusion and Sapient's killing of a magus. Adam didn't look forward to relaying the information.

20

UNEXPECTED REUNIONS

J *uly 1991*

BY FORCE OF HABIT, Landon Vent pushed his senses as wide as he could while he and Elaina walked through the quiet forest surrounding Sand. They had the forest trail to themselves, but caution wouldn't allow him to let down his guard. The battle against the unformed from a year ago remained fresh in his mind. Many Wrin had died in the conflict, many close friends, and although the unformed no longer lurked around Sand's border, Landon remained wary.

The evergreen trees, verdant and bright in the late afternoon sunshine, towered above and all around them like the pillars of a temple. The humid warmth of the summer air, damp and heavy, mixed with the scent of sap.

Landon stepped carefully along a pencil-thin forest trail, listening carefully to the world around him. He caught the scrabble of claws on fallen leaves and pine needles as a small animal ran away from his approach. Birds trilled from close by, likely thrush. He also heard Elaina's soft footfalls, the stutter of her limp marring her once graceful gait. Landon tried not to notice it. She had her dark hair pulled back in a ponytail, and the sun lit her dusky skin, her pretty features, and revealed the faint freckles on her nose.

The two of them walked hand-in-hand, and her long dress swayed with every step she took. She stumbled on the uneven ground, and he steadied her. She smiled "thanks," her dark eyes crinkling. The battle against the unformed had cost Elaina dearly, and while she'd come far she had a much longer way to go until she was fully recovered.

Concern for her was why a sword remained sheathed at Landon's waist, and why his hand remained on its hilt. *Undefiled Locus* was the blade's name, or at least that was what the necrosed had called it, right before Landon and Aia had killed the creature. Maybe it had some deadly properties. The fragmented memories of the holder he'd once been, Pilot Vent, said it was the case, but if true, Landon hadn't discovered them. For him, *Undefiled Locus* was nothing more than a simple sword, one he could wield, and that only competently.

"Granny Castor is expecting us for dinner tonight," Elaina said, interrupting his reverie.

Landon held back a sour expression. He and Elaina's grandmother had come to an agreement, but Granny Castor had yet to forgive him for what they both knew he had to do. He had to leave Elaina, and he might never make it back.

"What's wrong?" Elaina asked, picking up on his unhappiness.

Landon didn't want to tell her. He dreaded her reaction. His tension increased, and despite the peaceful forest around them, the sense of calm amongst the trees, he found himself unable to hold still. He twitched at every sound, every unexpected scent.

"You have to leave," Elaina said, somehow guessing what he had to do. He should have known. She had ways of learning things. Maybe it was part of her Wrin gifts.

"It won't be forever," Landon said. "It shouldn't be. I hope not." He spoke quickly. "William . . . I feel his call." He remembered his brother more clearly now, not in the dim fashion he once had, and his memories all spoke of love. William needed him, and Landon would always answer the call of blood.

Elaina placed a hand over his, the one resting on *Undefiled Locus*. She brought them to a halt. "I always knew this would happen. You told me."

Landon regarded her in surprise. *When did I tell her? Or did she learn it on her own?*

Elaina took in his features and laughed, low, throaty, and knowing. "I knew when you would arrive in Sand, and I've known for several months that you would have to leave."

Landon realized his eyebrows had risen in further surprise. "I didn't know you had the gift of prophecy."

She gave him a crooked grin, the one he loved. "I don't, but knowing when you'd come was something that echoed in Sand's *lorasra*. It told me a mighty warrior, a being of blood and bone, would protect Sand's fields. That's how I knew of your arrival."

Landon blinked. "A being of blood and bone," he repeated. "That sounds . . ." He searched for the right word. "Ominous. Is that why Granny Castor doesn't like me?"

Again came the low, throaty chuckle. "She doesn't like you because you stole her only granddaughter's heart. You know that. But the being of blood and bone part meant that you could fight in ways that we cannot."

Landon accepted her words with a shrug. "How did you know I had to leave?"

"You've been restless ever since Aia and Shon left. It's only gotten worse since the winter, when you learned about William's worries regarding Arylyn. It didn't take prophecy to tell me why. And I also understand why you have to go. Your brother needs you. I accept that."

Landon breathed out in relief, glad that Elaina understood what he had to do. "I'm a lucky man."

"We're both lucky," Elaina said. With that, they continued walking.

"I wonder how William's doing," Landon mused a short while later. "He's an *asrasin* by now."

Elaina seemed to withdraw into herself, wary and worried, and Landon wanted to kick himself. While the Wrin had been created by the *asrasins*, they didn't trust their creators. They never had.

Elaina shook off her reticence. "I'm sure he's doing well," she said. "Other than whatever he's involved in that requires the power of a holder."

They continued through the forest, and as they walked, a new recollection came to Landon. "Aia and Shon always used to talk about how powerful their humans were, Rukh and Jessira." He chuckled dryly. "You'd think they were the greatest warriors ever born the way those two talked about them."

Elaina graced him with a teasing grin. "Are you worried you won't measure up?"

Landon managed a tight smile. He *was* worried, but not in the way Elaina meant. Aia and Shon were powerful. They'd been instrumental in beating back the unformed.

"What's the real reason you're worried?" Elaina asked.

"I'm worried about what's waiting for me on Arylyn. What could possibly be so bad that William needs my help when he already has Aia and Shon?"

"And he also has the Kesarins' humans, Rukh and Jessira?"

"Exactly."

Elaina tucked her hand against his side. "I don't know, but you'll handle it like you handled the unformed. Other than the necrosed, there's nothing more dangerous."

Guilt crested within him. He'd never told her about Shet.

TRAVAIL HIKED a lonely path along an evergreen forest east of Janaki Valley. The slender animal trail he followed ascended and descended through the hills and hollows of Arylyn's higher elevations. Birds trilled, their songs filling the gaps in the forest, and the air remained cool and relatively still since the surrounding trees shuttered the gusting wind. The bright scents of pine, cedar, and aspen mingled with that of moss and loam. Vagrant sunbeams dappled parts of the canopy, but the forest floor remained cool and shaded. Dew glistened on leaves and needles, gathering as wetness on the trail.

Travail walked the path, brushing past needles and tree limbs. Every now and then he ducked his horns beneath low-lying branches, twisted his large frame when the trail constricted. All the while, his staff struck the forest floor in a regular pattern, echoing like a slow-beating heart.

Travail loved it here, the coolness of the weather.

While humans were enchanted by Arylyn's tropical beauty, he found the warmth distressing. With his thick fur, it was simply too hot for him on most parts of the island.

Travail paused when he crested a rise and reached a break in the trees. Through a gap in the canopy, he glimpsed the majesty of Mount Madhava. The island's largest peak ascended in a series of rocky rises, green forest along the base giving way to gray granite and eventually to a white-capped peak made of ice and snow.

Travail pondered the mountain. As a troll, he enjoyed solitude and cool elevations, but he'd yet to climb Mount Madhava. Perhaps today would be a good day to correct that oversight. His decision made, he set off for the mountain.

Several hours later, he heard footsteps resounding on the trail ahead of him, not the padded movements of an animal but the sound of boots striking the ground. Once more Travail paused, searching out with his senses, wondering why a human was out here in this backcountry. By the timing and loudness of the boot strikes, he reckoned the person was a man.

And he approached.

Travail waited at a dip in the path, relaxed in a sun-dappled hollow. He rested his staff against his shoulder, curious about the person coming his way. All the humans resided in Lilith or Janaki Valley, and sometimes a few had to take the rugged trails leading to the northern watchtowers during their martial work, but none ever came this way. It was one of the main reasons Travail was here to begin with: for the solitude.

An itch began in the forefront of his mind, something he'd never before experienced. The desire to meet the man coming toward him rushed over Travail, a pull like gravity. He'd never experienced that, either. He gritted his teeth against the calling, keeping his feet planted in place, unsure what was going on.

A few minutes later, a man crested the hill overlooking the hollow.

The sensation to meet him abated, replaced by startlement. The man resembled a tall, leaner version of William, with the same dark skin and hair and similar features. Older, though.

"Hello," the man said with a grin. "My, but you're a tall one. I'm Landon."

"Or you're a short one," Travail said, instantly warming to the man. He even sounded like William. "I'm Travail." His nose twitched in curiosity. "You remind me of a friend. William Wilde."

The man's grin broadened. "It's why I'm here. He's my brother. You wouldn't happen to know his whereabouts, would you?"

"Landon Vent?"

"That's me," the man said, still smiling.

A ripple of joy caused Travail to grin. *Wait until I tell William. He'll be so happy.*

"Can you take me to him? I'm a bit lost."

Travail didn't answer at once. Other understandings clicked in his mind, and he grew distracted. He recognized now the earlier sensation he'd felt, the itch in his mind, the desire to rush forward and greet the man. Landon was a holder, which explained Travail's response to him. Travail recalled a story told by his mother when he was young, about the reaction many trolls had when they came in contact with holders, the immediate warmth and trust.

Another question arose in his mind. How had Landon arrived on Arylyn? The anchor lines were far away at Linchpin Knoll. Maybe he reached the island the same way that Aia and Shon had? Some place near Mount Madhava?

Landon tilted his head to the side as if in thought. "You're awfully quiet."

"I'm thinking."

"You're a troll, right? Y'all do a lot of thinking."

Travail nodded, dipping his horns while still struggling to come to grips with the unexpected arrival of William's brother. "Pardon me, but how did you come to Arylyn?"

"I took the anchor line from Sand, same as Aia and Shon. How are they, by the way?"

"They're doing well. Grown tremendously since coming to Arylyn."

"Really?" Landon sounded both surprised and happy. "Aia always used to say she was a tiny kitten."

"She and Shon are both almost my height now," Travail said.

Landon barked laughter. "Well how about that?" He shook his head in apparent rueful disbelief. "About William?" he reminded Travail.

Travail disregarded the question. Caution reared its head. "When Aia and Shon came from Sand by anchor line, they ended up miles from here. Why didn't you?"

"Yeah, I get it," Landon said. "You're probably thinking I should have ended up in the same place as them." He shrugged. "The thing is, the anchor line from Sand always twists around. It never takes a body to the exact same place twice." He laughed. "Good thing it didn't dump me in the ocean, right?"

Travail chuckled, unable to hold onto his wariness. He liked Landon. "Let's go find William."

≈

You're shifting around too much, Aia heard Jessira tell Shon. *Stand still.*

Shon grumbled like an angry kitten, and Aia chided him. He really should know better.

I don't like wearing a saddle, Shon complained.

I know you don't, Jessira said in a soothing voice, *but I need you to do this for me. We need it if we're ever going to fight together again as a team.*

In spite of her words, Shon continued to shift about.

Idiot, Aia thought.

As demonstration to her little brother of how a proper Kesarin should behave, Aia remained unmoving and steady when Rukh placed a saddle on her back. Despite her best intentions, she still shuddered when Rukh tightened the saddle's cinches. She didn't like wearing anything other than her fur any more than Shon. She only allowed the riding accouterments because it kept Rukh on her back when they fought together, something they hadn't done during their entire time on Earth.

Of course, they hadn't been able to until now. Not only had they been separated, but when Aia had first come to this world she'd been reborn as a literal kitten. Only in the past few months had she and Shon regained their full Kesarin stature: seven feet tall and over twenty-five feet from nose to tail. They'd even reclaimed their speed.

Her Human cinched the last belt. *Too tight?* Rukh asked.

Aia twisted her back and bounced up and down a bit. The saddle stayed in place, not biting into her shoulders or chest. *It's fine.*

Ready? Rukh asked.

We'll find out soon enough, Aia said.

She stared down the long, gray line of Sita's Song, heart already pumping with budding excitement. They planned on riding through Janaki Valley, one of her favorite places in all of Arylyn. It would be their first ride together. The sun stood warm in the early morning sky. Mount Madhava soared, and best of all, the scent of cows and goats carried on the steadily blowing breeze. Janaki Valley always held the most wonderful aromas, and Aia licked her lips, wondering if she'd have the chance to hunt and eat during their time outside today.

Go ahead and mount, she told her human.

Rukh vaulted into the saddle, clutching her ribs with his legs and grasping the reins attached to the halter looped around her face.

Aia shook her head and rolled her shoulders, settling everything into place. She grinned, flicking her ears in anticipation. She hated the saddle, but she missed riding with Rukh even more, especially during battle. The way she clawed through their enemies, Rukh slashed and burned them, and the two of them destroyed all their foes with no one able to stand against them. *Here we go.*

She slowly paced forward, moving at a leisurely pace, letting

Rukh reacquaint himself with her motions. She accelerated into a slow trot.

Do you want to go faster? Rukh asked, a challenging note in his voice.

Aia chuckled. *I always want to go faster. Hold on!* She dashed down the road, reaching her best speed in seconds. Her muscles bunched and lengthened. The wind roared in their passage. Her eyes squinted, her ears flattened, but her vision and hearing remained intact.

Rukh whooped. *I missed this!* he shouted in her mind, sounding joyful. He leaned low, head pressed near her shoulder.

In anyone else, she would have found the presence of teeth near her neck unsettling, but this was Rukh, her Human.

Aia slowed down after a half-mile, growing winded, and easing to a halt. She breathed hard, gulping deep lungfuls of air. With a rueful shudder, she realized she was out of shape. *That won't do.* She'd have to run more often, regain her stamina.

While she recovered her breath, she and Rukh waited on Jessira and Shon. They watched for them, and her brother must have finally decided to co-operate with his Human because here they came, rushing forward like a diving hawk.

Aia was pleased to see her brother also blowing hard when he pulled up next to her and Rukh. *You're out of shape,* she said to him.

Shon growled, flashing his teeth in annoyance. Jessira patted his shoulder.

Aia felt bad about teasing her brother, and she rubbed the corner of her mouth against his head. *We both are. We need to run like Kesarins are meant to.*

Shon rumbled agreement, mollified.

Rukh rubbed her neck and chuckled. *You'll get back to who you once were,* he said. *You've already got your size, strength, and speed back. Stamina should come easily.*

Jessira laughed. *Do you remember when we ran across the Hunters Flats?*

Yes, Rukh said, finishing her thought in that way they could.

And Li-Choke actually thought he could keep up with us since Aia and Shon were carrying us.

Aia grinned at the memory. She missed Li-Choke. The noble Bael had been her friend, the best of his kind.

Shon had recovered his breath, and Aia was ready to go. *Are you ready to run some more?* Aia asked her brother.

I was born to run some more, he replied in a pompous tone.

Aia laughed at him. *Then follow and keep the pace.*

She took off, and Shon raced after her. Jessira whooped. So did Rukh.

Aia grinned at her Human's delight. She liked making him happy. Even more, she liked when he made her happy. He would *have* to let her hunt a succulent cow or goat after this. And later on she'd expect a proper chin rub.

She ran on, down Sita's Song, over smooth stones that begged her to go faster, past farms and farmers and their delicious livestock. One especially tasty-looking goat caught Aia's attention, plump and juicy. Her mouth watered.

An instant later she felt a presence in her mind. Someone she hadn't seen in months. Shon felt it too, and he shouted to her in joy. They skidded to a stop, excited to share what they sensed.

Her excitement crashed when she heard Rukh cry out in surprise. He flew over her head, his shout trailing. He'd been unprepared for her lurching halt. Aia expected him to slam into the ground, but her Human surprised her. Rukh used his Talents and landed smoothly. Aia smugly noticed that Jessira wasn't quite as agile. She'd also been hurled over her Kesarin's head and landed on her feet, but she had to take a single step backward in order to maintain her balance.

Aia winced when Rukh glared at her and Shon. Her head drooped, and her ears flattened.

What was that about? Rukh demanded.

Aia's excitement recovered, and her ears perked. *Landon's here. On Arylyn*

∿

WILLIAM HEADED BACK TO LILITH, finishing his regular morning run along the base of a gully that cut through a stretch of hills east of the village. He'd already covered five miles and lifted logs up and down a hill, but he still had the stamina to sprint the last two hundred yards. He breathed steady the whole time, like Travail had taught, deep breaths in, deep breaths out. The dark shade along the long ravine kept him cool, but sweat still beaded on his face, soaking his shirt in the front and back.

On he sprinted, exploding out of shadow and into sunlight, slowing down when the dirt trail became a gravel track. Only a half-mile and he'd be back at Clifftop, where Serena, Jake, and the other lieutenants had training duty with the Irregulars this morning. William would take over for the afternoon session.

He slowed further, walking now, and had time to appreciate the beauty around him. The path followed the edge of a cliff, and, to his left a sheer drop-off plunged hundreds of feet to the Pacific. Even at this elevation, he could hear the pounding waves, a low rumble. The surf splashed skyward, spreading into hazy droplets that formed a rainbow dappling the cliff face.

William smiled at the lovely sight. He never got tired of Arylyn's beauty. Part of him wished he and Serena could get married here, but if they did Selene wouldn't be able to attend, which was unacceptable. She had to be there. He also wished his own family could have attended his wedding, but wishes like that were fruitless.

A few minutes later he reached Linchpin Knoll and noticed Travail seated on a boulder, his massive staff resting across his knees. What more fully captured his attention, though, was the man sitting next to the troll. William couldn't immediately identify him, but a niggle of recognition wormed its way up the back of his mind.

The man was tall and rangy, a nervous air to his posture. His clothes—a sturdy camouflage jacket and pants—weren't typical for the people of Arylyn. However, he possessed the dark hair and skin of someone native-born to the island. More features became apparent, and William's eyes widened. His heart gave a lurch of trembling hope.

Landon? How? Please, let it be him.

William missed his brother terribly, missed talking to him, hearing his thoughts, learning from him, having his wisdom and protection . . . all the things meant when someone said 'big brother.' Maybe Landon finally remembered his family. He hadn't the last time they'd met. Maybe that's why he was here now.

William prayed it was the case.

Landon and Travail spoke briefly to one another before stepping away from the boulder. They walked forward, Landon grinning the entire time. William's eyes watered. It was Landon's lazy smile, his brother's gait, his mannerisms. He found himself grinning in response, walking faster.

"Landon?" William said, hoping against hope that his brother knew him.

"Hey, boy," Landon said, using the nickname only he was allowed to use.

William's eyes watered further. When he reached Landon, his arms went out to hug his brother. He was even more overjoyed when his brother hugged him back. *He knows me*, he thought, but he needed to be sure. "You know who I am?"

Landon still held his easy grin. "Of course I do. You're my little brother. The boy." He put his hand behind William's neck and gave him a light clap to the side of his head, just like he always used to. "I understand why you're thinking I wouldn't know you, and I admit, I still don't know some of the things that are important, but I know enough."

William felt a sense of unreality. He'd dreamt of this moment for so long, never daring to let himself believe it might actually happen. "When did you get your memories back? What have you been doing all this time?" The questions tumbled out of his mouth.

"Aia and Shon didn't tell you? I'm gonna have to pinch those two rascals."

Some of William's excitement faded. Landon's smile and many of his mannerisms were the same, but Landon had never spoken like this, like someone from a Western.

"I know what you're thinking, about the way I talk," Landon said, apparently noticing William's hesitation. "You gotta remember, I'm your brother but I'm also Pilot Vent, the holder who became Kohl Obsidian. Pilot was born and raised in the eighteen hundreds. It's why I sometimes talk odd."

William's worry faded. He didn't care how Landon spoke. It was enough to simply see his big brother again. "Aia and Shon told us you had to fight some unformed in a village called Sand. They also mentioned a woman there, Elaina Sinith. I met her once."

Landon nodded, the grin back. "Yep. She mentioned it, too. She was right worried about you when you were in that circus."

William laughed. "*I* was right worried about me. Necrosed and all that."

"Well, that about gets you up to speed on what I've been up to," Landon said. "How about you? You aren't so little any more, boy." He stepped back, viewing William up and down before shaking his head. "You got yourself all muscled up and strong."

"He's also faster than anyone other than Rukh," Travail rumbled in his deep voice.

"Really?" Landon shot him an apprising regard. "Maybe we'll have to have a race before I leave. I'm a holder, remember?"

"You could still lose," Travail said. "William has the blood of a necrosed."

Landon frowned. "Then how's this Rukh fella faster than you?"

"That's a long story," William said.

Landon shrugged. "Maybe Rukh will tell it to me one of these days. For now, I guess I should find out why I'm here."

"What do you mean?" William asked. He thought his brother had come to Arylyn to visit him. Landon made it sound like it was for another reason.

"I told you I'm a mix of Pilot and Landon." Landon leaned in close, whispering as if relaying a secret. "But just between the three of us here neighbors, I'm more Landon than Pilot."

William had a million questions about that, but he didn't have a chance to ask them.

Landon spoke on. "Anyway, the Pilot part of me felt a disturbance that said I needed to come here." He grinned again. "I felt a disturbance in the Force. Isn't that what you used to say, boy? You and your dork friends?"

William grinned at his brother, not caring about the crack about dorks. His big brother was back.

"Y'all gonna tell me why you need a holder?" Landon asked.

William answered. "We've got trouble coming."

"What kind of trouble?"

"I'll give you the condensed version." William didn't know exactly where to start, so he started at the part when he was kidnapped to Sinskrill.

Landon's easy grin fell away long prior to the point when William reached his story's end. "You've been through it, haven't you, boy?" Landon's mouth tightened with unhappiness. "I'm sorry I couldn't have helped you in all that, but I'm here to help you now."

"Come with me to Lilith," William urged. "The others—you remember Jason, Jake, and Lien—they'd be thrilled to see you."

Landon laughed. "I still can't believe that you're best buds with Jake Ridley. The two of you used to go at it like two cats fighting over fish."

"You'll come?" William asked.

Landon shook his head. "I'd love to, but this was always meant to be a short visit. Maybe next time."

Disappointment crushed William. Talking to his brother for only a few hours wasn't enough. He wanted more. A week wouldn't have sufficed.

"Come to my wedding, then," William blurted, and told Landon of his engagement to Serena.

"You're getting married?" Landon asked as if in disbelief. "Mom and Dad would have loved that."

"Will Elaina be able to come?"

Landon's face darkened. "About that. Likely not. She's got a powerful distrust of *asrasins*. All her kind do."

"But you'll be there?" William pressed Landon.

"Course I will. I said I would, didn't I?"

Landon! Landon! a pair of excited voices shouted.

"That would be Aia and Shon," Travail said, obviously picking up on the calls of the Kesarins as well. "Perhaps now you'll believe me when I tell you they're almost as tall as I."

Moments later, Aia and Shon sprinted around a corner.

"Good gracious, they are big," Landon said, his voice awestruck.

William did a double-take when he saw Rukh and Jessira riding the Kesarins. "Big enough to carry passengers, apparently."

Landon whistled. "Well, look at that."

William tugged his brother forward. "Come on. Let me introduce you to Rukh and Jessira."

21

A WEDDING AND REUNION

J *uly 1991*

JASON REMOVED a small plant from its pot and set it in the hole he'd dug. Next, he refilled the hole, careful not to stuff the dirt down too hard. He'd done that the first time, and Jessira had gently corrected him. But gently from her felt like Rukh shouting. Jessira had always been kind to him, but for whatever reason he'd always found her intimidating. Truth was he still did. He gave the plant a drink of water and was done.

On to the next hole. He shuffled on his knees a few feet over, not bothering to stand or take a break. He had no idea what kind of flowers or bushes he was planting. Greenery wasn't his thing, but he was happy enough to help out. Getting the landscaping done right was one of the final touches needed to get William and Serena's wedding venue finished.

They'd chosen the *saha'asra* in West Virginia for the location, reckoning it was the only place where Selene could also attend the wedding, which was important to both of them. They also wanted privacy, and Mr. Zeus had taken care of that. He'd created a small braid that convinced any folk staying in the surrounding cabins to go visit family for the weekend.

Jason finished planting another flower, and after this one he stretched his back, lifting his face to the morning sun that beamed from the midst of a blue sky untroubled by clouds. No breeze blew but that was fine. The day was comfortable, warm but not muggy and oppressive like summers could be.

He glanced around. Lien and Serena worked a few feet away, the two of them painting a small wedding arch. The girls laughed about something, and Jason watched them for a few more seconds. Lien had changed a lot since Sinskrill's attack. She'd always been blunt as a hammer, and if she didn't want to do something she wouldn't and she'd tell you why it was dumb. Now she was more mellow, more understanding and less quick to anger. Gentler really.

Jason figured that death and loss must change a person. It had certainly changed him. Or maybe Mink had. He didn't know, but it also didn't matter. He liked himself better now. He was happy, but he hated that people had to die for him to come out of his shell.

He gave his back another stretch, trying to work out the cramps. He'd been bent over for an hour now, planting things, and he couldn't wait to be done with it. He hated gardening, farming, anything to do with growing things. He perked up when Lien spoke to Serena, words he was glad to hear.

"I can take care of the rest of this if you want to help Jason," Lien said.

Jason viewed the two women in rising hope. Another pair of hands would make the planting go twice as fast.

"You sure?" Serena asked Lien.

"I'm fine. We're almost done anyway," Lien said.

Jessira and Julius stepped out of a log cabin right then, the same one Jason and the others had stayed in before all this mess started. Rukh worked on the home's front porch, replacing some rotten spindles in the railing.

"Thanks for helping me with the kitchen sink," Julius said to Jessira.

"You're more than welcome," Jessira said. "I only wish I could stay and help some more, but I need to help with the Irregulars." She said her goodbyes to everyone. An instant later she linked to the anchor line, tethering to it and striding onto the rainbow bridge in that martial yet feminine way she had. Her hips swayed.

"Stop staring," Serena said, plopping down next to him. She took one of the hand hoes and started digging a hole.

"It's hard not to," Jason said. "She's got this weird way of being scary and pretty at the same time. It's kind of, I don't know, fascinating, I guess."

Serena grinned. "William says the same thing."

Jason got back to digging a hole. "You think Rukh is scared of her like the rest of us?"

"If he's smart, he would be."

Jason noticed that Julius had gone to help Lien with the arch. His eyes narrowed in speculation while he watched them. He'd seen this before with the two of them, how they worked well together, whether it was fixing up Lien's old townhouse or helping with other things. He gestured at them with his chin. "What do you think is going on there?"

Serena paused, her eyes briefly skimming where he indicated, and resumed her work. "Nothing. They're friends. That's it."

"How do you know?"

"Because Lien said so. Now leave it alone. It's none of your business."

Jason continued to eye Lien and Julius. They shared a laugh, and his heart lifted. He hoped it meant something more than Serena's brusque "Nothing." He wanted to see his friends happy. "I think they get along well. You know what I mean?" He waggled his eyebrows suggestively.

Serena sighed in disgust. "You *are* a gossip."

"That's not true. I just want to help people figure—"

"I think you should let them figure it out on their own," Serena said. "If there was anything to figure out, which there isn't."

Jason thrust a finger in the air in triumph. "Which means you think there's something to figure out."

Serena rolled her eyes. "I literally just said the opposite of that." She elbowed him in the ribs. "And I came here to help you with the plantings, not gossip. Let's get back to work."

Jason furtively rubbed his ribs. She'd elbowed him hard.

"What's William doing while we're stuck out here with all this work?" he asked.

"Running the Irregulars," Serena said. "Now more work, less talk." She pointed to Jake and Daniella, who planted flowers on the other side of the arch. "They're almost done with their section."

Jason grinned. "At least you can't complain when I say those two make a good pair."

Serena seemed to stare at Jake and Daniella in contemplation, wearing a faraway, unreadable smile. "No. I can't complain about that."

"What's with the smile?" Jason asked.

"I guess I'm happy to see them happy. I hurt Jake. I worried for him. It's good that he found Daniella."

"Well, that's how I feel," Jason said with a measure of challenge in his tone. "I only want my friends to be happy."

Serena gave him a sly grin. "You mean like you are with Mink. We've all noticed how she brings out the best in you."

Jason had no response, and he felt his face redden. He didn't know what it was, but while he loved gossiping about everyone else —in the privacy of his thoughts, he readily admitted he *was* a gossip —he didn't like people gossiping about him.

Serena chuckled at his lack of response.

～

SELENE SAT between Mr. and Mrs. Ridley at Serena and William's wedding. They were bracketed by John and Elliot. About twenty other people were in attendance, give or take a few, and they sat on rows of white chairs angled along on both sides of an aisle that ended at a white arch decorated with pink and purple flowers. Selene didn't

know what kind of blossoms they were. Serena was the horticultur-
alist in the family.

Of greater importance to Selene was that she had a chance to
speak to the people who mattered the most in her life: Serena,
William, Jake, Jason, Mr. Zeus, her grandmother . . . A few others. She
missed them terribly. She missed Arylyn. It might be months or
longer before she saw them again.

Grief threatened to drown her, and she struggled to shut it down.
It was hard, and she tried to distract herself by glancing around. The
last time she'd been to this *saha'asra* it had been winter, when everything looked glum and gross. Spring had thawed and enlivened the
place with new growth and green leaves, and summer maintained
and deepened the colors. Someone had even planted fresh flowers
and shrubs.

Selene wished she could have helped with that. She wished she
could have done something—anything—to make Serena's big day
every bit as special as her sister deserved.

But she couldn't. She lacked *lorethasra*. Her own father had
burned it out of her. She could already feel the pain of being here,
seated within the *saha'asra*. It began as a dull ache in her stomach. In
a few more hours she'd have a pounding headache.

Selene viewed Elliot askance, wondering if he was having the
same problem. He likely was, but he wouldn't care. He was overjoyed
at spending time with his parents again. He hadn't seen them in
many months. They'd never been able to visit him in the Far Beyond.
They were magi who could only take a few hours in the rest of the
world. Any longer, and they'd die. *Nomasras* didn't help them like
they did other *asrasins*.

Selene tried to shake off her morbid thoughts. She reminded
herself that today was Serena's wedding. It was a day to celebrate, and
she could tolerate a little stomach-ache to see her sister happy.

Mr. Ridley leaned over. "How are you doing, Tiny?" he whispered.

"I'm doing all right," she said.

"We managed to snag one of the cabins for tonight. It's outside
the *saha'asra*, so you'll be fine. You'll get to see your friends and family
even after the wedding."

Selene grinned.

"Shh," Mrs. Ridley said. "It's about to start." She gasped. "Look at him."

She'd never seen a troll before, and she and Mr. Ridley sat in shocked silence as Travail slowly paced down the aisle, turning about when he reached the arch. He still only wore his leather loincloth, but at least he'd polished his horns. Their charcoal color had a luster Selene had never seen on them before.

Next came Mr. Zeus and Fiona. They halted on either side of the arch.

Selene's lips tightened. They looked so much older than she recalled, especially Mr. Zeus. The two of them had also lost a lot of weight. Everyone had. No surprise there. They were probably consumed with worry about how to stop her stupid father and Lord DumbShet.

Selene's gaze went to Elliot and his parents, who were Irregulars. They'd be part of the force that invaded Sinskrill, and she worried for them. Would they make it back? Would he see them again? Maybe this would be the last time the three of them saw one another.

Her eyes darted about as she realized the enormity of what her friends and family intended. Panic threatened. Her breathing became shallow. Her flittering gaze centered on Rukh. She liked him and Jessira. They were like a favorite uncle and auntie, and when Rukh smiled at her, her fear receded. His entire demeanor conveyed the promise that everything would be fine, that today was a good day, a day of celebration.

He winked, and the last of her panic popped like a soap bubble. Selene took a deep breath, calming down. She made a vow then. While the thread of her life would be different from what she had hoped and expected, she would still find a purpose in it. She would find her own way to joy.

William and Serena began a measured walk down the aisle, and Selene set aside her worries. Today *was* a good day. She'd make sure of it, no matter what it took.

SERENA HELD William's hand as they paced down the aisle toward the wedding arch. It was a perfect summer day, warm but dry, and the sun was happily shining. Birds sang from the surrounding forest. A gentle wind rustled the leaves of the nearby trees and the oak centered within the meadow. Dew and moisture from last night's rain glimmered in the sunshine. Her friends were all here. So was her family, including Selene.

But in this moment the only person Serena cared about was William, his hand in hers, his place by her side. He was handsome in his tuxedo, blue like Arylyn's sky, with black shoes and a white shirt. He looked like he was trying to prevent a wide-open grin from stealing across his face.

Serena felt the same way. Marriage on Sinskrill was a contractual arrangement, a union meant to improve one's standing. Nothing personal. Just business. That's what she had always expected from her future husband. She never thought she'd marry her best friend and love him so fiercely she couldn't imagine life without him.

But there it was. For some reason, God graced her with a chance at happiness. She hummed "Gloria," thanking the Lord she'd always hoped to serve for giving her this day.

She caught William's questioning glance, and she smiled at him. That broke his control, and he grinned. She pressed herself closer to his side and whispered so only he could hear, "Thank you." She meant the words for both William and the One to whom she prayed.

WILLIAM HAD to let go of Serena's hand when they reached the wedding arch. He gave her a wink and let his fingers trail in hers when they separated.

She looked lovely in her wedding gown. Nothing frilly though, a simple, white dress that contrasted beautifully against her dark skin. She'd also gone without a veil, choosing instead a small garland of jasmines woven into her hair. The lush scent drifted with her every step.

Travail—the troll had been the obvious choice to officiate the wedding—gestured for them to step closer.

William couldn't stop smiling. In a few minutes, he'd be married, but before the ceremony started he took a moment to reflect on those in attendance. Jake had his arm draped across the back of Daniella's chair and wore a toothy grin. He flashed a thumbs up. Jason and Mink held hands. Selene smiled, too, but William sensed a wistfulness to her humor. Mr. Zeus stood next to him and Fiona next to Serena. Their eyes were bright with joy.

Ms. Sioned, lovely but frail, sat in the front row and blew him a kiss when he glanced her way. William noticed Landon showing up then, taking a seat at the back of the audience. He gave his brother a brief nod of acknowledgement. William's throat tightened. He wished his parents could have been here with him. He sensed Landon might have felt the same way, given the shininess in his brother's eyes and the frequency with which he blinked.

Travail cleared his throat, and William took a deep, cleansing breath. It was time for the wedding to start.

TRAVAIL FINISHED William's part of the ceremony, which was a mix of the Christian conventions in which the young man had been raised and Arylyn's own traditions. Next, he addressed Serena and indicated for her to place a ring on William's hand. Moments afterward, he got to say the words he had wanted to speak ever since he learned that two of his favorite humans were going to wed.

Travail smiled widely. "I now pronounce you wife and husband. You may share your marriage's first kiss."

He couldn't tell if it was Serena who reached for William first or the other way around, but regardless, the two of them shared a chaste kiss that quickly became much more.

Someone hooted encouragement. *Jake.* Truth to tell, Travail wanted to do the same. Pride filled him at what William and Serena had accomplished together. After all their trials, it was a wonderful thing to witness their achievement on this most joyous of days. They deserved their happiness. They'd earned it.

SERENA TOOK a break from dancing and dropped into an unoccupied chair between Jake and Jason.

"Where's William?" Jason asked.

"Dancing with Selene," Serena said. She formed a small braid of Air, fanning herself. "What about Mink and Daniella?"

Jake pointed to the wooden dance floor they'd laid out on the meadow. Mink danced with Julius while Rukh held Daniella. A four-piece band from Arylyn played a lively beat.

"Those two are going to wear a hole in the floor," Jake said.

"Who?" Serena asked. "Mink and Daniella?"

"No. Rukh and Jessira," Jason corrected. "I don't think they've stopped dancing since the music started."

Serena noticed Jessira dancing with Mr. Zeus, who blushed the entire time. She grinned at the old man's discomfort. Jessira might be as old or even older than Jason's grandfather, but she appeared far younger, was beautiful, and was also taller.

The song ended, and William and Selene came off the dance floor, both of them laughing.

"What's so funny?" Serena asked as the two of them sat down next to her. As wonderful as the day had been so far, seeing her sister again, especially seeing her joyful, made it that much more special.

William explained. "Selene was telling me about a student at St. Francis who kept going on and on about the evils of witchcraft. When she told him magic came from God, he tried to get Mr. Meron—you remember him?"

"The Vice Principal?" Serena asked.

"Yeah, anyway, he tried to get Mr. Meron to suspend Selene for promoting vice and denying virtue."

Serena failed to see the humor in the story, and she glanced from William to Selene in confusion.

Selene picked up the tale. "Mr. Meron's mother is a practicing Wiccan. He told the dude—"

Dude? When did Selene start using slang like 'dude'?

"—that he couldn't suspend me for believing something he also did, but he could suspend the dude for being a dumbass. His words." Selene cackled.

Jake and Jason, who were listening in, broke out in laughter.

"Mr. Meron," Selene wheezed. "You know how serious he is."

Her words set off a fresh course of laughter.

Serena chuckled politely, still failing to see the humor in the story. Thankfully, William saved her from her confusion by offering her a hand.

"Care to dance?" he asked.

Serena rose to her feet, grateful for the excuse to leave.

"You didn't get the joke, did you?" William asked during the short walk to the dance floor.

"I'm guessing it's one of those things where you really have to know the people in question to get it."

They stepped onto the dance floor at the same time that a song ended and a new one began. It was reminiscent of big band music, and Serena laced her fingers into William's. They swirled into a foxtrot.

Serena lost herself in the motions and movements of the dance, glad like she had never been before in her life. She found herself grinning anew.

The song ended, and the next one was a ballad. Their movements slowed to a sway, and Serena rested her head against William's shoulder. She felt his heartbeat against hers.

"Thank you," William said, whispering into her hair.

"For what?"

"For marrying me."

Serena looked into his dark eyes, wanting him to see the surety in her own, the love she held for him. "Thank you for giving me a chance to marry you."

22

FALSE DECISIONS AND LIES

J *uly 1991*

AXEL SAT upon the Servitor's Chair in the Throne Hall, waiting impatiently for his brother to arrive. As usual, dimness filled the room, the only light was the gloomy illumination from whatever meager sunshine penetrated the stained-glass windows forming the ceiling. The darkness reflected Axel's mood, the same sour sensation which ruined all hopes and dreams for the future. For over four years he'd known the truth about Shet, and in all that time he'd fought to see Sinskrill survive, guided the mahavans along the only avenue that would allow his people to endure Shet's return.

And they'd failed him. Over and over again. First with William's and Jake's escape. Then the magi raid that freed Travail and Fiona. And most recently, the failed attack on Arylyn that had accomplished some damage but not nearly enough.

Certainly not enough to impress their Lord, who would come

with anger and pitiless contempt. He'd destroy them all, destroy Axel unless the Servitor took a chance.

He'd have to lie and deceive as never before.

The doors to the Hall opened, and in marched Adam, his spine stiff, face bland, and no weakness ruining his proper mahavan bearing. Axel silently applauded his brother. If he had fifty warriors like Adam, he would have crushed Arylyn. His Secondus strode past the gold-enameled columns holding up the ceiling and halted at the base of the dais, kneeling respectfully.

"Rise," Axel said.

Adam stood. "You summoned me, my liege. What did you wish to discuss?"

Axel didn't answer at once and kept his features unreadable. Over the years of his rule, he'd allowed some measure of emotion to creep across his visage at times. It didn't matter what the other mahavans thought of him. He ruled their lives. He didn't need to hide his feelings for fear they could exploit some perceived weakness. Of course, his current predicament was one of weakness, but no one else needed to know that. "We must talk about what comes next," he eventually said.

"What comes next?" Adam asked, his confusion clear.

"You've dreamt the signal for our anchor line, and we know the magi have come to Sinskrill in order to scout our forces. They likely have a certain confidence about what they face. You also know all this is as I intended."

Hopefully, overconfidence, which I'll use to crush them.

Axel leaned forward, wanting to impress his next instructions. "Now comes the harder part. We must learn when the magi intend their invasion of our home."

"How?" Adam asked, his tone curious and respectful.

"Can you not ask Serena to dream the information to you?"

Doubt flitted across Adam's eyes. "She has little love for me or anyone from Sinskrill, and less trust. I don't believe she's likely to betray the people she's chosen as her own."

Axel reckoned the same, but it didn't hurt to ask. He contemplated what he wanted of his Secondus. *Ask Serena for a favor?* He mentally scoffed at the notion. Asking felt like begging, and Servitors didn't beg. They ruled. Nevertheless, even the hardiest oak bent before a stinging wind. "Then we must pretend to ally with the magi," he told his brother. "You must convince her we speak the truth. Only by knowing their timetables can we also plan accordingly."

Adam hesitated. "It will not be easy," he said, hedging his bets and wisely unwilling to make false promises.

Axel commended him for his reticence. *If I only had fifty like him,* he thought again with a sigh.

"What should I tell her to ease her suspicions?" Adam asked.

Axel answered with the truth, but it was a lie by omission. "It is as you have long warned me: Shet will destroy us all. We must convince them to unite our forces because separately, we shall surely fall."

"Convince them?" Skepticism tinged Adam's tone.

"Convince them that we're considering it," Axel amended. "Anything to cause them confusion. It will work."

His brother's eyes narrowed, and he wore the demeanor of a man searching how to carry out his lord's commands. He knew better than to disobey.

"I will dream to her," Adam said, "but I have little hope she will believe us."

"As long as she *does* believe you, that's all I need," Axel said. "Once the magi are upon Sinskrill, nothing else will matter."

Because once the magi are on Sinskrill, I'll pave Shet's first steps on our world with their corpses. Or set the demon upon Shet, weaken him enough for the World Killers to attack. And once my enemies have diminished themselves, I will strike.

~

SERENA SAT UP CAREFULLY, not wanting to awaken William. She replayed the dream she'd just received. As before it had come from Adam, and he'd sent it tonight of all nights, her wedding night. She wanted nothing on this most important of evenings to remind her of Sinskrill, but apparently it wasn't to be.

She slipped on a robe and padded to the room's only window. It offered a view of the West Virginia meadow where she had recently wed. She considered Adam's sending while staring into the gentle spring night. She and William shared the same cabin as when they first came to this *saha'asra*. Peace reigned over the field. Dawn was hours away, and the world was quiet and dark. Clouds had moved in overnight. They shrouded the moon. From the surrounding forest, a stray breeze rattled limbs and rustled leaves, including those of the oak centered in the middle of the field. The wind created a soft wash of sound like a wave breaking. Serena noticed that the wedding site had already been broken down; the arch, chairs, and dance floor returned to Arylyn.

"What's wrong?" William asked.

Her eyes went to him when he spoke. He sat up, and she wished they could go back to bed and forget the dream. *Why can't we have one night of peace?*

"What's wrong?" William repeated.

His question jolted her out of her thoughts, and she recalled the dream once more before answering. "Adam says that the Servitor wants an alliance."

William groaned. "He had to tell you that tonight?" He smacked a pillow. "Just one night without any worries. Is that too much to ask?"

"I know," Serena said in sympathy. She felt the same way.

He sighed. "What do you think we should do?" he asked, climbing out of bed.

Serena turned back to the window, her arms crossed. "I don't know."

William's arms went around her, and she leaned her back against his chest. "We'll have to tell the others," he said.

She stiffened. She didn't want to speak to anyone about anything tonight. Perhaps it was selfish, but tonight was supposed to be for her and William alone; not anyone else, and certainly not anything to do with Sinskrill.

"But not tonight," he said, whispering the words in her hair. "Come back to bed. We'll tell them in the morning. They can figure what to do then."

She turned in his arms. "We're still taking time off from training?"

She needed to hear him say it. She needed the break. They all did, and she'd been anticipating these days alone with William for weeks now, ever since he proposed. Time passed swiftly, pressed upon all of them. This would be their last break before the invasion.

William nodded. "I think we've earned our vacation, don't you?"

"We have, but this is important. September's not far off." She examined his features. "You don't think they'll need our help?"

William exhaled heavily. "I don't know. Maybe. We can stick around and help them figure out how to respond, but I'm guessing they can learn it on their own."

"Probably," Serena relented, "but I'd feel better if we help out however we can. As soon as they realize they don't need us, then we can get going."

William smiled in response. "Good. Because during our time off, I was planning on doing a whole lot of nothing."

Serena's smile transformed into the one of secret amusement. She clasped her hands behind his neck. "Doing absolutely nothing sounds boring."

SHET LISTENED CAREFULLY as his close friend and servant, Sture Mael, relayed information about the state of his rising empire.

"The elves of the Apsara Sithe don't realize it yet, but they've signed their own death warrant," Sture said with a malice-filled smile, obviously glad to see the overly proud woven receive their long-deserved comeuppance. The gesture stretched the scar running from the corner of his mouth to his jaw in a gruesome fashion.

Shet remembered when Sture had received the injury. Shokan the Forever Cursed had delivered it, almost ten thousand years ago. He'd done it after Shet, Sture, and Sapient had killed Sira. Shokan had seen her fall and grown enraged. He'd slain two of Shet's titans in the blink of an eye and nearly ended Sture and Sapient as well. He'd failed, but Shet had been forced to retreat. He still recalled the shame of having to escape by the anchor line between Earth and Seminal.

Shokan might have killed him then, but Shet had played the final trick up his sleeve. He'd sundered the anchor line between the two worlds, trapping his great enemy within the strange universe of the rainbow bridge. Shokan had died, but Shet hadn't come out of the battle unscathed. He'd been thrown forward in time, broken in body and easy meat for the Mythaspuris who, after twenty years of war against him and his surviving titans, had managed to chain him to this very mountain, imprisoning him for the past three thousand years.

Shet mentally flinched at the memories. Even gods knew pain and fear. The only grace from those terrible years was knowing that the Asparas, Yakshas, and the utterly foolish dwarves of the Elasamara crèche had activated the Orbs of Peace, Shet's final revenge upon his enemies. As a result, the Mythaspuris were no more.

Shet pulled away from old, painful memories. Ironic that in this place of all places, this mountain where he'd once been chained, he'd found a safe haven from which to rebirth his empire.

He and Sture stood together on a balcony overlooking the large plaza where Shet occasionally held court. The Throne of the Eternal rested on a dais down below while necrosed, vampires, ghouls, and goblins wandered the square. However, his great tawny dragon, Charn, was nowhere to be seen. He was with Cinder and Anya, helping them capture the last of the missing Orbs of Peace from the Calico.

"The Apsara have granted us free access across their lands?" Shet asked.

Sture shook his head. "Not yet. They are too proud to allow it."

Shet nodded. "As elves have ever been."

The wind blew hard then, icy in the mountainous heights. It barely stirred Sture's close-cropped white hair and caused no discomfort to either god or titan. The gusting breeze also lofted the scents of ice, smoke, and iron, and Shet mentally nodded approval. His blacksmiths worked around the clock to forge the weapons powering his ever-growing, ever-hungry army.

"The agreement with the Apsaras allows us access to the Gideon River. From there, we can travel north and bring pressure to bear upon the Gandharva Federation. Once the humans are dealt with, we can swing around and destroy the elves." Humor laced the usually humorless titan's voice. "It is to our everlasting benefit that the elves, dwarves, and other races have forgotten humanity's importance."

"All too true," Shet agreed. "And that oversight will cost them. Within a decade, the Apsaras will be slaves, or they'll be broken like the dwarves of the Surent Crèche." Two months ago, that small kingdom of dwarves had dared defy Shet, spit in the face of his authority. His response had seen every dwarven man, woman, and child of their capital village crucified. The rest of the kingdom had quickly fallen in line.

His terrible retribution had been seen and feared by all the powers of the world. And in a few short months, far less than the five years he'd once promised the foolish mahavans, including the Servitor, Shet would return to Earth and reclaim his birthright. Following that would come Arisa, where his daughter, son, and their companions had died. He'd bring that world to heel as well.

Sture was apparently far less certain of Shet's timeline than his lord. He hesitated. "I am concerned. Once the last Orb breaks, the humans of the Gandharva Federation will have unfettered access to their *lorethasra*. You know how powerful they can become."

"We were both human once," Shet reminded Sture, "but ascending to our present station requires knowledge the humans of today lack, and more importantly, they also lack the will to accept pain."

"The humans have learned to endure the latter."

"And they still lack the former." Shet sneered. "Who will teach them? Shokan and Sira are dead, and no matter the name of their Federation, they aren't true Gandharvas. They'll die before they can master the power needed to defy us."

"My sources tell me *asrasins* have already arisen amongst the Gandharvas. They follow the code of our ancient enemies, the magavanes."

Shet blinked, nonplussed. "How is this possible? Who taught them?"

Sture shook his head. "I don't know, but other information arrives.

It states that trolls have roused, uniting with holders, and a black dragon has been seen."

Antalagore the Black. A spike of worry shot through Shet, but he quickly threw it off. "We always expected opposition," he said. "This merely confirms our wisdom in moving rapidly before that opposition can coalesce like a stone in a kidney and cause us more grief."

Sture nodded acceptance. "True, but I will form my own success rather than pray for it." He quoted one of Shet's favorite aphorisms, one he had ironically first heard from the mouth of Shokan.

"As you should," Shet said. "As we all should. Anything else?"

"The human, Cinder Shade, is to arrive in the next few days."

"Did he give any indication as to whether he and the elf succeeded in their mission?"

"None. He spoke through a *divasvapna* and simply indicated the timing of his arrival." Sture snorted derision.

"What of Charn?" His dragon was of utmost importance to Shet.

"He says your dragon chose to wing home on his own. He should arrive tomorrow."

Shet nodded, lost in ruminations and plans. What to do if Cinder and Anya were unable to recover the final Orb? It wouldn't be a disaster if the human and the elf failed, but it would make matters more complicated. He glanced at Sture. "He truly gave no indication of his mission's success?"

Sture shook his head. "The coward likely didn't even try to steal away the final Orb from the Calico."

Shet wouldn't show weakness before anyone, including his oldest friend, but the truth was that he didn't like to think about the Calico. He might even go so far as to privately admit that he feared her. Certainly he did Antalagore. When Shet had first burst forth from the mountain's imprisonment, he'd sought immediate dominion over everything around him. Blind luck had allowed him to capture the sleeping Charn, and flush with success, he'd gone after the Calico. It had been a mistake, one that had almost cost him his life. Only a weave sending her to the far side of the world had saved Shet. Later on, he learned that she also served as a Guardian to an Orb of Peace.

Shet leaned on a balustrade and tented his hands beneath his chin. "After we have the final Orb, Cinder and Anya will no longer be of use. I thought to keep them employed for certain tasks, but such a notion is no longer wise." His eyes went to Sture. "They will be formidable. We'll have to take them by surprise."

"I'll see to it personally," Sture vowed, a light of anticipation filling his features.

~

RUKH'S JAW clenched in irritation when Serena described her dream. Adam wanted them to believe that the Servitor sought partnership with Arylyn. This late in the day, with Shet ready to enter the world inside of a year or less? *Now* Sinskrill's ruler sought an alliance?

Highly doubtful.

The Servitor had another motive in mind, and the rest of Rukh's lieutenants who were still present at the *saha'asra* in West Virginia— Jason, Jake, and Mink—apparently thought the same.

Their impromptu meeting took place in Rukh and Jessira's cabin, held around the dining room table. The morning sun shone through the eastward facing windows, beaming sunlight into the front room and kitchen while a fire crackled in the hearth. Rukh had a pot of coffee brewing on the granite counter and had already cooked bacon and eggs.

Jake scowled. "I don't like it."

"You and me both," Jason agreed.

Mink took a sip of her coffee. "I think you're being too distrustful."

She spoke in a sarcastic tone, but Jason must have missed it. "You can't be serious," he said to her. "The Servitor is probably wanting—

"I know," Mink said, patting his cheek. "I was joking."

Rukh moved to where Jessira stood in the kitchen, making pancakes. He wanted the youth to figure out their next course of action. Jessira graced him a brief nod, agreeing with and under-standing his intentions. She flipped a pancake, adding it to the stack she'd already made. Rukh would have preferred dosas, but it wasn't his choice. William wanted pancakes.

"You already know there isn't a perfectly correct answer," Jessira said in a soft voice that wouldn't carry.

Rukh grinned, blowing on his coffee. He spoke equally quietly over the rim of his mug. "They'll figure it out."

Jessira shook her head, focusing again on the hot skillet. Another pancake was ready. "We'll have to land on an unoccupied stretch of land and push to the Servitor's Palace while locking their attention on the anchor line. That would be the simplest plan."

"It might be better if we could manage multiple landings," Rukh said, thinking about the situation. "The best place would be Village Bliss. If it's still unoccupied we shouldn't face much resistance, but we'll need a contingency if it is defended." He plucked a pancake off one of the stacks, reckoning he might as well eat now before the youth got to them. They ate like starving wolves.

Jessira wore a speculative look. "We'll have to be cautious about how we disperse our forces. We don't have enough warriors for more than two separate landing sites." She added another pancake to the stack. "What do you think about Adam's dream?"

Rukh grinned. "We'll tell him what he wants to hear," he said. "We'll give him a time and date for both the anchor line incursion and the beach landing." He imagined the Servitor's consternation when Arylyn attacked at an unexpected time. He hoped the news caused the man a heart attack.

Jessira elbowed him gently in the side. "You're taking too much pleasure in this," she teased.

"I'm not taking any pleasure," Rukh said in a wounded tone. "But I'll admit to shedding no tears if I hear of the Servitor's death."

"Me, neither." She gestured to the plateful of pancakes. "Make yourself useful and take these to those piranhas wearing human form."

Rukh picked up the plate. "You think they'll bite my arm off in their feeding frenzy?" He was only partially joking. He'd seen the youth tear into their food.

Jessira chuckled. "I'll pull you free if they try."

"That's not entirely reassuring." Rukh carefully set the plate in the middle of the lieutenants and yanked his hand back. They dove for the plate. Starving piranhas, indeed. However, even while stuffing their faces, the youth discussed their options.

Rukh listened in for a few minutes before adding to their conversation. "I agree about landing at Village Bliss, but there's an obvious problem: what if it's defended?"

"We might be better off if we can manage several landings there," William said. "There's a beach south of Bliss. We can come north and lay down suppressive fire on any defenders."

Rukh nodded agreement, pleased that William had figured out a way to deal with the problem. Of course, a more direct route, such as landing at Lake White Sun, might offer a better solution.

"And the cannons?" Jessira asked, arriving with the rest of the food, the bacon and eggs. "I mean our cannons. How will you haul them?"

Serena spoke up immediately. "Horses or bullocks. We can haul the cannons with draft animals."

Rukh hated the idea, although he recognized its necessity. His reluctance stemmed from his recollections of battles on Arisa when he'd transported horses and other animals across the Sickle Sea. Half the beasts had been sick with diarrhea, and the other half had barely enough strength to do more than travel a few miles before needing rest. "Have you seen what happens to a ship's hold when it's full of horses?"

"But how else can we do it?" Jake asked. "We could haul the cannons ourselves, but draft animals would be faster and not leave us wrung out from dragging heavy weapons around. We'll be fresh for the fight."

Rukh waved aside Jake's words. "You're right. Horses would be faster, but . . ."

Jessira finished his thought. "But you'll need to be prepared for some sick animals and a hold full of nothing good."

"Too bad we can't use pickup trucks," William said.

"We'd need some pretty stout ships to haul pickup trucks," Serena pointed out.

"And trucks won't function on Sinskrill. The mahavans' *saha'asra* is like Arylyn's: chemical reactions encased in metal don't work there."

William sighed. "Yeah, but they would have been a helluva lot faster than horses. And we wouldn't have to worry about them getting sick."

"What about the Servitor and Adam?" Serena asked. "What should we tell them?"

"Absolutely nothing," William muttered.

"Or we tell them exactly when and where we're landing," Jake said.

"What?" Mink said, sounding confused.

Rukh watched as Jason grew excited, apparently picking up on something. "No. Listen, it makes sense. We tell Adam the exact time and location and everything, but it's going to be nothing like what we actually plan on doing. We'll lie."

Rukh shared a pleased smile with Jessira. The youth had come far.

Mink grinned like a shark. "The mahavans will be looking the wrong way when we invade."

"There's still two problems," William said. "We still need to threaten through the anchor line—"

"Assuming my father hasn't changed the key," Serena interrupted.

William nodded. "Right. Assuming that. But we still need to pin their forces at the anchor line, whether the key is any good or not. That means we'll have to split our forces further. Can we do that?"

"We should be able to," Rukh said, although it would be a close-run thing. He still wished for another thousand Irregulars.

"What about the anchor line from Seminal to Earth?" William asked. "We still have to figure out how to shut it down."

The issue William raised was actually the most important element to what they intended, and as of yet they still had no way to fully accomplish it. Rukh had some notions. The book William had found, *Treatises on Travel*, held part of the key. The aether. Standing astride an anchor line. He now knew what it meant. So did Jessira.

They'd have to die, or at least their bodies would. It was a sacrifice they were willing to make. They'd already made it once in coming here. But it also wasn't enough. They still had to close the anchor line. It was the final mystery that needed solving.

Rukh scrutinized the others in the room, but no one had anything else to add. He rapped his hand on the table. "A problem for another time."

23

BATTLES FOR FREEDOM

J uly 1991

"THE HUMAN and his pet elf-woman should return later today," Sture said to Shet. The titan still believed he should have been the one to fetch the final Orb. He understood the Calico was dangerous, but risking her wrath was something Sture was willing to face. As a result, in his estimation the human and elf were no longer necessary for their plans. He was glad Shet finally saw matters in the same way. Cinder and Anya would be killed as soon as they offered the final Orb —assuming they'd managed to retrieve it.

Shet inclined his head in acknowledgment but didn't break his stride as the two of them swept through the crucible yards.

The broad space, wide and deep enough to race chariots, rang with clamor and curses. This was where the Shet's armies were forged, where violence spoke. The banner of Naraka—the name of Shet's citadel and empire on Earth—a black sun on a blood-red field hung proudly from the gray walls.

By habit Sture observed the ghouls and goblins, the weakest of
the woven, who formed the bulk of Naraka's armies. They were
trained here, forged into warriors who could maintain the battle. It
was necessary instruction. During Shet's long imprisonment, the dim
creatures had overwhelmed their prey through dint of far greater
numbers rather than skill or planning, and without such advantages
they tended to run at the first sign of trouble.

No more.

Such cowardice had no place in Naraka's armies, and the goblins
and ghouls would now be expected to wage war against the far more
powerful elves and dwarves, battle the enemy, and exhaust them
until Shet's more deadly servants—his titans, vampires, unformed,
and necrosed—could reap the killing blow.

Demons oversaw all the training of Naraka's armies, and Sture
nodded in approval of their fierce techniques. They faced their
charges with red-eyed glares and instructed them with guttural roars.
Flickers of flame passed across their smooth, chitinous skins, over
ebony horns and ashen wings, and down to cloven hooves. The stink
of sulfur filled the air as the demons exhaled smoke and ash.

Sture watched the black-armored monsters, considering their
origin: the realm of Rakshasa from which they derived their
surnames. They hated their imprisonment on Seminal, but pain
enforced their obedience. It was enough.

Shet wove Air, dispelling the demons' acrid stench, and Sture
maintained pace at his lord's side.

"Do we know if Cinder has the final Orb?" Shet asked.

"No," Sture said, his single word conveying his frustration. "He
only communicated their imminence." The damned human should
have done more, but he'd refused to answer Sture's questions. He'd
have Cinder's arrogant head on a pike once he'd made his final
report. It didn't matter if he had the Orb or not. Cinder's usefulness
was finished.

Shet grunted. "We need that final Orb. Thus far, we've rolled the
enemy, but our victories can be easily overturned if Antalagore
rouses and brings other dragons into the war."

The dragons. Shet had tamed Charn, but otherwise, the fierce beasts remained a wildcard, and whoever won their allegiance would go a long way to winning the war.

"Speaking of Antalagore, has he been sighted again?" Shet asked.

Sture flicked him a sidelong glance. "Only the one time."

Shet grunted, letting the matter drop.

Privately, Sture hoped the great, black beast had resumed his hibernation. "The lord of dragons will never be our friend," he began, "but should he remain slumbering, we will have far less to worry about."

"He will awaken now that I am free," Shet said, in the manner of utter certainty that only gods or the insane could manage. "We need to destroy the Orb before that happens."

"Or we need to kill him." A much better idea as far as Sture was concerned. "Kill every enemy" was his favorite phrase.

"Discover Antalagore's location and make it happen."

"I've tried," Sture said with a frustrated snarl. He'd sent warriors to all corners of the world, searching out the black dragon's lair. Unfortunately, the dragon's redoubt remained unknown, not even a hint could be discovered. It truly was a pity that his deceased brethren titans—Verde the Valiant and Duval of the Lightning—had been unable to slay the great drake all those millennia ago. They'd been assisted by Grave Invidious and Sapient Dormant, but the dragon had been merely injured, escaping after he killed Verde and Duval and nearly destroying the two necrosed as well.

"His wakefulness will make no difference once the final Orb is destroyed," Shet said. "Our powers will be unfettered then."

He and Shet exited the crucible yards and entered a long corridor paneled in dark wood and held up by a rounded, white-washed ceiling. Chandeliers held lumen globes to light the hall. This passage led to Shet's private quarters and those of the titans when they were in residence. A few scourskin slaves scurried about, maintaining Naraka's cleanliness.

"What of your plans for Earth?" Sture asked.

"It must be as it must be," Shet said. "I'll take the Servitor's body as my aether's vessel and shut off the poison that is slowly destroying

Seminal. It seeps from Earth to here. Much more, and it will over-whelm this world."

"They may know how to close the anchor line on their own and trap you on the far side," Sture reminded him. "Sapient has that knowledge. Others might possess it as well."

"Firstly, if they had the knowledge, they would have used it already," Shet said. "They would never allow me entrance to Earth. Secondly, as far as Sapient is concerned, you were right to question his loyalty. He no longer responds to my summons."

Sture started. He hadn't known. "What do you intend to do?"

"What do you suppose I'll do?" Shet asked with a smirk. "I will remind him of why I am a god and he is a worm. He will be submitted."

As it should be. Sture didn't approve of Shet's notion of accepting service rather than demanding submission. Had he the same power, he would have enslaved all who allied with him and destroyed everyone else.

"And thirdly, they'll never want me trapped on their side of the anchor line. I'd kill them all, and they know it." Shet grinned.

"I suppose so," Sture agreed with a chuckle. They continued down the relatively empty corridor. "We could simply close the anchor line altogether. With your power, you don't need the Wildness to do so."

Shet shook his head. "You know I will not. Once the anchor line opens, I'll have a chance to reforge it, remake it so it stays open like it was in ancient times. I mean to rule both Seminal *and* our birth home." His demeanor became prophetically grim. "And afterward, I'll take Arisa as well. The World Killers murdered my children. I mean to pay them back for that sacrilege."

CINDER STRODE next Anya through the empty halls of Shet's Palace. Their boots clicked on the white veined, marble floors as they marched toward the meeting which would go a long way toward determining Seminal's future. If they died here, that future would be bleak. If they survived, then Seminal might have a chance at true prosperity, all peoples this time.

He'd had hidden the final Orb of Peace within the *null pocket* sewn into his cloak, but not the one he currently wore. Right now, the Orb was far away, safe and part of their ploy to escape unharmed from Shet's Palace. Nevertheless, Cinder needed the object destroyed. So did Anya. Its power was the reason they remained trapped on this world. The Orb sapped Cinder's strength, pressing upon him like a fog, dulling his powers and thoughts. It left him empty, weaker than he should be.

On one side of the hall in which they traveled, a row of windows offered a view of the ranged mountains stretching north of the Palace. Sunlight glinted off snow-capped peaks and rocky shoulders. The light reflected through the window and brightened the white-washed hall. Not that the corridor needed it. Numerous chandeliers hung from the barreled ceiling, and bright lumen bulbs lit the hall.

They reached an atrium at the intersection of two passageways. A groin vault contained a set of frescoes, all of them images of Shet offering benedictions to the poor. All of them a lie.

"You're certain about this?" Anya asked as they continued on. "Once the final Orb is destroyed, humanity will rise and the elven empires will likely fall. My mother will fall. It will be the loss of great beauty."

Her thoughts on the matter shouldn't have surprised him, but somehow they still did. Anya had been an elf for decades now, over a century. Her time with them had left a mark on how she reckoned matters. "Elves should never have had empires," Cinder said. "Remember who they were originally meant to be."

"They've outgrown their creators' intentions," Anya said.

"Have the dwarves outgrown their creators' intentions?" Cinder challenged, his words snapping with irritation. This wasn't the first time they'd had this argument. "Beings of peace and tranquility who've become a byword for quarrelsome and petty."

"Perhaps not, but the elves haven't become less than what was intended."

"But humanity has. You've seen their cities. Even the finest of them would be a hovel on Arisa. The Orb holds them back, keeps them enslaved. It has to be destroyed. We need it destroyed if we're to ever save this place and find our way home."

Anya made a moue of disappointment, but at least she let the matter drop. A moment later she spoke again. "Remember to say nothing when we enter the courtyard," she warned. "We have to keep Shet's focus on me when you send the signal."

"I know the plan," Cinder said, his voice tightening with suppressed annoyance. In their prior lives, when they'd gone by the names 'Rukh' and 'Jessira,' she wouldn't have continuously reminded him of such simple facts.

She did now, which confirmed a yawning truth Cinder had first recognized weeks ago, even before their long journey to the Calico, and he feared what it meant. He worried that he'd lost his wife forever, that their love was dead. After all, how else to explain her inability to accept him as Rukh, her husband? She didn't trust him, disliked him really.

Anya placed a hand on his forearm and drew him to a halt. "I do trust you," she said, intuiting some of his thoughts, but not all of them, not the way she once had. "But you have to remember, I lived over a century without you, waiting for you, fearing you'd never arrive or that you'd already arrived but had died. I had to learn to fight on my own. Those habits aren't easily washed away."

She'd said as much before, and hearing it again did little to settle Cinder's disquiet. His skepticism must have shown.

"Cinder, believe me. I want this as much as you."

"Do you?" Cinder doubted it. She loved the elves too much, saw herself as one.

"I also know what you wish, that we could reclaim what we once were to one another. But now isn't the time to have this conversation."

In that moment a large part of Cinder's heart died. *What we once were to one another?* Her words had the sense of finality. He struggled to contain his grief and had to hope that maybe she spoke as she did because she didn't have her full memories. She didn't realize it, but it was the truth.

He also recalled the lessons of his youth, of his training in the

House of Fire and Mirrors, of his devotion to dharma. His teachings allowed him to crush his grief beneath the avalanche of what he knew needed to be done. *I'm a cold winter lake.* "I know the plan," Cinder said. "Make sure you know your part in it."

"Believe it or not, I truly do want what you do." Her green eyes shone with honesty, and she surprised him then. One hand slid to take his and the other cupped his face, caressing it.

Such a gesture of affection would have seen him dead in any sithe throughout the world, and his emotions roiled. *Why now? Why never once during our journey to the Calico, after I told her I remembered our life together?* Until this moment she'd never offered him anything but a smile, not even a held hand. He'd come to expect such coldness from her. To receive her touch now left him feeling like a desert-dried flower drowning beneath a blessing of water.

It was too much, and Cinder jerked his hand away from hers. "We have a mission to complete," he growled. He marched away from her. He didn't have time to wallow in mopiness and longing. Millions of people depended on their actions today.

Anya swiftly caught up with him. "Cinder," she said, her tone sharp. "*Cinder.*"

Cinder halted and glanced at her askance.

She spoke more softly, pleading. "I haven't been fair with you. I know it, but can we discuss it after?"

He snorted derision. "What do you wish to discuss?" He strode ahead of her again. "Let's get this done."

Anya didn't bother replying, which was for the best as far as Cinder was concerned.

He longed to see his children again. It felt like he'd spent three lifetimes away from them. He tried to convince himself that it didn't matter that he might do so without Jessira by his side.

Anya and Cinder walked to where Lord Shet awaited them on his courtyard throne. She flicked her gaze about. The last time she'd been here, the courtyard had contained nothing but tan flagstones and monsters. The monsters remained, but sometime in the past few months a long aisle of green grass had been planted to break up the monotony of the stone. The narrow lawn extended from a portico, through a nest of seething unformed, necrosed, goblins, and other assorted monstrosities, all the way to the throne itself.

Any who visited would have to traverse that gauntlet of threatening creatures, leaving them unmanned and shaken by the time they reached Shet.

Anya sighed to herself. Shet forever sought fear and coercion as the currency of his rule, but his techniques of intimidation had never worked on Anya, not in the past and not now. Neither did the woven cause her any trepidation, nor the fiery demons ranged around the throne. They wouldn't touch her. They couldn't. Not until Shet received the final Orb of Peace.

As she marched forward, head held high and straight, she noticed an absence: Sture was missing. But not the tawny dragon, the one Cinder had insisted they take to help steal the Orb, a dragon whose help they ultimately hadn't needed. He lay near the throne, curled like a cat sunning himself.

In addition, she noticed a sapling rearing behind the throne. It was new. The tree—a cedar of some sort—would likely tower over the rest of the palace, including the turrets and spires, when it reached its final height. A giant of its kind.

How apropos.

Shet liked everyone to know his importance. Everything he owned had to be bigger and better than any such similar item anywhere in the world. The conceit extended to Shet's physical build, which really didn't need to be so wastefully massive. It had to be a burden to maintain such a large physique.

Frankly, Anya found such displays pathetic. Only those unsure of themselves required them.

"You mean like how your elven mother makes new visitors crawl to reach her throne?" Cinder whispered.

Anya stiffened at his words. Not because his observation struck a nerve—she recognized the truth in it—but mostly because Cinder was supposed to remain silent. He was their means of escaping the palace, and they wouldn't manage it if he spoke. Shet might take too deep a notice of him.

Cinder smirked. He didn't have to speak for her to sense his amusement.

She'd unintentionally heard his thoughts. Doing so still caused consternation, left her unsettled and unfocused. She swallowed down a bolus of longing for her husband. Cinder looked and acted like Rukh, but he wasn't him. There were little details that showed the difference. Her husband had always been patient with her. They hardly ever disagreed or argued. And in battle, he had known better than to rush headfirst into a fight. In fact, as she reckoned matters, *she* should be the one to take on the greatest dangers while Rukh remained behind to defend her blind spot.

Cinder, by contrast, always argued, and he always dashed into danger, into the heart of conflict, always leaving Anya to protect his back. Truth be told, at least in this he *was* like Rukh: he never required her help. He crushed his enemies, destroyed them utterly.

A wave of emotion and thoughts flooded into her from Cinder, most of them dealing with her stupidity. She flicked him an outraged gaze. "What do you mean that's the exact opposite of the truth?" she demanded.

"We'll discuss it later, remember?" Cinder said, his tone mocking.

Anya's hot-blooded nature, so at odds with her elven heritage, reared its head, and she wanted to argue with him.

"Eyes forward," Cinder snapped.

Shet reclined in his throne. He clasped his black spear across his lap, and the right side of his face remained burned and masked, an injury Cinder claimed to have caused before he'd been cast adrift on the broken anchor line between Seminal and Earth. The god uncoiled himself to his full height. "Thank you for returning my dragon to me."

Anya briefly gazed at the tawny dragon draped in front of Shet's throne. Could he truly be who Cinder claimed? It sounded impossible.

Anya shook off her considerations. Shet required the entirety of her attention. "He was instrumental in our escape from the Calico."

"Was he?" Shet mused. "Odd that Charn hasn't spoken to me of his adventures with you."

"I was unaware the dragon could speak at all," she replied, daring to add a note of challenge to her tone. She would humble herself in front of this so-called god, but she was still a princess of the Yakshas. She would only bend so far.

Cinder silently urged her caution, communicating through the strange link they had. It was similar to what she and Rukh had possessed, which she hated. She didn't want to share her thoughts with anyone other than her husband, and given how he'd abandoned her, not even him.

Shet was talking again, and she had to refocus her attention on his words.

"I assume you have the final Orb?"

Anya nodded. "We have it, my Lord. It is safe."

"I don't sense its presence upon your person."

"You wouldn't. We didn't bring it with us."

Now would come the interesting part. If Cinder truly could speak to the Calico—if she was also who she claimed—they would soon know. If not, they'd soon be dead.

Shet scoffed. "You seek to bargain for your life with the location of the Orb?"

"If our circumstances were reversed, would you not do the same?"

Shet threw his head back and laughed. "Our circumstances can never be the same. I am a god. I'll kill Cinder, and you'll watch. I'm sure you'll be happy to tell me what I need to know then."

He languidly lifted a hand, preparing a weave meant to burn an avalanche to steam. Before he could complete the motion, Cinder attacked. He rushed into a cluster of necrosed, his sword blazing white as the sun. Two fell in the span of a blink. Another clutched a severed arm that pumped black blood. Woven monsters closed in on his location.

Anya cursed. There he went, acting in a most unRukh-like fashion. And there went the plan.

"Halt!" Shet shouted.

The throng of monsters paused their attack. Shet growled a word old in the old language, *"thraven"*—step back—and his creatures did.

"Safety," Cinder demanded. "We'll give you the Orb, and you'll let us go."

He was still speaking, and Anya wanted to throttle him. The plan had been for her to do the talking while he summoned their escape. He was ruining it all.

Shet smirked. "You will rue this day for the rest of your short lives. I could have offered you a merciful death, but instead, you have chosen pain. I am a god, and gods do not bargain. I will have the Orb's location while demons slake their thirst upon your body and your will. Agony shall be your payment, and you'll beg to tell me the Orb's location."

Anya swallowed heavily. A promise of pain from Shet wasn't a threat to be lightly dismissed.

Cinder apparently thought otherwise. He tilted his head as if in thought, and Anya had to do a double-take. *Rukh?* Cinder spoke. "But gods do fear."

An instant later, a roar shattered the morning quiet. The tawny dragon shuddered. Seconds later a winged shape, the Calico, flew toward them, swifter than an arrow.

Anya breathed out relief.

Shet viewed the oncoming dragon without apparent worry. "No matter how you've convinced her to help you, she can't save you."

"She doesn't have to," Cinder said. "She has the final Orb. Touch us, and she'll hide it away so deeply you'll never find it. You'll never free yourself from its grip. You'll always be weak."

Shet shook his head. "You are mistaken. She brings the Orb to me. I can sense its presence on her. I'll strip it from her corpse." He pointed to Charn. "Kill her."

Charn awoke, yawning mightily as he uncurled himself. He blinked at Anya.

You must remember, a voice spoke in her mind, one she'd long thought to never hear again. It came from the tawny dragon.

She trembled. *How can this be?*

The dragon seemed to evince rueful disbelief at her ignorance.

Silly human. I'll explain later. The dragon scooped up both her and Cinder. With great flaps of his wings he ascended to where the Calico waited. Shet shouted in outrage and confusion, ordering the tawny dragon to descend. The Calico kept her place with slow beats of her wings. Something dropped from her claws, a globe that Shet snatched out of the air.

"I promised to bring you the final Orb," Cinder shouted down to him. "Consider this my promise kept."

Shet's grip briefly tightened on the stone in his hand until it shattered. "It is done. My power is unfettered," he said, sounding gleeful. A predatory glare replaced the happiness, and he stared skyward at Cinder. "I don't know how you tamed the Calico, but—"

"I didn't tame her," Cinder interrupted. "She's my friend. Her name is Aia. You remember her? She remembers you." He pointed to Charn. "And his name isn't Charn. It's Shon."

Shet wasn't the only one to gape.

24

REBELLION

A ugust *1991*

SAPIENT SAT upon moss-covered stones and watched the placid waters of Lake White Sun. Waves rustled against the shore, splashing close to his position, but he didn't bother to move. Running water no longer threatened to undo him. He'd healed himself of that weakness. Clouds hung over the world with vast wings of gray, and a soft breeze rustled the lake's water and the surrounding forest. Otherwise no other sounds disturbed Sapient's contemplation. Animals instinctively knew to stay clear of him.

He pondered his past and his future, reflecting on how close he'd come to obtaining his goals. Only a few more feet, and he would have seized four *asrasins*, including the strange boy who somehow possessed the skills of a holder. Only a few more feet and he would have snagged a legendary prize, power enough to defeat a dozen Servitors. No heights would have evaded his grasp. With such puissance, perhaps he could have reworked the lines of force within his body, ascended like Shet and his titans and challenged them for supremacy. Instead, he'd only managed to capture the delicious *lorethasra* of a single *asrasin*. It was enough to satiate his hunger, but it could have been so much more.

He sighed in disappointment.

At least he now had enough power to heal that which had grown putrid and wasted. He breathed deep, his lungs filling more easily with precious air than they had in uncountable centuries. His heart beat steadily, and his blood flowed smoothly, rather than turgid and pus-like. Sapient examined himself, pleased by the lack of ulcers corroding his alabaster skin. He flexed fresh muscles. His arms had a more proper shape and length. They no longer dragged low and ape-like. His claws gleamed black and unbroken. He'd even grown hair.

The last was an unnecessary affectation, but Sapient didn't care. Gangrenous though his *lorethasra* stayed, he had plenty to spare. More importantly he couldn't accept this half-life of continuous decay and decomposition. He longed to be whole, to be who he had once been: a woven of grace and speed. And why not? After all, his ancient foes Shokan and Sira had been restored to life, so why not Sapient? Why could he not become who he had once been? Not a mawkish slave to Shet's whims or a holder who forever bent his knee to those less dominant, but a woven of true power and beauty who ruled?

Why not me?

Time passed, and Sapient came to a set of decisions. First he would have his revenge upon the Servitor. He couldn't live with the knowledge that a mere *asrasin* had humbled him. The man would have to die. Second, Shokan and Sira would also have to die. Their just punishment had been decided upon thousands of years ago when they'd left him to his fate following his transformation into a necrosed.

But not yet. They still had a role to play. Besides, murdering them ... He didn't enjoy the notion, not like he once had.

Sapient rose to his feet, nodding to himself as he strode away from the lake, his movements more graceful than they'd been in millennia. Seconds later he neared his home, the cavern in Sinskrill. He meant to husband his strength, rest until the magi came to

Sinskrill. Then he'd kill as many *asrasins* as he wanted, become more terrible than he'd ever dared dream. He'd even call his necrosed and share with them a bountiful harvest. And with his power, he'd lead them against—

A directive crashed across Sapient's mind. It arrowed across the void, shattering his thoughts like a boulder smashing kindling. It was a command he'd heard before and successfully ignored.

He would do so again.

Sapient crashed to his hands and knees against the pain, unintentionally bowing before the author of the command. *Such vengeful fury.* Shet. The god demanded *Undefiled Locus*, his greatest weapon, for when he returned to Earth. The instruction reminded Sapient of the god's need, and the Overward silently vowed to ignore it. Why give the god what he most desired? What had Shet ever done for him?

Nothing. Sapient had been transformed from a holder into a necrosed, freed from one servitude but bound to another. He'd been left to rot as a diseased husk rather than made whole and mighty. Shet should have done better when he remade Sapient's life, the weaving the god had forged into the core of his Spirit.

Fresh anger at his betrayal at the god's hands coursed through the Overward's veins. It allowed him to fling off Shet's command, and he straightened with a shudder, rolling his shoulders in relief.

It was then that an unfortunate tribe of unformed, all wearing the aspect of wolves, padded through the forest. Five of them.

Sapient saw them before they spied him, and the desire for murder filled him. He raced forward, silent but for the footfalls of his pounding feet.

The unformed heard him when he was still yards away, but the idiot creatures didn't flee. They chose to fight.

Sapient's curving claws gutted two wolves in seconds. Another he decapitated, gulping down *lorethasra* before the creature died. The fourth bit deep into Sapient's calf. He stove in the woven's skull. The final unformed displayed wisdom. It leapt away from him, transforming into an eagle. Wings clapped as it desperately sought to flee.

Sapient hurled the head of the decapitated unformed and

knocked the bird from the sky. He was on it before it could do more than squawk.

He crushed it under foot, adding the creature's *lorethasra* to his own, which lightened briefly before quickly resuming its blackish hue. He then stepped to the other unformed. They barely lived, but alive still meant they had *lorethasra* to steal.

Sapient fed, and while he did, he reached a final understanding. His earlier disinclination at killing Shokan and Sira was wise. Only they could prevent Shet's return to Earth. He'd have to ally with them. They were the only ones who could stop Shet, stand athwart the anchor line from Seminal and prevent the god's crossing. Another notion crossed Sapient's mind, and his plans firmed. The boy would be the key. It was lucky he hadn't killed him. Sapient needed his assistance.

ADAM PACED beside his brother while the two of them walked outside, alone on the battlements, both bent low against the knifing wind cutting deep at the heights. The Servitor leaned on Shet's Spear while Adam drew his cloak more closely about himself. Clouds possessed the sky, obscuring the sun behind a dismal gray wash, but at least the unceasing drizzle had temporarily abated. Puddles rippled under the force of a stiff breeze, and stray drops of water splashed onto Adam's boots.

To the west, Village White Sun hunkered like a beaten child. A crenellated wall, twenty feet in height, three feet thick—wide enough for a battlement—surrounded the last home of the mahavans. They'd finished it several days ago. Adam peered more closely at the village. Golden light poured from many of the windows, and from most of the chimneys rose smoke. It drifted on the breeze as both drones and mahavans alike settled in for the night. The two groups had been forced to share the village, which was filled to bursting.

Adam noticed the path the Servitor took ran close to the Judging Line, the place where traitors were hurled from the Palace's highest point. The fates of those set loose were determined by the swirling winds. It was said that the innocent would settle to the ground with no injury while the guilty would smash to oblivion against the hard walls of the Palace and the unforgiving ground. Unsurprisingly, in all of Sinskrill's long history, no one tossed from the Judging Line had survived the fall.

Adam hid a shiver. He knew the truth about himself. Treason lurked in his heart, and he worried his brother would somehow discover it.

"Has Serena told you any more about the time and place of their invasion?" Axel asked.

"You know she hasn't," Adam replied. "And she likely won't. Her heart is weak." He didn't believe the last. In his mind, Serena had made a bold, rational decision and profited greatly from it. But many others—the Servitor, for instance—thought otherwise.

"She and her sister both are weak," Axel said.

Adam grunted in reply.

Axel's voice softened. "I never intended to harm Selene." He spoke in a near whisper, and if Adam didn't know better he might have thought regret laced his brother's words. The Servitor fell silent, but when he spoke again all trace of softness had been wiped clean. "Dream to Serena again. We need to know the timing of their intentions."

"She won't tell me," Adam said, recalling the supposed dates Serena said Arylyn would invade. "Or at least I find myself unable to believe what she says."

"And you are wise to do so." The Servitor flashed a smile. "But now we know they will certainly attack, and we know when it likely *won't* be."

"As you say."

Axel shot him a questioning look. "You disagree?"

Adam considered how much he could or should say. He'd risen to become Secondus of Sinskrill, heir to the Servitor's Chair, achieved all that he could have ever wanted, but the success tasted like ashes. Sinskrill would soon be destroyed, either by the magi or by Shet or both. He was the Secondus of a dying realm. The recognition loosened fear's grip on his tongue.

"No matter what we learn, we both know the odds are against us," Adam said. "The new mahavans are coming along, but they won't be enough. When the magi arrive against us, we won't be able to stem their tide, even with the demon."

Axel rapped the steel heel of the Spear against the battlement. "You think I don't know this?" he demanded.

Adam refused to be cowed. Fear of what might happen to him had kept him quiet for too long. "I'm certain you do, but your knowledge hasn't offered you insight or wisdom into how to keep our people safe. We face annihilation."

"And what would you have me do?" Axel growled. "*Truly* ally with the magi?" He snorted derision. "We both know I won't, not now and not ever. They have wounded me too grievously with everything they've done to Sinskrill, stealing Fiona and Travail."

Adam scowled. "Then why did you have me dream this last time to Serena?"

Axel smiled. "Because you're the only one who has a chance to earn her trust. Serena may let slip a secret that will see us victorious."

Axel was mad. Adam saw it now, but for the sake of self-preservation he kept quiet.

"Or would you prefer I beg for Shet's forbearance?" Axel continued. He made a derisive noise. "He'll slay us for such a request."

"He'll slay us for our failure," Adam reminded him.

"Which leads us back to the quandary in which we find ourselves," Axel said. "We cannot ally with the magi. We lack the numbers to fight them. And Shet will kill us for our failures."

Adam kept his emotions in check although he still struggled with the notion that his brother thought they could defeat the magi. "What do we do?" he asked, his voice drone-flat.

"We survive. We find ourselves caught between an impossible enemy and an overwhelming foe. We should stand aside and let them battle one another."

It sounded foolhardy, especially because Adam knew the Servitor's pride wouldn't allow him to stand aside when the magi invaded Sinskrill. He'd fight them, not invite them in to battle Shet. In that moment temptation to defy the Servitor, the man who had led them to this disastrous place, coursed through Adam, but in the end he set it aside. "Yes, my liege." He felt like a coward while he spoke the simple sentence.

Axel took his words as acquiescence. "Have any of your spies amongst the unformed seen anything regarding Sapient?"

"I received the one report I told you," Adam said, reminding Axel of the dead magus. Knowing the Overward had killed an *asrasin* still left Adam disquieted.

"He no longer answers my summons," Axel mused. "Henceforth, we should consider him an enemy."

Adam wanted to roll his eyes. They should have always considered the necrosed an enemy. He kept his thoughts to himself, though. He'd already spoken as bluntly as he dared to his brother. He couldn't afford to press his luck.

WILLIAM REACHED the top of a gentle rise and settled into his morning run. He breathed slow and steady when he exited Clifftop and rounded past Linchpin Knoll. Under the influence of the bright, happy sunshine William pushed harder, went faster. He pumped his arms and legs, accelerating. His heart beat more strongly. Blood flowed. Air filled his lungs.

William continued running. He never slowed his pace. He could maintain it for miles. Only Rukh, Jessira, and Travail could have kept up with him. Actually, they would have left him in the dust, but no one else could have managed his speed.

Which had been a problem in the beach-landing training session yesterday. They meant to use swift attack boats for the Sinskrill attack, punch through any defenses, and create a beachhead at Village Bliss' docks. William was supposed to command their forces.

But his adrenaline had been up, and he'd rowed too hard, braided too powerfully. His boat had surged ahead of the others, alone and unsupported. In a real battle, his crew would have been shredded if the mahavans had gun emplacements set up to defend Village Bliss.

He'd have to be more careful to dial back the energy when the true invasion occurred.

It was coming. Only a few weeks. Arylyn was a frenzy of activity as the magi prepared for the inevitable clash to come. They had yet to solve the final puzzle—how to close an anchor line—but most everything else was good to go. The Irregulars. The plans. Rukh and Jessira, who'd battle Shet upon the anchor line. Arylyn was ready. Best of all, they still had months before Shet could make good on his promise to return to Earth. If they left for Sinskrill now, they could capture the island and at their leisure figure out how to shut down the anchor line.

William jogged on, considering the battle to come, and all the while, he unconsciously rubbed his wedding ring. He still wasn't used to wearing it, but he also couldn't imagine not having it on his finger. Or living with Serena. He'd moved into the cottage by the lagoon, and he loved waking up next to her, sharing her home, seeing her every morning and night.

An insistent knocking interrupted his musings, a feeling of someone rapping on the door to his mind. It distracted him and he slowed, uncertain as to what he was feeling. The sound repeated, a dull, echoing noise, and he slowed further.

Again came the rapping, and he ground to a halt, uncertain. He stood within a ravine, a dry gully with steep walls rising on both sides. A trade wind funneled through the passage, moaning like a wounded dog. A dozen yards ahead the dirt path exited the ravine, skirted a small stream and pond where beavers, otters, and frogs made their home.

The sound, a booming noise now, blasted into William's mind, and he went to his knees. Pain filled him. Something intruded on his thoughts. An image grew in his mind, an albino creature with dark hair, pitiless black eyes, and gleaming ebony claws at the end of well-muscled arms.

Sapient Dormant. The Overward of the necrosed. He'd killed Rail Forsyth. There were more details. The monster appeared healed and healthy.

He snarled at Sapient. "Get out of my mind."

Sapient chuckled. "So impatient. Do you not wish the treasures I offer?"

"I want nothing from you." William focused on his breathing, furious at the Overward's presence. Instinct from the red-eyed beast in the back of his mind told him how to expel the creature: a blast of Spirit.

"Be easy," Sapient said, holding up a hand as in a peace offering. "I don't seek a battle with you. At least not yet. I offer you something we both want."

William wasn't fooled. Whatever Sapient wanted couldn't be good. The pain receded. William had control of it, and he rose to his feet. "I want anything from you," he repeated, readying himself to throw off the Overward's intrusion.

"No?" Sapient asked in a wry tone. "You don't desire the means to close Seminal's anchor line?"

William kept a grip on the weave of Spirit meant to kick Sapient out of his mind, but curiosity kept him from unleashing it. "Speak quickly."

"You discovered the book, *Treatises on Ranged Weapons*?"

William hid a start. *How did Sapient know about that?*

"I sent you that information," the Overward explained, sounding smug. "It was I who inspired you to search it out. Just as I sent you the anger that allows you to battle far past what you normally might."

William blinked at the notion. The idea of searching for the *Treatises* had come over him all of a sudden. One second, he hadn't known to hunt for it, and the next, he couldn't rest until he'd found it. The need to discover this unknowable something had only abated when he'd found the slim pamphlet, *Treatises on Ranged Weapons*.

Could Sapient have really been the inspiration for the search?

William mentally scowled. He didn't believe it. The Overward had to be lying.

"I can see the doubt in your mind," Sapient said, "but understand this: in another life I wrote the *Treatises on Ranged Weapons*. The knowledge in it came from me."

William still didn't believe him. "What do you want?" He readied the weave of Spirit again.

"I want what you do," Sapient said, speaking more quickly. "I want to see Shet denied entrance to our world. The anchor line to Seminal must be closed."

"Why?"

"I have my reasons," Sapient said.

"That's not good enough," William said. He'd never trust this creature. He brought the weave of Spirit into his hands, ready to unloose it.

Sapient spoke more quickly. "Shet made me into what you see now. I wish to pay him back."

William sensed much more to the story than what Sapient was telling, but for now, he let it go. "Why don't you close it yourself? You're already on Sinskrill."

"I would if I could," Sapient said. "But such skills are no longer mine to command. The ability to collapse an open anchor line is something only certain holders possess."

William pondered Sapient's words. "No longer yours to command, meaning you were once a holder." Understanding filled him. "So was Kohl Obsidian, right?" He studied the Overward. "Are all necrosed fallen holders?"

"Only the most powerful. That's all you need to know. What do you say to my offer?"

"And why do you think I can close the anchor line?"

"Because you're a rare *asrasin*. You have some of a holder's talents. I realized that in the months after I first touched you," Sapient said. "You'll find more answers in the *Treatises on Travel*. Find that book, and you'll learn what you need to know."

William grimaced in disgust. *The Treatises on Travel.* He'd once thought that book could help, but it had turned out to be a bunch of gibberish. "I've read it already."

Surprise and speculation took hold over Sapient's features. "How? It is written in Arisan."

Arisan. That was the language of Rukh and Jessira's world. How did Sapient know about that?

Sapient's startle faded. "I see. You didn't read the original. You read a translation." He nodded. "You need the original. I believe you know two who can read it. The answers you seek will be found there." He smiled slyly. "Or you can allow a connection between the two of us, and I can implant the knowledge directly."

William readied his braid of Spirit again. "I'll kill you when we meet again."

"Or you'll die trying."

Enough. William unleashed the weave of Spirit. In the same moment, Sapient flicked his hand. He sent his own weave toward William, and it touched the surface of his thoughts. The braid, diseased and gross, angry and full of self-loathing, sought to burrow deeper into William's mind. The touch of it made him want to vomit.

William's weave thankfully broke the connection between the two of them, and Sapient's image faded, but a sense of the Overward persisted.

Knowledge and fury. The red-eyed beast growled. William's heart pounded. His vision grayed, and he had to breathe deeply, let the anger wash through him. Minutes passed. He continued to breathe with great inhalations, and slowly his vision recovered. His heart no longer raced. He no longer panted, but sweat poured off him, making his shirt cling to his chest and back. His legs felt rubbery, like he'd sprinted to the top of the Main Stairs.

William touched his head. A pain lingered there, and he realized that knowledge from Sapient's weave persisted in his mind.

He knew how to close an anchor line, at least part of what was needed. Maybe the book, *Treatises on Travel*, would confirm his new learning. He glowered. The information might be the key to winning this war, but he despised how he had come to learn it.

RUKH AND WILLIAM waited alone in a *saha'asra* in Arizona, next to a small lake with no one else about. The summer sun beat down like an anvil, baking the dry desert floor. Rukh wiped the sweat beading on his forehead. The temperature sweltered, and heat shimmers filled the various hollows of the undulating landscape. All around them, cacti spread their spiny arms.

"You're sure about this?" Rukh asked.

William shrugged. "I don't know. You remember where the information came from, right?"

Rukh nodded. He remembered. William had learned it a few days ago when he'd been out for a jog. *Sapient Dormant.*

It was an unforgivable violation, and Rukh vowed that the next time he saw the Overward he'd end the creature.

Nevertheless, despite his hatred for the source of the knowledge, he also felt they had no other choice but to test it out. He'd listened when William explained what he'd learned from Sapient and immediately sought confirmation through his original copy of *Treatises on Travel.* He found the portion that described anchor lines. It had been in the third section of the book, a chapter titled *"Termination Through Vivid Luminescence."* This time, when Rukh read the section he realized that "Vivid Luminescence" referred to the Wildness, the strange weave only holders could create. It could kill a necrosed, undoing the weave holding the monsters together, and close an already open anchor line.

The knowledge was exciting, and Rukh was more determined than ever to master the weave himself. He needed to learn how to create the Wildness on his own. With it he could do so much, maybe more than simply close an already open anchor line. Maybe the Wildness could destroy one as well. Perhaps Rukh could use it to eradicate the anchor line between Earth and Arisa. Maybe he could prevent Shet's daughter from ever crossing over to his home.

But first they had to test the Wildness, and Rukh prayed it would work. It had to. He felt time slipping away. The anchor line between Earth and Seminal wasn't supposed to open for many more months, but he sensed it might not be the case. Something, an instinct, told him time was not on his side. The invasion of Sinskrill *had* to commence in the next few weeks.

The satellite phone pinged, and he answered. It was Jessira.

"I'm ready," she said, speaking in her confident contralto.

"Same here," Rukh replied. "Link the anchor line."

"Will do."

Seconds later, a black line split the air. It rotated, displaying a flat rectangle filled with a kaleidoscope in the shape of a door. A bell tolled, and the colors merged, transforming into a rainbow bridge.

"The anchor line is open," Jessira said. "I'm tethered to it. Should I move on to it?"

"No," Rukh said. "Let's see if William can close it."

William took a settling breath. "Here we go."

Rukh prayed to Devesh. *Please let there be something to what Sapient said.*

William glowered at the open anchor line, his jaw clenching.

"What is it?" Rukh asked.

"I can feel the anchor line. I can see the weave, but every time I try to grab hold of it the damn thing slips away."

"Are you supposed to grab hold of it?"

"That's what the book said."

Rukh pursed his mouth as he recalled the passage in question. "The book didn't say 'grab hold.' It said 'attach.'"

"What's the difference?" William said, sounding annoyed.

"Apparently it's the difference between success and failure," Rukh said. "Study the anchor line more closely. It's made of Spirit, Earth, and Fire, correct?"

"Yes," William replied.

"Earth attaches to Water, and Fire attaches to Air," Rukh said.

William viewed him in surprise. "They do? How do you know?"

"The *Treatises on Travel* referred to another book, *The Lore of Itihasthas.* I read about the connections there."

"Why didn't you mention it before?" William asked.

"Because I only read *The Lore of Itihasthas* last night," Rukh answered. "Now be quiet and focus. Create a weave of Spirit, Water, and Air that can attach to the anchor line."

William grunted. "That's going to be hard."

"Life usually is."

More minutes passed. Jessira checked in again. William continued to peer into the distance.

"How are you doing?" Rukh asked.

William didn't answer at once, but after a couple more seconds he grinned in triumph. "Watch."

Lightning crackled down his arm and he pointed. A smell of sulfur suffused the air as the anchor line flared. An instant later it flashed apart like paper tossed in a forge. Ashes hung motionless before waning away like water evaporating.

"Excellent." Rukh let out a relieved breath. *One task down.* He called Jessira. "Open it again and lob a rock across when we tell you." He didn't want to test William's abilities on the living. Who knew what would happen when something was inside an anchor line when it collapsed? Seconds later, the anchor line flickered to life once again. He spoke to William. "Let me know when you're ready."

Far quicker than the first time, William indicated his readiness.

"Send it across," Rukh told Jessira.

William took on an air of utmost concentration. A rock the size of a grape plopped through the anchor line and landed on the ground.

William scowled. "Damn it."

"What happened?" Jessira asked.

Rukh told her.

"Well, that won't do," she murmured.

"What was different?" Rukh asked.

"I could attach that weird weave you told me to make, but the Spirit portion of the anchor line bulged when the rock was passing through it. I saw it. It was a lot thicker. I wasn't ready to braid something to match it."

Rukh considered the situation. Not for the first time did he wish he had the ability to see Spirit like a *raha'asra*. Everything would be a lot easier if he could.

"I want to try again," William said.

Rukh spoke again to Jessira. "Toss another stone."

William exhaled heavily. "Here we go." He stared ferociously at where the anchor line would open.

Rukh chuckled. "It's not your enemy."

William wore a rueful expression. "Right."

A second later, a black line split the air. It rotated, forming an open anchor line.

"Here it comes," Jessira said.

William pointed his finger. Lightning flashed down his arm, crackled into the anchor line, and it flashed apart.

"The rock flew back through the anchor line," Jessira said.

Some of Rukh's worries eased, but he wasn't yet ready to call today's experiment a success. "Tether to it and try to keep it open," he told Jessira.

"Give me a moment," she said. Seconds later she'd opened the anchor line again. "I'm ready."

"Me, too," William said, jaw clenched in effort.

"Try to keep it open," Rukh told Jessira.

She had no chance. The anchor line flashed apart even faster than before.

William whooped.

Rukh shared his joy. They had a way to close a tethered anchor line.

"I think I should practice more," William said.

Rukh agreed. "We'll keep going as long as you can." He spoke into the satellite phone. "Toss another rock."

"I've got a better idea," Jessira said. "I'm going to send a cockroach through. Let's see if there's a difference on something living."

An instant later, the anchor line opened.

"On a count of three, I'll send the cockroach," Jessira said.

An idea occurred to Rukh. "No," he told Jessira. "Count to three and then throw a stone."

"Why?"

"I want to test something. I want to see how long it actually takes an object to traverse an anchor line."

"Good idea," Jessira replied. "On three then. One. Two. Three."

Rukh started counting. He reached four when the stone exited the anchor line and clipped his boot. Four seconds to travel from Arylyn to Arizona. He wondered if the travel time was a fixed period or dependent on distance. It was an experiment for another day.

"Well?" Jessira asked.

Rukh explained what he'd discovered. "Send the cockroach through this time."

"On three again."

She reached three, and William waited a beat before lightning crackled along his arms again. The anchor line incinerated into ashes, and Rukh wondered what happened to the insect Jessira had sent across.

"The cockroach came flying out the anchor line right before it closed," Jessira informed him. "Still wiggling its ugly little antenna."

"I think I can do this," William said, smug and deservedly basking in the glow of his success.

"I want you to teach Jake and anyone else who can learn what you're doing," Rukh said. "Start with me. Tell me what to do. We'll see if I can create the Wildness."

25

FINALIZE PLANS

S *eptember 1991*

JAKE DREW DANIELLA to a halt in front of a broken down shack. Before the mahavan attack, the house had been a single story dwelling resting on a narrow yard halfway up Cliff Fire, which reared behind it. Stacked stones, some of them crumbled, formed the walls, and broad windows—most of them broken—interrupted the lines of the gray rock, allowing plenty of light and offering views of Lilith Bay. It was one of the many homes the mahavans had destroyed, and the previous owners had all died in the attack. No one had asked to inhabit it, and once Jake had seen it—he'd been searching Lilith for a house of his own for the past few weeks—he knew it was the right home for him. He'd immediately asked the Council for the rights to the property.

Jake smiled proudly as he gestured to the hovel. "What do you think?"

Daniella slowly paced the front of the home, distaste or confusion or both evident on her face. "Why are we here?"

Jake didn't let a little thing like her initial dislike of the ruined house cause him much disappointment. There was more to the structure than what could be seen on first inspection.

He took Daniella's hand and led her across the front yard. They had to high-step the mess of weeds that had taken over the lawn. Overgrown hedges and shrubs formed a ragged border along the property's perimeter. A beam of sunshine lit the structure, and Jake's hopes that Daniella would see the home's potential dimmed. Unfortunately, the light didn't make the house more attractive. Instead, it merely highlighted all the work the home needed, shining on broken masonry, pouring through the gaping holes in the walls, and bringing stark relief to the shattered roof. At least it had a deep front porch. Daniella liked those.

She brightened when they returned to the front of the home. "I see it now. You're moving out of Mr. Zeus' place? This is your new home. How wonderful."

She'd guessed the truth about the home but not the entirety of it. *Thank God.* Jake had thought about what he wanted for a long time, especially after William and Serena's wedding.

"I'm thinking it's about time I moved out," he said. He'd actually thought it was time for over a year now, but with everything up in the air he hadn't been able to fit it into his schedule. "With William moving in with Serena, Mr. Zeus and Fiona married, and Jason hardly home anymore—"

"He and Mink make a good pair," Daniella said with a warm chuckle.

Jake shrugged, not wanting to talk about Jason and Mink right now. "Anyway, I've never had my own place, and I like this one."

"Then I approve," Daniella said, taking both of his hands in hers and smiling happily.

Jake laughed. "That's not what you said a little while ago."

"I never said anything negative about your home," Daniella protested.

"But you thought it."

Daniella waved aside his observation. "I wasn't sure what you had in mind."

"What *did* you think I had in mind?" Jake asked.

"I honestly didn't know," Daniella said. "I thought we were going out for a romantic dinner since we leave for Sinskrill in a week."

Even more, Jake didn't want to think about the upcoming invasion. "Well, that's another reason why I brought you here tonight." He led her to the back yard.

"To help you rebuild your home?" Daniella teased.

"No. For this." He eyed her closely, anticipating her response.

Daniella gasped.

"You asked for a romantic dinner."

A hand went to Daniella's mouth and her eyes grew shiny.

Jake smiled. Her reaction was everything he hoped it would be.

The back yard remained every bit as ruined as the front, but centered within it, Jake had placed a table holding a number of covered dishes and two chairs. They rested under a rebuilt trellis. The lattice remained bare, since he'd yet to plant the vines meant to grow through their bars.

Jake tried not to preen, but he couldn't help it. "What do you think?"

Daniella kissed him on the cheek, her eyes still shining. "It's lovely."

He helped her take a seat at the table and uncovered the dishes: chicken marsala, mashed potatoes, and eggplant sautéed in garlic butter.

Daniella inhaled deeply and made approving sounds. "You made all this?"

Jake eyed her in surprise. "You know I can cook, right? I learned."

"I know."

"And for dessert," Jake lifted off the cover to the final dish. "Strawberry cheesecake."

Daniella's eyes widened when she saw the dessert. It was her favorite, and her delight increased momentarily, until a speculative air came over her. "Are you sure you don't have something else planned?"

Jake shook his head, leaning on his Sinskrill training to hide his emotions. "No. Nothing. I just wanted to make you dinner."

"Well, it smells delicious," Daniella said, wearing a bright smile. "Let's eat."

Jake nodded, doling out the food and pouring the wine.

"Thank you for this," Daniella said, gesturing to the food.

"You're welcome," Jake said. "But it's me who should be thanking you. For everything you've done for me."

She squeezed his hand in understanding. "Well, since I got you to cook me dinner every now and then, it all worked out."

Jake smiled, and they ate, talking about their friends and simple matters, and when they finished their meal, he cut into the cheesecake, placing a slice on Daniella's plate.

She stared at it, nearly salivating.

Jake laughed.

"What?"

"You look like a wolf about to eat a bunny."

"I like cheesecake," Daniella said with a shrug. She was about to dig into her dessert, but her eyes narrowed right then.

Trepidation filled Jake. Daniella could figure things out about him like no one else, and he'd really wanted the final element to be a surprise.

She stared at him, head tilted in thought. "A romantic dinner. My favorite dessert, and a new home that has a deep porch."

Jake mentally sighed, knowing there was no way to hide the truth from her. He stood and reached into a pants pocket to withdraw a small box, one that held a ring.

A WANING CRESCENT moon reigned amidst streamers of clouds and a sea of stars, beaming upon Arylyn and Mr. Zeus' back yard. Candles burned on the table under the pergola; floated on the small pond fed by the rivulet trickling down the cliff face; and nestled upon candle holders hung from the branches of several trees. A gentle breeze stirred leaves, rustled fronds, and occasionally wafted the aroma of jasmine. For most everyone here, it was a final night's gathering before tomorrow's departure for Sinskrill. It was Mr. Zeus' idea.

William glanced about, searching for Serena, but he found it impossible to find her with all the other people around.

Maybe she's inside.

Jake and Daniella were talking to Mr. and Mrs. Karllson, and William smiled when he noticed the flash of a diamond on Daniella's hand. He caught Jason and Mink slow dancing to the haunting melody that Rukh played on his mandolin. Jason leaned close and kissed Mink's cheek while they swayed. William grinned. The two of them deserved their happiness.

He noticed Julius, Ward, Mr. Zeus, and Fiona sharing a conversation, and he went to them. "Have you seen Serena?" he asked.

"I think I saw her go inside," Ward answered.

"Thanks," William said.

He was about to head in when Serena and Jessira stepped outside. Jessira murmured something to Serena and went to Rukh's side.

"Were you looking for me?" Serena asked William.

"How'd you guess?" he asked.

"Call it a woman's intuition," Serena said with a crooked smile.

"We need to get going. We've got an early day tomorrow. All of us do."

Travail approached. "I must leave soon as well," he said, obviously overhearing William's words to Serena. "My blessings and prayers for you and your safety in the coming hardships." He rested a gentle hand on their shoulders, squeezing softly.

William gripped the troll's hand. He wished Travail could come with them, but the troll wasn't a true warrior. Despite his size and power, he'd only get in the way.

Travail waved to the others and exited.

William and Serena also said their goodbyes and headed back to their cottage. They walked hand-in-hand. William illuminated their short journey with a braid of Fire and Air that formed a cool, silvery flame floating ahead of them.

The Guanyin came into view, and Serena didn't pause at the bridge's crest. She stared straight ahead, never once turning to look down the gorge at the titanic figures.

William did his best to contain his amusement. Her lingering fear of the statues still made him laugh.

"I know what you're doing," Serena said. "You can stop pretending you're not snickering."

"Sorry," William said with a grin that wasn't at all apologetic.

"I'm sure you are." Serena's voice was as cool as the flame lighting their way.

They walked on and soon reached Lilith Bay. A bustling trade wind tugged at their clothes, caused the ocean to rustle against the golden sand. The water glistened under the crescent moon.

Serena sighed. "Tomorrow is really going to happen."

It was, and William wished it wasn't. He didn't want to kill, and he really didn't want to be killed. He wanted serenity and joy, but the only way to achieve them would be through carnage and killing. It didn't seem real though, the coming battle for Sinskrill. Not even now, when in a few short days, everyone would be in place, and they'd begin the battle for their futures. Blood and grief would flow.

"You're not saying much," Serena said. He caught her glancing at him askance, her features unreadable, but he sensed an underlying rage.

He told her what he'd been thinking, the unreality of the battle to come, but the anger emanating off of her never changed. If anything the sense of fury increased. William grew concerned, not sure what had her so upset. "I really am sorry about laughing about the gorge," he offered, actually contrite this time.

Serena shook her head. "That's not why I'm mad. I'm mad because we have to fight again."

William felt the same way, and he hugged Serena. "I know. I hate it, too."

The words seemed to do the trick, and Serena relaxed against him. "Hate might carry us through what's to come," she said.

"And love will help us learn to live again afterward."

Moments later, they reached the swampy warmth of the jungle, and the world quieted. The wind barely stirred the trees, and the canopy hid the moon. Another ten steps a sound entered William's mind, one he knew well. He halted.

Sapient.

Serena regarded him with worry and confusion on her face. "What's wrong?"

"Someone wants to talk to me."

Understanding took hold of her, and she glowered. "The Overward. Be careful."

The knocking at his mind became more insistent, and rather than fight against the Overward, William relaxed. He wanted to hear what Sapient had to say. A vision of the albino monstrosity entered his thoughts, and he briefly pondered how he must appear in the necrosed's mind. "What do you want?" he demanded.

"How rude and uncouth," Sapient mocked. "No warm greetings for your dear friend?"

William didn't have time for this. He nearly shut his mind to the Overward, but Sapient held up a hand.

"A brief span of your time is all I require," the Overward said. "What do you imagine will await your planned invasion? The Servitor hasn't been idle."

William stilled his thoughts and drew deep on his Sinskrill training to flatten his features and posture. He couldn't have the necrosed guessing what he knew. "Why don't you tell me and save us both some time."

He didn't expect the necrosed to actually do what he asked, but Sapient surprised him. "I've not seen everything the Servitor and his mahavans have accomplished, but I can tell you this: the key to Sinskrill's anchor line remains unchanged." Sapient's demeanor grew crafty. "Do you know why?"

William considered how much to tell the Overward. He didn't know what game the necrosed was playing, but he decided to speak the truth and find out. "Because he wants us to come through."

Sapient applauded with a slow clap, as if congratulating a particularly stupid student. "Well done. And what do you suppose he has waiting on the other side?"

William glowered. "Like I said before, why not just tell me and save us both the time."

Sapient laughed, a gruesome sound. "Fine. Have it your way. The

Servitor has twenty cannons and a number of mahavans and woven near the anchor line. He has all of this protected by a number of *karimijas*."

William had never heard the word. "What are *karimijas*?" He couldn't believe he was actually having a conversation with the Overward.

"Shields."

"Do they look like gray globes?"

"You know of them?" Sapient sounded surprised.

William remembered what Serena had told him about the globes, the shields created to protect the Sinskrill fleet. "I've heard."

"Then my work here is done." Sapient dipped his head. "Prepare yourself."

William viewed the Overward in suspicion. "Why are you helping me?"

"I have my reasons. There is one other thing awaiting you, but I think you should have the pleasure of discovery. By the way, you wouldn't be interested in telling me the time of your arrival?"

"No."

"Fair enough." The Overward's presence swiftly faded.

"What was that about?" Serena asked.

William explained. "He sure sounded eager for us to attack Sinskrill, but . . ." His brows furrowed in uncertainty, "I get the sense that he doesn't want me to die."

Serena's brows pinched, and her gaze took on a disconcertingly intense air. "I doubt it. We both know he means to kill us—magi and mahavans both—while we're busy fighting each other. It would be nice to kill him first."

William wholeheartedly agreed.

Manifold listened quietly as Sapient discussed what he'd learned about Shet, Shokan, and Sira. He stood alongside the rest of his brethren, a little more than a handful now with the deaths of Rue Defiant and Charnel Blood. Manifold scowled when Sapient described Shet's betrayal. He had little love for the Overward and less trust, but in this he sensed that the leader of the necrosed spoke true. Shet had forged the first necrosed from the shells of broken holders and others, remaking the woven through an endless agony of desecrated *lorethasra*.

But even for Manifold, who had started life as a magus, his rebirth had been no less painful. Grave Invidious had been his creator, and that ancient necrosed had rent a once kind-hearted magus into a pustulant evil. It was a transformation to make the angels weep.

But not Manifold. The pain he'd endured was nothing next to the power. He often reminisced about his first murder, when he'd killed his first *asrasin*. The delicious taste of stolen *lorethasra*, the power flowing through his veins, the sense of invincibility when Antalagore's fire failed to fell him. . . . Magnificent.

Most days it was enough for him to forget who he'd been, but on some days—rare days—it wasn't. Some days Manifold more clearly recollected what it meant to be an *asrasin*. He remembered the feel of his pure *lorethasra*, the grace and glory of it; to fly and Heal.

But Manifold was a necrosed now, and for thousands of years he'd told himself that his heart had no room for regrets. *Lies.* His regrets refused to heed his wants and needs. Over the interminable years they'd chosen to speak ever more loudly.

Manifold pushed aside his vagrant thoughts and focused on the Overward's speech. Sapient spoke of Shokan and Sira, claiming they yet lived, that he'd battled them directly, and they remained as powerful as memories and legends reported. They'd even created a new holder from the meat and bones of an *asrasin*.

They lived when Shet promised he'd slain them.

Manifold's fury grew heated. What other truths had the god hidden?

Sapient clearly felt the same way. "All along I believed Shokan's curse to be the cause of our lingering torment, but if Shet lied about their deaths, why should we take him at his word?"

Brine Killed, a relatively young necrosed, somewhat shorter and thicker-hewed than the others, opened his mouth to speak. An instant later he closed it. He'd always been diffident. It didn't matter that he'd once been a prince, born to a line of *rishis* who had ruled what was now India. They'd lost their kingdom to betrayal and savage war, and when their heavenly palace fell, Manifold remembering finding the child Brine, lost and alone, and forging him into a necrosed. Brine probably hated him for it.

The youthful necrosed spoke at last, his voice deep like Manifold's. "You don't believe that Shet will avenge our suffering?"

Sapient snorted. "I don't think he remembers our suffering. He promised to cure it, but why would he care? He's become a god, but I still remember when he was nothing more than a powerful *asrasin*, one of many. We were fools to believe his lies."

"You were a fool," Manifold said, enjoying the chance to deliver a small insult to the Overward. Sapient was the most powerful of them. Smarter, too, but he'd always been too sure of his intellect. "I always held doubts."

And he had. Sapient might have rolled over like a submissive dog whenever Shet ordered him about, but Manifold had once been a magus, a *varuna* of renown, as much a friend and ally of Shokan and Sira as any, and he'd had always wondered if Shet had truly been able to kill those two. Sapient had claimed to see Sira fall, but while she'd clasped a hand to a grievous wound acquired during a battle in the heart of an anchor line, the Overward could never say what exactly happened to her afterward. The same with Shokan. He'd disappeared from all knowledge, wounded and presumed dead.

Apparently the rumors of his demise had been wildly exaggerated.

"Does it matter which of us had doubts and which of us didn't?" Sapient snapped in Manifold's direction. "The facts remain unchanged. Shet lied to us about Shokan and Sira. His words cannot be trusted."

"What do you advise?" Brine asked the Overward.

"When the magi enter Sinskrill, and they will. Trust me. It will be soon. I saw it in the boy's mind. We will enter as well—all of us—and we will consume any *asrasin* or woven we come across."

"We could have already done that if you simply told us the key to Sinskrill's anchor line," Brine said, overcoming his diffidence.

Sapient shifted about, staring at the ground like a scolded child, clearly bothered by something. "The Servitor is a more powerful foe than I initially realized."

Manifold didn't allow his surprise to show. *Had Sapient been defeated by a mere* asrasin? It should have been impossible, but apparently not, based upon Sapient's unhappiness.

Perhaps the Overward wasn't as deadly as he had once been.

"But his time is past," Sapient continued. "We can take the Servitor and all who fight alongside and against him. We'll kill them all. In the heat of conflict and in the confusion, they'll die at our hands."

"To what purpose?" Manifold asked. "Shet is still coming. And you say Shokan and Sira are here already."

Sapient waved aside his words. "In time we can manage Shokan and Sira. Once we kill enough *asrasins*."

Again, Manifold hid his derision. Shokan and Sira could never be hand-waved aside as unimportant. They were deadly.

The Overward still spoke. "As for Shet." Sapient's knuckles cracked when he fisted his hands. "I have my hooks in the boy I spoke of. He is both an *asrasin* and a holder. And he can close the anchor line to Seminal before Shet ever crosses over."

"The powers of both an *asrasin* and a holder?" Manifold let his skepticism show. "The knowledge, will, and skill to close an anchor line died out long ago."

"Nevertheless, the boy possesses the necessary attributes. I fought him. He has what is required." Sapient's grin broadened. "If you don't believe me then ask Grave Invidious." He laughed. "If you can figure out how to make a corpse speak."

An asrasin *with the powers of a holder? Impossible.* "How can such a thing be?" Manifold demanded. He wasn't yet ready to believe in this fable.

"I don't know," Sapient said, surprising Manifold with his willingness to display ignorance. "But he has what is required. It is enough, and while he labors at his task, we'll aid Shokan and Sira. They'll stand athwart the anchor line and defy Shet."

"And afterward, we'll destroy the victor," Brine breathed.

"Precisely," Sapient said. "My pet will close the anchor line while Shet battles Shokan and Sira, possibly trapping all of them. And whoever survives that clash and manages to break free will be weakened. They'll be easy fodder for our claws."

The other necrosed murmured approval. Manifold did, too, but his thoughts were elsewhere. *If an* asrasin *can become a holder, can a necrosed be healed? And what would that mean? What would become of me? Would I be rendered weak?*

Manifold didn't know, but he longed to learn. He was tired of this immortal life of constant decay. The smell enough was revolting. He listened with only half an ear as Sapient further discussed his schemes.

Manifold came to the slow understanding that for what he required, he might have to betray Sapient. He couldn't let anyone kill Shokan and Sira, either before or after their battle against Shet. They were the only ones who could heal him.

26

DANGER BECKONS

S *eptember 1991*

JESSIRA EYED the island rising out of the Norwegian Sea with trepidation. An instinct within her told her she and Rukh might not make it through this coming conflict. Something bad was going to happen. She could feel it in the core of her being, the heart of her that had already given so much. She and Rukh had left behind everyone they knew and loved—their children and family—all to save a world that wasn't theirs. And their battles wouldn't end here, and Jessira wished it would.

Haven't we done enough?

Or maybe it would end here. Maybe fate had something else in mind. Maybe they wouldn't see this battle through like they had all the others in times past. Maybe this time they'd finally answer the call of the singing light and join with Devesh and earn peace.

It wasn't likely. Jessira recalled the murals in Meldencreche. They spoke of her and Rukh's future as Sira and Shokan—the Lady of Fire and the Lord of the Sword—of further fighting and endless battles. Jessira was tired of it.

She noticed when Serena sidled next to her. "Are you all right?"

Jessira shook off her morbid thoughts, hoping it was only nerves. "I'm fine."

The two of them stood on the bow of one of the twenty ships meant to carry nearly four hundred magi—Agua Battalion—onto the shores of Sinskrill. The ships surged toward the island, cutting across the iron-colored waters of the Norwegian Sea. Wind and spray lashed, and gulls cried even this far out. A drab curtain of clouds filmed the sky, and rain fell. *A perfectly normal Sinskrill day.*

Serena watched the island, her features unfathomable, but Jessira sensed tension in the other woman. "I knew I'd have to come back here after we saved Fiona and Travail," Serena said. "I always knew we'd have to face Shet." Her jaw clenched. "I hope this time really is the last. I'm tired."

Jessira didn't respond. She shared Serena's feelings. After all, she'd been thinking along the same lines only seconds earlier. But whining about what she wished for wouldn't get the work done. She pushed away her thoughts, shoving them aside so she could concentrate on the task at hand. She formed a weave of binoculars, a skill she'd finally mastered following Sinskrill's attack, and regarded Village Bliss' empty bay in the near distance.

She immediately noticed the heavily fortified gun emplacements near the harbor. Her lips pursed. William's report hadn't indicated that the village was defended. She also noticed a number of strange animals wandering the docks and streets. Individually, they wouldn't have been worrisome, but the combination of eagles, wolves, and bears was an unnatural mix. There looked to be fifty of the creatures.

Unformed.

Jessira watched as well the screeching gulls keeping pace with the fleet. She questioned how many of them might also be unformed.

She shook her head. It was an impossible question to answer, and she resumed her study of the village. Further into Bliss, she noticed odd, man-shaped shadows skulking along the edges of narrow lanes and alleys, always keeping to the darkest parts of the hamlet.

Serena had binoculars to her eyes, too. "I'm counting fifty unformed and some weird shadows. I'm not sure what they are."

"They're a welcoming party," Jessira said. "It seems the mahavans are expecting us."

Serena let go of her binoculars. "What do we do?"

Jessira viewed Village Bliss through narrowed eyes, considering the impediments to the safe landing of her fleet. She deliberated their options and quickly reached a decision. However, rather than speak her thoughts, she wanted to hear Serena's first. Plus, it was an opportunity for the girl to come up with an alternative course when the first option was denied. "What do you think we should do?"

Serena didn't answer at once. She examined the shoreline with a frown of concentration. "We can't go against those cannons," she said. "They'll chew us up. And with that many unformed and those shadow-things, we'll have a tough time forcing a beachhead. We need maps."

Jessira nodded agreement and led them to her cabin, where she already had a large map of Sinskrill pinned to a centrally placed table.

Serena traced the island's eastern borders, pointing out their current location. "We can land south of Bliss. It'll be harder, but from there we can march overland to Village White Sun."

It was a good idea, but Jessira had always been one to go for the kill if possible. "We could do that, but if we're going after an undefended harbor, why not land closer to the objective?"

Serena tilted her head in consideration. "Where are you thinking?"

"The base of Lake White Sun."

Serena's brow creased. "But that's at the bottom of a cliff. There's also a large waterfall to take into account, not to mention it might be defended. It won't be easy making landfall there."

"It'll be difficult, but we can manage it. We've trained for it," Jessira said. "As for whether it's defended, I think it unlikely." She gestured to Bliss. "With the forces the Servitor has already committed here, and the forces he's likely holding back to defend White Sun and the anchor line, it's a risk worth taking."

"If he has even one or two cannons . . ." Serena said.

"We'll send the smaller attack boats first," Jessira said. "Those aboard should be able to dodge the incoming fire and set up the beachhead. From there, we can eliminate any cannons." She pointed to a line on the map. "Plus, there's a trail from the base of the cliff to the top. We'll still be able to haul our cannons up and utilize our bicycles."

The snorting of horses and bullocks down in the hold seemed to emphasize her words. The animals had made the journey through the various anchor lines and across the Norwegian Sea without significant complaint, far less than Jessira feared, but she still shuddered at the mess they'd made below deck.

"We'll still have mobility and firepower," Serena mused, apparently working through the possibilities and agreeing with Jessira's plan.

"Yes, we will. See it done," Jessira ordered.

Serena saluted. "Yes, ma'am."

~

WILLIAM and close to eight hundred magi—Terran Battalion— sweated under a burning sun outside a *saha'asra* in Australia. Red cliffs soared all about, and boulders and sparse bushes littered the otherwise bare desert floor. A heat-haze shimmered in the distance, and a bead of perspiration trickled down William's neck, past his collar, and down his back. More collected under his arms, on his chest, and on his forehead.

Rukh, who stood nearby, appeared unaffected by the heat. Not a surprise. William didn't think the man knew how to sweat.

Murmurs like the buzzing of bees hummed from the Irregulars. Their nervous energy seemed to crackle upon the air as they stood next to or atop their wagons, sat on their bicycles, all of them waiting for what they knew was to come.

War.

For most of them, this would be their first time in battle, and William worried for them. He hoped the training they'd undergone would be enough, that they could carry through with their mission despite all the horrors they'd soon have to face. The officers chosen to command the units would have an especially difficult time of it. Most of them had never seen battle either, and these virgins—Rukh's word —had to ensure that their warriors didn't freeze in the face of adversity. The officers would have to urge the others on, push them through carnage and calamity.

William knew all too well what they would experience. He'd endured more of it than he cared to recall: the blood, the death, the stench of killing. It would mark these young warriors, and they'd never be the same again. Many would die. Others would face horrific injuries. And some would carry wounds carved into their souls that might never heal.

William closed his eyes and took a moment to pray for those gathered here with him or on the boats approaching Sinskrill. He especially prayed for Serena. He hoped she never lost her smile of amusement.

"The concern you feel is natural," Rukh said in a soft voice, one not meant to carry. "It's the curse of command to send good men and women into harm, to know many of them might die and others might never recover from their injuries." He ran fingers through his short, black hair, staring into the distance, thoughts obviously distant. "I know it well, and I pray this is the only time you will ever have to carry such a burden." He nodded firmly, a sign that the topic was ended. "Let's review the plan one last time. Once we commit, there's no going back."

As Rukh's executive officer, his XO, William had helped develop the overall strategy, and once the battle began, he would then help adjust the tactics. They'd already had to alter the latter when they found out Jessira would be landing at the base of Lake White Sun. It would actually make their jobs easier if she managed it. Doing so would allow their units—Terran and Agua Battalions—to combine more swiftly and aim a hammer blow at Village White Sun and the Servitor's Palace. As soon as Jessira called in, telling them she was onshore, they'd attack.

"We'll send in armored vehicles first," William said. "The wagons with mounted cannons. We'll use them to create a breach." He wished again that *saha'asras* didn't have a weave built into them that rendered impossible any chemical reactions encased in metal. *That fragging weave.* Modern guns and artillery would have allowed this battle to go so much easier. He said as much. "I'm still worried about what's waiting for us on the other side of the anchor line."

"We'll know when we cross over," Rukh said. "What of Sapient? You trust him? Do you think he spoke truth about the cannons and shields on the other side of the anchor line?"

"I don't trust him, but I think he was telling the truth about what we'll find. It makes sense."

"He named the shields *karimijas*," Rukh said. "I don't know that word."

"We'll have to destroy them, whatever they're called."

"The first few minutes will be critical," Rukh said. "Those in the wagons will have to hold long enough for the rest of us to cut into their flanks and destroy these *karimijas.*"

"If it comes to that, we also have iron balls to punch through the shields."

"I imagine they'll be ready for that particular ploy this time," Rukh said. "It worked on Arylyn with the Servitor's ships, but I doubt it will today. Once we've engaged the enemy, we'll have to determine their weaknesses and kill them."

William figured the same. "What if we wait on Jessira to flank the mahavans at the anchor line?"

Rukh shook his head. "Agua will likely have their hands full. The Servitor had to have seen the fleet. He'll recall his woven from Bliss. They'll attack her forces as soon as they figure out where they are. They might even find a way to contest the landing on Sinskrill."

William shuddered at the thought. If that happened, it would make their mission even harder. "We're on our own then," he said softly.

Rukh smacked his shoulder companionably and smiled. "We're never alone. We're brothers. We'll fight as one. We'll break through as one."

William hoped Rukh's words would turn out to be prophetic and not simply something to calm his nerves. Another dark thought came to him. "We still don't know about this demon. Sapient never talked about it, and Adam didn't dream about it, other than that one time."

Rukh folded his arms. His nostrils flared in clear irritation. "Yes. It is a pity we couldn't learn more."

William agreed. The demon—its name alone was bad enough—but no one knew how powerful the creatures really were.

Minutes later, Serena called on the satellite phone. "We're landing. No opposition," she said. "Give us about four hours to disembark and reach the top of the waterfall."

"Understood," William said. He collected a few more details before passing them on.

Rukh gestured. "Gather the commanders. It's time."

William didn't have to shout for the other captains. They already waited close by. Rukh passed on some last minute instructions to them, and Terran Battalion got underway.

Horses snorted, whips snapped, harnesses tightened, and the wagons rustled forward. Clouds of dust drifted, and they entered the *saha'asra*.

AXEL WAITED ALONGSIDE HIS MAHAVANS, fingers tightly gripping Shet's Spear. The white wood remained cool despite the red runes glowing like burning coals. Today was the day. The magi were ready to launch their invasion. Serena hadn't bothered to confirm the timing with Adam. Not that he'd expected it. However, a fleet of ships had been sighted near Village Bliss.

Which meant they were coming.

Several months ago Arylyn had sent an advance scouting party onto Sinskrill, and the unit had escaped the island through Bliss' harbor. Thus, as Axel figured matters, it was also the most likely place where they would try to re-enter the island. His prediction had proved prophetic. The unformed had seen a fleet of ships charging hard for the village's harbor.

However, several miles out, they'd changed course.

Again, it was exactly what Axel had expected to occur. He'd planned for it. Along Bliss' harbor, he'd rigged what an invading fleet would take to be fortified cannons, all of them ready to launch withering fire on any ships that dared enter too close. Axel had also commanded a number of woven to make their presence easily seen within the village. The Servitor wanted the commander of Arylyn's fleet—whichever of the World Killers it happened to be—convinced that Bliss was heavily defended and thereby avoid the village.

In reality, the cannons had been props, and the supposed crews of *asrasins* manning them nothing more than clothed unformed. All of the woven assigned to Bliss could be easily recalled to wherever Axel required.

The ruse had worked—which was as it should be. The ships now sailed south, but they'd find that none of Sinskrill's other harbors would offer them a safe place to land. They were either too small or too far from the Great Way to provide quick and easy access to the Servitor's Palace, which was the magi's ultimate destination. They needed to be at the place where the anchor line to Seminal linked to Earth.

Axel reckoned the ships would then have no choice but to make for the harbor below the Servitor's Palace. It was the only place that made sense. Axel wished he could be there to witness their reaction upon discovering the surprise awaiting them. Cannons lined the Palace's harbor, and submerged chains, ones easily raised, would deny the vessels easy maneuvering and also prevent their retreat. Devon Carpenter, the Prime of Village Bliss, commanded there, and he would see the invading magi fleet destroyed.

Perhaps then, when Shet saw the fortitude of his mahavans in the face of adversity, he would grant them mercy. Or at least spare Axel's life, since he was the most important reason for today's impending victory. It would be his power that denied the magi their attempt to breach Sinskrill here, at this field where the various anchors lines attached to the island, to where the magi would likely send the majority of their forces.

Out of habit, Axel inspected the area around the encampment. This was where he'd positioned the bulk of his mahavans. Three hundred and fifty warriors filled the meadow, and his heart swelled. He'd done well in training them. While almost every one of his *asrasins* were young to the title of 'mahavan,' nevertheless, they sturdily gripped their weapons or waited alongside cannons, ready for the fight to come. No fear ruined their perfectly controlled features.

Restless and impatient, Axel's gaze flicked about the camp, ensuring that the gray globes—the *karimijas*—were properly positioned. The magi might bring their own cannons, but it would do them no good. His shields would repulse their attack. Then he'd answer their assault with fire of his own and call in the unformed to swoop into the carnage and kill even more magi. The enemy would be scurrying about in confusion and terror. Axel smiled. And then would come the final weapon at his disposal.

It had required a great deal of work on Axel's part to fashion such a defense, but in the end he knew it would be worth it. He nodded in satisfaction. *Yes. My people are ready.* The magi would come. They would discover this field defended with cannons and shields. And the magi would die. The only thing left to do was collect the corpses.

He noted Adam making his way toward his position.

"Everything is in place, my liege," Adam said.

"Good. When the magi knock upon our door, we'll greet them with all the friendliness they deserve."

Axel noticed when Adam merely grunted, neither agreeing nor disagreeing with him, and he understood his Secondus' reticence. Not for the first time did he wish his brother's dream of a temporary alliance between magi and mahavan could have taken place. It would have been glorious, and he imagined the veneration he would have received from leading their combined forces in an assault to defeat Shet and close the anchor line to Seminal.

But it was not to be. Such a dream was a fantasy, and a person couldn't live in their dreams.

~

JAKE HOPPED onto the running boards of the lead wagon. The front end was the chopped up cab of a pickup truck. Its flanks were armored in sheets of heavy steel, and an attached windshield was similarly protected, leaving the driver a narrow view. A cannon hunkered in the bed along with five magi. All the wagons were similarly kitted out.

Jake leaned into the cab.

Deidre Mason, a blacksmith by trade, had the reins. She was a small, stout woman, and right now she seemed nervous, licking her lips. She faced the anchor line William had opened, which was cranked as far as could be managed—thirty feet wide, over twice its normal width.

Jake had no idea how William managed it, something about instructions passed on by Sapient Dormant. Whatever. However he did it was good enough for Jake.

He searched along the line of wagons and bicycles. Everyone was sorted out, spaced properly and ready to rumble. He sighted Aia and Shon. Neither Kesarin was comfortable—they were actually scared—about voyaging aboard a ship, and they'd both decided to enter Sinskrill by the anchor line. Rukh stood near the great cats, on the bed of a large wagon with a mounted cannon, talking to the small group of Irregulars. He could have handled the cannon on his own. He was a *thera'asra* now, or maybe he'd always been one, an über-powerful *asrasin*. Or maybe he was a special type of *raha'asra*. Again, whatever. Jake was just glad Rukh was on their side.

He returned his attention to Deidre, who still looked nervous as a cat in a room full of dogs. Maybe she needed a pep talk.

"You know what to do?" he asked.

Deidre nodded. "Push through the anchor line, go fifty feet, spin us about, and cut loose with the cannon. Keep on going from there."

"That's the plan." Jake slapped her helmet. "The rest of us will be right on your tail. You won't be fighting alone. You'll blow through the mahavans, and we'll celebrate our victory tonight."

Deidre gave him a sour smirk. "But we're the lucky ones who get to go first, right?"

Jake affected a wounded tone. "You get to go first because you're so pretty and tough. The rest of us will be hiding behind your skirts."

"Get out of here." Deidre chuckled, shoving him off the running board. "Honest women have honest work to do."

Jake laughed. "Stay safe," he told the former blacksmith. "Kick some ass but save some for the rest of us."

He knew it wouldn't be as easy as their banter made it out to seem. They all knew it, but he also hoped Deidre would survive the battle and get to go back to doing what she once had. He wished it for all of them. But for that to happen they first had to take care of this one last problem. They had to kick the shit out of Shet and his fragging Servitor.

He stepped down the line of wagons until he reached his unit, the Skullcrushers. All of them rode bikes, and their helmets were decorated with the same image of a fractured skull. The Skullcrushers were part of Terran Battalion's cavalry. They could have maybe rode horses, but learning to fight while mounted wasn't something they had time to master. The bicycles would have to do, and the Skullcrushers' job was to get through the mahavan lines, find the shield-globe things—*karimijas*, William had called them—and destroy them. They had to be quick about it, too, because as long as the mahavans could hide behind them, they'd rain hell, safe and snug while Jake's people died.

He wouldn't let that happen. Not a chance. The mahavans wouldn't win this battle. This time they'd go down, and Jake would make sure they never got up. This time they'd die—permanently.

A high-pitched whine like feedback on an open mike ripped across the air. Jake winced. The noise exploded across the *saha'asra*, commanding everyone's attention.

Rukh had created the sound, and he sat upon Aia, well above the ground, waiting for the Irregulars to quiet. His cat growled, a deep thrum felt more than heard, and she looked flat-out menacing. Aia was bigger, badder, and faster than any animal had a right to be, and Jake was glad she liked him.

Rukh spoke to the Irregulars. "I know many of you have never tasted battle before, but you soon will. It is the most terrible of teachers. Fear will clutch your hearts. Terror will wreck your will, but understand this. You will not go alone into this wicked heart of darkness. Your brothers and sisters will light the way alongside you. Follow your commanders. Trust your training. All of you individually are worth ten of the enemy. And together." Rukh grinned now in triumph and pride, fist in the air. "Together we are invincible. No force, no Servitor, no *god* can defeat us. We will end this day victorious and with our enemies dead!"

Roars of approval met his words.

Rukh continued. "Never doubt our purpose, for it is righteous, and I say we will not go quietly into the long sleep. We will lash the enemy and bring him ruin. And through the blood and agony to come we'll restore our home, make right what our enemy threatens to destroy. We fight for freedom, for our beautiful past, and even more brilliant future. We begin!"

More roars met his words.

Jake pumped his fist and shouted along with the others. He called out last second instructions to the Skullcrushers, reminding them of their purpose and their position in the attack. He fist-bumped all of them before strapping on his helmet, straddling his bike, and getting ready to go.

He saw Deidre and a half-score of armored wagons rumble toward the anchor line. The Skullcrushers would be part of the wave following.

Deidre's wagon entered the rainbow bridge, and Jake took a deep breath. Butterflies flitted through his stomach, and a finger of fear slithered up his spine like a worm. He said a final prayer then, reaching for calm. He and the Skullcrushers pushed forward.

It was time.

Jake reached the anchor line, shooting through the doorway. His body elongated, stretching to its uttermost limits. He accepted the pain, ignoring it.

On the other side, he catapulted into a maelstrom.

27

THE INVASION OF SINSKRILL

Adam exhorted his mahavans to fight harder, to give more. The high wall his brother had insisted upon was proving its worth. It gave the cannon crews an excellent vantage point from which to rain death on the incoming magi. That, combined with the shields Axel had installed, allowed the mahavans to pin down the Arylyn forces, maybe even kill them all.

But it wouldn't be easy, nor would it be swift.

Dirt blasted as shells exploded into the magi, who tried to return fire—cannons mounted on wagons—but it did them no good. Their munitions proved incapable of penetrating the *karimijas*. Each time the magi fired a *nomasra* the gray globes flickered to life, creating a web that crackled and snapped, absorbing the impact. Right now, the best the enemy could manage was to hurl aside the mahavans' incoming fire.

Axel, who observed the battle from a few feet away, spoke, sounding pleased. "We have them pinned down. Continuing firing while I deliver the killing blow."

"Yes, my liege," Adam said.

Axel pointed Shet's Spear at the gray sky, the ever-present clouds above Sinskrill. Wind whipped about the Servitor. His cloak billowed. High in the air, a hole opened in the steel-colored curtain, swirling, chaotic, and lightning-laced. From within it came a mad voice, the sounds of garbled words echoing.

Adam shivered at the cacophony. No human or woven could have made that noise. It was utterly mad. Or utterly, incomprehensibly sane.

The hole in the sky expanded and something pressed through, something dark, oblong. It finished its extrusion and plunged toward the ground. Adam watched, aghast. He knew what it was, but in his heart, he'd always hoped that Axel would set the creature aside, that his brother would leave her slumbering.

Originally there had been seven hundred of these monstrosities brought to Earth, and this was the last of them. The husk of this one had been left slumbering for thousands of years, but now the shell was occupied, and she was awake. As a result, whether or not the mahavans won this battle against the magi, their only hope afterward might lie with Shet. He was the only one who could defeat this black-hearted monster.

The oblong shape took on definition. Legs separated. Arms unfurled. Wings snapped open. Adam realized with a start that while he knew she was female, he didn't expect it to be so obvious. *An hourglass shape and breasts.*

The mahavans and magi had ceased firing while the creature descended, all of them aghast. All of them knew what it was that had extruded from the sky, and it horrified them. Black chitin armored her form. Smoke drifted from her nostrils, and fires coiled around her horns.

Her descent slowed, only a little, and she crashed to the ground, landing on her feet. Her knees flexed on impact but she still struck with a sound like thunder. The ground shook, a wave spilling magi to the muddy earth.

The Arylyn forces were the first to shake off their shock. They opened up their cannons, firing point-blank at the monster. She shrugged off their attack and proceeded to tear into them.

"Why?" Adam demanded of his brother, horrified by what he was seeing.

"It was necessary," Axel said. "Shet will see our fearlessness and honor our courage." Adam made to speak again, to deny his brother's irrationality, but the Servitor cut him off with a chopping motion. "It's done. Accept it. I am the Servitor, and this is my will."

Adam wanted to spit in his brother's face. The demon was a creature of evil. He sensed it now. She wouldn't be satisfied with killing magi alone. She'd come after the mahavans as well. All this he wanted to say, but cowardice locked the words away. And like a coward, he meekly accepted his orders. "Yes, my liege."

"I leave the rest of these vermin to you," Axel said. "More magi beached near Lake White Sun. I go there to destroy them."

JESSIRA'S FORCES finally made it to top of the switchback slope that marked the passage from the base of Sinskrill's escarpment at Lake White Sun to the top the cliffs themselves.

The landing had been difficult, with rough waves threatening to batter their ships against the unyielding stone, and the wall of water from Lake White Sun's thundering waterfall kicked off unpredictable winds. All of it served to delay their progress, stretching their disembarkation far longer than they intended.

And once they landed, loaded down with all their supplies, the climb to the top of the escarpment hadn't been any easier. Winds whipped the narrow trail, and a downpour had almost entirely halted their ascent. They'd had to grind their way upward, inch-by-inch, foot-by-foot, but finally, here they were at the crest.

Jessira examined the scene surrounding her. Four hundred magi clambered aboard bicycles and wagons. Many of the latter had cannons strapped to their beds.

Serena had her ear to the satellite phone, her brows furrowed in concentration. She nodded at whatever William was saying to her. "I hear you. Stay safe." She hung up the phone.

"What's Terran Battalion's status?" Jessira asked.

"The mahavans have them pinned down at the anchor line. The Sinskrill forces are hunkered behind a wall surrounding the anchor-line field. It's protected by those gray globes we saw before. They're doing their best to punch through." She made a moue of dissatisfaction. "William is worried that Rukh might take the mahavans on by himself."

Jessira fought a wry smile. *Of course he will.* She still couldn't tell if Rukh always went after the most dangerous enemies because of the challenge of it or because he was really concerned no one else could handle the peril. Maybe it was a bit of both.

"Do they need our help?" Jessira asked.

"I don't know. William said they had a plan to break through."

Jessira considered if she should send the Aguas to the anchor line anyway. After a moment of thought she decided against it. "Gather up our forces," she told Serena. "We'll head toward Village White Sun. That way we'll still be close enough to offer support if the Terran needs us but also be in a position to prevent the mahavans from sending their own reinforcements."

Serena called out the orders, and seconds later bullocks grunted and groaned as they strained to get the rubber-wheeled wagons moving.

It was a short journey from Lake White Sun to the village, but every foot of it was overland with no trail or road to follow. They inched forward, and Jessira held in her impatience at their slow pace. She rode in a wagon—Daniella drove—in the middle of Agua Battalion's caravan and kept her eyes focused on the terrain around them.

This area of Sinskrill was devoid of trees. Only heather and low-lying vegetation covered the ground. The flora also hid deep recesses among the rugged rises. Heavy boulders, some of them large enough to pass for small hills, lay scattered about, making travel even more difficult. To their left, wind ruffled the waters of Lake White Sun.

Jessira's walkie-talkie—all members of Agua Battalion carried one—chirped.

It was Serena. She rode toward the front of their caravan. "We've picked up the road. The Great Way."

"Roger that."

Minutes later, Daniella flicked the reins when their wagon also reached the Great Way. The bullocks lowed, picking up the pace. Their hooves struck the paving stones in sharp, regular notes.

Jessira grimaced when they bounced over a rough patch. The Great Way wasn't much smoother than the rough terrain they'd exited seconds earlier.

On they traveled, entering a shadowed copse of evergreens, pine, and cedar. A whistling gust sprayed water from the damp needles and leaves of the surrounding trees. Sinskrill's gray gloom deepened.

Red fire flowered at the front of the convoy, catching Jessira by surprise. A series of explosions, a staccato sound erupted. A second later the wagon on which she rode rocked. Smoke poured skyward from up ahead as the convoy slithered to a halt.

The walkie-talkie came alive. Voices crowded over one another, shouting for information.

Jessira cursed. The command staff should know better. She shouted into her walkie-talkie. "Silence! What happened?"

Serena answered. "The Servitor and an unknown number of mahavans have blockaded the road. We're trying to retreat."

Jessira thought quickly. The Servitor and his Fire. He could destroy them all in these tight quarters. "Fall back. Leave the vehicles if you have to. Get clear."

"Yes, ma'am."

The magi at the front of the convoy exited their wagons and retreated. Jessira watched in approval as they faced forward, defending while slowly giving ground. *Good.* They were following their training.

Now it was time to deal with the Servitor. Jessira owed him for what he'd done to her on Arylyn. This time she'd come prepared.

"What do we do?" Daniella asked.

Jessira stepped out of the vehicle. "Gather units. Bring them forward. I need to know what's going on." She spoke into the walkie-talkie, passing on more orders.

Afterward, she darted toward the front of the convoy, zigzagging and hunching over to make herself a smaller target. Fifty yards up the road she saw Serena crouched alongside a cluster of magi, all of them sheltering behind their vehicles.

More explosions roared, and Jessira stumbled, caught her balance, and pressed forward. Growling fires raged ahead of her. Smoke clouded the passage through the copse. Jessira could barely see five feet in front of her. She braided Air, pushing the smoke away from her face.

She reached Serena. Fifteen or so wagons, most of them destroyed, stood between them and a dim set of figures. The Servitor and his mahavans.

Jessira scrutinized the situation and swiftly came to a decision. "Get the Agua organized. Co-ordinate with Daniella. Take care of the mahavans. I'll handle the Servitor."

⌇

RUKH TOOK in the scene around him. Disaster threatened. The wagon on which he'd been riding had been shot to pieces. A number of them had. None of those on bikes had yet managed to make it outside the killing field. They defended against the enemy fire as best they could. Blood soaked the field. Smoke belched from vehicles engulfed in flame. Animals struggled, crying in pain. The reek of burning wood and loosened bowels mingled. A good quarter of the magi were down.

They were trapped. A high wall, one that William's report hadn't included, surrounded the field into which the magi exited the anchor line. If not for the inexperience of the mahavans—the bulk of their veterans had died on Arylyn—all might have already been lost.

As it was, the situation was dire.

The mahavans had them pinned down, and a horned creature, monstrous, black as sin, and tall as a tree raged through the Irregulars. She—the creature was definitely female—had the wings of a bat, an overbite of fangs, and claws like scythes.

The demon. It had to be.

She tore into his forces while the mahavans laid down killing fire from behind the safety of stone and their shields.

A new plan was needed.

Rukh shouted for William's attention. His young lieutenant was busy shrugging aside the mahavan shelling, battling to keep the enemy's fire off the magi warriors, every one of whom were struggling to survive.

"Form a defensive line," Rukh told William. "Focus on the maha-vans. They don't know how to wield their powers as well as the Irregulars."

"They're doing a good job so far."

Rukh gripped William's shoulder. "Trust me. They're inexperi-enced. They'll break. They've only been successful so far because we're trapped, and they're invulnerable behind their shields. The moment we shatter their protection, they'll fall apart." Rukh pointed to the sky. "Aim the cannons at a high angle. That should get our munitions clear of the shields. Once they do, bring the shots around. I want them approaching those globes from the rear."

"What about that thing?" William gestured to the black-armored monstrosity.

Rukh viewed the creature. He'd battled things tougher than a demon. "I'll kill it. Settle the warriors. Get the cannons aimed. You'll have to take charge of them for now."

"Yes, sir," William snapped off a salute. He spun about to gather warriors to his side, shouting orders.

Rukh called for the Kesarins, who snarled in anger at all the turmoil around them. *Aia! Shon! The demon.*

We see her, Shon said.

Rukh shot toward the monster. He sourced his *Jivatma,* moving faster. Aia and Shon took different angles. They'd arrive first.

The demon must have sensed their approach. She stopped what she'd been doing—gulping down the head of a magus. Blood drooled down her chin as she flung the corpse aside. A ripple of black flames extended from a clawed hand. The fire solidified into a war-hammer the same color as her glowing, pus-hued eyes. The demon flared her wings and grinned, gesturing them onward.

Fragging bastard. Aia and Shon snarled agreement. Rukh sourced more deeply, Shielding and blurring forward. He now moved as fast as the Kesarins.

Aia leapt for the monster's throat. The demon leaned out of the way. Rukh feinted at the creature's right flank, aiming an attack at the hand holding the war-hammer. At the last instant, he was forced to roll under a blow that would have blasted through his Shield. He regained his feet and landed a solid strike against the demon's knee. His sword resounded as if he'd struck a boulder. A moment later, he had to spin out of the creature's grasping reach.

He needed more *Jivatma*. He drew deeper and formed the Wildness. He'd finally mastered the weave a few weeks ago. Lightning snarled, rippling up and down his blade. The blade hummed and glowed, whining with every movement.

The creature laughed when she saw his sword come alight.

Aia charged at the demon's back. The monster swung the war-hammer, barely missing his Kesarin.

Rukh used the distraction to attack. The demon blocked his leaping overhand strike with the haft of the war-hammer. Rukh landed and sent a horizontal slash at the demon's thigh. Even imbued with Wildness, the sword didn't penetrate. He might as well have struck stone, unable to even scratch the creature's chitin. Rukh didn't have time to consider other options.

With a viper-fast counterstrike, the demon sent an underhand swing at Rukh. He braced himself, strengthening his Shield. It wasn't enough. He was still flung through the air. He soared through the sky and landed on his feet, bending his knees to absorb the blow. He still slid back a dozen feet. His chest ached from the demon's strike, but he ignored the pain. He readied himself.

The demon calmly walked him down. "Is that the best you can do?" she growled in contempt. "You are weak, World Killer." She loomed over Rukh.

Shon reached the demon and managed to clamp his jaws on an ankle. With a jerk of his head, the Kesarin managed to throw the monster off balance.

Rukh hurled a white-hot Fireball at the demon as she stumbled away. It splashed across the creature's chitinous armor, causing it to smoke.

The creature tilted her head as if in thought. Understanding filled its eyes. "I recognize you. We've battled before, in history's depths.

Thrice. You were a more formidable foe then. My father will be pleased to learn of your demise."

Rukh disregarded the demon's apparent recognition of who he'd once been or would be. It didn't matter. Work needed doing. If the Wildness and a Fireball didn't work, he'd need to draw on other weapons. He sheathed his sword.

Rukh sourced more *Jivatma* and created a weapon taught to him by the First Father from Arisa, one he'd first used against the Sorrow Bringer. He formed a Bow. It glowed silvery in his hands. He hauled back on the limbs, took aim, and struck the string, a motion like plucking a mandolin. A quicksilver light, liquid and trailing embers, screamed across the intervening space.

It struck the demon in the chest. White light traced across the monster's torso. It etched her form like roots seeking purchase. An instant later it pierced the creature's armor. Black blood bubbled, and smoke wafted from a deep wound. The demon screamed in pain and fury. She stared in disbelief at the wound in her chest. Her gaze lifted, and her eyes were full of outrage. Rukh smiled a crooked grin of satisfaction. This time it was he who urged the monster on. *Come on, ugly.*

The demon gave in to her anger and thundered toward Rukh.

Be ready, Aia warned.

To my left, he told her.

A handful of yards away, Aia attacked the demon's flank. She crashed into the monster, throwing the creature off balance. The demon fell on its side. She sought to cave in Aia's chest with a swing of the war-hammer, but the Kesarin was too fast and darted away.

Shon harried from the other side, and the demon thrashed around, seeking to crush her tormenters.

At the same time, Rukh again fired his Bow. Another bolt of quicksilver tore toward the demon. This time the monster managed to defend with her war-hammer. The Bow's arrow was smashed aside.

Aia growled. *I grow tired of running from this thing. Kill her and be done with it.*

The demon levered herself up to a knee, and regained her feet. She took a deep inhalation before exhaling in a rush. A torrent of withering fire, green with flecks of putrid yellow, blazed from her mouth. The air grew superheated, shimmering.

Rukh took it on his Shield, shunting it aside and pushing forward. The demon's flames splashed across the ground, incinerating and despoiling whatever it touched. The ground wept pus. Rukh noted all this distantly with a snarl of fury.

He attacked. A Fireball mixed with a Bow formed a Spear, another weapon from his home world, another Talent from the First Father. A golden bar formed in his hands. Rukh launched himself at the demon with a *Jivatma*-powered leap. He stabbed the golden bar, and it extended toward the demon. The Spear cracked the creature in her horned head, puncturing deep inside. The monster's head snapped back.

The war-hammer drifted away into ash and smoke. The light left the demon's eyes, and she slumped to the ground, collapsing. Her body slowly withered. Flakes of black ash wisped off her chitin. A vague, bruise-colored cloud might have lifted off her corpse, but Rukh couldn't be sure.

Rukh slumped with fatigue. That hadn't been an easy battle.

WILLIAM SHOUTED commands to the Irregulars, gathering their attention while Rukh went to battle the monster, the demon. The magi remained pinned down by the mahavans' intermittent fire. The shots came haphazardly, as if the Sinskrill warriors didn't know how to form their braids correctly. Their aim was off, too.

It was like Rukh said. The mahavans were inexperienced, and it was that inexperience that allowed the Irregulars to repel most of the *nomasra* shells sent their way. Nevertheless, despite the magi's best efforts, they were still getting chewed up. They couldn't last much longer.

The ground reminded him of a moonscape. Ragged holes, large enough to lose a wagon, littered the field. Thunder rumbled. Fire crackled all about as vehicles burned. The magi had to change the odds. They couldn't hunker down like turtles and hope to hold out. They had to land a blow.

It was those gray globes. William scrutinized the devices, trying to figure how best to destroy them. They were set on steel poles, evenly spaced upon the stone wall surrounding the field. Those had to be destroyed. Straight steel shells like what the magi had used during the battle in Arylyn didn't work. The mahavans had figured a way to defend against them.

Maybe something else will work.

William drained Sinskrill's *lorasra* below one of the globes and released a blood-red tinged silver stream to his side. The sensation made his stomach roil, and he distractedly noticed the grass wilt where the bloody fluid struck. His focus, though, remained on the fragging gray globe. He hoped cutting off their source of *lorasra* would weaken the shield, but no luck. The *karimajas still* sent out webs of shielding.

Damn it! There went the easy solution. He'd have to try Rukh's plan.

William hunched low, and crab-walked his way to where he saw Jason huddled behind a destroyed wagon.

"What do we do?" Jason shouted.

For an instant, William wanted to say "Damifino," but he gathered his thoughts. "Pass the word. Form a defensive perimeter. Concentrate fire and defense."

Jake arrived, sliding to a halt. "Yeah, but what about the shields?" He must have heard William's words.

"Elevate the cannons to sixty degrees. The shells have to clear the shields. We can guide them in from there. Aim for the back side of those globes and destroy them." William glanced around. "Where's Mink?"

Jake answered. "Injured." At Jason's pinched expression of fear, he hurried on. "It's just a broken arm." He pointed to where the anchor line remained open. The wounded were being evacuated through it while fresh magi poured through to replace them. "She's already been sent back to Australia."

Jason's face relaxed.

"Get the Irregulars in position," William said to them. "Now!"

Within minutes, the magi managed to form a defensive perimeter behind a ring of wagons. They muscled them into place, under heavy fire the entire time. Half the Irregulars got the vehicles and their cannons into position while the others did their best to defend against the mahavans.

"Tracer rounds over the shields," William reminded them, instructing the cannon crews on what he wanted done. "We need to know how high up they go."

Seconds later Jason shouted the answer. "Got it. About thirty feet up, and we're clear."

William called out more orders to the cannon crews. "Concentrate fire east. Phosphorous shells."

"Yes, sir." Jason said.

Seconds later, five *nomasras*, streaked into the sky. They blazed a trail, white as the sun and reverberating like blowtorches. They arced above and beyond the wall.

Now comes the hard part. William silently urged the *nomasras* to find their target.

The shells bent their flight, aimed back toward the wall.

Fifty feet.

Two of them shuddered. They diverted away from the wall.

Thirty feet.

Another one dipped and spun, punched straight down. William distantly noted a white fire briefly blaze where the *nomasra* must have struck the ground.

Fifteen feet.

The final two continued on. They twisted in the air but couldn't be pushed away. They ended up striking at the same time, blasting away behind the wall. Two globes cracked. Fire rippled across the wall, a flash of light.

An opening.

"Cannons ready. Normal *nomasras*," William said to Jason. "Take down those walls." He sought out Jake. "Get the bikes up. There'll be a breach. Get through it. Swing around and kill whatever gets in your way."

Jake snapped off a salute and gathered riders.

William called over Ward and Tam. "Get some crews together. Do exactly what Jason did. Open that hole, and gut those bastards."

"Yes, sir," they said in unison.

Something heavy crashed into the field. The ground shook.

William shot a worried look, wondering what new danger had arrived. He exhaled in relief when he found the source of the commotion. Rukh had taken down the demon. The monster had fallen and was no longer moving.

Thank God.

An instant later, Ward whooped. His crew had carved open a breach. "Send them our regards," he said to the crew under his command.

"Will do," someone replied.

More cannons boomed. Jason's, Tam's and Ward's, and many more. Broken stone blasted outward. Dust bloomed skyward. The wall crumbled. Mahavans cried out in pain and shock.

"Fire at will!" William exhorted the other cannon crews. "Get that wall down." He found Deidre Mason. "Get some wagons through the breach and flank the mahavans."

Deidre shot off.

Jake and a score of riders swept toward the opening Jason and Ward's cannons had created. Five wagons followed them, Deidre spurring them onward.

For the first time William felt hope they might actually pull this off. This place was likely to be the most heavily defended area on Sinskrill, and the cannon crews were taking apart the wall. More bikes and wagons poured through the anchor line, and lieutenants and sergeants directed them to the breaches. Fewer magi needed evacuation.

The mahavans fought on but the heart had been taken out of them. They were the ones who likely formed the bulk of the Servitor's forces.

Except . . .

Where were the unformed and the vampires? William shot his

gaze all about the wall. He only spotted mahavans. Where were the fragging unformed?

His eyes went skyward. To the east. He finally saw them. A large flock of birds winged their way. Eagles or falcons. Strange shadows seemed to ride the air behind the birds. They were still minutes away. There was time to get ready.

"Watch the sky. We've got incoming," William warned the Irregulars. The unformed he knew how to kill. The vampires, though. Was that what those weird, shadowy things were?

The birds came on. Once overhead, they tucked in their wings and fell like bullets.

William drew on his *lorethasra*. He formed a braid of Fire and Air before connecting it to Sinskrill's disgusting *lorasra*. A weave took shape, thick as a rope. It hissed and sizzled over William's shoulders and chest, rippling like lightning. A dozen other Irregulars had similar weaves.

As one they thrust their arms up, hands aimed at the unformed. Lightning arced toward the creatures. Fifty of the unformed were instantly incinerated. Their corpses fell like a strange hail, a thump here and there. Smoke wisped off their bodies, and the smell of burnt meat that reminded William of roasted chicken mixed in with all the other stenches.

The remaining roughly thirty unformed landed, apparently unhurt. The shadowy things, though, continued to circle, a dozen of them.

28

STRIKE AND COUNTERSTRIKE

Shet paused before exiting the citadel proper into the outer courtyard. Golden sunshine lit the world at the mountain's peak, but at these heights it possessed no heat. Rather an icy wind blustered, deepening the chill. Shet ignored it. Cold didn't touch a god. He stared into the empty courtyard. No one else was present. *As it should be.* He'd ordered the plaza cleared out. Even the battlements were empty. No one was allowed to witness what he did today.

Shet stood alone, feet shoulder-width apart, his freshly formed golden staff braced against the ground and considered his new weapon. Only a week old, but he'd already tested it and found it to be far more useful than the black spear he'd been forced to wield after breaking the bondage of the Mythaspuris.

Freedom.

He wished he had someone with whom to share what he'd become. His daughter and son, for one. His wife, perhaps. How he'd loved them. But his children were dead, and his wife had betrayed him, unable to accept the glory he'd managed to achieve. In the end, she'd denied she ever loved him, claiming to have cast him out of her heart. He often mused over what had become of her.

Shet even missed Charn, the dragon Cinder and Anya had wrested from him. The beast had been mute like many of his kind, but his presence had been comforting, soothing in a sense. He, too, was gone, and it went without saying that Cinder's claim that Charn was actually Shon was silly. Shon had been Sira's Kesarin. He'd been a cat, not a dragon.

Shet threw off his maudlin thoughts. He had no room for such frail meanderings, especially on today of all days, when he'd force open the anchor line between Seminal and Earth. In the natural course of events the linkage between the two worlds wouldn't open for another few months, but Shet was vastly more powerful now. He could force the issue. And he had to. His plans on Seminal hadn't yet come to fruition. The pesky humans of Gandharva, the elves of the Yakshima Sithe, and rishis of Bharat were proving troublesome. Not to mention Cinder and Anya and their sentient dragon allies. Fearsome foes threatened. Too many troubles occupied his time.

He needed to do away with as many of them as possible, beginning with Earth. He had to protect Seminal from Earth's aether and save this blessed world whether anyone recognized his wisdom or not. Of course, the acclamation would eventually come, and if he got to inflict some long-overdue punishment on traitors—both the maha-vans and magi—it was only just and proper.

He entered the black-walled courtyard, and it struck him then, the bleak nature of his home. He didn't like it, and he recognized that he'd erred in much of Naraka's construction. While he'd designed his palace to strike fear in the hearts of those who groveled for his blessings, he should have imbued his home with a greater sense of beauty and grace. Rather than powerful and intimidating alone, his home should have also striven to convey majesty and grandeur. He'd failed in that regard, unable to balance that symmetry of emotions when erecting his citadel. Only in the incorporation of the various arches, arcades, and ribbed ceilings throughout the palace's interior had he created a semblance of grace.

Of course, in some regards, he *hadn't* failed. For instance, the Throne of the Eternal. It hunkered atop the dais, alone and nacreous, glimmering in the noonday sun that beamed ineffectually at these heights. His throne dominated the courtyard, and combined with the chill air, the ambassadors and important personages visiting here were often deeply unsettled.

Which was what Shet wanted.

Those coming to him should understand that they arrived as supplicants. Their visit would see them broken of their pride. Such as the last delegation. It had been from the island nation of Marut and its primary inhabitants, the kapis, the monkey-like descendents of the god Vaanar. They'd shivered in terror the entire time.

Weaklings. Once the kapis had been fierce warriors, but now they were knee-knocking cowards.

How the world had changed during his long imprisonment. Those who had once been powerful were now impotent while those whose only purpose was to serve thought themselves kings and emperors. They deserved humbling, these arrogant lessers who dared consider themselves his equal. It was a punishment thousands of years in the making.

But first there were today's events to tackle. Earlier, the Servitor had journeyed to Seminal and spoken of an impending incursion of magi. The puny *asrasin* claimed the enemy massed along an anchor line leading to Sinskrill and would arrive at any moment. The Servitor claimed he would rout the invaders, but Shet doubted it. He'd long since lost all faith in the Servitor. The man was a liar. Indeed, he was a weakling, and while Shet traveled to Earth and dealt with the fool, his captains, the Holy Seven, would maintain control of Seminal and advance the plans they'd discussed. He trusted them to do his will.

In that instant, five of his titans, Sture Mael, Garad Lull, Tomag Jury, Liline Silt, and Drak Renter, entered the courtyard, exiting from a white entrance on the other side of the black-walled courtyard, shutting the heavy, oaken door behind them.

Shet awaited the arrival of his captains, and Sture spoke without preamble. "We have everything in place to protect your form during your time on Earth."

Shet expected nothing less. "Hide it well. It shouldn't take me long to destroy Arylyn and Sinskrill."

"The anchor line will remain open on its own?" Drak asked. He was young to his post, lean and handsome, with long hair, dark and dank. He sometimes forgot himself, asking questions when he required no answer.

Such as now. Nevertheless, Shet humored the young captain. "Of course. On its own it will stay open for exactly three Earth days. I'll cleanse the poison from that planet and stabilize the anchor line." He smiled. "After that, I'll eradicate Sinskrill and Arylyn. Then will come Seminal and any who dare challenge my rule on any world."

"Yes, my Lord," Drak said, bowing slightly.

"You understand your orders?" Shet asked his arrayed titans.

"We are to seek alliance with the rakishi," Sture said. He struggled with an emotion, frustration probably. "They insult us. They've disregarded our entreaties."

The rakishi. The children of the long-deceased nagrisi—sinewy warrior woven—and the rishis. The rakishi were another who thought too highly of themselves.

"Kill their oldest," Shet ordered. "Their most powerful. The ones they call Shrewds. Perhaps when their mightiest are spasming around a gutful of steel, reason will calm their arrogance."

"As you will," Sture said.

"The spiderkin continue to press hard against the elven empires of the Apsara Sithe," Tomag said. The powerful titan, muscular and blond, with a plethora of swords, daggers, and other weapons hanging from his belt, appeared thoughtful, but behind his considering demeanor lurked an idiot.

His twin brother Tormak was no better. Cannon-fodder is how Shet considered them. In fact, if not for the power possessed by the brothers, he might have long ago done away with them both. In truth, he had no use for dullards, but Tomag's and Tormak's capabilities on the field of battle couldn't be ignored or discarded.

"Let the spiderkin bleed the elves," Sture said to Tomag. "When each side is weakened, we'll sweep forth and destroy them both."

Shet imagined the satisfaction to come. "Elves, spiderkin, boastful rakishi and other woven . . . They'll all pay the price for their hubris."

Liline, his lovely, cruel captain, opened her mouth to speak, but

Sture cut her off. "Cease your prattling. A greater task awaits our Lord. Attend him."

Shet nodded appreciation to his friend and general. "Observe." He sourced his *lorethasra* and sent a surge of Spirit at the place where the anchor line would open. It ballooned out, undulating like a heat haze to those with the vision to see. "The anchor line opens."

A white line, more vivid than the Wildness, split the air. It sizzled like water hitting hot coals, rotating into the shape of a doorway. It was easily tall enough for Shet to step through and wide enough for the other titans to walk abreast of him. A coruscating welter of colors took minutes to condense into the proper shape of a rainbow bridge, and when it did a bell tolled and a hot wind rolled off the open doorway. The billowing power tickled Shet's nostrils.

He fought a desire to sneeze, distracting himself by more tightly gripping his staff, considering and anticipating the destruction he'd mete out to his enemies. Too long had he left their betrayal unpunished. Too long had they left him to rot. Too long had they escaped judgment. Finally, they'd learn what it meant to anger a god.

"It is time," Shet intoned. He concentrated, forced his attention inward, creating a thick braid of Spirit, a rotating double-helix. He quickly added threads of Fire attached to Air and Earth to Water. In moments, the weave was complete. It spun in the vault of his mind, ringing like wind chimes. Ironically, he'd learned the braid's creation from Shokan. It was a weaving only a *raha'asra* who was also a *ther-a'asra* could form. The most powerful woven could manage it also, but that was of no consequence.

Shet's Spirit slipped out of his body but somehow retained possession of his staff.

This was different from the anchor line that the mahavans of Sinskrill used to travel to Seminal. That one only allowed their minds to make that journey. This one allowed much more. It allowed the travel of one's aether, *Jivatma* as Shokan called it. Shet tethered to the anchor line and stepped upon it. The world shattered like broken ice as he passed into an endless night.

~

THE RUINED bulk of Clarity Pain, Shet's original place of worship, surrounded Sapient and his necrosed, all ten of them. They stood in the throne room. Vines penetrated the chamber, spreading fingerlike tendrils along the ceiling. From the poisonous green growth blossomed small, white flowers carrying the musty aroma of a fresh grave. The unlamented corpse of Grave Invidious remained where he'd fallen, near the throne. The deadly spiders who'd webbed much of the chamber had long since scattered when the necrosed had entered the hall. They knew well enough to give wide berth to those who couldn't die. This was where the necrosed had been born, where Sapient had been transformed from a mere holder into a being of power.

The other necrosed held back from him, shuffling about in nervousness and excitement. All except for the massive Manifold Fulsom. He stood directly behind Sapient, his fetid breath stirring the Overward's dark hair.

Sapient ignored Manifold's overly close presence and concentrated on what needed doing. He linked to the anchor line leading to Sinskrill, and a black line split the air in front of him. It rotated and a doorway formed, one filled with coruscating colors. Sapient sent the key.

"You're certain this will lead us to Sinskrill?" Manifold dared ask.

Sapient immediately backhanded the large necrosed, not appreciating his close proximity and unwilling to allow his powerful subordinate to question his authority.

Manifold rocked on his heels, took one step back, resettled himself, and glared.

Sapient stared the larger necrosed in the eyes, silently challenging him.

Manifold dropped his gaze. "My apologies, Overward."

Sapient didn't reply at once. He kept his attention hard on the other necrosed. Seconds passed. "Apology accepted." He resumed facing the anchor line.

By now the wildly shifting colors had taken the shape of the familiar rainbow bridge, and Sapient set aside his recent confrontation with Manifold. On the other side of the anchor line awaited a feast, one of the utmost deliciousness. No necrosed had ever partaken of such a wondrous repast. The magi would soon attack Sinskrill. Sapient had seen the coming conflict with his own eyes. A fleet charged Sinskrill, boats filled with juicy *asrasins* just waiting to be consumed.

Sapient shivered in excitement. He'd only returned to the Far Beyond in order to collect his brethren. He needed them to share in the coming the banquet. He needed them powerful for the task ahead of them. By himself he couldn't fight all his enemies: the Servitor, Shokan, Sira, and possibly Shet. Plus, he had to ensure that the boy holder denied Shet's admittance into Earth.

Sapient tethered to the anchor line, sensing when the others did so. "Kill everyone you come across," he said by way of final orders.

He stepped onto the anchor line. The world became glum and silent.

In the distance, Sapient saw a doorway. It seemed to stretch farther and farther away. A tunnel extended beyond and behind him. His body frayed, torn into the now familiar pain of travel. He ignored it. An instant later, the doorway snapped into place.

Sapient exited into the heart of a battle.

He immediately killed an *asrasin*. The woman had been standing next to a firewager, a cannon, mounted on a wagon. He drained her *lorethasra* as her life failed. He stretched limbs that hummed with fresh power. His mind sharpened, and his thoughts brightened, growing clearer.

Four other *asrasins*—a mixed group of men and women—stood beside her. Sapient's brethren followed on his heels and killed them as well.

Braids of Fire and Earth gripped him. Sapient cut them with barely a thought. He wanted to laugh. Hundreds of *asrasins* huddled in the ravaged field that contained Sinskrill's anchor lines. His brethren spread out, each prepared to kill and consume as many *asrasins* as they could.

Sapient made to join them, but unexpected caution reared its head. He took in details. The boy holder commanded the *asrasins*, magi apparently. He had already taken note of the necrosed and shouted orders. Within seconds, Sapient's brethren found themselves attacked on all sides. Their progress slowed.

The boy ignited his sword. *The Wildness.*

A flicker of worry climbed Sapient's spine. The doubt transformed into fear when his regard fell upon a titanic corpse that lay unmoving roughly fifty yards away. Black chitin the color of dried blood armored the creature, but even now it crumbled apart. Batwings extended off her back, and short, vicious horns protruded from her head. Her eyes would have been the color of corruption.

Sapient knew what the monster was: a demon, and someone had slain it. Only Shokan could have managed the feat. The Lord of the Sword was near.

Sapient shot his gaze about the field, searching for Shet's great foe, the one all necrosed counted as their greatest enemy.

There!

On the far side of the meadow, he battled. Many millennia ago, Sapient had fought Shokan and had been easily bested. He'd also battled the Lord of the Sword and the Lady of Fire more recently and barely survived the encounter. He had no intention of facing his once-friend a third time.

To the west, onto the war-torn field opened another anchor line. Sapient's gaze snapped in that direction. Through the anchor line stepped a man. No. Not a man. A holder. Another one. He shared features with the boy. Perhaps a brother. And he also wielded a sword.

Sapient recognized it. *Undefiled Locus.* It burned with the Wildness.

The two holders reached one another and fought side-by-side, battling Brine. They looked to overwhelm him fairly soon. Sapient scanned the field and saw Shokan destroy two necrosed in the span of seconds.

Even with the fresh power of a newly killed *asrasin* coursing through his veins, Sapient knew he couldn't defeat so many foes. It was time to retreat. He sprinted for a hole in the wall surrounding the field. The four other necrosed who still lived apparently recognized the same wisdom that he did. They broke off their attack and followed his retreat.

CINDER CROUCHED ATOP AIA, hunched in a saddle while she drifted on currents of icy wind. He ignored the cold and ran his fingers along a ruffle of soft calico fur that ran from his dragon's wagon-sized head to where her wings emerged directly behind her shoulders. Cinder still wasn't used to her appearance. She was a dragon, but in his mind, she should be a Kesarin.

A hard gust of wind twisted her about, and Cinder had to grip the sides of her long neck more tightly. The ground was a long way down.

I won't let you fall, Aia said.

I know. It's only that—

You like to be in command of a situation?

Cinder chuckled ruefully. *Yes.*

They floated high in the sky, miles above Shet's palace, unknown and unnoticed as they rode the currents. Clouds obscured their presence. A hundred yards away Anya rode Shon. A fierce line of concentration knitted her forehead as she closely watched the palace below them.

Despite the lack of sunshine, Anya's crown of golden hair glowed. Cinder traced the lines of her sharply pointed ears. Those features and her slanted eyebrows marked her as an elf. Her choice of species was the best decision she could have made upon entering Seminal, but now her choices were far wider. Anya could have become human again. Cinder could have helped her make the transition. With his memories and powers restored, he knew how.

She'd chosen otherwise.

He sighed. She'd also made other choices he wished she hadn't.

Give her time, Aia advised.

She's had decades, Cinder said. *If anything, time has hardened her heart against me, against who we once were.*

Aia had no response to that, and they stared at Shet's outdoor courtyard. Small breaks between the fluffy, white clouds gave them glimpses of what occurred below.

Cinder sensed something happening, and his senses heightened. He quickly wove binoculars. Shet, Sture, and four other titans stood in the courtyard's heart. Something swirled to life in front of them.

The anchor line to Earth.

Aia plunged downward, Shon following close behind. Seconds into their freefall, both dragons pulled up sharply.

The palace is warded against us, Aia said. *We can't land.*

Cinder measured the distance to the ground, already considering the necessary weaves. He sourced his Well, the housing of his *Jivatma*, conducting heavily from it, able to use it like no human in thousands of years. A heady sense of invincibility filled him, but he ignored the sensation.

He had to get down there. Shet was already through the anchor line. Everything depended on stopping the god. *I'll take care of the ward,* he told Aia. Cinder loosened his grip and slipped out of his saddle.

RUKH Aia shouted. She darted after him.

His name was Cinder. Rukh was who he wished to be, but only Jessira could give him his name back. And that wouldn't happen any time soon.

Cinder braided Air to Earth, hardening his skin and shielding his face. Maybe she'd forgive him one day, but until then he had a Trial to complete. The wind still whistled past his ears but it no longer burned his eyes.

Aia reached his side, wings tucked tight as she fell next to him.

Cinder noted Shon shoot downward as well, Anya still in the saddle. Cinder's focus, though, remained on the courtyard. It grew larger. The titans became recognizable. There had been five of them outside, but two had retired into the palace, taking Shet's body for safekeeping. The ones left were Sture, Liline, and Tomag.

What are you doing? Anya shouted in his mind. *You'll die.*

An elf would. I won't, Cinder shot back.

She had no reply to that, but he sensed anger bubbling in her mind.

But the titans, Aia protested.

Cinder knew the odds against Shet's captains weren't good, but he'd have to hope for the best. *I can take them.*

Not without Jessira's help, Aia said.

Anya, Cinder corrected.

You're being foolish. Aia reached out with a clawed hand, threatening to pull him aboard. *You have to leave your body. How can you do that while battling Shet's captains?*

Cinder shifted away from his dragon with a blast of Air. *Leave it,* he told her. *The plan is unchanged. Do your part and fly us to safety when it's time.*

He noticed Shon still plunging toward the courtyard. Anya climbed to the edge of her saddle. She held Shon's tawny fur in a loose grip, apparently readying herself to leap off of him.

This time it was Cinder's turn to demand to know what she was doing.

I'm only doing the same as you. You'll have to catch me before I hit the ground. She released the saddle and arrowed downward.

Cinder cursed under his breath. Nothing for it now. The titans had noticed them and held their weapons at the ready.

Cinder stretched his senses until he could see the ward blocking the dragons. It mostly contained Water, a dragon's bane. But add Air and Earth to the Water along with a healthy dose of Fire, and the ward should disintegrate. He could manage it once he was inside the barrier.

It was dangerous to attack this way, but he'd always been foolhardy. Jessira had always said so.

You're still foolhardy, Anya said, speaking through the link provided by the dragons.

There was no time to answer. A blistering line of Fire rippled toward him. Cinder batted it aside. More weaves came at him and Anya.

Aia and Shon ripped the attacks apart.

The titans scattered, giving themselves room to maneuver and fight, possibly worried about the dragons. Aia and Shon banked sharply, pulling up before they struck the ward.

A hundred feet to go. Cinder blasted Air, slowing his descent. He hardened muscles and bones, stiffening them. It would be a hard landing, but he could take it. He slowed Anya's descent as well. Her more fragile elven frame couldn't be reshaped like his.

Cinder landed. Blue flames shot out of Sture's eyes, rocketing his way. Cinder slapped it aside with a braid of Air. He instinctively ducked, sensing the storm of swords threatening to skewer him. Tomag Shield-Breaker's trick, one he'd learned from Shet. Cinder conducted more *Jivatma* and Shielded. Liline shot steel slugs. They materialized in front of her hands, fired faster than bullets.

Cinder took them on his Shield. He responded with fire of his own, sending a sizzling cord of lightning. She gave way. Sture arrived, sword slashing. Cinder blocked, slid a thrust, and shot a sidekick. He flung the titan halfway across the courtyard.

Anya landed and Shielded. She unsheathed her sword and took off some of the pressure on Cinder. Tomag sent a misty green serpent with venomous fangs at her undefended back. In one motion, she spun and cut the snake off at the head. The serpent dissolved into acid that hissed as it etched the courtyard's stone floor. Anya flung a pattern of sparkling light directly into Liline's face, causing her to fall away. She then attacked Sture, who'd rejoined the battle.

Cinder finally had time to release the weave he'd been holding, the one meant to dissolve the ward. An instant later, it came apart in a hiss of steam.

The dragons roared and descended to the courtyard. The titans wisely backed off, no longer attacking. They watched from a safe distance. The odds were no longer in their favor.

Cinder moved to stand before the open anchor line. He created the weave he'd discovered long ago, a braid whose spine was a double-helix made of Spirit. To it he added fine threads of Fire-to-Air and Earth-to-Water. He sensed Anya doing the same.

Wind chimes rang in his mind when he finished the weave, and it glowed, reflecting something far off and glorious.

His aether slipped out of his body, Anya only a moment behind. She reached for him, and he accepted her touch. It was something automatic, something they'd done without thinking when they'd called themselves Rukh and Jessira: to reach for one another and share everything.

Time stopped. Aia and Shon stood unmoving, mouths agape in mid-roar, flickers of fire frozen in front of their nostrils.

Anya's heart and memories opened for Cinder. He saw her decades of loneliness, the bitterness they engendered, the despair. For the first time he truly understood the pain she'd endured on his behalf, on *their* behalf. Words couldn't convey his grief. He didn't know how to apologize.

She slammed shut the window on her emotions. *Stay out of my mind,* she told him, her voice hard and angry.

Cinder mentally sighed. *So be it.* Their thoughts remained connected, though. She hadn't entirely broken the link. *We need to fight as one,* he said to her.

How? she asked, her voice sounding suspicious.

Like this. He created a braid, one from his Caste on Arisa: an Annex. He prayed she'd accept it. It would be their best chance at surviving Shet.

She let his weave touch her, and they Annexed.

A languid peace stole over Cinder. In his mind's deepest recesses, he remembered himself as Rukh Shektan, a son of Ashoka. His thoughts drifted, as if a film of fog covered them. All his regrets stilled.

29

PAYBACK

Serena ordered the magi away from the battle between Jessira and the Servitor. Those two fought like gods descended to Earth, ravaging one another with blows hard enough to crack a mountain. Instead, she did as Jessira had ordered: focusing on the warriors opposing her magi. Fifty mahavans and a score of unformed, most of them in the form of tigers, had come in support of the Servitor. They sheltered on a small rise, boulders protecting their backs. It was a good defensive posture, but the Irregulars had them massively outnumbered. Agua Battalion would chew them up, assuming no more units entered the fray in support of the Sinskrill forces.

Serena recognized some of the mahavans facing Agua Battalion, drones during her time on Sinskrill, friendless and powerless until the Servitor gave them all a second chance. Based on how well they sourced their *lorethasra*, their flickering Fire, trembling braids of Earth, and shuddering weaves of Air and Water, they were poorly trained. She might have felt sorry for them, but she was a warrior, and she had a mission to complete. These mahavans opposed her. They'd helped the Servitor kill her friends, whose burnt bodies she could see. Their corpses littered the ground ahead of her, torn apart like their wagons and oxen.

These mahavans and woven were a large part of the reason why. Their faces were blank of emotions, but Serena could sense their fear. They knew death was coming, and she'd deliver it to them. A simple plan came together in her mind.

Serena called for Daniella and Lien. "Take fifty magi," she told Daniella. "Go after their left flank. Draw them out." Next she addressed Lien. "Take another fifty with you. Once Daniella has their attention, attack from their right."

"What about you?" Lien asked.

"Once the enemy engages, I'll hammer into the heart of their forces. We'll crush them in between our units."

"That doesn't account for the unformed," Daniella said.

"I'll have forty in reserve. We'll kill them all."

Daniella and Lien snapped off salutes and went to gather their units. Serena waited for them to get into position. The plan should work. The mahavans didn't have artillery to provide covering fire while the magi charged. She might have used her own cannons, but at this range it would have been too easy for the mahavans to plug their muzzles with one of the many boulders lying around.

Daniella began her assault. There was no more time for planning or second-guessing. Explosions and shouts soon followed. Dirt and mud blasted skyward. A cold drizzle started. The rain couldn't drown the stench of sulfurous Fires that quickly filled the air. Serena watched the mahavans form a pair of straight lines. Their previous trembling braids became firm. They defended against Daniella, smoothly and without panic. These new mahavans were better than Serena realized. She'd have to commit more of her forces. She called up the reserve to buttress her own unit, recognizing that they might be needed sooner than anticipated.

Lien's company attacked. The unformed went after them. Lightning flashed at the woven, but it didn't slow them down. More explosions, snarls, and roars filled the air. A tiger leapt onto a magus, ripping out his throat. An elephant inhaled a braid of Water. He swelled. An instant later, he contracted, shooting the braid back, a torrent from his trunk, drowning another magus. An eagle tore out the throat of an Irregular. Individual battles broke out. Serena saw Lien get cut off. She desperately lashed out with whips of Fire, burning a buffalo who transitioned into a falcon. The woven resumed his attack in the form of a charging rhino. Lien barely escaped by throwing herself to the side.

Serena studied the line of battle and cursed. She had hoped the Sinskrill forces would be broken apart by now, but they continued to defend well, their line intact. Daniella's and Lien's units, on the other hand, were getting chewed up. Serena had no other option. "Attack!" she shouted.

She led her initial seventy Irregulars and the reserve in a straight-ahead charge at the Sinskrill forces atop the hill. Some of the unformed spun to face the danger, and as soon as they did, Lien put down two of them. Fifteen mahavans shifted about to defend against her charge. They tore the ground with hissing weaves of Earth and washing braids of Water. More mud exploded. Three Irregulars went down screaming, chests caved in or bodies set alight. More fell. Serena closed her mind to the carnage and death screaming all around her.

She focused on the mahavans atop the hill. She had to reach them. Nothing else mattered. She leapt over the braids and deto-nating earth, dodged whistling arrows of Air and burning lines of Fire. *Closer.*

Serena lofted boulders and stones at the mahavans, anything to distract them. Other magi followed her lead. The mahavans faltered in their defense.

Only a few more yards.

Serena reached the hill, clambering it quickly. Seconds later, she was in the midst of the mahavans. She rolled under a sword aimed at her neck. In one motion, she unsheathed her own blade at the same time that she regained her footing. She blocked a thrust. A diagonal strike was slipped and parried. A blade cut into her bicep, and she fell back, cursing at the pain. She sensed movement to her side and ducked. A bear reared over her. She launched a slice that nearly took off the creature's leg at the knee. The bear collapsed when his limb would no longer support him, roaring in anguish.

Something rammed her in the spine, slamming her into the ground. She spun about and realized a dead mahavan had crashed into her. She pushed him off, regaining her feet.

More magi had gained the hill. The pressure eased, and Serena was able to step back and take in the battle. The mahavans and unformed were crumbling in the face of her unit's pressure. Daniella's Irregulars had also found their footing. They neared the hill's crest, about to break through the mahavan line. Some of the Sinskrill warriors ran. Lien's unit had similar success. They'd destroyed the bulk of the unformed. The surviving woven creatures retreated, winging in the direction of Village White Sun and the Servitor's Palace.

A few more whiplashes of Fire and bolts of Air, and the battle was over.

Serena's eyes went to where she'd last seen Jessira fighting the Servitor. She saw her commander clutch her chest as if in pain. Blood flowed from one of her thighs, and her lip had split. The Servitor stood yards away from Jessira. A bruise bloomed across his temple. His mouth hung open, and he panted heavily. But his Spear remained leveled, triumph written upon on his face.

Serena shouted to the Irregulars. "Get him!"

JESSIRA COULD HAVE ORDERED the magi to help during her battle against the Servitor, but they would have only gotten in the way. Or worse, they would have died. She chose instead to fight the Servitor by herself. Not that she wanted to. While she and Rukh had continued to grow in power during their time on Arylyn, Jessira wasn't sure she was ready to take on the Servitor. She remembered his abilities, but she wouldn't fear them. She reckoned he had the greater strength and matched her speed, which meant she'd have to use skill and guile to defeat him.

"Shet may fear you, but I do not," the Servitor said. "I've already defeated you once, in the heart of your home no less."

Jessira recalled the battle on Arylyn and her lips thinned in anger. Yes, he'd knocked her unconscious, but he'd also attacked when she was busy battling his mahavans. She'd been unprepared. This time was different. Jessira flashed the Servitor a smirk. "And I've defeated you once before as well, when we stole Fiona and Travail out from under your nose. What do you say? Best two out of three?"

The Servitor spun his spear in a circle, red flames growling, trailing the weapon's length. He slammed the butt into the ground. "Come on then, World Killer," he snarled.

Jessira rolled her shoulders, drew her sword, and from her Well, she conducted *Jivatma*. It resembled a pure lake, untouched and a summer-sky blue, bringing with it a heady sense of invincibility and deeper life. The gray world of Sinskrill brightened. Shadows no longer hindered her senses. Colors became more vibrant, sounds more distinct, smells sharper. Jessira formed a Shield and readied a Fireball in her off hand. She also created the weaves for a Bow and a Spear, ready to release them at an instant's notice.

She conducted more *Jivatma*, and time slowed. Jessira readied to hurl herself forward in the eye-blurring fashion of a Kumma-trained warrior, even if she herself wasn't of that fabled Caste.

The Servitor rushed at her, dirt and mud spraying behind his heels. He moved nearly as fast as Rukh might have managed. But Jessira was ready for his speed. She threw the Fireball, not expecting it to connect, and it didn't. It screamed the short distance between them, but the Servitor batted it aside with his spear and kept on coming. She now had a gauge of his reflexes.

The Servitor leapt at her, weapon aimed at her heart. She slid to the side, both hands on the hilt of her sword as she blocked a back-swing. Their weapons came together with a hollow ring.

The runes on the spear flared hotter. The fires spat against her Shield, and Jessira gave ground, needing distance. The Servitor didn't give it. He was on her too swiftly. She couldn't bring the Bow or her braided Spear into the fight, but she kept them at the ready. She ducked a horizontal slash that transitioned into a straight thrust, taking the attack on her Shield. Green webbing rippled to life, sparking and buzzing. The blow threw her off balance.

Fragging unholy hells, he's strong. Jessira reset her feet.

The Servitor pressed against her defenses, his spear whistling. Jessira parried an overhand blow but was too slow to defend against the under swing. Her Shield slowed his spear, but the butt end still took her in the gut, rising to slam into her chest and then her mouth. Jessira's head snapped back. Ribs cracked, and her upper lip split. She gasped, struggling for breath. Blood leaked into her mouth. Her vision grayed.

Fear and anger brawled within her. She should have seen the blow coming. She needed distance before he attacked again.

She desperately plucked the Bow's string, and a silver light shot at the Servitor. He paused. *Thank Devesh.* The light whined, a high-pitched sound, crossing the distance and ramming into Sinskrill's ruler. The Servitor had a type of Shield, and it held for a moment, but the Bow still blasted him off his feet. He launched fifteen feet through the air, landing on his back, flipping over onto his stomach. He slid but managed to hold onto his spear.

Jessira took the break to Heal her ribs as best she could. They still hurt, and she struggled to take a deep breath, but it was the best she could do. She distractedly noted the battle between Agua Battalion and the Sinskrill forces but lacked the time to pay it any further attention.

The Servitor regained his feet. His white leathers were ruined, covered in mud and muck. He glared at his filthy clothing, appearing angrier at that than anything else. He shook off the filth as best he could. Blood trickled down his face from where the Bow had clipped him on the temple.

He aimed the spear, and Jessira knew what was coming. She drew more deeply from her *Jivatma*. This time she was ready. The Servitor sent a blistering line of Fire. It roared like a blast furnace, hot enough to bore through a mountain. Jessira launched her counter, a line of Earth, thick as a hawser. It impacted his Fire, capturing some of its heat. More importantly, it blasted the Servitor's weave aside.

Jessira charged in behind her line of Earth, going on the attack.

She feinted a slash. He bit. She adjusted the blow. It would have cut him across the chest, but at the last instant, he managed to bring his spear into position to defend. She tried to follow up, but he was ready for her this time. Steel clashed against the flaring wood of his spear. She sent a diagonal swing, which he deflected. An overhand blow had her sliding aside. She sent a slash. He parried and sent a straight thrust. She punched it away, and her sword slid down the haft of his spear, threatening to slice his fingers. He flinched, disengaging. His weapon dipped, leaving his chest unguarded.

Jessira didn't bite. It was a trick. She pretended to chase his feint with a short thrust. He set his spear to snap her sword aside, but she'd already brought her blade to guard. The Servitor was over-extended now. Jessira carved a deep line across his bicep. She took a shallow slice to her thigh for her troubles.

They both withdrew, staring at each other from a distance of fifteen feet. The Servitor had his spear leveled and ready, and a crooked sneer twisted his face. He was trying to project confidence, but Jessira wasn't fooled. She was damaged, but so was he, and if the battle came down to one of will, she'd win. Of this she was certain. Jessira grinned at him then, wanting him to know it, too. She sent a line of Fire at him.

He glowered, crossing his arms and blocking her braid. He leapt back twenty feet. Weaves of Earth, Air, and Water chased him. A slicing motion with the spear tore them apart. More formed.

Jessira glanced back. A number of Irregulars charged the Servitor.

Her heart nearly stopped. The Servitor would attack them. Kill them. They couldn't defend against his power. Jessira stepped forward, prepared to defend the magi. She never needed to.

The Servitor glared at the onrushing Irregulars, and a second later he transformed into an eagle, winging west. He clutched the spear in his talons.

Jessira breathed out in relief.

"Are you all right?" Serena asked. She'd been at the head of the charging magi.

"I'm fine. Or I will be. Give me a moment to Heal myself." She still watched the Servitor. The man was a small dot now. "We'll call that one a draw."

～

THE BATTLE WAS FINALLY TURNING in favor of Terran Battalion. All of the necrosed broke for a hole in the wall, and Jason was heartily glad to see the last of them. The mahavans also abandoned the field. They streamed away from their battlements, likely heading for Village White Sun. As for the unformed, those who had survived the lightning sent against them dashed about, slashing and clawing at any magus they could get ahold of. The well-trained members of the Terran Battalion reacted instantly. They were used to dealing with the creatures from the prior battle on Arylyn. The Irregulars brought the battle to the body-altering creatures, fighting in small units of three or four magi, isolating the woven and cutting them down.

But a more deadly peril threatened.

Vampires, or at least that's what Jason figured them to be, drifted above the battlefield. They were tall men and women, pale-featured and flying upon wings made of ever-fraying shadow. Their clothing was perfectly tailored for their slim, elegant frames, but rather than the black garb that Jason might have expected, their pants and shirts were colored in loud reds, blues, and yellows. Gold circlets set with diamonds held back long, dark hair. They surveyed the fighting with cold, gray eyes.

Based upon a signal only heard or sensed by the creatures, the vampires opened their mouths, jaws unhinging like snakes and displaying lines of dagger-like teeth. They screamed, the sound high-pitched and piercing. It washed across the battlefield, pulsing fear and paralysis into the hearts of those still fighting.

The Terran Battalion threatened to come undone. After everything they'd fought against—the killing field, the demon, the necrosed—the vampires were too much. Jason tried to clamp down on his own fear. He searched around for Rukh. *Where the hell is he?* His fear escalated when he couldn't see their commander.

"Courage, son," Tam said. He stood nearby and clapped Jason on the shoulder, staring him in the eyes.

The fear unclenched, and Jason gave the old Marine a nod of acknowledgement.

"Be ready!" William bellowed from a dozen yards away. "They're only another flavor of monster. We'll send them straight to hell."

His words broke Jason out of his spell, and other magi seemed to take heart from his words.

The vampires slowly descended, screaming the entire time as they circled toward the ground.

"Light them up!" William shouted.

Jason did as ordered, sending every kind of braid he could think of—Fire, Earth, Water, and Air—against the woven monsters. He cursed an instant later. The braids had no effect. The creatures became wispy, transforming into something ephemeral, like a holographic image, and his weaves simply passed through their elegant forms. Air and Earth couldn't bind them, and Fire and Water couldn't harm them.

William called an end to the attack, and the vampires smiled then. Their mouths split into sinister grins. One of them, a male, lunged at an Irregular who tried to stumble away, but the vampire flew forward, his feet floating inches off the ground. She thrust with her sword, but he swayed aside, sashing forward again to rip out her throat. He proceeded to chew on her face.

William screamed inarticulately, unloosing a bolt of bone-white Spirit, one as pure as any Jason had ever seen.

The vampire went wispy, but William's braid of Spirit took the monster through its chest and didn't simply pass on through. It seemed to fill the vampire, and the creature's slim features quickly grew bloated. His entire body expanded, and the vampire shrieked, a high-pitched scream like a saw cutting wood. Light leaked out of every one of his pores. He flashed once, and a small pile of ashes marked where he'd been standing.

A brief silence took over the field. The vampires appeared shocked. Their demeanor of vicious pleasure had drained away, replaced by uncertainty and maybe fear. As one, they stared at the ash pile of the fallen vampire before turning their gazes toward William, anger now filling their visages.

"Get them," Jason shouted. He shoved any nearby Irregulars into motion. "Use Spirit. It'll kill them."

Landon stepped up to William's side, a plain longsword in his hand. He spun the blade in a circle, igniting it with the Wildness.

Jason did a double-take. When had Landon arrived? He had no further time to wonder. A pair of vampires had localized on him. He and every magi standing nearby shot bolts of Spirit at the vampires. Their weaves were thin and weak compared to William's and did little more than irritate the vampires. They quickly had to give ground.

The vampires advanced, confident again.

Landon was suddenly there between Jason and the vampires, his longsword ablaze and crackling like a lightsaber. Fear again took hold on the vampires' faces. One of them said something, but Jason couldn't make out the words. The creatures brought up clawed hands and black currents shot from their fingers, hissing like a dozen rattlesnakes. The streams twisted toward Landon, but he slashed the dark lines into ribbons with his glowing sword. The vampires snarled, and Landon rushed them before they could recover. One he skewered, and the other he beheaded.

After Landon finished off the vampires, he faced Jason with a crooked grin. "It ain't easy killing these bastards, but somebody's got to do it." He glanced to the side and his smile faded. "Gotta go, friend." He rushed another three vampires who threatened a cluster of magi. Their weaves of Spirit were thicker than what Jason could manage, but they still did little more than slow the creatures down.

Landon laid into the vampires, killing them before they even noticed his presence. Meanwhile, William fired bolts of Spirit at the vampires, especially the ones who sought to flee by flying away. They were unsuccessful. William burned them all. Seconds later, the field was free of the creatures.

It was over.

Jason breathed out in relief, chuckling.

William approached then, speaking rapidly. "I'm leaving Jake in charge. Get him on the walkie-talkie."

"Where are you going?" Jason asked. "And where's Rukh?"

"He had to leave," William said. "He said the anchor line is opening sooner than expected. He has to be in the Throne Hall to stop Shet. I've got to get there, too. I'm the only one who can close the fragging anchor line."

Jason pointed to the hole in the wall. "The necrosed escaped. Should we pursue?"

William shook his head. "You won't be able to stop them. They'll tear the Irregulars apart and gain strength with every *asrasin* they kill. Landon and I will deal with them if we have time, but the Throne Hall is more important."

Jason accepted William's words. "Any orders you want me to pass on to Jake?"

"Hunt down the mahavans, all of them. We can't let any of them stop Rukh and Jessira from doing whatever they have to at the Throne Hall."

Jason nodded. "Yes, sir." Fighting mahavans he could do. All those other monsters, though. They were for people like William and Landon.

William and Landon mounted up on a pair of bicycles and left the field in a cloud of thrown mud and torn grass.

Jason withdrew his walkie-talkie and got hold of Jake. He passed on William's orders.

"Understood," Jake said. He paused a moment before passing on his own set of commands. "Clear the wounded, but leave a detachment at the anchor line. We have to maintain control of the field. It might end up being our only way off this fragging island."

"Copy that, sir," Jason said. He finally had a moment to take in the battlefield. It looked like the meadow had been chewed up and spit out. Nothing remained but mud and torn grass. A drizzle had started, but it did nothing to squelch the acrid smoke that drifted all across the field from the many places where it had burned. Multiple holes had been punched into the mahavan's wall. Rubble littered the ground, as did the bodies of dozens of magi. Some lay in repose, clearly dead. Others moaned, shouted, or screamed in grievous injury.

Jason swallowed back his sorrow. The battle had gone about as bad as could be expected, and he had a lot of terrible work yet ahead of him.

30

BATTLEFIELD REUNIONS

Wil128illiam pedaled hard alongside his brother. He'd worried that Landon might not be able to keep up, but his concern proved unnecessary. His brother rode at his right hip, face focused and breathing easy. The two of them hurtled down the rugged road that led from the anchor line to Village White Sun. Minutes later, William saw the trail he was looking for. Travail had shown it to him years ago during his training on Sinskrill.

Five miles as the crow flies from here to the Palace.

The path they needed branched off to the left, overgrown and barely visible. Weeds choked it, but taking it would shave a few miles and many minutes off their journey. They took the trail, bouncing over the rugged terrain. Mud kicked up, vegetation slapped at their ankles, but they hardly slowed, pedaling hard while descending a hill. They wended through a scattering of boulders that rose higher than their heads.

William's bike shuddered and juked with every sharp turn, but he maintained his balance. The clouds had grown thicker, and the day felt like it was slipping into twilight. An ill wind kicked up, chill and cutting. It bit through William's jacket, but he paid it no attention.

He slowed when the trail took them into the depths of a forest, narrowing until they had to ride single file. The light dimmed further, but at least the trees cut down on the wind. William stayed in the lead. He knew where they were headed. Every now and then a gust ripped through the canopy, shaking branches, needles, and leaves. The trees, soaked by a previous rain, splashed icy precipitation. Some of it showered William in the face.

He wiped off the water, disregarding the cold.

"Where are we going again?" Landon asked.

"To the Servitor's Palace," William answered. "That's where the necrosed are probably headed, too."

"How do you figure?"

"Remember I told you I share a connection with Sapient?"

"Yeah?"

"That's how I know."

The trail ascended a hill in a twisting fashion. Thick roots carved the path, threatening to buckle their front wheels and dump them off their bikes. William hopped off his bike and ran it most of the way up the hill. Mud squelched with his every step. He slipped, nearly fell, but pushed on as fast as he could, breathing smooth and steady. All the running and wind sprints had been worth it.

They had to get to the Throne Hall. That's all that mattered. Even stopping the necrosed wasn't as important. Rukh and Jessira would handle the Servitor and Shet, and he'd shut the anchor line. That was the plan.

They crested the hill's summit and exited the forest. Spread out before them was Travail's old field from when William had been enslaved on Sinskrill. His heart dropped. On the other side of the meadow were five necrosed who appeared to be having an argument. One huge brute faced off against Sapient, who was easily identified by his albino skin.

William cursed. They'd didn't have time to fight the necrosed. He also didn't think they could handle five of them on their own, especially with Sapient tossed into the mix. He gestured for Landon to retreat down the trail, but one of the necrosed, a female, noticed them. William sighed when she barked to the others and pointed.

"Well, there goes that," Landon said, not sounding the least bit worried. He set aside his bike and unsheathed his sword. William recognized Landon's blade from Sapient's dreams: *Undefiled Locus*.

Three necrosed charged, but Sapient and the larger one held back. In fact, they didn't move at all. Hope twitched across William's mind. If Sapient and the other necrosed stayed out of the battle long enough, maybe he and Landon could take out the others. They could handle three. He hoped.

William readied his weapon.

Landon ignited the Wildness and grinned. He indicated the necrosed with his chin. "Come on. Let's have some fun."

William couldn't help it. He grinned back at his brother. Despite the terrifying circumstances, joy filled him. He'd missed his brother. "Let's do it."

He ignited the Wildness as well, and his blade crackled. The two of them shouted incoherently as they charged the enemy. William knew that only the Wildness could kill the necrosed, but other weaves could slow them down. He drew on his *lorethasra*. Air slammed into a relatively short necrosed, hurtling him into the tree line. The other two leaned into William's wind, countering it somehow.

No more time to think. The necrosed had arrived.

William ducked a clawed swipe. The necrosed he fought, a dark-skinned monster, shot off a front kick. William dodged. He sent a feint at the creature's legs. The necrosed hopped back.

The monster eyed him warily. "We thought all your kind dead." His voice was deep and surprisingly mellifluous.

William didn't bother answering. The creature was trying to buy time for the third necrosed to re-enter the fray. William didn't allow it. He got in range of the smooth-voice necrosed.

The monster swung an overhand left. William blocked. The necrosed pulled short his blow and sent a right cross. It would have ripped off William's face. He ducked, called up Earth, and trapped the creature's feet in a mix of clay and mud. At the same time, Fire dried the material to a consistency of concrete. The necrosed lurched off balance. He fell forward, arms outstretched.

William stepped to the side, angled a downward strike, and decapitated the necrosed in one blow.

Landon had dealt with his necrosed, the female, as well. The third one finally arrived but ground to a halt on seeing them and the two dead necrosed at their feet.

Good. The monster's hesitation gave them time to regroup. William's gaze flicked about, searching for Sapient.

There!

The Overward raced toward the Servitor's Palace, but the big necrosed still hadn't moved. He gazed at them with arms folded and a calm visage. The necrosed who William had earlier thrown into the forest flicked his eyes from William to Landon and back again. He snarled and ran into the trees.

"What do we do with him?" Landon asked, gesturing toward the big necrosed.

"We kill him."

They marched toward the last necrosed. William recognized him from one of Sapient's shared thoughts or memories. His name . . . It tickled the back of his mind. *Manifold Fulsom.*

The necrosed watched them approach. "I won't fight you," Manifold said. "You mean nothing to me. I only want Shokan and Sira. They are the only ones who can heal me." A note of pleading entered his voice. "Will you allow it?"

William pulled up short. He never expected to hear a necrosed ask for anything, especially in such a tone of supplication. The begging confused him, and his mind recoiled. What did Manifold really want? It couldn't be as simple as what he was actually saying. "Tell me why we shouldn't just kill you instead."

"I wasn't always like this," Manifold said, gesturing to himself. "I was once otherwise. I wish to be healed of the pain of being a necrosed. Shokan and Sira can do that."

William rolled his eyes. He shouldn't have expected a more noble reason for why Manifold wanted to be spared. He hadn't grown remorseful for all the evil he was sure to have done in his life. He only wanted his own personal pain to end. "That's not good enough."

Manifold grinned, a gruesome sight of misshapen teeth. "Then how about this. I know you want to shut the anchor line to Seminal. Sapient taught you how, but Sapient has his own motives."

"What does Sapient want?" Landon asked.

Manifold's features became crafty, and he addressed William. "He wants power. There is a way for him to attain it. He'll betray you. I won't. I'll defend you. I've already done so once." He pointed to Sapient's distant form. "He would have killed your holder brother if not for me."

William didn't believe the necrosed, and he brightened the Wildness. "No deal."

The necrosed shook his head. "You show a considerable lack of wisdom. I've killed seven *asrasin* today. I've consumed their *lorethasra*. I am more powerful than you know." He exhaled heavily. "Nevertheless, I will help you regardless of your desires toward me."

William prepared to fight, but the big necrosed never gave him a chance. He thundered away, running in the same direction as Sapient, toward the Servitor's Palace.

"We're going to chase him down and kill him, right?" Landon asked.

William watched the swiftly departing necrosed, and a niggle of worry trickled down his spine. They should have just attacked and killed Manifold. Now they'd have to deal with him later, possibly in the Throne Hall. It was the last thing they needed.

A moment later, he shook his head. The monster ran as fast as Rukh. "I'm doubting we'll be able to catch him before he gets to the Palace. We'll roast him then, if you get my meaning."

Landon grinned. "I never got your meanings."

William smiled while they jogged to retrieve their bikes. "That's because you weren't smart enough to keep up with me."

Landon chuckled as if all the world's troubles meant nothing, and they shared a laugh, one that only brothers or the closest of friends could share.

∾

THEY'D LONG AGO INVENTED bicycles on Ashoka, but the ones there were primitive in comparison to those on Earth. The ones from Rukh's home weren't good for anything other than city use, and even then they generally rattled out a person's teeth in the process. He still remembered the first time he had seen a proper bicycle. It had been in Cincinnati, several years ago. He'd stopped dead in his tracks, immediately understanding what it could mean for a warrior: an unmatched range of movement across even the most rugged of terrain.

Rukh had fallen in love. The bicycles on Earth, especially mountain bikes, would have been useful on Arisa, certainly in the cities but even more in the Wildness where the Sorrow Bringer and her Chimeras had once ruled. It still struck him as amusing that those terrifying parts of Arisa shared the same name as the holder-based blend that could kill a necrosed.

He recalled that a handful of the woven monstrosities had attacked the magi and escaped through a breach in the wall. He had to hope that the Irregulars could handle them. He also had to hope that William would make it to the Throne Hall in time. The boy was strong and resourceful. He had the entire Terran Battalion to back him up. Plus, Landon, another holder, had arrived. Between all of them, they should be able to see William safely to where he needed to be.

The odds would have been even better if Shon had relented and stayed with William, but the Kesarin had refused. Jessira had been injured battling the Servitor, and Shon wouldn't go anywhere but immediately to her side. Aia wouldn't stay back, either. As a result, all three of them raced for the Palace, Rukh riding a sturdy mountain bike, bracketed between the two Kesarins, Aia to his right and Shon on his left.

Rukh hoped they weren't too late. They had little time left, maybe only minutes, before the anchor line opened, and he cursed anew. On this day of all days, the anchor line decided to open? It was the worst fragging luck. Even a few more hours would have made their mission that much easier to accomplish. A few hours more and they would have rolled the mahavans and waltzed to the Throne Hall with plenty

of time to spare. But no. Bad luck had to intervene and make a difficult task that much harder.

We could go faster if you rode me instead of that contraption, Aia
said.

I need both of you free to fight at your best, Rukh replied.

He pedaled on, following a narrow trail that Aia had somehow
picked out. It went in the direction they needed to go. Clouds thickened, and the sky darkened, taking on the mournful air of a funeral.
A stiff breeze kicked up as Rukh descended a heather-covered
hillock. The wind threatened to spill him off his bicycle, but he maintained his balance.

They reached the base of the hill and entered a copse of scraggly
evergreens. The air stilled here, wind blocked by the canopy. The
only sound was that of the Kesarins' pounding paws and his bicycle
tires sucking through the mud and dirt. They exited the copse in time
to catch a gust that rattled branches, pine needles, and leaves. From
their rain-soaked boughs showered a collection of water.

I hate rain, Aia muttered.

Jessira is near, Shon said. *Serena is with her.*

Where? Rukh asked.

Follow, Shon replied. He accelerated ahead of Rukh, darting
across his path.

Aia peeled off to join her brother, and Rukh pedaled after the
Kesarins.

They cut across the slope of a moss- and ivy-strewn hill,
bypassing stones and boulders. The sounds of shouting, of cannons
booming, and fires raging reached them. They crested the peak, and
a wide bowl of fallow farmlands reached out in front of them. The
Norwegian Sea glistened, indigo and reflective. What caught his
attention, though, was the scene of furious battle in the distance.
Smoke and flame wreathed Village White Sun, but as far as Rukh
could tell, not much damage had yet been done to the hamlet. Agua
Battalion had taken up a nearby position.

Closer at hand were Jessira and Serena, pedaling alone on a pair
of bicycles toward the Servitor's Palace. They paused and waited until
Rukh and the Kesarins reached them.

He checked Jessira for injuries, studying her carefully. He needed her fit and ready for the battle against Shet. More importantly, this was Jessira, his wife. He hated seeing her hurt.

"I'm fine," she said, acknowledging his worry. "Really. I already Healed myself."

"Just making sure," Rukh said. He scrutinized Village White Sun. "Who's in charge there?"

"Julius," Jessira said. "Daniella's his second. We had things in hand, and I figured they could handle the rest. I know time presses."

Rukh nodded sourly. "Doesn't it always?"

"It does make life interesting," Jessira said with a laugh like wind chimes.

Shon drew himself up. *We fought a demon,* he announced proudly.

I heard, Jessira said, rubbing her Kesarin's chin, *but we're not done fighting.*

Time's burning, Rukh said. *There are probably about fifty maha-vans left at the Palace. We'll Blend and slip past them.*

"Where's William?" Serena asked, speaking aloud.

"He's on his way," Rukh said. "Landon's with him. Let's go."

They had covered a mile when Aia's ears flicked. She slowed, drawing the rest of them to a halt. *William and Landon are coming.*

Shon rumbled approval.

Moments later, William and Landon pushed out of a small stand of trees. They raced down a hill, pedaling like mad fiends and whooping like little boys. They accelerated up a small hill and flew through the air when they reached its summit. They landed with a clang and kept on coming.

Rukh grinned. *That looked fun.*

"It does look fun," Jessira agreed, sensing his thoughts and smiling his way.

William and Landon arrived seconds later, skidding to a stop. Aia and Shon moved to William's brother, and while the Kesarins appeared lazy and aloof in their manners, Rukh sensed their excitement.

He wiped the smile off his face and addressed William. "Report."

William's grin fled, and he snapped off a salute. "Jake and Jason finished off the mahavans around the field. There were some vampires and unformed, but we had them routed by the time Landon and I left. We also ran into some trouble on the way here." He described a battle against the necrosed and the strange offer made by one of them. "What do you think it means, sir?"

Rukh shrugged. "No idea, and I don't care. We'll figure it out after we stop Shet."

They broke off the Kesarins' reunion with Landon and resumed their journey to the Servitor's Palace.

They soon reached their destination and left their bikes at the base of a shallow rise. Rukh and Jessira formed Blends, Linking and widening them to encompass everyone in their unit. They climbed the small hill and intently observed the Servitor's Palace.

Rukh formed binoculars, considering the damage. Something had punched through the portcullis and gate. Both structures had been tossed into the courtyard, twisted and torn and lying atop a number of corpses. More dead littered the ground, all of them apparently ripped apart.

The necrosed. It had to be them.

From deeper in the Palace Rukh caught the sound of battle, men and women shouting, screaming in desperation.

No one manned the battlements or the gates. The way inside was open.

~

IN THE END the Irregulars smashed through the Sinskrill forces around the anchor line, killing most of the mahavans, unformed, and vampires. A lot of necrosed, too. But Terran Battalion's death toll had also been horrific, hundreds dead and wounded. And from what Jake heard, Agua had also taken heavy casualties. Something about an ambush by the Servitor.

Jake wanted to link with Agua, but he also had to maintain control of the recent battlefield. As a result, he left a guard force of a hundred magi at the chewed-up meadow housing Sinskrill's anchor lines. Ward commanded them. He'd hold the field and evacuate casualties to the hospital tents in Australia.

Meanwhile, Jake led the remainder of Terran Battalion toward Village White Sun, where the last of the mahavans had holed up. Hopefully, this would be where this nightmare that had begun on a lonely road in Cincinnati would finally end. More, he prayed that the price they'd have to pay to take Village White Sun wouldn't be any steeper than what they'd already endured.

Jake crested a hill, and the village's fields stretched before him. Cannons crouched upon the farmlands like misshapen toads, but their barrels were quiet, not currently in use. Agua's crews stood about, unsure what to do other than glare at Village White Sun.

"Why isn't any one firing?" Jason asked.

"I don't know," Jake answered. A fog of smoke drifted across the village's battlements, but he counted eighteen cannons mounted on White Sun's walls. They weren't doing anything but sitting there either. They hunkered, menacing but silent, while the mahavans stared at the magi. "Leave the Terran here. Let's figure out what's going on."

"We should have gone with William and Landon," Jason said. "They'll need our help."

Jake agreed. In fact, if he had his way he'd already be pedaling pell-mell for the Throne Hall. But duty called, and he had to take care of this last battle.

A raindrop hit his cheek, and he glanced skyward. The day had grown dark with heavier clouds moving in. A cold wind kicked up, frothing the indigo waters of the Norwegian Sea, and he shivered. He hated it here, the cold, the gloom, the memories, and nothing would ever change that fact.

They asked a group of magi for directions to the command center and eventually came across Julius, Daniella, and Karla. The three of them leaned over a table containing a large map, glancing up when Jake and Jason arrived. Daniella flicked him an assessing gaze, a question on her face.

"I'm fine," Jake said in response to her unspoken query. "You?"

"Right as rain," she replied, her tone light and airy.

Despite her answer, Jake stared hard at her. She hadn't been injured, but she'd seen death today. She'd killed. He wanted to know she wasn't hiding some secret wound, a hurt no one else could see. He wanted to smooth her pain away.

"What's the situation?" Jason asked Julius.

Jake did his best to set aside his concern for Daniella and focused on the map, needing to understand what was going on. A number of markers indicated their forces and those of the mahavans.

Julius pointed to the line on the map that represented White Sun's wall. "They've got about five hundred mahavans in the village."

Jake frowned. That didn't sound right. He did the numbers in his head, counting up how many mahavans they'd killed at the field. The Terran had taken out over three hundred, and he'd heard Agua had killed a little more than a hundred in a series of running battles at Lake White Sun. Toss in the ones remaining in the Palace—Jake figured there were about fifty of them—and it meant there were at most five hundred people left in Village White Sun. But they couldn't all be mahavans. Many were probably drones, and a lot of them children.

"There aren't five hundred mahavans left," Jake said, explaining his calculations. "At most they've got about two hundred. The rest are drones and children. We can't kill *them*. They're defenseless."

Karla nodded firm agreement.

"And we won't," Julius said. "We won't bomb the village, only the wall and any who take up arms against us."

Jason exhaled heavily. "I want this over."

"We all do," Jake said, "and with the Terran added to Agua, we'll have the mahavans outnumbered almost three to one. We should be able to end things quickly."

"I wish it were that easy," Julius said. "They still have those damn, gray globes along their wall. We can't get through them. It's why we're sitting out here picking our noses. It's a stalemate."

"What about coming in through the harbor?" Jason asked.

"Same problem," Karla said. "They've got that approach defended with those globes, too."

Jake realized it was the same situation the Terran had faced. So maybe they could use the same solution. "William had us aim our cannons at a high elevation and bring the munitions around to strike the globes from behind. They aren't shielded in that direction. Concentrate fire there, and we might be able to blow a hole in the wall."

"It'll put us in range of their cannons," Daniella said

"But it's also our best plan," Karla said.

Julius nodded. "I agree. Let's go with it."

"Where do you want the Terran?" Jake asked.

"Hold them in reserve for now," Julius said, "but I want you and Jason on a cannon crew. You know where you're aiming, and you're also the most powerful magus we have for Spirit."

Jake still wanted to get to the Palace. He felt they might be more needed there than here. "As soon as we show you what to do, Jason and I are heading for the Palace."

"Understood," Julius said.

More orders were snapped out, and Jake and Jason joined a cannon crew.

"Here's to hoping for a lucky first shot," Jason said.

"Definitely," Jake replied.

There were four other cannons in close proximity to their own, and forty magi spread out in a loose arc, clusters of eight around each weapon.

Jake faced the village, studying it but unable to make out many features. Acrid smoke, gray and eye-watering, lingered over White Sun from when Agua had earlier tried to penetrate the shield. In addition, a twenty-foot wall hid the village. Mahavans patrolled the battlements, and Jake noted how few of them there were. He lowered his estimation of how many remained. A lot less than two hundred.

"You ready?" he asked Jason.

"Whenever you are."

"Let's give it a go."

Jake judged the distance needed to be in range. It would put them several hundred yards from the wall. Even the mahavans couldn't miss from that close. But it's where they had to be. *Take a punch to give one.* "Forward the cannons fifty yards," he ordered.

Within minutes the mahavans began bombarding their position. The shells landed in front of them, behind them, to the sides, and all around but nowhere close. Explosions showered towers of mud. Fires briefly flared before Sinskrill's omnipresent dampness put them out. More sulfurous smoke drifted across the field.

Jake viewed the magi units whose job it was to defend the cannons. "Is that your work?"

One of them shook his head. "Nope. They just have bad aim."

Jake chuckled. Maybe this really would be easy—He immediately cut off his line of thought. No reason to jinx things.

"Increase angle by twenty degrees," Jake ordered.

Within seconds the cannons were loaded, aimed, and ready. Jake held a thin line of Spirit, clamping the *nomasra* shell in place while the rest of the crew lit it with their Elements. Jake waited.

The *nomasra* glowed more brightly. When the shell was ready Jake released it, but kept it tethered the entire time. He watched it soar over the battlements. *Now to bring it around.* He changed the direction of the *nomasra*, altering its course, aiming for base of the wall. The shell disappeared from view, and an instant later it exploded. A sound like thunder echoed across the field as the wall shook and debris lofted in a plume. A crack appeared, snaking from the foundation to the very top.

The other crews were similarly successful with their shots. More cracks fractured the battlements.

The mahavans still fired their own cannons, and this time their aim was better. Some of the shells detonated close by.

Jake kept his attention on the wall. "Keep firing," he said.

Several minutes later, another set of shells launched skyward. They descended, striking the wall's foundation, one after the other in a staccato pattern. Debris blasted into the sky. More thunder rumbled. The cracks became fractures. The wall crumbled, large openings formed in slow motion. Screams reached them from unlucky mahavans who either fell from the battlements or found themselves battered by flying debris. At least three globes crashed to the ground, smashing like broken eggs.

Julius brought more cannons forward, taking advantage of the breach. Explosions filled the air, an unceasing welter of noise. A drizzle started. The cannon crews maintained a steady rate of fire. More breaks formed. Dirt and ash clouded the air.

Jake's crew had to take a breather. So did Jason's. The two of them stood and watched as the magi tore into Village White Sun's wall.

"I sure hope we don't have to go in there and do house-to-house fighting," Jason said.

Jake nodded in distraction. Worry for what was happening at the Servitor's Palace occupied his thoughts. That's where the most important battle was taking place. He couldn't stay any longer, and he went to Julius. "I'm heading out. You got this?"

Julius gave a tight nod. "Go. We'll finish them off."

Jake searched about for a bicycle and quickly found one. Jason must have had the same idea. They mounted up and pedaled away from one battle and toward another.

31

CONVERGENCE

T his last battle wasn't going to be easy. William could tell. He surveyed what he could of the Palace's courtyard beyond the broken portcullis. The bodies of a number of mahavans lay strewn about like debris. Nothing moved. Blood seeped from gaping wounds. Farther inside, past a set of doors torn off their hinges, he heard screaming. It mixed with the cacophony of cannons booming from White Sun.

"It's probably the necrosed," Rukh said, breaking the silence and confirming William's own supposition. "There's probably two or three of them in there. We kill them if they get in our way. Nothing slows us down from getting to the Throne Hall. Drop everything you don't need."

William followed Rukh, slithering down the hill and dumping his pack, canteen, bow, and quiver. He kept hold of his sword and satellite phone. Serena stood close by. She no longer hid her emotions as she once had. Concern and fear furrowed her features. He hoped she'd never have to be afraid again. Maybe after today she wouldn't be.

She noticed his attention and stared at him wordlessly.

He had so many things he wanted to tell her, but all of them spoke of his fear for her, his terror that this battle would be her last—or his. She didn't need to hear that, and he kept the thoughts to himself. Instead, he stepped close and hugged her. "Stay safe," he whispered into her hair.

Serena leaned away from him, the hard lines of her worry giving way to her wry smile of secret amusement. "I always try."

His heart beat faster when she grinned at him, and he drank in the sight of his wife, her smile, her eyes, her everything . . . His life would be pointless without her. "Stay safe," he repeated.

Serena slowly reached up to cup his face. A serious air took over her features. "Don't die."

Jessira interrupted them. "It's time to go."

"Yes, ma'am," William said. He broke away from Serena, but maintained a position by her side.

"Let's roll," Rukh said.

They dashed down the hill, raced across the bridge spanning the moat, and into the courtyard. The Kesarins took point, Rukh and Jessira following directly behind. Landon came next and William and Serena defended the rear.

William's eyes flashed, taking in the scene. Dead mahavans everywhere. Beyond the twenty in the center of the courtyard, he spied more who must have tried to exit the barracks. Boulders had crushed them flat. The by-now familiar stench of fresh death—blood and other liquids—polluted the air. William formed a filter to keep out the stink. A few mahavans moaned pitiably, but they didn't have time to help the injured.

They rushed on, and within the Palace they found wide halls paved in gray marble and more corpses. The mahavans inside had been torn apart. Gouges rent their chests. Some were missing limbs. All gazed sightlessly.

A few could have been dried corpses left out in a boiling sun. If William didn't know better he would have thought them killed months ago.

"The necrosed have fed," Rukh said, gesturing to the withered bodies. "They're power grows with each death. Be cautious."

They reached a broad staircase. It spiraled to the Palace's higher floors. More screams echoed down, and more mahavans littered the steps, all of them bearing terrible wounds. Their leather armor, dark with blood, hadn't saved them. Nor had their swords, which were bent into twisted shapes as if someone had smashed them against the stone corners of the hallways.

They reached a landing and took a corridor leading off of it. The walls here were a plain white, illuminated with lamps hung at regular intervals. Fine rugs muffled their footsteps. Rukh whispered for them to slow down and give everyone a chance to catch their breath. The number of dead mahavans had decreased. Only a handful now, blood still oozing from fresh wounds, lay unmoving in this hall.

William figured the number of dead or dying mahavans they'd now passed numbered close to fifty. The necrosed, however many there were, had destroyed everyone they came across. He figured it had to be the Overward and Manifold. With all the mahavans they'd killed and consumed, he worried at how powerful they were now.

Serena must have been thinking the same thing. "How are we going to kill these necrosed?" Her voice had become drone-flat.

You've fought these monsters once before, Aia said. *You survived the battle and your enemy did not. This will be no different.*

William tried to take heart from her words, but his doubts persisted.

"We have to keep going," Rukh called when they reached a staircase at the end of the hall.

They ascended. William knew from his time as a prisoner here that they neared their destination. The stairs ended at the landing to another hallway, and at the far end would be the double doors leading into the Throne Hall.

The Kesarins' pads fell heavily as they surged up the stairs. Rukh and Jessira were quieter, and Landon was utterly silent. William took deep breaths. His heart pounded. He realized he couldn't hear any other sounds but that of their travel. The screams had fallen silent.

"We're getting close," Serena said.

They reached the top of the stairs. The large doors leading into the Throne Hall lay on the ground, torn off their hinges and resting ten feet inside the room.

Rukh called for them to slow.

Angry voices came from the Throne Hall.

AMONGST THE VOICES Serena heard emanating from the Throne Hall, her father's was the most readily identifiable. Arrogance didn't merely lace his tone, it suffused it. The others—there were two other voices—were less readily recognizable, but one sounded cultured and elegant while the second one reminded Serena of stones grinding in a mill. One of them had to be Sapient, and the other was likely Manifold Fulsom.

Rukh drew them to a halt. *Aia's allowing us to share one another's thoughts. The anchor line will open soon.* He addressed William. *We'll protect you against the Servitor and the necrosed. I don't know what they'll try to do, but stay out of it. As soon as you feel the anchor line start to open, let us know. We have to get through it before Shet exits.*

Make sure to shut it behind us, Jessira said. *All we have to do is hold Shet at bay and you should be able to eventually collapse the anchor line.*

You'll need Undefiled Locus for some of that battling and all, Landon said, unsheathing his sword. *I heard from the fella I took it off of that it's a nomasra that lets an asrasin wield his Elements more powerfully than normal. It's likely to do you more good than me.*

He and Rukh swapped blades, and Rukh gave the rune-marked longsword an experimental twirl and slash. Serena had never seen a sword like it before. The blade had a fuller on each side, and a cool, crystalline glow emanated off it. It left embers of white light in its passage, as if it already contained the Wildness within its metal.

Thank you, Rukh said. *It's beautiful.*

Like I said, it's got a tad more bite than your pig-sticker, Landon said with a grin.

Rukh smiled back. *I think I like you.*

You ought to, Landon said. *I just gave you my sword. I'll want it back whenever you're done using it.*

Rukh gave the sword another twirl and slash. *I'll try to remember that.* He addressed them all again. *Landon and Serena will take on one *of the necrosed. Aia and Shon will go after the other one. Jessira and I will handle the Servitor.* He glanced at them. *Ready?*

Nods met his question, and they rushed into the Throne Hall. It was as Serena remembered: a long, rectangular room held aloft by a bevy of gilded columns. The ceiling contained murals and stained glass images of Shet in various poses, and the dim light of the late afternoon eked through the wide windows lining one side of the Hall. It did little to rectify the gloom.

The Servitor stood upon the dais at the far end of the room, next to his Seat. He clasped Shet's Spear at the ready. Two necrosed faced him. One was a dark-haired albino—Sapient—and the other was a massive brute—Manifold. Both appeared healthier than any of their kind Serena had ever seen.

The three occupants of the Throne Hall had been eyeing one another mistrustfully, but the necrosed spun when Rukh led them at a charge into the Throne Hall.

Manifold's eyes widened, and hope lifted his gruesome features. "Shokan. Sira," he breathed. "You truly live."

Sapient's face blanched beyond its customary pallor. He viewed Aia and Shon in horror. "You're dead. I saw it."

Serena had no time to wonder at the necroseds' strange responses.

From the Servitor's Spear blasted a shimmering weave of Fire. It twisted on its axis. Rukh moved in a blur and took the blow on *Undefiled Locus*. His face appeared clenched in anticipation of pain, but it never happened. His sword sucked in the braid, glowing brighter for a second.

Serena's father never had a chance to launch a second attack. Sapient leapt at the dais. The Servitor took a single step back, whipped the Spear in a circle, and batted the Overward aside with the iron-shod heel of his weapon.

"We have no disagreement with you," Manifold said to Rukh. "I can help. You only need—ahh!"

The Servitor had blasted the distracted necrosed off his feet with a weave of Air. Serena ducked as Manifold flew past her. The necrosed smashed into a golden pillar.

"The anchor line," William shouted. "Get to the anchor line! It's the throne. It's opening."

Rukh pointed his sword at the Servitor, and a white-hot line blurred toward Serena's father. The weave impacted in a low-pitched drumbeat against a green web, a Shield like Rukh and Jessira's. The Servitor grunted, forced backward. The line from Rukh's sword keened. A second later, it hammered through the Servitor's Shield, and he catapulted off the dais, his clothes smoking.

"Come on," Jessira shouted. She urged everyone to the dais.

Sapient was already there, blocking their passage. Serena had no chance to curse the necrosed. Aia shoved the Overward aside, bullying him out of the way.

A flicker of rainbow-hued light played across the dark marble of Shet's throne. The image passed so swiftly that Serena wasn't sure she had actually seen it. The statue of the god's six-armed warrior persona loomed closer.

Another flicker from the throne.

Serena caught movement in the corner of her eyes from the base of the dais. The Servitor. He slowly rose to his feet. Flagstones hurtled their way. Serena desperately nudged aside as many with as she could with a blast of Air. The rest got through, but promptly bounced off a Shield Jessira had erected.

The Servitor shouted.

Serena's jaw dropped in shock. Her father battled Manifold and Sapient. The Overward hurled the Servitor out of the way. Unimpeded, both necrosed rushed toward the dais.

"Keep going," Jessira urged them all.

A many-colored light played across the throne. This time Serena knew she'd seen it. The light grew brighter. A line split the air. Serena held her breath, waiting for it to rotate and complete the anchor line.

She heard William gasp. "I can't close it. Something's trying to get through."

"Let it open," Jessira said. "Rukh and I will tether to it. Slam it shut as soon as we get through."

"You cannot do this," the Servitor shouted from the other side of the room. "You don't know what he'll do to us before he kills us.

Death will be a mercy." He held out the Spear and a bolt of Fire exploded from its leaf-shaped blade.

Rukh extended a hand, and the Fire shattered against his Shield, one that encompassed all of them. He swung *Undefiled Locus*, pointing the tip at the Servitor. From it shot a heavy weave, thicker than rope. It contained all the Elements. The Servitor sought to deflect it with the haft of his weapon.

Instead, Shet's Spear sheared through the middle. The Servitor gaped momentarily before the weave slammed into him, tossing him into a pillar. He slumped, unconscious. The fiery runes emanating off the two halves of his broken spear faded to simple black lines.

Rukh spoke to William. "Ready?"

William nodded, and sweat beaded his forehead.

The line in the air slowly rotated, and a doorway became apparent. It swirled with a myriad of shapes and colors that took on the image of a rainbow bridge.

Rukh, Jessira, and both Kesarins surged onto the anchor line. A flash of white fire signaled their passage. Footsteps thundered up the stairs, and Serena gasped as first Sapient and then Manifold roared past her. They never slowed. They, too, leapt at the anchor line. Their bodies collapsed to the ground in front of the rainbow-colored doorway, though, appearing lifeless. Something pus-colored then sped from their corpses and through the bridge between worlds, vanishing into infinity.

Serena had no idea as to the meaning of what she'd just witnessed, nor did she have time to figure it out. She turned to William, who had his jaw clenched as he strained to close the anchor line. She silently urged him on.

Seconds passed, and the rainbow bridge slowly faded. Sweat broke out on William's forehead. He grimaced, his teeth displayed in a rictus of effort. Next, the anchor line rotated until the door was no longer visible. Only a thin line splitting the air above the throne remained, but it never entirely receded.

William sagged. The absence of noise sounded thunderous.

"Do you realize what you've done?" A voice spoke from the back of the Hall. *The Servitor*. He'd recovered.

Serena realized she, William, and Landon were alone with her father. Even together they were no match for him. He'd kill them. Oddly, the notion raised no fear. After everything she'd been through, fear didn't easily find purchase in her heart.

The Servitor paced toward them. "You've damned us all. Shet will kill the World Killers and everyone with them. Then he'll cross over to our world and kill us, too." He brought the remnants of his spear to the ready. "But perhaps he'll forgive me if I offer him your corpses as recompense for his troubles."

PAIN BECAME the entirety of Rukh's awareness. His body boiled and blistered. He felt like his soul burned. It lasted only an instant, but it seemed endless. The anguish began the moment he leapt through the anchor line, the same as the last time he'd journeyed between worlds. A person's physical shell couldn't take the travel. For whatever reason, it was destroyed. Only the aether—a person's essence—could survive such a trip.

The Kesarins weren't immune to the transformation, either. Judging by their howls of pain, Aia and Shon experienced the same horrific torment. Rukh turned to them, immediately noticing that they remained powerful felines. It was as if through the act of living, the body somehow stamped an impression of itself on their aether. A fiery glow emanated off their fur. Rukh noticed a silvery color rising above his own skin.

Jessira took a shuddering breath. While her body was gone, her appearance was relatively unchanged, only a golden glow about her to mark the difference. She remained otherwise as she had always been from the very first time he'd seen her: indomitable, proud, and beautiful. She glowered at nothing in particular. "I'm never doing that again," she vowed.

Agreed, Shon said.

Rukh took a moment then to gather his bearings. Above and all around him loomed a sky of black, smooth and reflective like glass, extending to the limits of his vision. Pinpricks of bleeding lights dripped illumination through the darkness like luminescent rain-drops. Close at hand behind him, a sliver of light marked the bridge's termination, but ahead, it extended into the darkness and was lost. Beneath his feet spread a rainbow-hued bridge no thicker than a beam of light but wide enough for an army with room to spare on either side. Colors constantly shifted underneath his feet. They formed cloud-like shapes that whispered and gave images. He viewed graceful figures—elves—kneeling in front of trees crowned with liquid leaves of silver moonlight and golden sunshine; another was of a desperate figure with half a hand who bore a white ring and battled in the heart of a volcano against a foul figure crowned in darkness. He also saw Arisa, and a pang of longing clutched his heart.

"Why would you endure such pain, Shokan," a deep, cultured voice asked. "You should have simply freed your aether when you stepped on the anchor line between worlds."

Rukh spun about. Sapient Dormant and Manifold Fulsom had followed his group onto the anchor line. A bubbling, pus-colored glow streaked in black surrounded the two figures. Otherwise, they, too, were utterly unchanged. Sapient had been the one to ask the question.

Manifold's face brightened, and he spoke in a gravelly voice. "I see it now. Their aethers tell the truth. He isn't Shokan entirely. Neither is she Sira. They don't possess all their memories."

Rukh didn't have time for this. He readied to attack the necrosed.

Sapient held up his hands. "We don't seek battle with you. We will help you stop Shet. That is your purpose, is it not?"

"Why should we trust you?" Jessira asked the necrosed.

The two creatures shared a brief appraisal before facing Jessira.

"Because we speak the truth. You saw us fight the Servitor," Sapient said, apparently speaking for both of them.

Rukh realized there was no further time for discussion. From the other end of the anchor line, something approached, something powerful enough to warp the bridge. It was an oppressive force, like a wind presaging a swiftly moving object, felt long before it was seen. A shining, red light barreled toward them. It gradually gathered into the form of a man, a titanic being who towered over even Manifold Fulsom.

Shet.

The god ground to a halt, standing tall and straight, garbed in a white shirt trimmed in silver and wearing gray pants tucked into black boots. Muscles stretched beneath the clothing. Shet's features were perfect, more beautiful than handsome, but on the right side of his face, a terrible burn marred his perfection. He loosely held a golden staff.

Rukh drew as deep as he could on his *Jivatma*. The sword, *Undefiled Locus*, echoed his need, and a power surged. Rukh found himself floating in the stillness of a mirrored pool, his *Jivatma*. It was more vast than he recalled, perhaps an effect of the sword, every bit as wide and deep as it had been when he'd shed his flesh and battled the Sorrow Bringer.

He was ready. So were Jessira, Aia, and Shon.

Displeasure creased Shet's features. Lightning haloed his head. "Sapient and Manifold," he said, his voice deep and commanding. "I see you have taken the traitor's path." Rukh felt it when the god's gaze rested upon him a moment. It had a weight, a strange heft like the darkness of a cavern. Shet's attention lifted, focused again upon Sapient. "These allies of yours, I do not know them, but they will not avail you."

"How does he not recognize Shokan and Sira?" Manifold whispered to Sapient, his voice quiet enough that the god must not have heard.

"Recognition of others was ever a weakness of his," Sapient said.

Rukh sensed Jessira pace forward. She moved to support him on his right side while Aia and Shon did the same on his left. The necrosed advanced as well. Rukh regarded Sapient and Manifold, and the Overward dipped his head in seeming encouragement.

Again came Shet's gaze, and the god's eyes widened in recognition when he saw *Undefiled Locus*. He addressed Rukh this time. "That sword is mine. Give it to me. Now."

Rukh offered Shet a smirk. "Ask nicely."

Shet snarled. "You will remember those words and rue them dearly."

The golden staff was brought to the ready. Rukh silently cursed. He hated fighting staff-wielders. The last time had been against a portion of Shet's daughter. She'd also wielded a golden staff.

Shet attacked.

Six red chains hurled off the staff, shooting forward. Rukh strengthened his Shield, trusting it to protect him from the blow so he could give one. The chain struck like a boulder hurled by a giant. Rukh was blasted back, soaring through the air, back parallel to the ground, and over the heads of the necrosed. Gravity didn't work the same here, and he threatened to float away until Manifold grabbed his leg and slammed him back toward the anchor line's floor. Rukh twisted and managed to land on his feet.

Fragging hells! That was stupid. The others had more wisely dodged the chains. Aia closed on Shet from the left, Jessira from the right, and Shon from the center. The necrosed followed close behind.

Rukh drew deeply on his *Jivatma* and blurred back toward the god. *Undefiled Locus* glowed more brightly. On instinct, he conducted a Fireball through the sword. Shet, even in the midst of defense, clenched a fist. His Shield—Rukh hadn't noticed it before—brightened noticeably in a webbing of green. The Fireball impacted in a shower of flames and sparks.

Jessira traded blows with the god. Aia tried to rake Shet's thigh but he defended, slapping her paw aside. The necrosed flanked the god. Manifold took a gut kick, but Sapient managed to land a kick of his own. It rebounded off Shet's Shield.

Shet spun his staff, twirling it and causing the others to fall back.

Rukh arrived. He blocked a blow aimed at his head, slipped one aimed at his torso. His diagonal counter was parried. He spun with the blow and came around with an upward, rising strike. Shet blocked, both hands braced on his staff. Rukh's hands stung, but he ignored the pain, maintaining a firm grip on his sword.

The god pushed him back. Rukh momentarily allowed it, but when Shet's attention lapsed, he lanced forward. He evaded a thrust, barely managed to bring his blade back into place, blocking an overhand blow. He ducked a horizontal strike that would have crushed his skull, Shield or no Shield.

Rukh stepped back, and Shet didn't follow. Once again, Jessira and the others moved to support him. Lightning coursed through *Undefiled Locus* as Rukh ignited the Wildness.

Shet smirked. "The Wildness is a waste against me."

Rukh was about to attack again, but movement in the far distance, from the direction he assumed led to Seminal, gave him pause. A golden glow and a silver one sped their way.

Shet noticed it as well. He stepped back, awaiting whoever was coming. It looked to be a man and a woman.

Grief tore at Rukh when he saw their features.

32

FUTURES DECIDED

T wo more people arrived by anchor line, clearly coming from Seminal. They moved swiftly, and Jessira hoped they weren't Shet's reinforcements. As they drew closer, her fears went unrealized when she saw that their faces held the blank stares of a Duo. They unsheathed their swords.

They look like you and Rukh, Shon said.

Jessira had already come to the same shocked realization. She shared a stunned glance with Rukh. "How is this possible?"

Rukh's mouth twisted into a scowl, but he didn't reply.

Jessira sensed his answer, though. They'd failed in the past. It was the most likely explanation. It was why these other two who looked like their twins were here, arriving from Seminal. She and Rukh were fated to become the Lady of Fire and the Lord of the Sword in Earth's ancient past. Worse, it also seemed that they would be flung into Seminal and take part in another war.

Her heart trembled. *When will Rukh and I know peace?*

Shet eyed the new entrants with distaste and annoyance. "Cinder Shade and Anya Aruyen. You dare defy me?"

"We will always defy you," the two of them spoke in that synchronous, eerie way Duos had. They turned to Jessira and Rukh.

"Remember why you struggle. It will carry you through the Trials to come."

Shet did a double-take. "How is there two of you?" His eyes widened. "I see it now. Twins?" He snarled. "No matter. Come on then. I'll kill all of you."

Jessira had no time to process the god's confusion. The other Duo —Jessira's and Rukh's future selves—attacked Shet with the man taking the lead, leaping forward, sword aimed like a dagger. Chains burst from the god's staff. The man batted one aside, dodged another. The woman did the same.

Jessira started when Rukh spoke to her. "Come on. We have to finish this."

She knew what he wanted, and she reached for him. They Annexed, and peace smoothed her troubled brow. Her thoughts drifted until they were as distant as a dream.

Their Duo burst into action. It sent Primary attacking the enemy from the right while Secondary came at him from the left. Primary fired a Fireball. As expected, it impacted against the enemy's Shield. Sparks showered, obscuring Secondary's approach. She slammed a slash at the enemy's side. He deflected, a slight shift of his staff.

The Duo recognized allies. The Kesarins, Aia and Shon. The great cats mauled the enemy. He kicked them aside. In came the other Duo. They attacked with a combination of Elements and the sword. The enemy gave ground.

Manifold and Sapient gave chase. The god leaned backward from a gutting strike, twisting and snapping upright. His return, a side kick, launched Manifold aside.

All of this Jessira noticed through a mind clouded with fog. It wasn't important, at least for now.

Their Duo re-entered the fray, drawing *Jivatma* more deeply as it rushed the enemy. Primary deflected a red chain hissing with heat. Secondary aimed a strike, shifted away from an overhand blow, and blocked a swing of the staff. A *Jivatma*-powered leap took her inside the enemy's Shield. Her knee connected with the enemy's chin.

The god stumbled back, shaking his head and gaining distance.

Duo wouldn't allow it. Neither would the others. The Kesarins attacked. So did the necrosed and the other pair of warriors.

They converged on the enemy, who defended with chains and his staff. The Duo noted the god's more rapid movements. Metal rang. Sparks flashed. The god blunted blows, threatened to rip apart flesh with his barbed chains. He gestured them onward.

A Kesarin obliged. Shon raked the god's back.

Shet roared and flung the Kesarin aside. He smashed a staff into Aia, slamming her into the ground. She lay limp.

Both necrosed arrived.

Shet held them off with his chains, their barbed tips swirling about his staff like snakes and striking with cobra swiftness. Sapient fell, stunned by a blow to the side of his head. A crater dented his ethereal skull. Manifold tried to block a horizontal blow with an upraised arm. The chain snapped his ghostly forearm with a sound like a breaking branch.

The Duo re-engaged. Primary took the lead. He fired a set of Fireballs. The enemy's Shield easily handled the attack. Secondary used the distraction to leap over Primary, a Spear jutting from her hand. It didn't come close to landing. Primary took a deep cut to his forearm. Evanescent blood—red tinged with a silver hue—flowed, drifting on an unfelt breeze. Secondary missed a block. The staff clipped her leg. Something gave way. Primary took a shattering blow to the skull. His Shield buckled, and he went down. His sword skittered across the ground. Another chain snaked around and tore into a hobbled Secondary, ripping through the back of her knee. She fell, and pain broke the Annex. Jessira's awareness returned.

The other Duo relieved the pressure. They arrived in a storm of swirling steel. One of them managed to land a slash to Shet's shin. The god scuttled away, seeking space. The other Duo moved to flank the god. Aia still lay in a heap, but Shon rumbled to life, surging forward. Shet immediately whipped his staff about and clouted the Kesarin in the chest.

The Duo heard ribs crack. Shon roared in pain, wheezing as he stumbled away from the god.

Fury threatened to disrupt Jessira's ability to think clearly. She went to Rukh's side. He struggled to remain standing. They were losing.

"We have to keep the pressure," Rukh said, his words slurred.

Jessira didn't know how. Her leg leaked blood. It could barely hold her weight, and Rukh wasn't doing much better. His balance was off. Aia and Shon were injured. Same with the necrosed. The only ones still in the fight were the other two warriors, the ones she realized were likely a future version of herself and Rukh.

Rukh—her Rukh—tried to stand, collapsed to a knee, and she tucked her head under his arm, helping him regain his feet.

Shet and the other two warriors continued to battle, a non-stop clamor of clashing steel, clattering chains, and crackling Elements. Jessira watched, unable to do much more than that. The three combatants launched at each other and were hurled apart. A break in the battle.

"Cinder and Anya," Shet began, "Leave off this—"

The anchor line shuddered. Everyone still standing stumbled. The god viewed the slit that represented the way to Sinskrill. No one could fit through there.

Relief coursed through Jessira. William still had it closed, which meant he still lived.

Again, the anchor line shuddered, trembling this time. The shape of it lost hue and depth. Jessira could see around the anchor line, to the vast abyss beyond it.

Shet snarled. "Cretins. Do you know what you've done?" He glared at the anchor line's end.

Jessira and everyone else took the battle's pause to recollect themselves. The opening to Seminal continued to shrink. They'd won, but what would victory cost them? She stared at the other set of warriors. Their Duo had ended, and they stood apart. The man held a forearm pressed to a bleeding abdomen. He'd taken a blow meant for the woman. Blood also leaked from his temple, another gash he'd taken in her place. He limped, having trouble bearing weight on one of his legs. The worst, though, was the lack of love between the two of them, at least on the part of the woman.

Jessira sensed it. It was as obvious as sleet falling from a cold, bitter sky. She glared at her future self. *Why,* she wanted to ask. *How could you stop loving him?*

The woman regarded her, must have noticed her outrage, and her gaze went to the side. Shame flushed her features. An instant later, her visage firmed and she stared back at Jessira in unblinking certitude.

Shon levered himself upright. *"Speak quickly,"* he said, giving them the ability to speak to one another, mind-to-mind.

"You don't know what I've endured on his behalf," the woman said. *"But you will. You'll live it."*

"I don't care," Jessira said, disgusted by the self-pity she saw in her future self. *"You're a pathetic coward, and I will hate who I am to become. How could you throw away what we have with him?"* She wanted to hit the other woman. *"And whatever you endured, he would have endured a hundred-fold. You know this. Wretched filth."*

The woman's features went blank. Their conversation had occurred at the speed of thought.

Shet spoke. "I will do what must be done."

Chains whipped out. It smashed into the anchor line, shattering it. A red wave pulsed from the god's staff like an arrow of cold. It punched through the slit of Sinskrill's anchor line.

The blowback threw Jessira off her feet. She fell to the ground, but a second later she floated into the air. Her last vision was of Shet racing back toward Seminal. She saw the other two warriors give chase. Manifold and Sapient, too. The bigger necrosed scooped up *Undefiled Locus* on his way.

Her vision went blank. Memories came undone as she ascended through darkness, fell and twirled about, toward a shimmering light far away.

◆

WILLIAM BRAIDED HARD, holding the anchor line closed. It wasn't easy, but he managed. It would have been far easier if nothing distracted him, but such wasn't the case. Interruptions abounded. First and foremost was the Servitor. He held the broken halves of his once potent weapon, which were now a short staff and a shorter spear.

"You three will pay for what you have done," the Servitor said. His gaze slid over to Serena. "In this, blood will no longer suffice to protect you."

William caught Landon shaking his head. "That there's a man with a killable face, don't you think?"

William was too tired to laugh at his brother's observation. He was even more tired of the constant threats on his life, of having terrible creatures wreck his mind, of fighting for what felt like forever. He was tired, emotionally and mentally.

One more battle, though, and it would be done. "Talk's cheap," William said. He wove the Wildness, knowing his eyes had gone pure white, glowing with intensity. Landon did the same. "Shut up and fight," he told the Servitor.

"Whatever happens, we can't let him hurt William," Serena said to Landon. "He's the only one who can keep the anchor line closed."

"Use the Wildness to make yourself tougher," Landon advised him. "It won't make you stronger or faster, but it will make you harder to hurt. Let it flow into you."

William did as his brother instructed. He strengthened the Wildness further, pouring it into his sword and his flesh. The weave crackled and snapped within him, and William gritted his teeth. It felt like his muscles were coming off his bones. An instant later the braid soothed his pain, leaving him strong and able.

Not a moment too soon.

The Servitor attacked with bolts of Fire and whistling arrows of Air.

William pulled up flagstones, shielding the three of them. Serena cast her own lines of Fire. The Servitor easily slapped aside her attacks. The dais trembled. Stones ripped loose. William dove to the side when a rock the size of his head sped toward him. It smashed to powder against Shet's throne.

William descended the dais, Serena and Landon flanking him.

The Servitor advanced, inexorable as the tide.

"Get him," Landon said. He bum-rushed the Servitor.

William and Serena followed on his heels. Lightning crackled from Landon's sword as he tore into the Servitor. He swung wildly and without form.

William supported him, looking for an opening. Serena flicked a slash. The Servitor blocked but left himself open. William couldn't take advantage. He was out of position.

Landon could. He sent a perfect thrust through the Servitor's small mistake, stabbing into the other man's thigh.

The Servitor hobbled away with a glower. William prepared to step forward but felt a weave forming. Something deadly. He disengaged.

A pair of fist-sized balls of molten Earth screamed at Serena and Landon. She ducked behind a gilded pillar, and a chunk of it shattered. Smoke and pieces of rock exploded. Landon took the ball aimed at him on his sword. The molten Earth split on either side of him. One half crashed into a cluster of columns. The other scored a line across Landon's side. He shouted in pain as his skin blistered. Blood poured from the wound. Landon pressed a hand against his wound and somehow sealed it, probably a holder's braid. Nevertheless, he gritted his teeth, the pain on his face evident.

William's throat clenched when the column Serena hid behind shuddered. "Move!" he shouted at her.

She dove aside right before the column came down in a crash of rocks. The sounds echoed, and a fog of dirt obscured the air. His gaze darted about, finally locating Serena in a clear area many yards away. Her face was masked in blood and dirt. She struggled to her feet, keeping the weight off one foot.

He had no more time to spare for her. The Servitor had noticed him. They crashed together in a clash, his steel sword against the strange, white wood of the broken Spear. William slapped aside the staff portion, ducked the spear tip, feeling it graze through his hair. He rolled away from a backhand slash.

The Servitor wouldn't relent. William battled with all his skill. He used the speed and strength granted to him by the Wildness and Kohl Obsidian's blood. The Servitor easily kept up. William sought to lock the man away from his *lorethasra*. He might as well have held back a river in flood. His brief inattention almost cost him.

A whistling sound was his only warning. *Damn it!* He threw himself backward, barely evading a spear thrust. A rushing weave of Water would have ended him, but William managed to fall to the side. The braid blasted into a column directly behind where he'd been standing, causing the structure to crack along its entire length and fall in slow motion. William dove for safety, as did the Servitor.

The column smashed into the ground, and the floor buckled. Flagstones shattered. William's ears rang from the thunderous impact. A moment later, he covered up as chunks of stained glass from above shattered on the floor all about him. Several nicked his shoulders, a few pieces embedding themselves in his skin. Pain and blood flowed. Dust clouded his vision.

Landon arrived, exploding through a haze of dirt. The Servitor slapped his attack aside with a parry and counter slash. He attacked with the spear tip. Landon drifted to the side and prepared an overhand blow. The Servitor kicked him in the gut. Landon flew through the air and crashed into William.

They both slammed into the ground.

Fragging hell! William almost lost his grip on the anchor line to Seminal. He scrambled out from underneath Landon, who groaned. He didn't have any time to spare for his brother. The anchor line was too important.

Serena hobbled back into range of battle. She launched boulders and stones. Lines of Fire, whipping strands of Water . . . Anything she could find.

The Servitor defended against her braids and attacks, spinning the spear or staff as needed, but Landon used the break to regroup alongside William.

"He's a strong one," Landon said, clutching his stomach.

William didn't answer. He still had the entirety of his focus on the anchor line.

There was a lull in the battle when Serena hid again behind a column.

William found the Servitor addressing him and Landon. "You'll truly allow my daughter to face me alone?"

"Little busy here," William said. "Keeping the anchor line closed and all."

"You waste your time," the Servitor said. "Shet will kill your friends and tear the anchor line open."

"It's my time to waste."

"And your lives are mine to take."

"You ready?" Landon asked him.

William nodded. He finally had control of the anchor line. *Now, don't open again.* "Yeah, but it'd be nice if he just gave up and quit."

Landon laughed. "Now you're getting it."

They advanced, both of them limping, side-by-side, toward the Servitor, who readied the broken halves of the spear.

A voice spoke from the entrance to the Hall. "You haven't killed him yet?" It was Jake.

Jason was with him. "The hell y'all still playing around for?"

They must have come from the battle at the anchor line or the village. Hope surged through William. They only had to hold the Servitor off until the anchor line collapsed. He could feel it weakening already.

The Servitor's focus went to Jake and Jason, and William took the momentary inattention to attack with a line of Fire. Landon rushed forward, sword ready. As expected, the Servitor easily defended William's weave. He parried Landon's slashes and thrusts but never noticed the bowling-ball sized rock Serena sent hurtling at his head. Not until the last moment. The Servitor managed to break it apart, but shards of stone still cut across his face, momentarily blinding him.

He stumbled, flailing wildly. Landon ducked under the Servitor's wild swings and sent a short thrust across the back of the Servitor's ankle.

Jake and Jason arrived, harrying the Servitor like wolves pulling down a lion. Serena added her sword and weaves. The Servitor blindly defended.

William shouted, a blaze of fury powering him past reason. The Servitor, the man who had caused all this death and destruction . . .

The Servitor whipped staff and broken spear about, gaining space. William stepped past the others, into the pocket. *Take a shot to give one.* He parried the spear, took a blow from the staff to his chest that he only partially blocked with a hastily lifted rock. He pressed onward, snapping off a side kick that made the Servitor fall back.

Jake gestured, and a line of Fire erupted from his palm. It slammed into the Servitor's shoulder, spinning him about. Blood immediately soaked his ruined shirt, and he shouted in rage and pain.

William moved into range once more, placing himself in danger. The Servitor managed to evade a slash. He blocked another blow but fell for a feint. William angled a straight thrust to the Servitor's chest. It punched home. The Servitor's staff and short spear clattered to the ground, and William watched the knowledge of his impending death fill the man's face.

In that moment, pity warred with hate in William's heart, and pity won. Rukh would have wanted that of him. He stepped forward, easing the Servitor onto the crumbled floor of the crushingly quiet Throne Hall.

Serena arrived, her face a mask of blood and drone-flat features. She crouched next to her father.

The Servitor's mouth gaped. He blindly reached for Serena's hand, a silent plea on his features. She took his hand, saying nothing.

"I loved your mother," he said. "Remember that."

Serena's face didn't twitch, and she stayed silent as her father died. He breathed out his last, and she let his hand slip from hers.

William remained kneeling beside her, watching her, unsure what was going through her mind. He rested a hand on her shoulder, and she placed her own over his. "What do you need?" he asked.

The mask of her face cracked, and she buried her face in his shoulder. A single shudder was all she allowed herself before she pushed away from him and stood. He rose, too.

"It's done," Jake said in a disbelieving tone.

Jason laughed, his voice delirious. "We did it."

William sensed the anchor line bulge. He didn't know what it meant, but it couldn't be good. "Down!" He pulled Serena to the ground, protecting her body with his.

A red bolt blasted from the anchor line. It fanned outward, moving faster than thought. William's muscles clenched, bones threatened to break. Coldness seeped into his heart, and the world faded.

~

A WORLD of darkness screamed past Rukh's ears. The red wave from Shet. The rebound from his power. It had knocked Rukh off the anchor line, and he plummeted through a realm of strange lights, unable to tell in which direction he fell. Up, down, sideways. Gravity seemed to have failed. On went the rushing movement, and he didn't know if it would ever stop. It continued, longer than when he had traveled from Arisa to Earth. He could no longer hear Aia's or Shon's thoughts, lost sight of Jessira. He panicked. Life would be meaningless without her.

His body stretched, thinning, tearing. The mirrored lake of his *Jivatma* emptied, streaming away from him like a wispy, silver thread. At the limits of his endurance, a white light came clear. His essence slammed onto the rainbow bridge of a tethered anchor line.

He grunted in pain.

The white light grew larger, taking on the rectangular shape of a doorway. Rukh ran toward it, straining against what felt like a riptide. A last push, and he exploded into a world. Tumbled down a slope. Finally halted his fall. He panted, painfully regained his senses, and stood. He found himself on the edge of a cliff and froze in horror at what he saw.

A world caught in midnight and ruin. A broad plain where a titanic battle raged. Balls of green fire roared, exploding into clusters of people who flashed apart into ash. Streamers of white-hot pebbles howled like buzzsaws, whipping through the air and tearing apart both man and animal. Beams of light whined as they cut through stone and shields, leaving sprays of blood with each puncture. Small, red figures swarmed giants, tearing out bites of flesh. Warcats screamed challenge, and thunder rumbled in an endless peal. A massive mountain stood silent sentinel over the carnage.

Aia and Shon exited the anchor line. They slid down the hill, halting their progress next to him.

Where are we? Aia asked.

Why are they killing each other? Shon asked, confused and shocked. He must have noticed the battle.

Rukh didn't answer. His focus remained on the anchor line, the glowing rectangular shape of it. He waited, praying Jessira would follow. Seconds passed. Terror filled his throat. *Where is she?*

Relief flooded him when Jessira shot out of the anchor line. Her aether—something more than her *Jivatma*, her soul maybe. It still shimmered a luminescent gold. *She made it.*

Jessira exited the anchor line more gracefully than he had. She didn't fall down the hill, and she took in the terrible scene upon the plain. Her mouth dropped open in shock. "Devesh save us."

"Jessira," Rukh called.

Her gaze rested on him, but the horror of the battle still reflected in her eyes. Several seconds passed, and she shook her head, finally noticing him fully. She limped down the slope to his side and hugged him, her ephemeral body pressed against his.

Rukh held her close. He could have held her forever.

"Where are we?" Jessira asked, pulling away from him slightly.

"The past," Rukh said. "Earth's past. Thousands of years ago when we become Shokan and Sira." Bitterness edged his voice. Another world needed saving, and the burden of salvation once more fell on him and Jessira. He wanted to howl at the unfairness of it. Hadn't they given enough? Done enough?

When will we go home? Aia asked.

I don't know, Rukh replied. He found himself wishing that none of them had left Arisa, but if this was the time from which Shet's daughter originated, perhaps all this sacrifice would end up having meaning after all.

Jessira spoke. *The last thing I remember is Shet arriving.* She frowned in confusion. *Did we win?*

Rukh hesitated in answering. He couldn't remember, either.

We won, Shon said. *Barely.*

Despite the fact that it had been their aethers who had fought, they had taken damage in the battle. It was as if their actual physical forms had been injured. Aia's grace was gone. She limped, one limb bent awkwardly. Shon struggled to breathe, and Jessira couldn't bear weight on one leg. As for Rukh, a ringing in his ears stole his balance.

At least they'd managed to stop Shet. A blessing as far as Rukh was concerned.

"No rest for the weary," Jessira said with a tired sigh, indicating the battle.

"No, there isn't," Rukh agreed. A memory of what he'd done following the journey from Arisa to Earth reminded him what they required now. "We need to clothe our essences in flesh or we'll die." He pointed to the battle. "At least we'll have plenty of fresh corpses down there from which to choose our next bodies."

Jessira held him close, kissing his cheek. "We're still together, *priya*. I promise we always will be."

33

DÉNOUEMENT

Wiilliam blinked, awakening from whatever had knocked him unconscious. Something had bled through the anchor line. At least that's what it felt like. He couldn't be sure. He couldn't think straight, and his muscles twitched, firing spasmodically. A bone-deep ache pulsed throughout his body, and he groaned.

After a few minutes of lying on the ground, a thought triggered, and he forced himself into motion.

Serena.

With another groan, he rolled off her. His head throbbed like an anvil had been dropped on it, but he ignored the pain, praying she was all right. Blood, bruises, and dirt covered her face. He eyed her, panic rising. *Is she . . .* He peered closely, hoping to see a sign.

Serena shuddered, and some of his panic receded. Her eyes slowly opened, filled with confusion, but despite it she reached for him, her hand moving erratically.

William managed to gain enough control of his limbs to clutch her hand. He hoped that whatever had struck them down wouldn't leave them permanently impaired.

He glanced around the room. The others had also been afflicted.

They lay where they'd fallen, unmoving, and he worried they were dead.

More minutes passed, and William's lack of co-ordination slowly resolved. The twitching of muscles ebbed, and strength returned to his limbs. The headache lingered, but he felt well enough to stand. Serena and the others recovered at about the same time that he did, and they all struggled to their feet, groaning and stumbling.

"What the hell was that?" Jake asked.

William worked moisture into his mouth. For some reason it was cotton-dry. "I don't know. It came from the anchor line." He viewed the destruction all about them. The throne hall was utterly wrecked. Columns lay in shattered heaps. Many of the stained glass windows had crashed from the ceiling into broken shards. The floor was pock-marked with jagged holes, and a thick film of dirt covered everything.

"Is the anchor line closed?" Jason asked.

William couldn't tell. "Give me a sec." He focused as best he could, stretching his senses for the anchor line. When he'd first entered the hall, it had been so easy to feel it, impossible to ignore, throbbing like an infected wound as it pulsed Shet's disgusting *lorasra*. The throne had been its source, and William's eyes went to the crumbled dais. *Where was it?* He couldn't find it. Wherever he looked, he saw fragments of black stone, the remnants of where the throne had once stood. The battle must have broken it. His eyes widened in wondrous realization. The throne had been destroyed, which meant . . .

William quelled his growing sense of excitement and kept searching for the anchor line. He had to make sure. He searched out every recess and crevice. Nothing. He turned to the others. "It's gone," he said, teeth flashing in wild jubilation.

An exultant expression bloomed on Serena's face, dawning like sunshine after a thunderstorm. She let out a low-throated laugh of relief and shock. "We really did it? We stopped it all."

William understood what she meant. Everything they'd suffered, all the carnage, killing, and pain were over. The war was over. It was done, and they'd survived, triumphed. He let loose a glad shout, laughing as he hugged Serena, twirling her about, uncaring of the pain in his shoulder.

All the while, she grinned back at him. Swelling and bruises marred her skin, but they would heal. She was beautiful, and they'd survived the impossible. They had a lifetime of love ahead of them. No more fighting and war.

He laughed louder, only stopping when Landon cleared his throat pointedly. "Listen. I'm all for celebrations and all, but this don't seem like the place for a party."

William set Serena down. Landon was right. They had to find out if that red wave, whatever it was, had affected anyone else. They had to check on the Irregulars. Rukh and Jessira would . . .

He spun about to face the throne. It was destroyed. Everything around it ruined. He could barely make out the necrosed, their apparent corpses. *Rukh and Jessira. The anchor line. Aia and Shon.* The grief of unexpected loss sapped his joy. They hadn't gotten out in time.

Serena must have come to the same conclusion. She, too, was staring at the crumbled throne. Jake and Jason realized the truth also. An air of sorrow stole over their group.

"Maybe they aren't dead," Jake said. "Maybe they went to Seminal."

William hoped so. He hoped wherever Rukh and Jessira ended up, they would attain the peace they desperately deserved. He closed his eyes and sent a prayer for them. When he finished, he viewed the others. "We have to find out what happened to the rest of our people."

"They should be fine," Jason said. "We left them while they were crushing the remaining mahavans at Village White Sun."

Jake pointed at the Servitor's body, distaste evident on his face. "What do we do with that?"

Serena found a torn curtain and covered her father's body. "Leave him for now," she said. "We can take care of him later."

Before they departed the throne hall, they healed whatever wounds they could. William's shoulder remained painful but at least it no longer bled. Serena was able to bear weight more easily on her ankle. The five of them hobbled out of the throne hall, limped down the stairs, and walked through corridors lined with dead mahavans.

"Did y'all do that?" Jason asked, pointing to the dead.

"Wish we could say it was us," Landon answered, "but we found them all corpsified like that when we arrived. It was a pair of necrosed that did the killing."

"What happened to them?" Jake asked. "The necrosed."

"It's strange," Serena said, "but they fought on our side against my father. They even went through the anchor line. They said they wanted to stop Shet."

Jake viewed her in shock. He eventually shook his head. "Miracles never cease."

William still couldn't understand the motivations of the necrosed. Why *had* they fought against the Servitor and Shet? It made no sense, but a part of him wanted to believe that even with all the evil those two had done, maybe they still heard God's call every now and then.

"What are you thinking about?" Serena asked. "It looked like something deep." William explained, and Serena offered him her secret smile of amusement, but this one was mixed with obvious love. "Never change, William Wilde."

They exited the palace, stepping into the courtyard. There they found more dead mahavans, torn limb from limb, and he found his earlier hope—that Sapient and Manifold possessed some small kernel of goodness—tested. What kind of creatures could kill so gruesomely?

They left the palace grounds.

Night would soon fall, and clouds layered the sky in blankets of burgeoning darkness. No light shone within the palace, but William saw campfires burning at Village White Sun. There were dozens of them, and he exhaled in relief. "I think our people made it through." He set off for the village. It was time to see what all this victory cost them.

~

THEY REACHED THE VILLAGE—FINALLY. Serena had found a piece of wood to act as a staff, and she leaned on it, needing it to help her bear weight on her right ankle. She'd healed it as best she could, but it would be weeks before she'd be able to walk without pain. The rest of her was also a mess, cuts and scrapes all over.

Serena let William hold her hand, let him support her on her other side. She didn't mind, and in fact, she liked having him hold her up. It was comforting, and she needed it. She suspected he did, too. They limped along. Jake, Jason, and Landon fanned out to either side of them, shambling along as best they could.

William led them through the campfires where the Irregulars stood about, staring at them with pleading expressions, following after them. The Battalions had won the battle against the mahavans at White Sun, but everyone knew the most important one had taken place at the palace. All of their fellow magi begged for information, surrounding them.

William brought his group to a halt close to what was the camp's center. "It's done!" he shouted. "The Servitor's dead, the anchor line is closed. Shet never made it through."

His answer spawned a thousand shouts of joy, and the information raced through the camp with the speed of a rumor. By the time they reached the command tent, Julius, Daniella, and Karla had already heard the information. They stood outside, faces jubilant and clapping their hands as Serena and the others approached them. The entire camp applauded, shouting the glad news of their salvation.

William held up his hands, calling for silence. It took many minutes for him to gather everyone's attention. "We won a great victory tonight. All of us fought. We bled. But we overcame and did the impossible because we're mighty!"

Cheers met his words.

"But we also paid a terrible price for our triumph, and that needs to be the focus of what we do after today. Celebrate now, but never forget our lost friends."

More shouts and cheers came from the Irregulars, who eventually dispersed.

"We didn't know what was going on," Julius said when they pressed into the threshold of his campfire. "I thought we were done for when this wave of cold swept over us. All of us pretty much collapsed."

"It came from the anchor line," Serena said. "We still don't know what it means."

Daniella held Jake's hand, and she peered about. "Where's Rukh and Jessira?"

Jake flinched, and realization dawned on Daniella's face.

Serena answered. "They didn't make it." She leaned on her mahavan training, using it to suffocate her sorrow. Such emotions weren't weak, but she wasn't ready to face them yet.

Somberness deflated some of the group's joy.

"What about here?" William asked. "How'd it go?"

Julius appeared hesitant to answer. "We're still getting final reports," he said. "We've evacuated the injured, but the final tally of how many died . . ." He shook his head. "A lot more of our folk will probably still end up dying from their wounds."

"How bad was it?" Jake asked.

Julius grimaced. "Bad. It was the battle at the anchor line that hurt us the most. That demon thing."

"How many?" Serena pressed.

Julius swallowed heavily. "We lost twenty percent of our people. At least."

William's shoulders dropped. "You're saying we lost two hundred of our own."

Julius nodded.

"What about the mahavans?" Serena asked. The mahavans and drones of Sinskrill weren't her people, but this had been where she'd spent most of life. She'd always have memories of the place.

Julius shrugged. "Again, we're still getting reports, but it sounds like we pretty much wiped out the mahavans. We're guessing there's no more than fifty of them left. The rest are what they call drones. A bunch of them died, too. There's little more than a hundred of them."

Serena gritted her teeth at the information. The numbers represented more than simple arithmetic. They represented a tragedy. A ruinous war because her father was a coward and a cruel, despotic god had demanded a blood sacrifice.

~

OVER THE NEXT few days the Irregulars begin the long trek back to Arylyn. Many decisions remained, but they could wait. They never did find the final necrosed who'd entered Sinskrill. William reckoned he escaped in all the confusion. It was a worry for another day because the most pressing issue they faced—what to do with the people remaining on Sinskrill—still required resolution when the Irregulars readied their evacuation.

Adam Paradiso, the only survivor amongst Sinskrill's senior mahavans, made the suggestion that the drones be allowed to emigrate to Arylyn. "Our culture was poisonous to all of us," he had said. "I saw it long ago but didn't have the courage to speak my mind. I can now. Let the drones heal, become proper persons instead of slaves."

William promised to bring the proposal to Lilith's Council.

As for the remaining mahavans, Adam had another idea. "Leave them here. There's only a few dozen of us left. Let us rot together, alone and forgotten. We no longer pose any danger to Arylyn. Not now, not ever."

Jake had growled at the former Secondus. "We can make sure of that by ending all you evil bastards right now."

William knew his friend would rightfully never trust the mahavans, especially Adam, who'd almost killed him, but as tempted as he was by Jake's proposal, he couldn't allow it. With Rukh gone, he was the commander of the Irregulars. The decision was his, and he went with Adam's option. He wouldn't set the Irregulars hunting down the remaining mahavans and murder them. He'd had enough of killing. All of them had. The Village Council could make the final decision about what to do with Sinskrill.

Besides, he preferred to see his people safe at home where they could heal, which is what he ordered.

On a cruel day of wind and lashing rain, William gathered the majority of the Irregulars, and most of them left Sinskrill by the anchor line connected to Australia. Some took the boats, but before they departed William made sure all of the mahavans deep-ocean capable vessels were sunk and that the key to Sinskrill's anchor line was changed. He didn't want to give the mahavans an easy route to escape their island.

Months later, all of the wounded Irregulars were up and about, healthy and hale, and William hoped their souls recovered, too. It would be the greater challenge, probably years of healing ahead of them all.

Despite the victory over Sinskrill and Shet, for a long time a morose air pervaded Arylyn. It had been as Julius had feared: over twenty percent of the Irregulars had died. An entire generation of young people had been killed in the battles against the mahavans.

Mr. Zeus and many others openly wondered if the island's population would ever recover. Not every couple on Arylyn could conceive a child who had a connection to *lorasra*. The majority couldn't, and the Village Council worried about their future survival.

Their concerns were for another time.

William had other thoughts on his mind as he stood in the dining room of Mr. Zeus' home, staring into the backyard where a party went on. He'd been outside for a while, amongst the rest of the company for the past few hours, but he needed to retreat inside for some peace and solitude. Sometimes he wanted to be part of the party and sometimes he didn't want to do anything but watch.

Outside he saw lively conversations taking place between Serena, Julius, Ward, Fiona, and Mr. Zeus. They sat underneath the pergola. His wife looked like she was having a good time, smiling freely. She must have seen him through the glass because she met his gaze, holding his eyes, making sure he noticed when she tucked a strand of ear behind an ear.

William smiled, although the heart-racing sensation her simple gesture normally induced didn't occur. His feelings felt far away, flat and distant like they were covered in a layer of cloth. He figured he'd recover in time. This was his way of dealing with the grief and loss they once again had to endure.

Jason, Mink, Travail, Lien, Jean-Paul, and Thu spoke to one another, standing near the fire pit while Jake, Daniella, and Mr. and Mrs. Karllson smiled about something. It was good to see the Karllsons happy. They still grieved for Daniel, but at least overwhelming sorrow no longer carved their features in gloom.

Mr. Zeus said something to Fiona before slipping away to come inside. "Too many people?" he guessed, speaking to William.

"Sometimes it helps to watch instead of participate."

Mr. Zeus fell silent for a moment, his face inscrutable. "You've come far," he said after a moment. "I only wish the journey didn't have to be so terrible."

William shared the sentiment. "Me, too."

Mr. Zeus pointed to Serena. "At least you found yourself a lovely bride."

William smiled. "So did you," he said, pointing out Fiona.

Mr. Zeus laughed. "Love at my age." His features went inscrutable again. "You've sensed the loss in *lorasra*, haven't you?"

Leave it to Mr. Zeus to figure out Arylyn's eventual demise first, even if it was decades away. It wasn't a topic William wanted to discuss, though, at least not today. "Leave it alone. It's tomorrow's problem. Today's a day for celebration."

The door to the dining room opened, and in stepped Jake and Jason.

"What are you two gossips gossiping about?" Jason asked.

William answered without missing a beat. "We were wondering how long it would take you to kiss Mink when you thought no one would notice."

Jason gaped.

Jake laughed, shoving Jason. "You idiot. That's not what they were talking about."

Jason nodded, appearing sage now. "Yes, you're right. As serious as they seemed, they were probably talking about how long Daniella will put up with your bad breath."

"You jackhole."

William wanted to laugh as his friends began bickering. Some things never changed, and some things never should.

Again, the dining room door opened, and this time it was Serena who entered. "Travail's getting ready to leave," she said to William. "He wants to say goodbye."

"Be right there." William turned to the others. "Try not to kill each other."

He stepped outside into the bright sunshine. Wispy clouds drifted sedately in a blue sky. The smell of water and wet stone mixed with the sweet aroma of the fresh flowers Fiona had planted throughout the backyard. Palm fronds rustled under the influence of a soft breeze, and water trickled down the cliff face that formed the rear of the property, emptying into the small pond.

"William. It's been a lovely party," Travail said when he arrived, "but I fear it's time for me to make my departure."

William nodded, unsurprised. Travail didn't like large crowds, which, truth to tell, neither did William. Not now, anyway. He preferred the company of small groups of his friends.

"Are we still going running tomorrow morning?" William asked.

Travail grinned. "Of course." With that, the massive troll slipped his way through the other folk and left the party.

His departure seemed to signal the gathering's end. Next to leave were the Karllsons, Lien, and Julius. Following on their heels were Jean-Paul and Thu.

"We leave," the Frenchman said, hugging Serena and then William.

His husband, Thu, shook their hands.

Jean-Paul paused before they left. "Enjoy the rest of your day." He waggled his eyebrows and leered. "And your night, you newlyweds."

Thu sighed. "Come along, Jean-Paul."

Jean-Paul complained as they departed. "I was only joking. You know how I am."

"Sadly, I do," Thu said. They were soon lost to sight.

Others left until the only ones remained were William, Jason, Jake, Mr. Zeus, Fiona, and Serena.

William took in those who were still there. His first true friend, who'd taught him to be strong. His childhood enemy who'd become his greatest ally. The old man who'd showed him a world of magic. The old woman who'd feigned cruelty to protect him. And the woman he loved above all else.

He also considered those who'd already departed the party, along with those whose lives were forever gone. Sadness and joy warred in his heart in equal measure.

Mr. Zeus was right. He had come far, but what a terrible journey it had been. He wondered how Landon was doing. They had promised to stay in touch by traveling once a month to the *saha'asra* in West Virginia. So far, they had.

He also thought of Selene and made a private promise to go see her in a few weeks. The last time he'd seen her, she'd seemed happy, as if she was starting to find her footing.

Then there were Rukh and Jessira. He'd never know what had truly happened to them. Wherever they were, he said a prayer on their behalf. He also knew that they would have appreciated the honor done in their name. Arylyn's first birth following the battle at Sinskrill had taken place, and the baby, a girl, had been named in their honor: Russira. It was a made up name, but it meant everything to the Irregulars who'd served under Rukh and Jessira.

William gathered everyone's attention. "I'd like to say a few words," he said. "To those of us who survived, to those who passed, and to loved ones everywhere."

∾

MARCH 1992

WILLIAM STROLLED CLIFFTOP WITH SERENA, at peace and content in a way he hadn't been in so long. It was a sunny day full of promise. A gentle trade wind drove off any chance of humidity. It also gathered the smell of roasting meat from Jimmy Webster's restaurant and sent it drifting about. The aroma competed with the lush floral scent wafting from the strand of jasmines Serena had woven into her hair. The Triplets remained empty of clouds—no chance of rain—and the skies contained a depthless blue. Mount Madhava soared to the north, green at the base and a granite gray at the shoulders. Snow covered the peak.

Arylyn was seemingly unchanged.

There were many other folk out and about, and William slowed to greet them. His pause allowed Serena to stroll ahead of him, and he had to increase his pace to catch up with her.

He slowed a bit when the trade wind swirled her honey-colored dress, catching the fabric so it molded around her long legs.

Serena graced him with a knowing grin when he finally reached her side. She didn't call him out on his leering, though. She found it amusing. He loved that about her. "Has the council decided what to do with Brandon?" she asked.

"I haven't heard, but I'm guessing he'll be sent back to Sinskrill." It only made sense. Brandon had been part of Arylyn's invasion. Some things could never be forgiven.

Serena didn't respond, and William eyed her askance. "You disagree?"

She shook her head, the flowers shifting about. William unconsciously lifted his nose, inhaling the aroma of Serena's jasmines. In that moment, William wanted to take her in his arms and kiss her.

Once again, she smiled in amusement at him, obviously guessing his thoughts. "Stop thinking like that."

"Why? We're still newlyweds. We're supposed to think like that. It's in the contract."

Serena chuckled low and throaty. "Is that so?" She looped an arm inside one of his, gripping his elbow. "We'll see," she said, her words a promise.

They walked in silence, deeper into the village. A view of the empty enrune fields opened before them. They remained unused. Too many of Lilith's youth had been killed, and no one much felt like playing. Maybe they never would.

At least more of the village had been restored. The last of the damaged and destroyed houses had finally been torn down. A lot of the work had been through the efforts of Sinskrill's former drones. The council had decided to allow them to emigrate to Arylyn, and they'd been offered a chance to live wherever they wished. Most ended up housed in homes mixed in amongst the rest of Lilith's population.

Some magi had wanted the drones segregated in their own

district, but Mr. Zeus had adamantly opposed such a notion. "It'll become a ghetto if they're shoved off in a corner," he'd contended to the Village Council.

His arguments had carried the day, and the council had allowed the drones to settle in any empty home they could properly restore. They were also tasked with helping repair the damage done to Lilith. It would take them years to finish it all, since the drones had few talents beyond farming. At least they were learning and progressing. After being healed of their Tempering—Adam showed the magi how —the former drones had been taught to use their *lorethasra*. It was too bad that none of them had much skill beyond use of Spirit. They could only form the crudest of braids with the other Elements. Maybe that would also improve with time.

"Look. It's Jason and Mink," Serena said.

William grinned. Before the battle at Sinskrill, the two of them had spent almost all their free time together. Now it was worse. They hung on each other in every spare moment, kissing whenever they thought no one was paying attention. "When do you suppose they'll get married?"

Serena rolled her eyes. "I think you've taken up where Jason left off."

She meant he was acting like a gossip, and William didn't disagree. "That doesn't tell me when you think they'll get married."

"Not before Jake and Daniella," Serena said. "But before others. Beyond that, I'd leave it alone."

William ignored her advice and took a stab at guessing who else might be getting married. "You mean like Julius and Lien?" William figured those two might eventually see one another in a romantic kind of way, and if so, he approved.

Serena sighed. "I think you should do what I told you before: leave it alone. Everyone will figure it out at their own pace. They have time. We all do."

William fell silent, and they continued their walk. Serena was right. They did have time, but not as much as she thought.

Months ago, William had noticed a change to Arylyn's *lorasra*. It was weaker than before. Even the leylines pulsed less brightly, their colors muted as if the island's magic gradually weakened.

It had taken weeks more for William to be convinced that what he saw wasn't a figment of his imagination, that it was all too real. Arylyn's *lorasra* was inexorably fading. And whenever he created fresh *lorasra*, while that sense of loss lessened, it always came back. Not even three *raha'asras* could keep up with the diminishment.

Something was poisoning the island, all the *saha'asras*, in fact. William had checked. The *saha'asras* in West Virginia and Arizona showed a similar loss.

Jake and Fiona hadn't seen the problem yet, but they would. And if they reckoned the same as William, Arylyn had less than hundred years before the loss of *lorasra* became critical.

"Penny for your thoughts," Serena said. "You've been awful quiet."

William spoke without thinking, a lie leaping to his lips. "I was thinking how lucky we are to have peace and beauty."

Serena didn't appear convinced. She arched an eyebrow. "Really? I was expecting far deeper thoughts than that."

William didn't have a ready reply, and they entered a shadowed alley. No one else walked it. He caught Serena viewing him in challenge, and he drew her to a halt, wanting to explain what he'd noticed. He didn't want to destroy her happiness, but she deserved to know the truth.

He told her what he suspected. He shouldn't have been surprised when she took the news without even blinking.

Instead, she merely nodded thoughtfully. "Even if you're right, we'll find a solution," she said. "We always have before. Look at how we handled Sinskrill and Shet. We've already done the impossible, and if we can do that, your little problem will be nothing."

"But we only have—"

Serena placed a finger on his lips, shushing him. "It can wait for tomorrow or even the day after that. We have years to figure it out." She wore a warm smile and tucked a strand of hair behind an ear before looping her hands behind his neck.

William wrapped her in his arms, one hand on her waist and the other around her shoulders. He drew her close, knowing she'd allow it. He kissed her deeply, and his heart came alive. He remembered the first time he'd stepped into a *saha'asra*, how the world had brightened, his life starting anew. Kissing Serena was like that, and his heart soared.

THE END

AUTHOR'S NOTE:

Whew! It's hard to believe it's over, but that's the end of William and Serena's story . . . at least so far. Maybe there's more to what happens in their lives, but I think they've earned their rest. Of course, I thought the same about Rukh and Jessira, and look how that ended up. Regardless, I want to thank everyone who made it to the end of this series with me. I'm still humbled that so many people took the time to read the books. And speaking of gratitude, if you feel so inclined, I'd be really happy if you could leave a review on Amazon.

GLOSSARY

ARYLYN

D RAMATIS PERSONAE

AFA (NAME MEANS 'STORM') **Simon:** He is originally from French Polynesia and came to Arylyn in 1856 when he was 33. By the time William arrives, age has left him stooped and weak, but he somehow still maintains the lush gardens around his home. He is also the most creative *raha'asra* on Arylyn.

BAR DUBA: He is native born to Arylyn and possesses features typical of those types of individuals with Mediterranean dark skin and hair. In addition, he is the councilor for Cliff Air and is known to enjoy his food and dislike folk who are long-winded.

· · ·

BREAK FOLIAGE: A native-born magus who is also a born politician. He's a small, weasel-like man with a nasally voice who represents Cliff Fire on the Village Council. He and Zane Blood generally vote together, and Rukh can't stand either of them.

DANIEL KARLLSON: Native born, but his parents are not. They are Trace and Magnus Karllson, and he is their only child. When William was discovered in the Far Beyond, Daniel's parents were asked to help evaluate this potentially powerful *asrasin*. They wanted Daniel to experience life in the world outside of Arylyn's shores, but he was initially hesitant to go. At the time, he had no belief that the Far Beyond could teach him anything. It took Jason Jacobs, his best friend, weeks of hounding to convince him to temporarily leave Arylyn. Then Daniel saw *Star Wars*, and his world changed. He became a proud participant in all things 'nerd'. He also became a good friend to William Wilde and later on, he fell in love with Lien, who also accompanied the Karllsons to the Far Beyond.

DANIELLA LOGAN: Native born, but like her older sister, Karla, she has blue eyes. She doesn't like enrune and tends to be quiet until people get to know her.

EMMA LAKE: A young native born girl, and one of Selene's earliest friends on Arylyn.

FIONA APPLEFIELD: She was originally from England and kidnapped to Sinskrill when her *lorethasra* flowered to life. For decades, she was the only *raha'asra* on the island (other than the Servitor), and consequently, for the past sixty years, she has functioned as a battery for the rest of the mahavans. She is also Serena and Selene's grandmother.

. . .

JAKE RIDLEY: He was originally a rich snob, athletic, good-looking, and smart, but life hasn't been kind to him. Growing up, he and William disliked one another. Much of this is because Jake was a bully. Yet, he can also be quite charitable and loving, especially to his brother, Johnny. His rivalry and distaste for William continued through high school, but they managed to set aside their differences when they were both kidnapped to Sinskrill. There, the two of them forge a tight bond and become the best of friends. His parents are Steven and Helen Ridley.

JANINE DALE: A native born blacksmith.

JASON JACOBS: He was born in New Orleans to Randall and Amelia Jacobs but entered a *saha'asra* at age nine. In that moment, his *lorethasra* came to life. He would have died, but his great-great grandfather, Odysseus Louis Crane III (Mr. Zeus), discovered him. Jason moved to Arylyn, and that was also the last time he saw his parents or the rest of his family. He doesn't speak of why that occurred. He and William are close friends.

(*AN INTERESTING HISTORICAL NOTE: JASON' great-grandmother, Layla, was the only daughter of Odysseus and Edith Crane. Layla married a white Cuban Hispanic. They had seven children, including a son, Sonny, who married Julia, a member of the Cherokee tribe. Sonny and Julia had three sons and one daughter, Amelia—Jason's mother. She married Randall Jacobs, whose family hails from Scotland and Germany.*)

JEAN-PAUL BERNARD: A flamboyant, somewhat obnoxious Frenchman. He was once a pot-smoking hippie from Paris, France before emigrating to Arylyn. He loves to surf and taught Serena how to do so. She considers him one of her only friends on Arylyn. He is married to ThuDuc Thu.

. . .

JEFF COATS: A farmer murdered by the mahavan, Evelyn Mason, during her scouting mission to Arylyn.

JIMMY WEBSTER: A native born restaurateur. He owns and operates *Jimmy Webster's Restaurant*.

JULIUS O'BRIEN: He is originally from Montserrat, British West Indies, but his parents moved to Jamaica when he was young. He was a bit of a black sheep, falling into the Rastafarian life, of which his parents disapproved. Later, he chose to pursue civil engineering at Purdue University, but on a trip home to visit family in Jamaica, he came in contact with a *saha'asra* and had to emigrate to Arylyn. He helps rescue William and Jake from Sinskrill and later takes part in the battle to free Travail and Fiona.

KARLA LOGAN: Native born, but like her younger sister, Daniella, she has blue eyes and wears glasses. Her grandfather was a rector in the Episcopal Church in the United States. She loves enrune and often plays the sport with Serena and Lien.

LIEN SUN: She is originally from China, but as a teenager, she found herself on the wrong side of the Communist Party. She fled and ended up in a *saha'asra* in Beijing. Luckily, Peter Magnus Karllson was visiting the city at the time and saved her by bringing her to Arylyn. She originally stayed with Mr. Zeus for the first three years of her life on Arylyn, but when he moved to the Far Beyond to determine William's eligibility for Arylyn, she moved in with the Karllsons and pretended to be their foreign exchange student. She loves to sing but is a terrible singer. She also prides herself on not being a nerd, although she is one.

. . .

LILIAN CARE: Originally from England, she moved to Arylyn in the 1940s, shortly after the end of WWII. She once worked as a governess and has been Lilith's mayor for the past five years.

LUCAS SHAW: He is originally from Charleston, South Carolina and retains the accent of his blue-blood forebears. He emigrated to Arylyn in the 1920s. He is a member of the Village Council and represents Cliff Water.

MAXINE KNIGHT: She is originally from a small town in Indiana. She runs *Ms. Maxine's*, the best place for ice cream in all of Arylyn.

ODYSSEUS LOUIS CRANE III AKA MR. ZEUS: At the time of the events of *William Wilde and the Necrosed*, he is 134 years old, but he only appears to be in his sixties. He has a deep, soothing voice, a long white beard, and looks like a wizard. He emigrated to Arylyn in 1878 and married another emigrant to Arylyn, a black woman named Edith Naomi Merle. However, when their only child, Layla, proved to be a normal—a person without *asra*—they took her to the Far Beyond and raised her there. Edith never returned to Arylyn, though. She died in Mississippi, and Mr. Zeus has never explained how she passed away, although he's let slip that she died at the hands of a necrosed.

A MORE DETAILED biography of Mr. Zeus:
    Mr. Zeus's great-grandfather, Lucius George Crane, emigrated to the American Colonies in the mid 1700's. He settled in Savannah, a young town in what later became the state of Georgia. Lucius worked as a fisherman, but when the Revolutionary War erupted, Lucius joined the Continental

Army. Later, after the war's conclusion, Lucius bought land near Augusta and became a farmer, founding the plantation Aria. By the time Mr. Zeus' father, Odysseus Louis Crane II, inherited the plantation, it had five hundred acres of land and almost 35 slaves.

Decades later, the Civil War broke out, and Mr. Zeus's father joined the Confederate Army, serving in the 6th Regiment, the first unit mustered from the state of Georgia and commanded by a good friend of the family, Colonel Arthur Colquitt, whom his father had met while the two men were studying at Princeton. Mr. Zeus' brothers, both of whom were much older than him, joined the Confederate Army as well, but they were assigned to the 19th Regiment. His eldest brother, Joshua, was killed at Cedar Mountain, while Jeb died at Second Manassas. His father learned that they had expired when the 19th and the 6th both fought at Antietam. He wrote home to Mr. Zeus' mother (Miriam Francis Crane) that his heart was empty. All he had seen was death and suffering, and soon after, he died at the battle of Fredericksburg. Later, General Sherman burned Aria to the ground, leaving Mr. Zeus' family destitute.

After the surrender of the Confederacy, Miriam married Zachary Thomas, a local plantation owner whose entire family had also perished during the war. Mr. Thomas adopted Zeus and his sister, Ruth Esther, and moved the family to California in 1866. He wanted a fresh start and no memories of a way of life that had died in a flood of fire and blood. They moved to Santa Barbara, where Mr. Thomas took his remaining savings and bought land. He established an orchard and grew oranges. Within 12 years, the family was living prosperously. Mr. Zeus' mother had several more children, a girl, Susan and a boy, James. Ruth Esther married a local lawyer, the son of a well-to-do family that had been in Santa Barbara for many years.

As for Mr. Zeus, at twenty-six he was sent east to take a tour of Europe, but he never arrived. Instead, he came across a saha'asra in New York City, in a swampy field that would eventually become Central Park. His lorethasra came alive, and Afa Simon brought him to Arylyn.

PETER MAGNUS KARLLSON (AKA MAGNUS): He is from Sweden and

looks like his Viking forebears. When his *lorethasra* came to life, it broke his heart to have to leave his family. He spent years hating what had happened to him, but eventually Trace arrived, and his life changed. He married her within nine months of their meeting, and they have a son, Daniel. When William was discovered, they accompanied Mr. Zeus to Cincinnati in order to expose Daniel to the wider world beyond Arylyn's borders. In addition, Magnus discovered Lien in China and brought her to Arylyn prior to the events of *William Wilde and the Necrosed*.

RAIL FORSYTH: A scout in the Ashoka Irregulars.

ROBERT WEEKS: A native born blacksmith who helps build Arylyn's cannons.

SEEMA CHOUDARY: A small, quiet Indian woman originally from what became the Krishna District in Andhra Pradesh after the end of the British Raj. Her caste is Kamma, which Rukh and Jessira find interesting. She emigrated to Arylyn in the early 1900s when she was still in her teens and is the councilor for Cliff Earth.

SELENE PARADISO: Serena's younger sister, and they share the same parents. She is aware of this shared lineage—the fact that they're true sisters and that the Servitor is their true father. Until escaping to Arylyn, she didn't know about her grandmother, Fiona Applefield. William and Jake think of her as their little sister.

SERENA PARADISO: She was born on Sinskrill to Axel Paradiso and Cinnamon Bliss. However, at age 11, when she passed her Tempering, she was taken from Cinnamon and given to Axel's wife, Alaina, to become her daughter. She eventually became a bishan, but not until after she saw her birth mother, a woman she loved with all her heart, whipped to death in front of her eyes. This event is the main reason why Serena became such a hard, ruthless, and consummate liar.

SIONED O'SULLIVAN: She is originally from Ireland and came to Arylyn when she was twenty-three. She is a *raha'asra*, and William's and Jake's originally instructor in *Jayenasra*, the Beautiful Art. By the time William arrives on Arylyn, she is over 140 years old.

SILE TROY: Native born to Arylyn. He works as a farmer with a plot of land in Janaki Valley. His wife is Jennifer Troy, a singer and a baker, and his grandmother is Sioned O'Sullivan. Sile agrees to take on Serena as an apprentice farmer, acting as her master.

STACEY CLOUD: A scout in the Ashokan Irregulars.

THUDUC THU: Originally from Saigon, Vietnam, he emigrated to the United States as part of the Vietnamese boat people in 1978. Shortly thereafter, he emigrated to Arylyn. He is married to Jean-Paul Bernard.

TRASE KARLLSON: Born in Ethiopia, and her birth name is Hanan Malak Abdullah ('merciful angel' in Arabic). She was engaged to a family friend at age fifteen, but after she was attacked by her fiancé's older brother, she had to flee, fearing an honor killing. She entered a *saha'asra*, and its glory calmed her pain. She stayed there, preferring to die, but Mr. Zeus saved her. As a result, she has a deep and abiding gratitude for him. On Arylyn, she eventually met Peter Magnus Karllson. They have a son, Daniel.

. . .

TRAVAIL FINE: He is a young troll, only about 200 years old. He was tricked into coming to Sinskrill by a prior Servitor, and with his fear of open water, he was trapped there. As a result, he has a deep and abiding hatred for Sinskrill and all mahavans. Like all trolls, he is massively built, quiet and solitary, and a Justice. In addition, he was William's and Jake's protector and teacher during their time on Sinskrill, and they love him for his friendship. Fiona Applefield was once his bishan and has always acted in his best interests, although on Sinskrill they kept their friendship secret.

WARD SILVER: He is a native to Arylyn and master of multiple Elements: Fire, Earth, and Water and Spirit. He is young and is the one who eventually teaches William how to properly braid his Elements.

WILLIAM WILDE: Born in the mountains of North Carolina but moved to Cincinnati, Ohio when he was ten. As a result, his mountain accent sometimes still comes through. His parents, Kevin and Jane Wilde, were killed by the necrosed, Kohl Obsidian. It was assumed that his brother, Landon, was similarly murdered. These events started William on the long road to becoming an *asrasin*. He is also a *raha'asra*.

ZANE BLOOD: A native-born man who has an overabundant sense of self-worth, much of it undeserved. He is the councilor for Cliff Spirit, and he and Break Foliage are allies on the Village Council.

HISTORY

THE ISLAND WAS DISCOVERED in 7545 B.C. At the time, it was volcanic and uninhabitable, but in 6257 B.C., a small colony of *asrasins* was eventually established there. Most were magavanes—followers of Shokan—and fleeing the *Nusrael*, the catastrophic war amongst the *asrasins*. At the time, the island was a relative backwater given its active volcanism, tortured landscape of flowing lava and erupting sulfur vents, and its meager *lorasra*. As a result, it was largely ignored during the worldwide war. However, as the battles raged on, other *asrasins* who had once scorned the island chose to settle there.

THE *NUSRAEL* eventually settled down to a low-level conflict, and the island was once again forgotten as many of its inhabitants rejoined the larger world. But as the millennia passed, more and more *saha'asras* were slowly bereft of *lorasra*, and Arylyn became one of the few places in the world that could sustain the life of those with *lorethasra*. It was permanently settled in 2039 B.C. with the founding of the village of Lilith. The volcano at the island's heart was put to sleep through the *asra* of the dwarves, and several *sithes* of elves beautified the place when they planted forests and jungles on the once barren hills and valleys of Arylyn.

IN THE CENTURIES THAT FOLLOWED, with the ongoing failure of all the world's *saha'asras*, the island was conceived as the final home of the magi. A *sithe* of elves and *settling* of dwarves—the descendants of those who had helped tame the island—was allowed to live there as well. By 533 AD, no other community of magi existed in the world.

STILL, the passage of time did not leave Arylyn untouched. The *saha'asra* dwindled, the *lorasra* faded, and the elves and dwarves living there eventually died out. They became nothing more than Memories. The island's magi population shrank as well, and by the time William Wilde enters the island, it has become a shadow of its former self, although its inhabitants don't seem to realize it since it remains a place of peace, beauty, and grace.

GOVERNMENT

LILITH IS GOVERNED by an elected council with one councilor representing each of the five Cliffs upon which the village is built. The councilors serve for three years. The mayor who oversees the government is chosen in a village-wide election. Lilith, though, basically governs itself without much input from the Village Council. This was actually the intention of Lilith's founders.

THE CURRENT VILLAGE COUNCIL:
Mayor: Lilian Care.
Cliff Air: Bar Duba
Cliff Fire: Break Foliage
Cliff Water: Luke Shaw
Cliff Earth: Seema Choudary
Cliff Spirit: Zane Blood

GEOGRAPHY

CHARYBDIS WAY: A narrow pass that cuts across the western slopes of Mount Madhava. It is south of the Jaipurana Pass, and the Riven Road extends through both of them.

CHIMERA SEED: A blocky bridge that connects Cliff Spirit with Cliff Water. Carved into the posts of the bridge are figures of fantastical creatures who Rukh and Jessira recognize as Chimeras from their home world of Arisa. No one knows how such carvings came to be.

. . .

ELVEN TOR, the: A large, rocky hill where the Elven Memory comes to collect those who are on their pilgrimage to examine Arylyn's history.

GUANYIN BRIDGE: A reflective, silvery bridge made of an unknown material. It traverses River Namaste at the base of Cliff Spirit where the river recollects after plunging down Lilith's cataracts.

JAIPURANA PASS: A mountain pass skirting the northwestern shoulders of Mount Madhava. It is north of the Charybdis Way, and the Riven Road extends through both of them.

JANAKI VALLEY: THE NAME MEANS 'MOTHER' in Hindi, and it is a mystical valley of fertile fields and lush orchards. It is where the bulk of Lilith's crops are grown, and all magi hold the valley in reverence.

LAKSHMAN BRIDGE: A stone bridge that traverses River Namaste near the enrune fields. The name may be derived from that of Rama's brother, Lakshmana, in the ancient Indian epic poem, the *Ramayana*.

LILITH: The only village in Arylyn. It is built upon terraces carved into five cliffs that overlook the Pacific Ocean. The five **Cliffs** are **Cliff Air, Cliff Fire, Cliff Water, Cliff Earth,** and **Cliff Spirit,** and each one is bifurcated by a set of Main Stairs. They also all contain a number of smaller stairs and bridges to connect the various terraces of each Cliff.

   Clifftop: The area atop the Cliffs. It's Lilith's industrial and mercantile core.

   The Village Green: The heart of Lilith. It sits at the point where

Clifftop eventually runs into the Main Stairs of Cliff Spirit and that portion is shaped like a ship's prow.

LINCHPIN KNOLL: A small hill near Clifftop where all the known anchor lines that connect Arylyn to the rest of the world are located.

MOUNT MADHAVA: It is the only true mountain on Arylyn, visible from nearly every vantage point on the island. It had once been an active volcano until a *settling* of dwarves calmed it. The descendants of those dwarves would go on to live in a set of villages they built within the mountain's broad shoulders.

RIVEN ROAD: A rugged road that branches off Sita's Song north of Janaki Valley. From there, it extends around the western and north-western shoulders of Mount Madhava by passing through Charybdis Way and then Jaipurana Pass. From there, it leads to Arylyn's northern beaches and watchtowers.

RIVER NAMASTE: The river that feeds Janaki Valley. The waters collect from the foothills that surround Mount Madhava. From there, the river flows through Janaki Valley and tumbles over the cataracts, spreading like a fine mist across Lilith's Cliffs before recollecting at the base of Cliff Spirit. The waters then sweep north through a narrow canyon lined with statues of great figures from Arylyn's past.

SCYLLA PASS: A mountain pass on the northwestern slopes of Mount Madhava. It branches of the Riven Road and parallels Jaipurana Pass before rejoining Riven Road north of Jaipurana Pass.

. . .

Sɪᴛᴀ's Sᴏɴɢ: A long road that runs through Janaki Valley and all the way to the southern base of Mount Madhava.

Vɪʟʟᴀɢᴇ ᴏꜰ Mᴇʟᴅᴇɴᴄʀᴇᴄʜᴇ: It was the last, living dwarven village on Arylyn before the dwarves became a Memory. It sits within the bulk of Mount Madhava and the Dwarven Memory resides there.

MISCELLANEOUS

Oɴ Aʀʏʟʏɴ, those who wish to progress in a profession start out as apprentices. From there, they become journeymen. Finally, they become adepts, or masters.

Eɴʀᴜɴᴇ: The national game of Arylyn. It utilizes speed, physicality, and skill with *asra*. The latter is actually the most important attribute for success in enrune.

Tʀᴇᴀᴛɪsᴇs ᴏɴ Tʀᴀᴠᴇʟ—A Translation: A translated book about anchor lines.

Tʜᴇ Iɴᴛᴇʀᴠᴇɴᴛɪᴏɴ: A very boring book about the *Nusrael*. William discovers it in the library. The librarian advised him to never open the book's pages, but William didn't listen. He sometimes wishes he had.

SINSKRILL

SINSKRILL DRAMATIS PERSONAE

ADAM CARPENTER (WENT by the name Adam Paradiso in the Far Beyond): The powerful Secondus to his true brother, Axel. He was also Serena's Isha during her pilgrimage as a bishan in the Far Beyond.

AXEL CARPENTER: Raised to the status of Servitor over twenty years ago when he successfully managed to claim the Servitor's Seat. He is the unopposed leader of the mahavans.

BRANDON THRUM: Born to two nameless drones. He is a Walker and was once Serena's fiercest supporter when he thought she might become a Village Prime.

DARREN PYRE: Fire Prime. An old mahavan. He served as Adam's Isha.

DEVON CARPENTER: Prime of Village Bliss.

EVELYN MASON: An intense, young Rider with auburn hair that billows about her head when her passions run away with her. She was also once Serena's supporter on Sinskrill, but she now wants nothing more than kill Serena, who she believes a traitor.

GOLD IMBUE: Tender Prime. Like all mahavans, he can be casually cruel.

.   .   .

Hannah Yearn: Captain of the *Deathbringer*. Competent but risk-averse and Brandon replaces her command of *Deathbringer* before the battle at Lilith.

Josiah Danks: The foreman who replaced Justin Finch upon his demotion.

Justin Finch: A Sinskrill foreman who disliked William and Jake enough to fight them. He was broken to the rank of peasant for striking those considered of higher rank than him.

Mary Commons: Justin Finch's fiancé before he was broken to the rank of peasant for fighting William and Jake.

Rail Swift: Rider Prime. He is a known coward who hides during a conflict.

Sherlock Carpenter: Prime of Village Paradiso on Sinskrill. He died shortly after lashing Jake.

Thomas White: A Tender occasionally in charge of William and Jake during their time on Sinskrill.

Trina Batter: Walker Prime. She often works with Darren Pyre, the Fire Prime. They have a true son, Aaron Batter, who is a Spirit Master, which is an embarrassment to both of them.

Tristan Winegate: A young Tender who had initially supported

Serena in her bid to become a Village Prime. He died at the teeth and claws of a small tribe of unformed.

HISTORY

THE ISLAND WAS FOUNDED as a refuge for the mahavans in 3659 BC but not permanently settled until 1943 BC. Originally Sinskrill was a barren land with a climate similar to the Faroe Islands. As a result, the first inhabitants had to import much of the fauna and flora. They planted tough grass and heather to hold the soil of the lowlands and then forested the hills with lodge pole pines, spruce pines, feltleaf willows, black cottonwoods, green alders, beech, caneloes, and hard log marten. The work might have gone easier with the aide of a *sithe* of elves. However, since mahavans tend to enslave any woven race they encounter, that proved impossible.

NEVERTHELESS, the island flowered. It is known that at one time, tens of thousands of mahavans once called Sinskrill home. This included Amethyst, a smaller island off the coast of Sinskrill. However, a combination of the fading of the world's *lorasra* and the foolish importation of several large, powerful tribes of unformed led to the devastation of the mahavan population.

BY MODERN TIMES, all of Sinskrill's northern villages have been abandoned, and so, too, was Amethyst. The only remaining places of habitation exist along the island's southern coast. The rest of Sinskrill has been given over to wilderness. In essence, the island has returned to its roots as a rocky place full of rugged mountains. It has once more become a hard place for a hard people, a fact in which the mahavans take great pride.

. . .

OF NOTE, there are no rats, mice, frogs, gnats, or mosquitoes on Sinskrill. The early settlers wisely chose against allowing pests onto the island.

GOVERNMENT AND SOCIAL STRUCTURE

THE GOVERNMENT IS FAIRLY simple in that the Servitor is the island's unquestioned sovereign. This unchallenged rule is felt to be ordained through the will of Sinskrill's god, Shet, who supposedly chooses the island's next ruler upon the death of the prior Servitor. This happens when a mahavan manages to sit upon the Servitor's Chair for a full minute, thus earning Shet's blessing. Any mahavan can make the attempt but lack of success can be painful and earn the enmity of the new Servitor. As a result, it is generally only the Secondus who tries for the Chair, and from that point on, the newly raised Servitor—regardless of whether they are male or female—is referred to as 'liege', and they take the surname 'Carpenter'.

OF COURSE, like all places, Sinskrill contains politics and a wise Servitor plays each faction against the others. In this case, the wise Servitor plays each *collegium*—around which mahavan society is structured—and their respective Primes, against one another.

EVERY MAHAVAN BELONGS to a single *collegium*, and there is one for each Element. In addition, the various *collegia* have different levels of respect amongst the overall mahavan population.

THOSE BELONGING to the Fire Master *collegium* are known as Seres. They are the finest warriors on Sinskrill, with training in unarmed and armed combat. The Air Masters are called Walkers, and they are the Servitor's spies. They are also in a constant conflict with the Seres for dominance in Sinskrill. Those from the Water Master *collegium* are known as Riders. They cleanse the water of impurities, such as heavy metals that seep down from the northern mountains as well as *lorasra* that flows from Shet to Sinskrill. The lowest ranking *collegium* belongs to the Earth Masters, who are known as Tenders. They are essentially farmers.

As for the Primes, they are mahavans of note who are given command over a *collegium* or one of Sinskrill's villages. In this case, Paradiso or Bliss since the Servitor rules Village White Sun directly. The village Primes are also adopted by the Servitor into his/her family and take on the surname 'Carpenter'.

In addition, there is a fifth group of mahavans, Spirit Master, or Spiritualists. However, they are of quite limited power and prestige and are not afforded an independent *collegium*.

Of interesting note, Servitors tend not to live as long as other mahavans, and no one knows why. Some have speculated that it might be due to the fact that upon their elevation, a newly made Servitor is transformed into both a *thera'asra* and a *raha'asra*, a fact not widely known.

An even less known secret—one known only by Servitors and a few of their most trusted subordinates—is that, in addition to their abilities as *asrasins*, all Servitors have the power of an unformed.

*It should be noted that mahavans believe themselves to be superior to all magi, especially when it comes to physical conflict. Recent events have not borne out this viewpoint.

SINSKRILL MISCELLANEOUS

BISHANS: Shills who have progressed deep into their training. They are tested a final time at age eighteen after their pilgrimage, and those who pass are made mahavans. However, just as important as completion of the pilgrimage is *how* such an accomplishment was managed. It is the latter that often determines into which *collegium* a newly minted mahavan is accepted.

DEMOLITION: The Servitor's ship.

DRONES: This is the status of all children at birth, including those born to mahavan parents. Their status remains unchanged until the age of ten when they are given three attempts to pass a Tempering. Failure on all three occasions leads to stripping where they still have some of their *lorethasra* but can no longer link to *lorasra* in any meaningful fashion.

From that point on, their life path is forged and they work as peasant farmers, largely under the regulation and control of the Tenders.

*ALL DRONES TAKE the surname of the village in which they were born. In addition, boys are eventually sent to a different village from their birth.

LORD SHET: The god of Sinskrill. He is also the lord of *raha'asras* and master of all Elements. His compiled wisdom is found in *Shet's Counsel*. Most *asrasins* believe him to be a myth.

. . .

Isʜᴀ: One who trains a shill or a bishan.

Mᴀʜᴀᴠᴀɴs: the elite *asrasins* of Sinskrill. It takes years of forging to create one. Once a bishan is elevated to the status of mahavan, they can exchange their village surname for that of their parents, or even that of the *collegium* into which they were accepted. Most choose family.

Sʜɪʟʟ: A drone who has passed their Tempering. At age fifteen, shills are retested and those who pass become bishans. They have two chances to pass and failure leads to stripping.

THE FAR BEYOND

DRAMATIS PERSONAE IN THE FAR BEYOND

WIZARD BILL'S WANDERING WONDERS

The circus that William, Jason, and Serena join in order to temporarily escape Kohl Obsidian.

Bɪʟʟ Lᴏɴᴅᴏɴᴇʀ: Portly co-owner of *Wizard Bill's Wandering Wonders*. He gave William, Jason, and Serena jobs when they were on the run from Kohl Obsidian. He's married to Nancy Londoner, and he enjoys his beer. Known as Mr. Bill by his employees.

. . .

DUBROVIC FAMILY OF TUMBLERS, the: A supposedly famous family of tumblers from Croatia. In reality, all of them are American gymnasts who are unrelated to one another and thrown together by the manic madness of Mr. Bill for his circus.

ELAINA SINITH: a beautiful, mysterious woman who claims to be a witch from a village called Sand. This inevitably leads to the joke that Elaina is a 'sand witch'. She works at *Wizard Bill's Wandering Wonders* as a fortune teller.

JANE SMITH: Seamstress at *Wizard Bill's Wandering Wonders*.

JIMMY HANSON: The cook at *Wizard Bill's Wandering Wonders*. He's not too bright but very loyal to Bill and Nancy.

LUC DUBROVIC: A gymnast who is supposedly the head of the famous Dubrovic Family of Tumblers from Croatia. In reality, his name is Stanley Wilson.

NANCY LONDONER: The tall, slender co-owner *Wizard Bill's Wandering Wonders*. She was the one who pushed her husband, Bill, to give William, Jason, and Serena a chance to join their circus.

ST. FRANCIS HIGH SCHOOL

*THE HIGH SCHOOL THAT WILLIAM, Jason, Jake, Daniel, and Lien attended. Serena joins them at the beginning of their senior year.

PRINCIPAL ALFRED WALTER: School principal.

. . .

MRS. GERTRUDE NELSON: Biology teacher. She has a pet boa and William is terrified of the reptile.

JEFF SETTER: Defensive captain of the St. Francis High School football team.

MRS. JENNIFER CLANCY: English teacher. She is later put on bed rest during her pregnancy.

MRS. KATHERINE WILKERSON: William and Serena's homeroom teacher. She has a yearly winter sweater contest that she holds right after the Christmas holidays.

LANCE OWENS: Wide receiver on the high school football team. Jason dusts him in a sprint, which earned him the interest of Coach Rasskins.

MR. MIKE FARTHER: Jason's homeroom teacher.

FATHER RICHARD JAMESON: Religion teacher who takes them to a church in Over-the-Rhine in downtown Cincinnati.

MR. ROBIN CLEATING: Substitute English teacher when Mrs. Clancy is put on bed rest.

. . .

VICE-PRINCIPAL ROGER MERON: A bulldog of a vice-principal who's more clever than most realize.

SONYA BOWYER: Jake Ridley's longtime girlfriend in high school. William had a crush on her until Serena walked into his life.

COACH STEVE RASSKINS: Head football coach at St. Francis.

STEVEN ALDO: Part of Jake's group of friends at St. Francis. As such, he's not expected to show much in the way of friendship toward William, but he subtly does so anyway.

MR. THOMAS CALLAHAN: American History teacher who speaks like it's still the 1950s.

OTHERS

AIA: Once a small kitten who helped kill Kohl Obsidian. A Kesarin. She is bonded to Rukh.

HELEN RIDLEY: Mother to Jake and John Ridley. Married to Steven Ridley.

JOHN AARON RIDLEY: Jake's little brother, who used to go by 'Johnny'. He was born with a neurodegenerative condition that has slowly limited his mobility. Jake loves him fiercely.

. . .

SHON: A Kesarin. He is bonded to Jessira.

STEVEN RIDLEY: Father to Jake and John Ridley. Married to Helen Ridley.

THE WOVEN

*ALL BEINGS who are created through the work of *lorethasra* and *lorasra* are collectively known as 'woven'. In addition, most woven have an instinctual understanding of the Elements that *asrasins* lack. However, once a task is identified, it is often the *asrasins* that accomplish the deed. For instance, in the founding of Arylyn, once the dwarves and elves showed what was needed, it was the magi who performed the work.

ANTALAGORE THE BLACK: The greatest of all dragons. He betrayed Shet and was eventually killed by Sapient Dormant for his treason. Or so it was once thought.

DEMONS: Mysterious and more powerful than the necrosed. Psychotic, and utterly evil, they live for torment. They may not actually be woven. They are great enough to give the Servitor's pause.

DWARVES: Mountain dwelling woven. They live in large matrilineal villages, which they name a *settling*. Their ability to bring calm and peace—a skill they share with those around them—extends to the dragons who often share a mountain range with them. Shet has a special hate for dwarves.

· · ·

ELVES: Live in large groups they call *sithes*. Generally smaller than humans but swifter. Arrogance is often an adjective associated with them.

HOLDERS: Creations of the magavanes. Holders are woven assassins who were meant to kill other *asrasins*, specifically mahavans. Their greatest weapon is the Wildness, an ability to impart energy into their weapons and render them capable of cutting through nearly any weave or substance.

LANDON VENT: He is the merged consciousness of Landon Wilde, William's older brother, and Pilot Vent, the holder who became Kohl Obsidian.

NECROSED: Monstrous woven created thousands of years ago by Shet at his fortress, Clarity Pain. They were meant to be the antithesis of dwarves, bringing fear rather than calm, and death rather than peace. Since holders were assassins meant to kill *asrasins*—specifically mahavans—Shet wished to turn their power on the magavanes. Thus, he captured a large group of holders and tortured them until he created the first necrosed, **Grave Invidious**. Shokan, though, placed a curse upon the necrosed, such that they are in a continual state of decay and rot.

NECROSED CAN ENTER long periods of catatonia, measured in decades, before cycling to awareness, and when they do, an insatiable hunger for flesh and *lorethasra* fills them.

THE EXACT NUMBER of necrosed is unknown but it is likely small. Nevertheless, all woven and *asrasins* fear the necrosed, and it is believed that no one except a holder can kill one of the undying monsters.

KNOWN NECROSED:

Charnel Blood: Powerful necrosed. Killed by Rukh and Jessira.

Grave Invidious: The first necrosed and the keeper of Shet's temple, Clarity Pain. He was also the protector of Shet's sword, Undefiled Locus and was killed by Landon Vent.

Kohl Obsidian: He was once a holder named Pilot Vent but was transformed into a necrosed by Sapient Dormant, the Overward of the Necrosed. Kohl would go on to kill William's family, thus setting William on the road to becoming an *asrasin*.

Manifold Fulsom: A large, powerful necrosed.

Rue Defiant: Female necrosed and as ancient as Manifold. Killed by William.

Sapient Dormant: Overward of the necrosed. Created by Overlord Shet. He was born in Clarity Pain, and one of his first acts was to supposedly slay the dragon, Antalagore the Black.

SALACHAR RAKSHASA: A demon roused by the Servitor.

SCOURSKIN: Extinct on Earth, but their species still lives on in Seminal. They are a short, blue skinned race of woven with heads that look like catfish. They live off of *therasra* and are among the stupidest and weakest of all woven.

TROLLS: Powerful, intelligent woven. They are universally massive and have horned heads. Throughout history, they have served as Justices, possessing an ability to see to the heart of the matter and render a judgment that can never be forgotten. It is a power all *asrasins* respect. Of interesting note, they procreate by parthenogenesis.

. . .

UNFORMED: Shape-changing woven. They can take on the form of nearly any animal, regardless of size. They generally live in small tribes of 40-50, which are led by a Prime—either male or female. Each Prime is supported by a Secondus, a powerful ally who can later become a threat.

They have a first name and a last name, the latter of which is that of their tribe.

However, their surnames frequently change since unformed move about quite often. Their allegiances shift from tribe to tribe, whose territories also tend to change rapidly. As a result, unformed don't bother remembering their lineage. It is unimportant. For unformed, nothing is truly fixed.

ONE BITE from a Prime can transform nearly any other woven into an unformed. Only *asrasins*, holders, and necrosed are immune.

KNOWN PRIMES:
 Jeek Voshkov
 Arcus Elder

*AN INTERESTING ASIDE:

Most of the dangerous animals on Sinskrill, such as wolves, are actually unformed. In addition, the bears, who come over from Amethyst, are also unformed. The unformed were brought to Sinskrill long ago by a Servitor whose name was intentionally forgotten.

DEFINITION OF TERMS

*BRIEF HISTORY OF *ASRASINS*: It is thought that many of the gods and goddesses of the ancient pantheons, such as those from Sumeria, Babylon, Egypt, and China were actually *asrasins* of some sort. Those ancient warlords waged horrific wars of conquest, dominance, and enslavement upon the rest of the world, especially normals, those without *lorethasra*. But when Shokan inspired the magavane servants of the mahavans to overthrow the rule of Overlord Shet, an event known as the *Nusrael*—the Catastrophe—the *asrasin* control of the world began to crumble.

ASRA: Magic or more specifically, enchantment.

ASRASIN: General name of the magic practitioners. In ancient times, *all* children of a single *asrasin* parent had the potential to become an *asrasin*. In the modern era, this certainty has been lost. Nevertheless, there are still several ways to become an *asrasin*. Most commonly, a potential wielder of *asra* is born within a *saha'asra* to *asrasin* parents. Then there are those who have the potential to become *asrasins* but are born outside *saha'asra*. These individuals generally lead normal, unremarkable lives, although many mention that prior to their arising as an *asrasin*, they experienced frequent bouts of ennui, as if they are perpetually unfilled. However, if such an individual is exposed to a *saha'asra*, their *lorethasra* awakens, and they have to go to live in a *saha'asra* that contains a sufficient amount of *lorasra* to sustain them or face imminent death. The only two such places today are Arylyn and Sinskrill.

BRAID: A magical spell or creation. Also called a weave.

CLARITY PAIN: Overlord Shet's temple stronghold and palace where he created the necrosed.

. . .

COUNCIL OF MAGAVANE: The *asrasins* who fought to free humanity. They were inspired by Shokan and Sira. Later on, they became the progenitors of the magi of Arylyn. Interestingly, prior to Shokan's and Sira's arrival, most who called themselves magavanes were servants of the mahavans. An unsubstantiated rumor states that the magavanes also enacted a plan to slowly drain the world's *saha'asras* of power to further erode mahavan dominance.

FIVE ELEMENTS, the:
　Fire: crackles and smells like sulfur.
　Air: hisses and pulses as it distorts the air.
　Earth: rustles like ivy shifting about.
　Water: possesses a rushing sound, like a breaking wave.
　Spirit: white but with flecks of color that are reflective of an *asrasin's* natural moral tendencies.

FAR BEYOND, the: the world outside the borders of a *saha'asra*.

GREAT DYING, the: The one hundred and eighty-five year period of time in the Middle Ages when most of the magical races perished. Most historians date the Great Dying to approximately 1209-1394 AD. The cause is unknown but likely due to the ongoing fading of the various *saha'asras* throughout the world.

JAYCIK KORNAVEL: Author of the *Lore of Itihasthas*. He is reputed to have been a magavane and personal friend of Shokan and Sira.

JAYENASRA: The Beautiful Art. An ancient word to describe the use of *asra*. The term has fallen out of use.

· · ·

Ley lines: Arterial or root like systems that extend from primal nodes and spread *lorasra* throughout a *saha'asra*. They can become corroded or corrupted over time and are maintained through the work of adepts in the Elements of Water, Fire, and Spirit. However, proper repair or installations of new ley lines can only be done by a *raha'asra*.

Lorasra: The *asra* contained within a place. It is a phenomenon that *asrasins* use to create their braids and weaves. When it is polluted, it is called *therasra*.

Lore of Itihasthas, the: Author Jaycik Kornavel. A book written sometime between 6200-5000 BC about the *Nusrael* and ancient *asrasins*.

Lorethasra: The *asra* or magic contained within a person. *Lorethasra* rests upon five primeval Elements: Earth, Air, Water, Fire, and most importantly, Spirit. In essence, these are the five Elements of classical Buddhist thought, but what the Buddhists thought of as 'void', *asrasins* recognize as Spirit. All *asrasins* can bend these Elements to their will, although they are usually only adept at two or perhaps three of these forces.

Magavane: *Asrasins* who were inspired by Shokan and Sira and came to believe that mundane humanity deserved more than enslavement. They formed the Council of the Magavanes and fought the lords of the Mahavana Axis.

Magus: Name for those *asrasins* from Arylyn. They descend from the magavanes.

. . .

MAHAVAN: The ancient *asrasins* who once ruled the Earth. The greatest of them was Shet. In their view, all lesser *asrasins* and woven are fit for nothing but servitude. As for normal humans, those without *lorethasra*, they were meant for nothing more than slavery. The mahavans eventually formed the Mahavana Axis as a counter to the Council of the Magavanes.

MAHAVANA AXIS: The enemy of the Council of the Magavanes.

NOMASRA: Any object imbued with *lorasra*.

NUSRAEL: "THE CATASTROPHE". The ancient war among the *asrasins*, the beginning of which was heralded when Shokan inspired the magavanes to fight for freedom.

OVERLORD SHET (*SET as Egyptians called him*): The greatest and most powerful of all mahavans. At one point, he was the acknowledged, unchallenged ruler of the world. For now, he resides on Seminal and is still the god of the mahavans of Sinskrill.

PRIMAL NODES: *Nomasras* that are repositories of *lorasra*. From a primal node, *lorasra* extends into a *saha'asra* through ley lines, which can variously be likened to an arterial or root system. Primal nodes can only be created by a *raha'asra* or a skilled adept in Spirit.

RAHA'ASRA: A type of *asrasin* who can create *lorasra*. Such an individual is often quite powerful.

SAHA'ASRA: Places of magic.

. . .

Seminal: A mythical world where Shet is said to have fled following his defeat at the hands of Shokan and Sira. Little is known about the world except that *lorasra* is said to be unconstrained there. Somehow, it is perpetually made, and the plants and creatures of this world have adapted to it in their own fashion. However, the *lorasra* is so potent that it can be too much for even an *asrasin* to safely use. There are said to be lakes of *lorasra* in Seminal that are deadly to all creatures.

Shokan: The great enemy of Shet. The Lord of the Sword. Husband to Sira, the Lady of Fire.

Sira: The great enemy of Shet. The Lady of Fire. Wife to Shokan, the Lord of the Sword.

Thera'asras: Asrasins who are masters of all Elements. However, their control of Spirit isn't at the same level as a *raha'asra's*.

Theranom: Special *nomasra* vessels specifically designed to contain *therasra*, which would otherwise pollute the environment.

Therasra: *Lorasra* that has become polluted from use. It can easily destroy the environment by distorting trees, bushes, plants and even animals and people.

Undefiled Locus: Overlord Shet's sword. The weapon was somehow turned against him during his final battle with Shokan and Sira, thus leading to his defeat. Shet left Undefiled Locus within the heart of

Clarity Pain, guarded by Grave Invidious, the greatest of his necrosed, until the god's return.

WOVEN, **the:** Magical races created by *asrasins.*

SEMINAL

ANYA ARUYEN: Jessira reborn as an elf on Seminal. How she ended up on that world remains a mystery.

CINDER SHADE: Rukh reborn as a human on Seminal. How he ended upon that world remains a mystery.

LORD SHET: Also known as the Lord of the Mourning and Shet the Eternal. He is the mythical god of Sinskrill, and a figure of legend who battled Shokan and Sira in a long ago age on Earth. Somehow he was defeated and trapped on Sinskrill.

THE HOLY SEVEN: Shet's great servants, also called titans.
1. **Sture Mael:** The Indomitable. Mountain Tamer. He is the greatest of Shet's titans. He was once Shet's bishan.
2. **Garad Lull:** The Killing Smile. Handsome, cunning Titan. He is the one who tricked the holders into invading Clarity Pain.
3. **Tomag Jury:** Shield Render: Twin brother to Tormak.
4. **Tormak Jury:** Sword Breaker: Twin brother to Tomag.
5. **Rence Darim:** The Illwind. She and Liline Silt are the only female Titans.
6. **Liline Silt:** Water Death. She and Rence Darim are the only female Titans.

7. **Drak Renter:** The Fell Whip. He is the youngest of the Titans. *Dead Titans: Verde the Valiant. Duval of the Lightning.*

LANGUAGE OF SHEVASRA

THE ANCIENT MOTHER tongue of the asrasins. This is a partial list of some of the surviving words from that language.

ASRA: Enchantment.

ASRASIN: General name of practitioners of *Jayenasra*.

BISHAN: Young master. The term has fallen out of favor in Arylyn but is still used in Sinskrill.

HASTHA: The past.

ITI: That

ITIHASTHAS: That which has happened.

ISHA: Masterful instructor. A teacher in the ways of life. The term has fallen out of favor on Arylyn but is still used in Sinskrill.

JAYEN: Beauty made alive.

. . .

LOR: Secret. Hidden.

LORETH: Within.

MAGA: Servant of greatness.

MAHA: One who wields greatness.

MAYNA: Someone of interest.

NOME: That which is malleable.

NUSRAEL: Catastrophe.

RAHA'ASRA: Builder/creator

RASHASRA: Most High. God.

SAHA'ASRA: Place of magic.

SAHAR: Place.

SHEV: To submit.

.   .   .

SHEVASRA: The language spoken in ancient times. Translated as submission to *asra*.

SHEVELA: Submission.

SHILL: Incompetent or untrained person with potential. The term has fallen out of favor on Arylyn but is still used in Sinskrill.

THERA: One who wields power.

ABOUT THE AUTHOR

Davis Ashura resides in North Carolina and shares a house with his wonderful wife who somehow overlooked Davis' eccentricities and married him anyway. As proper recompense for her sacrifice, Davis unwittingly turned his wonderful wife into a nerd-girl. To her sad and utter humiliation, she knows exactly what is meant by 'Kronos'. Living with them are their two rambunctious boys, both of whom have at various times helped turn Davis' once lustrous, raven-black hair prematurely white. And of course, there are the obligatory strange, strays cats (all authors have cats—it's required by the union). They are fluffy and black with terribly bad breath. When not working —nay laboring—in the creation of his grand works of fiction, Davis practices medicine, but only when the insurance companies tell him he can. Visit him at www.DavisAshura.com and be appalled by the banality of a writer's life.